Doin' Dirty

Also by Howard Swindle

Jitter Joint
America's Condemned: Death Row Inmates in Their
    Own Words (with Dan Malone)
Trespasses: Portrait of a Serial Rapist
Deliberate Indifference
Once a Hero

Doin' Dirty

Howard Swindle

St. Martin's Minotaur
New York

www.minotaurbooks.com

Permission to quote lyrics from "Small Town Saturday Night," by Patrick Alger and Henry Devito, is granted by an agreement with Universal Music Publishing Group, Los Angeles, California.

Permission to quote lyrics from "For What It's Worth," by Stephen A. Stills, is granted by an agreement with Warner Bros. Publications, Miami, Florida.

Permission to quote lyrics from "Turn Out the Lights," by Hank Craig and Willie Nelson, is granted by an agreement with Glad Music Co., Houston, Texas.

Library of Congress Cataloging-in-Publication Data

Swindle, Howard.
    Doin' dirty / Howard Swindle.—1st ed.
        p. cm.
    ISBN 0-312-20389-6
        1. Police—Texas—Dallas—Fiction. 2. Dallas (Tex.)—Fiction. 3. Drug traffic—Fiction. 4. Alcoholics—Fiction. 5. Texas—Fiction. I. Title.

PS3569.W536 D64 2000
813'.54—dc21   00-040243

First Edition: October 2000

10 9 8 7 6 5 4 3 2 1

To Doctors Charles T. Richardson, John T. Preskitt,
Robert G. Mennel, and Robert F. Hebeler,
of Baylor University Medical Center, Dallas,
for giving me a second chance; and,

To my wife, Kathy Swindle,
and my daughter, Ashley Swindle Ingram,
for never giving up on second chances.

Nothing good happens in my books without the remarkable patience and deft, insightful touch of Kelley Ragland, editor at St. Martin's Press, and my longtime agent, confidante, and dear friend, Janet Wilkens Manus, of Manus & Associates Literary Agency, Inc. They're more critical to the process than black coffee.

Doin'
Dirty

1

Jeb Quinlin had done the best he could to put Brett Holman in prison for the rest of his life. Now, as he stepped down from the witness stand, he wasn't sure he'd done enough. Quinlin had testified about Holman's prints being found on the murder weapon, offered proof that he had bought the Smith and Wesson .38 from a sporting-goods store a week before the murder, and destroyed Holman's only alibi witness, a bottle blonde who wasn't nearly as eager to commit perjury after Quinlin had threatened her with a guaranteed ten years at Gatesville for the vial of cocaine in her purse.

Still, juries were dice rolls. They liked things neat and nice, with no loose ends. Hell, life was a loose end. Not black, not white, just a bunch of diffuse gray, which, often as not, obscured the truth like fog on a rock. Juries wanted motives, and Quinlin hadn't given them one. He knew why Brett Holman had rung Gerald Richardson's doorbell, then shot him three times in the face and chest when he opened the door. But *knowing* something to be true and *proving* it was a horse of a different color. The O. J. trial had taught him that, along with several judicial abortions of his own.

On his way out of the courtroom, Quinlin spotted a seat on the aisle and impulsively slid in. The stack of paperwork on his desk could wait a half hour. Pluck Watkins was the prosecution's next witness, and Quinlin figured Pluck would be worth hanging around for, particularly if he was sober. Pluck could give the jury the motive. If they believed him.

Pluck Watkins had been the Richardsons' gardener. Quinlin had found him just two days before trial, and even when he had, he wasn't sure about Pluck's abilities as a witness. The old man was nearly seventy, stooped and grayed, and spoke in a near-indiscernible black dialect. Worse, Pluck was a career wino. Drunk, he spoke his own language.

Pluck had been trimming hedges in the Richardsons' backyard when he happened to glance through the windows into Loretta Richardson's bedroom, catching the lady of the house and an equally nude Brett Holman doing the horizontal mambo.

Now, on the witness stand, Quinlin noticed, Pluck was nervous and edgy, which probably meant he was at least quasi-sober.

"You're appearing here to testify voluntarily, aren't you, Mr. Watkins?" the prosecutor asked.

"Not 'zactly, no, suh," the old man said earnestly.

"What do you mean, 'not exactly'?"

"Well, suh, that *dee*tective, Quinfield—"

"You mean, Quinlin?"

"Yas, suh," Pluck said, "he told me he'd put my sorry ass *under* the jail if I wudn't sober and tell the truth."

Quinlin felt his face turning red. He hoped Pluck stopped there, not volunteering that the detective had also promised him a bottle of Thunderbird if he showed up sober and did a good job on the stand. The assistant district attorney grinned and waited for the light laughter to end before moving along. Quinlin sensed the jury liked the old man, who clearly was trying to do his best, despite his alien surroundings. The prosecutor led him through the questioning, which put Pluck in the Richardsons' backyard with his hedge trimmers on that fateful day and, by happenstance, glancing through the window of the master bedroom.

"When you saw Mrs. Richardson and Mr. Holman in the Richardson bedroom, how were they attired?" the prosecutor was asking Pluck.

The old drunk looked at him quizzically but didn't say anything.

"Come on, Mr. Watkins," the assistant district attorney said, annoyed. "Don't be bashful. You can tell the jury. How were they attired?"

The old man's forehead wrinkled and he stared distantly at the ceiling.

Finally, the judge interceded. "Mr. Watkins, I can hold you in contempt and put you in jail if you don't answer," he said. "Now, answer the state's question. How were Mrs. Richardson and Mr. Holman attired?"

"Well, suh," Pluck said finally, "they wasn't a-tired. They was a-fuckin'."

The jury gave Brett Holman life.

As it winds its way south from Dallas, Houston School Road moseys through flat, indistinguishable farmland. South of Loop 635, decades of heavy farm machinery and neglect by county commissioners have turned the asphalt into a quilt of pits, ruts, and patches. Day or night, Jan Baynum knew the stretch of road by heart, veering over the center stripe by rote to dodge a pit, swerving to the sloping shoulder to avoid a rut. She'd made the same trip five days a week for more than fifteen years from her home in Lancaster to Baylor Medical Center in downtown Dallas.

On this night, the registered nurse was woefully late. It was 3:30 A.M. before she finally left the hospital, staying late because every bed in the sixth-floor cancer ward had been full and her counterpart on the overnight shift had phoned in sick at the last minute. Administering chemotherapy was exacting work, made even more difficult if the shift was short-handed; reluctantly, she had volunteered to stay over.

Jan Baynum would later put the time at about 3:55 A.M., when, just as she neared a curve in the road, she saw a pair of taillights appear almost spontaneously, as if they had just swerved onto the road from the ditch. Instinctively, she tapped the brakes entering the curve. That's when she saw the little sports car beside the road. As her car was almost beside the vehicle, the splash of her headlights swept across the silver sportster, and she thought she saw someone slumped against the glass on the driver's side. The tail-lights that had appeared so abruptly in front of her had already disappeared into the darkness.

She was a woman by herself, in pitch-black darkness on a lonely road, but the more she drove, the more she knew she had to go back. She was a registered nurse, after all, and someone could need help. She turned around and went back.

The nurse stopped on the opposite shoulder of the two-lane road, leaving her engine running and her headlights on. She removed her cell phone and dialed 911 but didn't push the send button. The phone was primed if she needed it; the push of one button would summon help. Cautiously, she approached the car and tapped on the side window. She could see the side of a man's head and his ear. When he didn't move, she opened the door gently, reaching over quickly to keep the man from slumping out of the car.

She put her fingers on his carotid artery but found no pulse. She couldn't see it in the dark, but she smelled the vomit. Jan Baynum pushed the send key on her phone and walked back across the road to her car to wait for the police.

She collected her wits. She almost forgot about the taillights that had appeared from nowhere and then vanished so quickly.

Nothing made Quinlin sleep better than a conviction. Now, the early-morning smells invigorated him, made him happy to be alive and up early, before the sun moved things ahead on its own agenda. For some reason, the clock moved more quickly in the light than in the dark. The smell of brewing coffee gurgling in the pot on the counter mixed with the freshness of sourdough bread toasting in the oven, all of which was overpowered by the aroma of bacon crackling in the microwave.

And there was Madeline, meandering obliviously through the logged kitchen and great room in nothing but a white Dallas Cowboys jersey and a pair of black panties, making it tough for him to concentrate on the five eggs scrambling in the skillet. Physical attraction was one thing. Lust, after all, was a dilemma with a twenty-minute solution. But whatever the intangible trait that lay beyond her skin-deep beauty, Quinlin knew it was the real reason Madeline had become habit-forming.

She took her customary position at the back window, peering intently through the faltering predawn darkness at the deer feeders twenty-five yards from the back of the ranch house. Deer moved early, and once they had discovered the corn in the two galvanized feeders, the backyard of Quinlin's house had become a regular stop. The ritual also became an anticipated treat for Madeline and Quinlin, who ate their breakfast in the nook at the back windows, watching the deer gouge and butt one another for their turn at the yellow corn in the troughs.

"Jeb, he's back!" Madeline yelled just as he was spooning the scrambled eggs from the iron frying pan onto a serving plate. "Get over here quick, before you miss him!"

Quinlin dumped the eggs onto the platter and moved quickly to the telescope at the back of the great room. The sun hadn't yet made its grand debut, but it was already diluting the darkness the way a hefty splash of cream lightens black coffee. He could see the right side of the buck's rack, then a portion of his muzzle through the crosshairs. He squinted over the magnifying glass to orient himself. The deer in the distant dawn was sturdy and big, his muzzle maybe even reaching Jeb's shoulders.

"Let me see," Madeline said, pushing Quinlin from his vantage point behind the telescope. "God, he's so beautiful. Can you imagine how many people have tried to put him on their walls? He's just majestic."

The buck didn't have a lock on majestic. Not with Madeline bent over the tripod, the Cowboy jersey clumped at her waist, leaving nothing to cover the black panties. It was sensory overload, with Jeb looking over her shoulder at the spectacular deer, then glancing down at a rounded butt that couldn't be contained by the pair of overtaxed bikini panties.

"This ol' boy's bound to be pretty good at staying alive," Quinlin said, still in his coarse, precoffee rasp. "He's a trophy all right. How many white deer do you see, anyway? I need to nail him before he gets away again."

He moved to the tripod that held his Canon Rebel, which was

already loaded with the fastest film he could find. He hoped for enough light as he focused the zoom lens and hit the motor drive. He had reserved a special place for Whitey's picture above the mantel on the native-rock fireplace. The motor drive roared, clicking off all thirty-six frames in only seconds.

As if the white buck instinctively sensed the intrusion, he meandered off behind a clump of blackjack oaks, taking the three does with him.

"You'd have missed Whitey if you hadn't finally listened to me," Quinlin said, grinning. "Told you it'd be worth your while to spend another night. But no, you just had to get back to town. So tell me, Ms. Meggers, how many sights like this do you see from *your* back door in the city?"

"Whitey's the only reason I've been hanging out here," she said, acting indifferent. "Now that we've got him on film, guess I'm fresh out of reasons for living like a part-time hillbilly."

"I think you mean redneck," Quinlin said. "There's a difference. Socially and politically. Tell you what. Leave your car out here and drive in with me this morning. While we're in Dallas, we'll get a doctor to look at that arm, too."

"What arm?" Madeline asked, clearly clueless.

"The one that I'm apparently twisting against your will."

Detective John Dabney appeared in the squad room with a cup of vending-machine coffee and carrying a large transparent plastic evidence bag with someone's personal belongings. Carefully, he put his coffee on the edge of his desk, then dumped the contents of the plastic bag unceremoniously onto a stack of unfiled police reports. Wallet, a BMW monogramed key ring with six keys, a Yale class ring, and small change. The young detective opened the wallet, spent several seconds counting, and announced to no one in particular, "Not your normal corpse beside the road. BMW Z-3 convertible, a cool three hundred fifty-seven dollars in knock-around cash, and dressed like Jeb's stockbroker."

Quinlin let the jab, an obvious reference to his new ranch and pickup truck and probably his girlfriend's money, slide.

"Where'd you find him?" Quinlin inquired from two desks away. It was early for the day watch, and the two homicide detectives had the Crimes Against Persons bull pen to themselves except for an old night-shift detective named Moon Mullins, who was dozing with his feet on his desk.

"Early this morning, on the shoulder beside Houston School Road," Dabney said. "Another ten, fifteen feet and he'd have belonged to Lancaster."

Quinlin grinned, remembering his rookie year as a detective. Gus Branson, a legendary old homicide detective, was two weeks from retirement. Branson's remarkable claim to fame was that he had

cleared every case he'd ever been assigned, though word in the
squad room was that some of his cases were about as shaky as the
old man's grip had become in his last few years.

Quinlin, in only his second week out of uniforms, watched incredulously one night as Branson dragged a corpse by its collar
across four lanes of Coit Road, then dropped it in a parking lot on
the westernmost reaches of the city of Richardson's jurisdiction.

"Richardson never gets any murders," Branson had said, dodging
a pickup on his return across Coit. "Hell, the body's been dumped
anyway. Doesn't matter where it lands. They'll probably be proud
to get one. Give 'em something to do."

"I'm figuring Mr. Carlisle here as a medical," Dabney said, bringing Quinlin current. "Not a mark on him. Vomited all over himself.
The JP ordered an autopsy, but it's gonna be a heart attack or
something. The good—and should I say well-heeled—die young."

Quinlin went back to his coffee and newspaper. An advertise-
ment left him shaking his head and muttering. The quad-cab, four-
wheel-drive Dodge pickup he'd bought three months earlier to
replace his bullet-riddled International Scout was fifteen hundred
dollars cheaper at a dealership in Denton. He pulled the felt-point
pen from his pocket and did the math, knowing he was going to
be even more pissed. Thirty-eight miles north to Denton, fifteen
hundred dollars. Yep, $39.47 a mile, that's what it broke down to,
one way. Could have saved some money on that trip.

"Uh-oh," the younger detective said ominously. He was holding
a small laminated orange card in the air when Quinlin looked up.

"It's a DPS press card, Jeb," Dabney said. "Says our stiff's a staff
writer for the *Register and News*. Somebody named Richmond Carlisle. Ever hear of him?"

"No, but it doesn't matter," Quinlin said. "You better hope like
hell it's a medical, else you just got your ass dropped in the grease.
The media takes it personally when something traumatic happens
to one of its own. Page one. Politically sensitive. Count on it."

Within the hour, Deputy Chief Jon Abrams, Dallas's chief of
detectives, walked into CAPERS, grabbed a red marker, and wrote
Richmond Carlisle's name on the erasable board under the heading
Quinlin/McCarren. Dabney, a plainclothesman less than three

months, was quietly relieved; Quinlin wasn't excited, but neither was he surprised.

Clint Harper answered on the first ring, producing a sigh of relief from Quinlin. Usually when he tried to reach the *Register & News*'s highest-profile reporter, Harper was out of town on assignment.

"They finally take the company credit card away from you?" Quinlin asked. "What you doing in town?"

"Naw, the editors are in a big circle jerk trying to figure out what my next assignment's gonna be. The executive editor apparently thinks I don't hum the company chorus. Thinks that I take too long to produce too little, so he's lobbying for me covering the SPCA or some other sacred cow of his. Meanwhile, I'm just hanging loose, waiting on a puff of smoke from the brain trust."

"Guess the aura from the Pulitzer's long gone, huh?" Quinlin said, to no response. "Tell you what, Clint. This isn't all social. Do me a favor. Go to your Human Resources, find out who Richmond Carlisle's next of kin is, and let me pick you up in front of the building in five minutes. We've got a problem. I'll run it down for you, what little I know at this point, but the bottom line is, your Mr. Carlisle's met his last deadline."

"Foul play?"

"Probably not, but we're not sure right now."

"Wouldn't rule out accidental suffocation if I were you," Harper said.

"What you talking about?"

"Accidental because Carlisle's got more than a healthy respect for himself, and suffocation because he's always got his nose up some editor's ass."

Quinlin laughed. "Take it you're not gonna be a pallbearer?"

"All of Richmond Carlisle's pallbearers are gonna be strangers."

Quinlin led the way to a booth at the back of the Farmers Market Grill. The café, a timeworn institution on the city's frayed southern edge, was in a lethargic idle between breakfast and lunch, and about a quarter of the tables were filled with malingering coffee drinkers. A curious odor of coffee and collard greens hung heavy in the air.

The detective caught the waitress's eye, held up two fingers, and slid into the side of the booth facing the door. Old habit. Quinlin didn't sit with his back to doors.

"I called our friend at the Medical Examiner's Office and asked him to pull out all the stops on your buddy," Quinlin said. "Berryman said he'd do the autopsy himself, which makes me feel a lot better."

Quinlin had also phoned Richmond Carlisle's next-of-kin information to his partner, Paul McCarren, who would put in the call to Carlisle's folks in Manhattan. Death notification was one of the cops' worse jobs. That's why they'd invented junior partners. Quinlin had handled his share of horrible news over the years. There was still the issue of notifying the dead man's employer, the *Register & News*, which Quinlin dreaded like a saltwater enema. A reporter's death—even if it ultimately turned out to be from natural causes—was guaranteed to become a "head shed" case, one that would get the attention of headquarters and all the brass who inhabited it.

It was the senior corporal's experience that the higher up the food chain the deceased had been in life, the more grief he caused in death. Garrett McWilliams, an erstwhile mayor pro tem in Dallas, had been a major case in point. McWilliams was a computer-software guru and a major contributor to a wealth of charities when he turned up dead on his own three-acre estate in Preston Hollow. Paramedics answering a 911 call found his nude body in the living room of his servants' quarters. The megamillionaire had been stabbed twelve times in his face and chest and his genitals had been mutilated, a fact his lawyers' "crisis team" had managed to withhold from the media. While the TV stations were playing the murder as a major whodunit for a week, Quinlan had found the killer in less than two hours: the twelve-year-old son of McWilliams's Haitian gardener and maid. The mainline politician and civic leader had sexually assaulted the boy earlier and had come back again. Faced with reliving the horror, the humiliated and terrified boy had gone into a frenzy with his mother's kitchen knife.

McWilliams's wife, aided by a SWAT team of the city's highest-dollar lawyers, refused to accept the boy's version. Indeed, the bereaved widow was less concerned that her husband's murder be cleared than she was in suppressing its motivation. Those kinds of headlines would virtually ensure she'd be treated like cubic zirconia at the next Crystal Charity Ball. Behind the scenes, Quinlin had spent hours defending his case—and the Haitian boy—against attacks from lawyers representing McWilliams's widow, who had even intimated that she would establish a trust for the boy if he would recant his story about her husband's predatory sexual proclivities. Only when Quinlin had dredged up yet another underage boy, who told the same story about McWilliams, did his widow drop her crusade. A juvenile court judge, in a closed-door trial, determined that the Haitian boy had acted in self-defense, and the boy and his family returned to their homeland.

In Richmond Carlisle's case, *Register* editors undoubtedly would make phone calls to chiefs' private lines to express their "concern." There would be mutual consternation between the power brokers who controlled the city's only printing presses and the politically appointed police brass. Air was thin at those heights, and gravity would take over. Shit would roll downhill in avalanches, which was where Quinlin always found himself in politically sensitive cases— up to his armpits in sewage.

The waitress appeared with two white mugs and a small copper-colored thermos of coffee. Judging from her twang, she was from some wide spot in deep East Texas, where she'd apparently gotten about twenty pounds too familiar with biscuits and gravy. She was a peroxide blonde with big hair, and her cowgirl butt was enshrouded in a pair of Wrangler jeans like a pair of shrink-wrapped hams.

"Don't reckon y'all want to bother with the menu, huh?"

"No," Harper said, anticipating her concern, "but if you'll let us borrow your booth here for a little while, we'll make it up in the tip. That fair, hon?"

She rolled her eyes in a "seeing is believing" look, did a pert about-face, and strutted her cowgirl butt to the waitress station, where she turned abruptly to make sure she still had an audience. She wasn't disappointed, catching Harper's eyes locked on her most prominent asset.

"Don't want to upset your natural-causes fantasy about Richmond," Harper said, sucking flame from a Bic into a Marlboro Lights, "but he was way over his head in some pretty heavy stuff when he croaked. Maybe just coincidence, maybe not."

"I'll let you enthrall me with the details if you'll let me bum one of those Marlboro Lights first," the detective said, looking around guiltily. "Madeline doesn't have to know anything about this. Staying off the booze is one thing; redlining *every*thing in my life is another."

"You're preaching to the choir," Harper said, passing the disposable lighter and a Marlboro across the table. "If I had to give up smokes right now, I'd be drinking again by nightfall. I've got to have *a* vice. Otherwise, I'd be as boring as you, Jeb."

"What can I tell you?" Quinlin said. "I'm a damned choirboy. Don't know why anybody would even want to associate with me. I wouldn't, truth be known."

Harper didn't mince words; it was one of the hallmarks of their long-standing relationship. They shot straight with each other, not having to read into the record such routine caveats as "Don't quote me on this" or "I'll lose my job if anyone finds out where this is coming from." The precautions were taken for granted over the years and, occasionally—but only when absolutely necessary—were protected by flat-out lies, even to lieutenants and editors. The relationship meant not only that Harper and Quinlin were professional colleagues but also that they drank and chased together in the not-so-old days.

"Richmond Carlisle was a prima donna without portfolio," Harper said. "He talked the talk, but he was lame on the walk. Bottom line, he was an Ivy League golden boy who ingratiated himself with our executive editor, sucked up to get good assignments, almost always investigative stories, and virtually, at least in my opinion, almost always missed the bull's-eye. He was one of those who wanted to use the *Register and News* as a stepping-stone to get to the hallowed *New York Times*. Mommy and daddy have some stroke with Brewster; I hear they own a substantial chunk of stock in the paper. So when junior graduated with honors from Yale, he landed in our newsroom like he was Pulitzer's bloodline. He's a pompous asshole. *Was,* I guess.

"Anyway," Harper said, "young Carlisle was meddling in a couple of things that could have gotten him in trouble. You read the stories a few weeks back about Bumpy Rhodes?"

"About Bumpy not having enough collateral to write all the bail bonds he's got outstanding?" Quinlin said. "Yeah, you guys cost him a cool half a million dollars and got his inside man at the sheriff's department fired, right?"

"Well, that was Richmond Carlisle's handiwork," Harper said. "Probably the best stuff he's done since he's been here. It was a throw-down series, all based on public record, and I hear the courthouse reporter actually got the tip. Carlisle just checked it out and it fell together. But it created some problems for Bumpy with the Bail Bond Board."

"Bumpy ended up naked, holding his crank on that one," Quinlin said. "And Bumpy's never been real fond of that posture."

"Yeah, but is Bumpy going to risk a thriving business just to get even with a schmuck reporter over a story that's already run?" Harper asked. "Been my experience that the real danger to a reporter is *before* the story runs, not after. Before it hits the print, that's when you can get some ribs broken. Afterward, well, that'd only bring the heat down on whoever you're writing about, and he's already in the floodlights anyway. And Bumpy knows he doesn't need any more exposure."

Quinlin knew Delbert "Bumpy" Rhodes mostly by reputation. Rhodes's reputation in law-enforcement circles was about as stellar as the Nightstalker's. Quinlin knew a detective in Robbery and Theft who caught Bumpy taking food stamps and child-welfare payments from the wife of a man who had absconded on one of his bonds. Bumpy, all 275 pounds of him, was puffed up and indignant, claiming it wasn't theft at all, just merely an "escrow account of sorts," until the fugitive turned himself in on the outstanding $100,000 bond. Rhodes returned the welfare proceeds and a grand jury declined to indict.

"Did Bumpy threaten Carlisle?" Quinlin asked.

"Bumpy threatens everyone," Harper said. "Probably did, but I can't see him following through, not with a reporter—and not after the story ran."

"You said Carlisle was working on a couple of things," Quinlin said. "What else?"

"Well," Harper said, "coming from where you come from, you're gonna know who he was messing with when he ended up with a tag on his toe. And you're gonna know why I told the executive editor he was full of shit if he thought I was going to baby-sit Richmond through the investigation. That's why the boss thinks I'm not a company guy, I guess. I don't know what the lead was, or where it came from, for that matter. Junior was being really cagey about what he had and where he got it. But he was screwing around with Clendon Colter and his boys."

Quinlin swallowed a mouthful of coffee and let out a low whistle. "The Colters," he finally said. "That's about as strong as it gets in this state. What, he couldn't find any crap on the governor?"

"It would have been easier," Harper said, "and probably a hell of a lot safer. That's why I think Berryman might find more than a congenital heart problem or a stroke. I tried to tell Carlisle that. . . ."

Quinlin was lost in thought. Yeah, he was intimately familiar with the Colters, or at least had been as a teenager growing up in Comanche Gap, where the Colters still headquartered their state-wide business conglomerate. He had gone to school with Buck and Wade, Clendon Colter's two sons. Even been to the famous Pan Permian Headquarters Ranch on several occasions when school classes would have barbecues and swimming parties at the Colters' Olympic-size pool. What he had seen was opulence beyond a young country boy's imagination. Jeb was the son of a divorced mother who had scraped by working the overnight shift, mopping floors and emptying bedpans, at a nursing home. But at the Colters, Mexican butlers moved among the students and teachers offering *cabrito*, tamales, and fajitas from trays that were gorged with exotic food, some of which, Jeb couldn't even pronounce.

Supposedly, Clendon Colter's main house was an exact replica of the governor's mansion in Austin. Two hundred yards away, a huge aircraft hangar sat beside an asphalt runway used exclusively by the Colters' Beech King-Aire. It was undoubtedly a Learjet by now, Quinlin imagined, since thirty years had passed. Rumor was rampant in Comanche Gap about how ol' man Colter came up with his untold millions, and vague speculation was that it wasn't all that legitimate. A younger Jeb Quinlin had dismissed much of what he heard as envy and wishful thinking. Sul Ross County was, for the most part, a relatively poor ranching county and it was understandable, he thought, that its residents would resent wealth in the midst of their bare-knuckled, hardscrabble lives.

"Can you find out for sure what kind of lead Richmond had?" Quinlin asked.

"I bowed out early, so it'll be tough," Harper said. "Particularly now that he's dead. But one of the many reasons I refused to participate is that the smug bastard wouldn't say. Just 'impeccable sources.' Well, that didn't cut it with me. That's not the way I play the game. A reporter doesn't trust me enough to tell me where his information's coming from, I don't trust him enough to work with him."

Quinlin was momentarily lost in thought. The sound of breaking plates brought him back. Across the room, East Texas was red with embarrassment, standing in the debris of broken dishes.

"Figure I'll drive out and visit the scene when I leave here," Quinlin said, "just to get the lay of the land. Tag along if you want. Our rookie assumed he was investigating a medical, and I get the feeling that the only thing Crime Scene did was take pictures. Between you and me, that could come back to bite us in the ass."

The detective eyed his watch; it was 11:30. "*After* I get something to eat," Quinlin added. In the almost year since he'd been sober, he'd been eating anything that didn't bite him first. He ordered a chicken-fried steak, mashed potatoes with cream gravy, pinto beans, collard greens, corn bread and homemade coconut cream pie. Harper opted for a cheeseburger and fries.

"You keep eating like this, you gonna make Bumpy Rhodes look like a runt," the reporter said.

"Doubt it," Quinlin said. "I got good metabolism. It's the only good side effect from being type A, and damned sure the only decent trait I inherited from my ol' man."

Before they headed for the crime scene, Harper pitched a ten-dollar bill on the table for East Texas's tip, noticed her eyeing him, and nodded to her on the way to the cash register, which produced a seductive smile.

"You know," Harper said, falling in behind Quinlin, "take fifteen or twenty pounds off that cowgirl, and you might be surprised."

"Wouldn't be enough," Quinlin said. "She'd have to lose the double bubble, too."

"You talkin' about the gum or the hair?"

3

Detective John Dabney hadn't been far off in his estimate. Richmond Carlisle's body and car were found precisely twenty-seven and a half feet from the sign on Houston School Road that said WELCOME TO LANCASTER. Houston School was the tiny vein that tied the once sleepy farm town—now a bedroom community—to the heart of Dallas's urban sprawl. Most of the traffic on the outdated country road came from people trying to get to Loop 635 without having to idle through the bumper-to-bumper congestion on Interstate 35, which ran parallel with Houston School about a half mile to the west. At night, when Carlisle's body had to have been left beside the road, the traffic would have been minimal, Quinlin suspected.

Quinlin lucked out, a natural by-product of the city of Dallas' slipshod towing policy. Carlisle's sports car was still beside the road, waiting for the on-call wrecker service to show up to haul it to Impound. Anticipating the likelihood of the little BMW still being there, Quinlin had grabbed the keys from Dabney before he left the squad room. He phoned Crime Scene to get them back to the scene, then called Communications, as if there were any real need, to delay the tow truck.

Slipping on a pair of latex gloves, Quinlin opened the passenger-side door and was hit square in the face by the smell of closed-up vomit. The stench forced him backward a half step, and he took a deep breath before he moved back to the car. Carlisle's mobile phone was still in the pedestal mount. If, in fact, the reporter had been overcome by some medical malady, its onset had been so rapid and devastating, he hadn't had time to make an emergency call. Yet, he—or someone—apparently had had enough time to pull onto the shoulder and turn off the ignition. Dabney didn't mention the witness finding the car running. Quinlin slipped the ignition key in and turned it. The battery was up, and the engine kicked off immediately. The gas gauge showed more than a quarter of a tank. The glove compartment was neat and orderly, and it held the owner's manual and warranties, along with copies of every main-tenance and oil-change receipt Carlisle had. The reporter appeared meticulous and businesslike in his auto records. Quinlin took it as a good sign. Maybe there were notes or calendars somewhere, too. The only untoward signs in the car's interior were smeared vomit stains on the steering column and the driver's seat, approximately where Carlisle's crotch would have been, and an oily smear on the otherwise-clean side glass where the reporter's head had apparently come to rest.

Quinlin popped the trunk. The only things beyond the spare and jack were a canvas bag with workout clothes, a towel, a rela-tively new pair of Reebok cross-trainers, and a Dell laptop com-puter.

"He was a technowhiz," Harper said, watching Quinlin eye the computer. "He's probably got fifty programs on there, telling him everything from when to pick up his dry cleaning to when to shit."

"Y'all were close, I can tell."

"Hey, I don't wish bad news on anybody," Harper said. "But I figure God's got some master plan. If He had a quota of people to take off the planet yesterday, I figure He must have started at the top, with Carlisle, figuring the world would somehow get by."

Quinlin took the bag and laptop to his car, parked one hundred feet behind Carlisle's BMW, and locked them inside. He'd turn over the laptop to Tech Services when he got back to headquarters. Hopefully, the portable computer would contain the notes or cal-endars Quinlin prayed existed.

On the way back to the Z-3, Quinlin stopped and examined the loose dirt beside the road. A pair of tire tracks lay at the rear of the sports car; it looked like there were others, too—probably Dabney's or the original marked sheriff's unit that had answered the nurse's original call. But these tracks were unusual. There had been a light overnight sprinkle, and the damp ground had absorbed the indentations of the tracks well. Judging from the width and the rough gripper-tread design, Quinlin figured they belonged to a pickup truck, maybe a four-wheel drive or a sport-utility vehicle. Either way, based on the track on the right-front side, the vehicle appeared to have a major alignment problem. The inside third of the tire was bald and devoid of tread. The detective made a mental note to get Crime Scene to take plaster casts when they arrived.

"We gonna run out to Berryman's now?" Harper asked.

"Got a better idea. I'll wait for Crime Scene; then I'll head to the ME. You, my charitable friend, can perform a real public service for your fallen colleague by going back to the *Register* and letting them know they've got a new opening for a reporter. That way, I don't get caught up in it, and, who knows, it might even improve the way they think about you."

"Employee of the month," Harper said, cynicism dripping. "I can see it happening."

"Leave me one of them Marlboro Lights before you leave."

"So, are you saying someone tried to choke Richmond Carlisle to death?" Quinlin asked. He found his eyes fixing on the dead man's throat as the corpse lay naked on the autopsy drain slab.

"No, that would be missing the point," Dr. Mark Berryman said. "What I'm saying is that I've found a faint bruising on his neck—at the base of his jawbone and directly beneath the lobes of his ears. The distance between the two bruises at either end of the jawbone approximates a man's outstretched palm, and it could have been produced by, say, the thumb and index finger, like so." The medical examiner stretched the palm of his right hand and placed it on the corpse's throat.

"See how the faint bruises line up with my thumb and index finger?" Berryman asked.

"But nobody was trying to choke him to death?"

"I don't think so. The bruises aren't deep enough to have had that kind of pressure. I found a lump on the scalp, just to the left of crown, about the size of a peach pit. It's a blunt-force injury, sufficient to have created a quarter-inch laceration and a tiny amount of bleeding.

"What I'm speculating *preliminarily*, Jeb, is that someone hit him in the head to overpower him," Berryman said, "and then quite possibly stuck their hand over his throat to hold his head forcibly in place, as if maybe trying to immobilize it or something."

"For what purpose?"

"That, I don't know yet. I've just gotten started."

Mark Berryman was the most down-to-earth forensic pathologist Quinlin had ever worked with. In the end, Berryman's findings would be firmly rooted in his microscopic world of subdural hemorrhages, plaque-riddled arteries, bloated intestines, and soot-stained gunshot wounds. But in the interim, when investigators desperately needed leads in their race against the clock, Berryman also gave them educated speculation.

Working his way through a body, Berryman would gather a symptom here, a manifestation there, and, ultimately, he would have a chain of clinical evidence irrefutable beyond a shadow of doubt. And, unlike human witnesses, the doctor's findings weren't subject to the deficits of human recollection, description, prejudice, or emotion. It was ironic, Berryman had once told Quinlin, that in life, human beings were cunning enough to concoct stories that best met their immediate needs, which in criminal trials generally meant survival or vindictiveness. But in death, stripped of their personalities, proclivities, and motives, their bodies told only the truth. If you just knew what to look for.

"You perform forensic pathology in death," the ME said, "but you end up with life's ultimate truth."

Quinlin studied the body on the drain slab. Richmond Carlisle had been handsome and sophisticated in life and, if you believed Clint Harper, more than a little arrogant and egotistical. But stripped of his Hugo Boss suit, Gucci loafers, and Yale class ring, Carlisle was just another naked mystery lying on a slab, the four-teenth this week, according to the erasable status board outside the pathology suites.

Whatever acute malady had led to his demise wasn't readily apparent. With the exception of the pronounced swelling around his eyes, which had spread to his forehead, the bump on the head, and the light bruising around his neck, the reporter's body was wholly unremarkable to the naked eye. He looked like he could have been injured in a minor fender bender.

"I was leaning toward natural causes before the lump on the head and the bruising on the throat," the ME told Quinlin. "Still could be, of course. Do your due diligence. Find out if he was into karate or some other martial art. And I'm assuming we can't rule out rough sex. Might ought to ask about that, too."

Berryman grinned at Jeb's determined look. "Relax," he said. "You'll be the first to know. I'll find it, whatever it is."

4

The ranch was everything Jeb Quinlin had dreamed about for years. Daylong stints of wrangling with witnesses, murder suspects, and police bureaucrats in the city, and he was more than ready for the one-hour commute to the country. The drive wasn't bad; surprisingly, it was actually therapeutic, an hour-long decompression from the day's psychic flotsam. The farther he drove southwest, the lighter the traffic, and he could feel the stress lifting from his body. By the time he pulled through the gated cattle guard to the little ranch outside Granbury, his nerves were settled. He was in a new world, *his* new world, and it was as far as he could get from chalk outlines, yellow crime-scene tape, bodies with gaping wounds, and blatantly lying suspects.

The gravel road ran a quarter of a mile from the cattle guard before it looped into a circular drive in front of the log house. The distance and the gradual downward slope of the land guaranteed the house couldn't be seen from the narrow highway, not that Texas Farm Road 4 carried all that much traffic anyway. Still, Quinlin particularly enjoyed the fact that he could awaken every morning and look in any direction without seeing another house or a speeding car, even take a leak off the front porch if he wanted. The solitude had always been part of the dream. He wasn't enamored with being a hermit. But over the years, he had become a human sponge that had reached saturation with society's dregs, trauma, and violence.

Actually, the ranch was more than twice the size of Quinlin's dreams. He'd always figured he'd be lucky if he could end up with fifty acres and a tiny one-bedroom loft cabin—and that only after he retired and cashed in his pension in a lump sum. He named it Lobo Mesa, which he had painted on a small sign at the front gate, in tribute to a lone wolf whose howl he'd heard the first night he spent on the property. The ranch was 125 acres of rolling caliche rock and blue stem grass, and laden in heavy clumps of live oaks, post oaks, blackjack oaks, and occasional be-damned mesquite. Already, Quinlin was spending his weekends chain-sawing the bigger mesquites and dousing their open cuts with diesel oil to make sure they didn't sprout again. Over time, the stumps would rot, and then he'd pull them up by the roots. The smaller mesquites, he pulled out with chains he attached to his antique little Ford tractor. Give a mesquite an inch and it'd metastasize like cancer, its shallow roots sucking all the moisture from every decent plant in its shadow.

The land sloped toward the middle of the acreage, where it met a deep, dry tributary of the Brazos River that was littered with heavy, rough caliche rock and lined by cedar. The creekbed flooded every time it thundered, but the powdery white caliche was so porous that water didn't stand for much more than a week.

The centerpiece of the ranch was the aspen-log house on the northern edge of the land. Its original owner had waterproofed the logs with clear varnish, preserving its natural buckskin tone. The house had a red galvanized-tin roof, a feature that Madeline particularly coveted during the thunderstorms, when rain would dance off the metal above her in steady, soothing patters. Full-length porches spanned the front and the back, and during rain showers, the two would adjourn to rocking chairs on the back porch to smell the wetness in the grass and listen to the rhythmic metallic drone off the tin.

Lobo Mesa wouldn't exist were it not for Madeline, and it was undeniable that her role in creating the opportunity had only complicated their lives more than ever. Though they both avoided talking about it, Quinlin suspected that Madeline, too, was growing as frustrated with the unspoken terms of their relationship as he was.

"Well, Mr. Macho, do you want to wait until you're too old to enjoy a ranch," she had taunted, "or do you want to swallow some pride and let me help make it happen now while we can still enjoy it?"

The 125-acre ranch ran $175,000, which, at $1,400 an acre, was more than reasonable, particularly considering that the price included the three-bedroom ranch house. Quinlin had received $100,000 from Sarah's life-insurance policy, a fact that made him feel even more guilt about his former wife's death. He'd almost waited too long to make up his mind on the ranch. The real estate broker had phoned on a Monday night to say he'd gotten an offer of $170,000, which had the owner leaning. Madeline had the money, no question, not only the $2.5 million share of her divorce settlement with Beau Meggers but also another $3.9 million in reward money from the feds for turning him in for money laundering. So when Quinlin told her Tuesday morning about the competing bid on the ranch, she had pushed him to make a counteroffer that very day.

"Look," she said, seeking a compromise he could live with, "let me pay half and you pay half. I'll give you the money; you put the land in your name. When you get your pension, you pay me off. Simple. Then it's yours, free and clear. No strings."

At the last minute, Quinlin had come up with a compromise to Madeline's compromise. The title to the land would carry *both* their names. He insisted on a contingent 7.5 percent note—the going rate, according to that day's business section of the *Register & News*—that specified he had an option to purchase her half outright "upon his retirement from the Dallas Police Department and at such time as his retirement funds become available." By paying half, he still had enough money to make down payments on the new Dodge truck and the old Ford tractor, which he got with a posthole digger and a plow. Without her name on the title and the interest-bearing note, he said, it was no deal.

Madeline had mortally embarrassed him at the closing on the property. Just after she had signed her name as co-owner of the new Lobo Mesa Ranch, she noted to everyone within earshot, "Jeb, Texas is a community-property state, which means that what's one's is the other's too. You do the right thing at some point and marry me, and you erase an eighty-seven-thousand-five-hundred-dollar debt. Is that an incentive, or what?"

Madeline's mouth—there was no guarding against it. Quinlin had felt the blood rush through his face and was left flat-footed and speechless in front of the seller, the closing agent, and the real estate broker.

But it was marriage, not debt, that was always barely beneath the surface of his thoughts. And he knew the same was true with Madeline, though they both had vowed not to discuss it, at least not now. As it was, she was dividing her time between her condo in Dallas and the ranch. Madeline complained that half her clothes were at the ranch, and when she needed an accessory to an outfit, more often than not, it was someplace she wasn't.

Fact was, he felt whole when she was around and splintered when she wasn't. Wasn't that what marriage was supposed to be about? Being whole and sharing? Caring about someone else more than you care about yourself? What a concept, he thought, particularly after he and Sarah had lived together like strangers.

Madeline joked about living like a "hillbilly in the country," but she had fallen in love with the ranch; that much was easy to see. He found her several times at the small corral, feeding the horses, and her walks inevitably led her to the stock tank, which he had stocked with bass. They routinely had sat on the grassy berm overlooking the tank and watched the sun go down; it was among the most tranquil times in his life.

Still, there were loose ends. Not a single pitfall that sabotaged a potential marriage, but an accumulation of snags that collectively made the proposal fraught with problems.

Both suffered guilt from what Quinlin called "blood money," his from his wife's life insurance, when she was murdered during one of his investigations, and hers from a bitter divorce and an IRS reward for putting her former husband in prison for twenty years.

"We need to get over this," Madeline had said during the last rendition of the recurring conversation. "What's lost in all this is that neither of us did anything wrong. We've got to stop beating ourselves up and live our lives."

But there was more than guilt that made each of them uncertain. They had met almost a year earlier, while both were undergoing treatment for alcoholism at Cedar Ridge Hospital. The ensuing year had been sober for both, but not without effort. Quinlin still felt the craving when he was under stress, which was about every other day. The pockets of every jacket he owned were filled with hard watermelon-flavored candy, which he popped in his mouth when he started thinking about Bud Light. Madeline had been a social drinker, and Chablis took over her mind late in the evenings, when she was relaxing. The forced sobriety frequently left them inexplicably moody and caught up in their own battles.

Both were still seeing counselors in aftercare and both occasionally caught themselves acting like a dry drunk. Not surprisingly for recovering alcoholics, both had come to view their drinking as *the* cause for everything screwed up in their lives. Stop drinking and life should be wonderful. There were still nig-naggling little pitfalls in daily life that they wrestled with, believing they shouldn't have to be coping with such tribulations now that they were sober.

One of the recurring tribulations was Madeline's oft-repeated opinion that Quinlin was "too damned old-fashioned, proud, and macho" to commit to a woman worth $6.4 million.

"I think you can't live with the fact that your wife would have so much more money than you," she taunted. "And I think that's ridiculous. If we got married, everything gets thrown into the same barrel anyway. What difference does it make, if we want to spend our lives together?"

Quinlin denied the allegation. "I just don't want another screwed-up marriage," he'd say. "We've just got to be sure this time, that's all. Besides, you can't say you don't still have some guilt about Beau; you've admitted it. I've still got some about Sarah; I admit that. We've just got to make sure we erase everything on the blackboard, that's all."

Quinlin's evasiveness about their relationship actually underscored the neon warning that both their counselors had repeatedly given them before discharging them from the hospital: "Don't make any major life decisions in the first year. Sobriety is a whole new episode in your life, and emotionally, you won't be able to make good decisions until you get your feet solidly beneath you."

The hitch wasn't love. That was the easy answer to the equation. The ranch was lonely without Madeline. He figured he spent most of his time begging her to stay longer. At times, he wondered if perhaps Madeline was right. Did he really have too much pride, he had to ask himself, to marry a woman worth millions? Would she ultimately expect him to quit the police department and become a "gentleman rancher"? Would he feel guilty every time he spent twenty dollars, knowing the money was hers? Would he be a "bought man"?

"You know," Madeline said one night a few weeks earlier, sitting on the back porch, "pretty soon we're not going to have our 'one-year moratorium' to use as an excuse, and we're going to have to talk about our relationship. You going to be up to it?"

Quinlin managed a quizzical grin and shrugged.

They were barely a month short of a sober year.

Skip Windom saw Jeb Quinlin coming through the basement door. He left his boots propped on the desk and drew another long sip of coffee from a cup that said BYTE ME. Windom, a civilian, headed the department's Tech Services Department, which kept the computers working. He was also as close to a bona fide computer expert as could be found in Dallas, having retired as a top engineer from Texas Instruments. Windom didn't wait for Quinlin to ask.

"Ain't good news, Jeb," he said, still not moving his boots off the desk. "Your man had Microsoft Word, Smartext, and Paradox. The shells are still there, but there's no data in them. He either had just loaded the programs and hadn't used them, which I doubt, or they've been purged, which is more likely. Sorry."

Richmond Carlisle's address was three blocks off the sixteenth fairway of the Park Cities Country Club. Quinlin's MAPSCO showed Regal View Lane on the boundary between Highland Park and University Park, an imaginary line made visually obvious by a preponderance of Mercedes-Benzes and stretch limos on the Highland

Park side and Lexuses and BMWs on the other. The boundary was a societal demarcation, Quinlin figured, a distinct barrier in the pecking order of the food chain. Haves and almost-haves, arriveds and getting-theres. Carlisle's condominium was on the BMW side of Regal View, tucked behind an ivy-covered six-foot privacy wall of beige brick. The driveway had an electronically controlled wrought-iron gate with a pedestal-mounted microphone at window level.

"Yes, ma'am, deceased, that's right," Quinlin repeated into the box. "We have permission from Mr. Carlisle's next of kin to examine his apartment."

Silence.

"Or," Quinlin added quickly, "we can go get a warrant and a couple of uniformed officers and come back. Whatever lights your fire."

The gate creaked open, and Quinlin steered the white Crown Victoria into the complex, following the terse directions given by the hoarse, faceless female voice in the microphone.

Whatever privacy the manager undoubtedly would have afforded Mr. Carlisle in life apparently was voided by his death. The chic but markedly disinterested property manager met Quinlin and his partner on the second-floor landing of the quadraplex, unlocked the door with her passkey, checked his file, and punched in four numbers on the security console to disable the security alarm. She wore a looping gold chain over a bulky black top with a pair of black stretch pants and black spike heels. Her black hair was shiny and pulled back, and deep red lipstick and white eye shadow made her severe and unyielding. McCarren asked Quinlin under his breath if she should be out during daylight hours. The younger partner also thought it strange that Zombie Woman hadn't asked how her erstwhile tenant had died. It was human nature, wanting to know every lurid detail of bad news.

"You can buzz me from the gate on your way out," she said, "and I'll lock up."

"So how much these dudes rent for a month?" McCarren inquired as she was turning her back to leave. He didn't have to schmooze; the door was already open. It was habit.

The property manager turned with a dramatic flair, and her eyes did a quick calculation. They apparently weren't impressed with the young cop, despite his navy Tommy Hilfiger suit, bone-colored shirt, and matching herringbone tie. "Like the old saying," she said, "You got to ask, you can't afford it."

The two detectives stood in the foyer, taking in all the trileveled condo they could see. McCarren speculated aloud that there must be close to three thousand square feet, enough to fit his entire house under the roof; there were more indoor plants than he had in his yard, front *and* back. The place was immaculate, and McCarren, himself a bachelor, marveled at how fastidious a fellow single man could be—until he found the note from the maid on a table just inside the door. "Señor Richmond," it said, "you have nada klorine for hot tubb. Too, you tell me dinner for how many guests, no?"

"This is all nice," Quinlin said, "but you're the computer expert. Let's find the damned thing and see if we got lucky."

Except for a couple of computer courses while he was getting his degree in criminology at the University of Texas at Arlington, McCarren had become computer literate on his own. Computers were his hobby; they also paved the way for an early promotion to detectives from uniforms. On his own time, McCarren had programmed his computer to show the frequency and likelihood of a serial rapist's next victim. Extensive stakeout teams, using his information, bagged the pervert, and McCarren had his detective's shield.

If McCarren couldn't unsort Carlisle's computer maze, they could still call on Skip Windom. But for purposes of testimony, Quinlin preferred a commissioned officer as a witness, rather than a civilian.

Carlisle's computer was in a top-floor study in the back of the condo. Quinlin stood on the balcony while McCarren worked on the computer. The senior detective looked down on a well-appointed common courtyard with a pink marble pool, a fountain, irrigated tropical landscaping, and a Plexiglas canopy with state-of-the-art exercise equipment. The backyard, Quinlin surmised, had cost more than his log house.

Richmond Carlisle had indeed been a computer geek, and his electronic toys filled one entire wall. His system was state-of-the-art, much more so than DPD's rickety old system, held together with baling wire, and McCarren quickly discovered that the programs were heavily passworded. Anyone as obsessive and meticulous as Carlisle, McCarren figured, had to have logged the access codes. He started in Carlisle's Rolodex under the *P*'s for password and PIN numbers. He tossed the unlocked lap drawer in the huge desk and the three drawers to the left. Finally, he found the codes typed neatly on a piece of paper taped to the underside of his leather desk calendar. The four primary PINs were RSC (Carlisle's initials), 1967 (apparently his birth year), 4217 (the last four digits of his SSN, according to the *Register & News'* Human Resources Department), and Bolshoi (for God only knows why). Like most people, McCarren noticed, Carlisle also used his birth year for PIN numbers on his savings accounts and credit cards, all of which were listed, by account number, on the same sheet. The detective was mildly disappointed. Most computer techies were more imaginative. They used byzantine passwords, unrelated and untraceable to any information contained on driver's licenses, birth records, or other documents someone might stumble upon.

The minutiae of Carlisle's life was contained in a microchip smaller than a pinkie nail, and with a few keystrokes, the details unreeled onto the oversized thin color monitor in front of McCarren. The passwords allowed him to plumb and prowl Carlisle's existence with extraordinary depth. Carlisle had paid his bills and done his banking electronically; he'd made his airline reservations on the Internet, talked frequently with the same people on E-mail, been a member of a Yale alumni electronic bulletin board, had his own Web site on a publishing net, bought his vitamins from electronic shopping nets, and downloaded apparently every nude picture he could find of Melanie Griffith onto a file he slugged GODDESS.

McCarren had spent hundreds of hours probing people's pasts. But, overwhelmingly, that research had been through interviews and public records. The uncommon computerized access to Carlisle's life made McCarren strangely uncomfortable, and he imagined himself as a Peeping Tom. Periodically and involuntarily, he looked over his shoulder. Quinlin sensed his guilt.

"It doesn't make it any easier that you're on official police business?" Quinlin asked. "Don't let it get to you. Law of averages says we should be able to catch an easy one every once in awhile. Besides, it's probably all gonna be for naught. Young Carlisle probably punched out on natural causes. He doesn't seem exotic or good enough to have pissed off anyone enough to kill him.

"And damned sure not the Colters," Quinlin said. "If that bunch had killed him, he'd be a missing person from now on. They'd have left him for coyote bait at the bottom of some canyon."

Hesitantly, McCarren continued to plumb Carlisle's computer. There was a computer fax from a friend in Philadelphia, and a junk fax from a Chinese restaurant offering carryout. The detective found a letter to Carlisle's family lawyer in New York, asking tax questions about restructuring his trust account, from which he apparently had been receiving substantial payments since his graduation from Yale.

And in a letter to a woman lawyer in Boston, apparently a former classmate, Carlisle had made veiled but unmistakable references to an abortion a year earlier. "Considering our life goals, your making shareholder in the firm and my getting to the *Times*," he had written, "it was wholly the only practical option." Now, it seemed to Carlisle, they were "headed in markedly different directions and our lives are singularly disparate." It was the most stilted Dear John letter McCarren could imagine. Carlisle apologized for feeling "that our relationship needs to be ended as expeditiously and painlessly as possible."

"Geez," McCarren said, "this bastard is a veritable fountainhead of emotion."

When McCarren noticed that Carlisle had been querying on the Net for interpretation of federal drug statutes, public corruption laws, and RICO, the federal Racketeer influenced and Corrupt Organizations Act, he pulled some of the responses from Carlisle's E-mail. He found nothing, however, that pointed to the identity of the source Carlisle had so zealously guarded, or information that source would have passed along about a bail bondsman or an assignment in Sul Ross County.

It was almost six when McCarren logged off the computer. Quinlin gathered the ream of printouts and then they headed down the stairs. Quinlin couldn't help himself. He opened the refrigerator door and scanned the contents. Checking refrigerators had become a habit six years ago, after he'd discovered five thousand dollars tucked in a manila folder inside a freezer. The cash, as it turned out, proved to be the payoff for a contract killing and the key evidence in sending its owner to the death house in Huntsville.

The inside door of Carlisle's refrigerator was loaded with vitamins and supplements, many of which bore Chinese characters. There was a carton of 2 percent milk, four quarts of orange Gatorade, and assorted condiments, but Quinlin fixed on several bottles of wine, the names of which he couldn't pronounce.

He wondered if he would ever get over the resentment of not being able to drink. Other people could handle it; it made him crazy. Furthermore, abstinence made him feel left out.

Making his way to the foyer, the senior detective noticed a blinking red light on the bar by the kitchen. A six-foot fern had hidden the pulsating light from view on his way in. The light was attached to a caller ID.

"Caller ID?" Quinlin muttered to McCarren. "But of course."

Quinlin hit the playback button on the answering machine. There were five messages: a woman wondering why Carlisle hadn't returned her call; a computer-generated voice selling cut-rate vacation packages; a whiny "Why don't you call" from his mother in Manhattan; the rebuffed woman again, more strident this time; and a man's voice. The man didn't identify himself, just said, "Call me. I've got something else you'd be interested in."

Quinlin quickly hit the save button, then reached in his coat pocket for his microcassette recorder. He replayed the message and taped it, then saved it again on Carlisle's machine. The corresponding caller, according to the digital readout on the caller ID, was David Cartwright, and it listed his phone number, a North Dallas prefix. Quinlin produced a notebook and pen. He sat on a bar stool and began going backward through the calls placed to Carlisle's condo, logging the names, numbers, and times. The machine had a capacity for ninety-nine calls, and it was filled.

Quinlin and McCarren would cross-check all the names and numbers on a database when they got back downtown, but Quinlin figured it would just be due diligence. David Cartwright not only had "something else" for Carlisle; he had called six times in nine days. All the calls had been after 9:00 P.M., and one was placed at 11:58 P.M. The last call had been made on the day Carlisle died.

"Great," McCarren said. "Who's Cartwright and what did he have for our boy?"

"Probably seaweed and ginseng. You know, we get lucky, we could still catch a natural causes out of all this."

Dr. Mark Berryman was on his third cup of black coffee and second package of vending-machine Oreos by the time Quinlin and McCarren answered his beep and appeared at Parkland's South-western Institute of Forensic Science.

The well-developed and superbly conditioned body of Richmond Carlisle had not yielded answers easily. The challenge had left Berryman exhausted, but the results—solving the puzzle—had also left him exhilarated.

"This poor bastard didn't die of natural causes," Dr. Berryman said.

Quinlin and McCarren looked at each other. They'd never heard Berryman use a bad word. He never cursed. Carlisle must be something special.

"And he died in unimaginable anguish, I'll guarantee you that."

The forensic pathologist led them through Carlisle's body in chronological order. The exterior of the body may have been distinctly unremarkable, but the insides, according to Berryman, were ravaged. And whatever caused the damage had had the equivalent effect of a neutron bomb, particularly in Carlisle's sinus cavity and the frontal lobe of his brain. Swelling in the frontal lobe was so extreme that it had forced the entire brain backward in the skull, shoving its very backside, the cerebellum, over the hole through which the spinal cord entered the head. Tissue in the brain and sinus cavity showed hemorrhaging, and necrosis, or decay, was apparent. Lymph nodes, the body's natural barrier against bacteria and other harmful microorganisms, were swollen or collapsed. The microscopic cells had swollen and ruptured. Cell membranes in his brain had been destroyed. And when the cells and vessels literally imploded under the invasion of the lethal substance, there had been a complete shutdown of coagulopathy, the body's natural clotting process. Bottom line, Carlisle's head was a bloated reservoir of dead tissue and blood.

Nor was Berryman's discovery of devastation limited to Carlisle's sinus cavity and brain. He'd found blood in the dead man's nasal passages and along his gums. There was blood in the lining of his heart and in his gastrointestinal tract, and tissue in both places had been destroyed.

"Only once in fifteen years have I ever seen similar damage," Berryman said, "and that had been confined to a patient's lower leg, about three inches above the ankle. Out of ignorance or fear, that patient hadn't sought treatment, and he died an agonizingly painful death strung out over three days."

"So Carlisle died of what, exactly?" Quinlin asked, straining for the bottom line.

"I'm coming to that," Berryman said, relishing the punch line. "You're not going to believe it, though."

The pathologist had relied on that episode from more than a decade earlier and thus had ordered blood work and a urinalysis on Carlisle. There was a marked decrease in red cells and platelets in the blood, and his urine showed blood, glucose, and an uncommonly high presence of protein.

Convinced he had isolated the cause of Carlisle's death, Berryman had lowered the high-intensity surgical lights to within twenty-four inches of the body and examined it with a magnifying glass. Meticulously, he'd examined every inch of skin and checked between his toes, under his nails, beneath his scrotum, in his armpits, and inside and behind his ears. With the aid of two lab techs, he'd rolled Carlisle's stiffened body over so that it was lying facedown and begun the process anew, pausing periodically at pimples, moles, and the dead man's anal cavity. Not finding what he was looking for, Berryman and his aides had rolled Carlisle onto his back again. The pathologist then pulled over a two-foot stool beside the examining table and moved the lights so they were directly over the incision he had made in Carlisle's face. Standing on the stool and bent over the body, he ran the magnifying glass slowly over the exposed sinus cavity. Not taking his eyes off the cavity, he reached up with his right hand and pulled the light until it bumped the back of his head. He asked for an alcohol swab and dabbed away at the tissue.

"There it is!" he had screamed as the two lab techs looked blankly at each other. "Son of a bitch! What'll these people think of next?"

Cleared of blood and fluid, the tissue at the uppermost point of Carlisle's nasal membrane, the portion that separates the nose from the sinus cavity, reflected a tiny pin prick. It had been made, Berryman knew, by a narrow-gauge hypodermic needle.

Except for an occasional break to use the men's room or to stretch his back, Berryman had spent five and a half hours hovering over Carlisle's body.

"Richmond Carlisle was murdered," Berryman now said to Quinlin and McCarren, "and whoever did it was one macabre son of a bitch. It's going to take maybe a week before the toxicology reports confirm this, but I'm certain that somebody injected him with snake venom. Through his nose."

"Whoa," Quinlin said. "You say snake venom? You've got to be shi—"

"Let me finish, Jeb," the pathologist said. "I'm so tired, I could pass out. Pending the toxicology reports, I'd say the venom was something from the Crotalus family, maybe a copperhead, but probably a rattlesnake, judging from the edema and swelling at the point of envenomation."

The invigoration from the discovery was gone from Berryman's voice now, and he just sounded bone-weary.

"This explains the bruising at the base of the jaw," the doctor said. "After striking him in the back of the head, I think somebody probably straddled him on the ground. I found some tiny granules of soil in the hair at the back of his head—we'll be taking a look at that later. At any rate, someone grabbed him around the neck with one hand and, I strongly believe, injected him with the other hand.

"Death would have been quick," Berryman said, "but not quick enough. Trust me. This guy died a horrible death."

5

Clint Harper's cubicle at the *Register & News* was larger than the others and even had a window that overlooked a fountain in a small park across the street from the newspaper building. On one of the two walls that wasn't a soundproofed fabric divider was a framed reproduction of a full-page in-house ad that noted he had won the 1993 Pulitzer Prize for investigative reporting.

Harper was typing steadily at his computer when Quinlin appeared in the doorway of the cubicle. Harper was a thorough reporter, and he'd already talked to the Berryman and gotten the results of the ME's autopsy.

"Talk about a bizarre cause of death," Harper said, his eyes taking in a last glimpse of the type on the computer screen before turning to Quinlin. "This is one for *Ripley's*. You think it's for real?"

"How often is Berryman wrong?"

"Yeah, right. I'll tell you this, though. If the Colters are behind this, they're a bunch of real sickos."

"That's what bothers me," Quinlin said. "I grew up around the Colters, and there's no question they're accustomed to having their own way about things. And there's no question they're ruthless as hell about business deals. You don't get where they've gotten by being nice guys. But injecting snake venom in somebody's nose? I don't think that's their style. Their style would be, at first warning, to get their task force of lawyers to come after Carlisle and the paper with threats of libel and try to turn this building into a four-story parking garage. They'd coerce, threaten and leverage behind the scenes—not kill, particularly not using snakes. They don't have to. That's the way power brokers get it done. This is way too blue-collar for the Colters.

"Given our two preliminary options," Quinlin said, "I'd still put my money on Bumpy Rhodes."

The bail bondsman was nothing if not crudely sadistic. Quinlin had once arrested a murder suspect, Reginald Worthington, who swore that Bumpy and his bounty hunters had tortured him for twenty-four hours before finally turning him in to sheriff's deputies. Known by some women on the street as "Mule" for certain legendary attributes that weren't all that apparent with his clothes on, Worthington was pulled out of a Houston brothel by Bumpy's bounty hunters. According to Worthington, Bumpy's boys had held him down while their boss slid handcuffs around his right wrist, then ratcheted down the left bracelet around the base of his penis and balls until his eyes bugged. They kept him that way, Mule claimed, for the 235 miles from Houston and threw him in the back room of the bond office for another half day before hauling him to the Lew Sterrett Criminal Justice Center.

"How'd your brass handle the news about Carlisle?" Quinlin asked.

" 'Bout like I expected," Harper said. "Implied, although unspoken was the fact that he would still be alive if I had adopted him for the Colter story. The executive editor, my greatest fan anyway, read me the riot act about following orders and being a team player and generally tried to make me feel like run-over dog shit. Same old stuff. Some of the staff, particularly the younger ones, who bought into Carlisle's debut-of-a-star routine, are convinced I'm just as guilty as the guy who murdered him. It's pretty chilly when I walk through the newsroom. The sentiment is that either I wimped out or I'm a prizewinning, arrogant asshole too good to work with a junior reporter."

"Well, Carlisle was a college graduate and old enough to vote," Quinlin said. "Sounds like he let his battleship mouth overload his motorboat ass. That's not your fault, no matter how they try to shake it out.

"So what's your story going to say? I mean, no viable suspects, just a cause of death. Even that's preliminary. Sounds pretty sketchy to me."

"It will be, but I don't have a choice. Brewster says we're going to be in the paper in the morning, then we're going to be in the paper in the morning."

Garrett Anderson Brewster—never just Garrett Brewster or Garrett A. Brewster—was the *Register & News*'s executive editor, a transplanted Brit who, despite more than thirty years on U.S. soil, still spoke the Queen's precise English with a pompous, contrived accent. Brewster had made no secret of the fact that without the publisher's support, Harper would be out of a job, Pulitzer or no Pulitzer.

Quinlin had heard about Dallas's highest-profile editor years earlier. A burglary detective he knew had investigated a break-in at Brewster's Highland Park mansion. Despite having a high-tech security system, the newspaper executive supposedly had forgotten to arm the system before leaving for a monthlong European vacation. The insurance claim had been well into the six figures and alleged some items, according to the burglary detective, that may well not have existed. The burglary dick figured it was a painless way to pay off a month's vacation in Paris and Switzerland.

"I'm going to need some official police comment for the story," Harper said.

"It can't come from me, not on one this big," Quinlin said. "I'll go to Chief Abrams when I get back to the station and encourage him to go on the record. This one's going to be too politically hot, and it needs a deputy chief. I doubt he'll say much at this stage, but I'll see what I can come up with. When's your deadline?"

"About two hours."

"Say, you know those handy-dandy commercial databases you guys got, where you can look up all the business holdings and secretary of state's records on the computer?" Quinlin asked. "How 'bout running the Colters and their business dealings for me? Just to see what we're dealing with here."

"Where you want to go with it?"

"Nuts and bolts," Quinlin said. "Nothing's too inconsequential.

I'm looking for relationships and holdings. Indictments, lawsuits, liens, bankruptcies, marriage applications, divorces, SEC filings, licenses, airplane and car registrations. In other words, I want to know every time the Colters have passed gas. Probably turn out to be a wasted effort, but we need to start somewhere."

"That's going to be a hell of a list," Harper cautioned, "just from what little I've heard about the Colters."

"There're three of them—Clendon, the old man, who'd be in his sixties, maybe even seventy. And then there're his two upstanding sons, Buck—and that's his for-sure, real name—and Wade, the little brother. Buck's my age, DOB somewhere around fifty-one, and Wade was maybe two years behind me in school."

Harper was jotting the information in his reporter's notebook.

"Clendon Colter has a thing about 'Pan Permian,' " Quinlin said. "He puts it on everything. That's where you'll find most of his holdings."

"What's Permian?"

"It's an oil field in West Texas," Quinlin said. "Word in Comanche Gap when I was a kid was that ol' man Colter was a wildcatter in the Permian Basin back in the forties and fifties, and supposedly that's where he made his first real money. And virtually everything he owns today still carries a version of Pan Permian, kind of a tribute to his good luck, I guess."

Quinlin remembered some of the Colter entities from a recent profile on Clendon Colter in *Texas Monthly Business*.

"There's Pan Permian Holdings, Inc.; Pan Permian Ranches; Pan Permian Land and Cattle; Pan Permian Development, which is into commercial real estate; Pan Permian Oil and Gas; Pan Permian Financial—that's his bank holding company; Pan Permian Air, his airfreight business; Pan Permian Freighters, a truck line; and Pan Permian Consultants. God only knows what that is. Oh yeah, there's even a Pan Permian PAC, a political action committee."

"The computer databases should be able to break all that out," Harper said, "but it's going to take me awhile. And I can't get started until I get this story and Brewster off my back."

"I'm running some traps on Bumpy Rhodes with some detectives and a prosecutor I know," Quinlin said. "Bumpy's fifty miles of broken glass, and, from what I'm hearing, he didn't appreciate—"

A woman with a grim face appeared in Harper's doorway.

"Mr. Brewster wants to see what you've got so far on the Carlisle piece," she said. "And he said to tell you that means *now*."

She did a curt about-face and was gone.

"Brewster's secretary," Harper said. "He hired her because the temperature of her heart was as low as his."

"So tell me this and I'll get out of your hair," Quinlin said. "Know a David Cartwright?"

"The FBI agent?"

"Beats hell out of me," Quinlin said. "How many David Cartwrights you know? And did Richmond Carlisle know him?"

"I only know one," Harper said, "and I don't know him well. Just another peach-fuzzed Young Turk for the feds. Wouldn't have a clue who Carlisle knew or didn't know."

Quinlin saw Harper writing the name in his reporter's notebook as he left the cubicle.

Quinlin was waiting at the cattle guard in 5:30 A.M. darkness when Larry slowed down, aimed his old pickup diagonally across Farm Road 4, and side-armed the newspaper squarely between the two upright fence posts and into the only puddle in the gravel lane. Quinlin cursed and grabbed the paper quickly. Even enshrouded in its plastic wrapper, the newspaper had sopped up the overnight rain like a sponge. He headed back down the lane in the International Scout which he still used to piddle around the ranch, and he made a mental note to tell the teenager to leave his paper in the mailbox from now on. He parked the banged-out Scout in the circular drive and paused on the wide front porch long enough to rub Bingo's ears. The Border collie lay on his belly, a soft sound coming from his black-and-white stomach. Smartest dog Quinlin had ever seen; maybe he could teach Bingo to snare the paper in midair like a Frisbee before Larry could destroy it.

Quinlin moved quickly inside, grabbed a cup of black coffee, and carefully spread the newspaper onto the kitchen table. The top third of the paper had turned to papier-mâché. Madeline, meanwhile, was requesting the features section, which had escaped with only a soaked corner.

Harper's story was on page one, above the fold and beneath a substantial headline that read REGISTER & NEWS WRITER FOUND SLAIN BESIDE ROAD. His eyes quickly scanned the story:

By CLINT HARPER
STAFF WRITER OF THE REGISTER & NEWS

A *Register & News* staff writer whose body was found in his car on a south Dallas County road Tuesday was murdered, according to a preliminary autopsy by the Dallas County Medical Examiner's Office.

Richmond Carlisle, a 31-year-old special projects writer, apparently was injected with snake venom before he was left in his car along the then-deserted Houston School Road, according to the medical examiner, Mark Berryman. The final autopsy has not been finalized, pending results of toxicological exams expected next week.

"The cause of death was unorthodox, gruesome, and painful," Dr. Berryman said. "That's about all that we're certain of right now."

Deputy Chief Jon Abrams, head of detectives for the Dallas Police Department, said the investigation into Carlisle's death, originally believed to have been the result of natural causes, is in the early stages and has produced no suspects or motive.

"Richmond Carlisle was one of the key members of our staff and possessed unlimited journalistic talent and potential," said Garrett Anderson Brewster, executive editor of the *Register & News*. "We are saddened and griefstricken over his loss and will leave no stone unturned in investigating the cause of his death."

The editor declined late Wednesday to say what assignment Carlisle was working on at the time of his death. "We're providing that information to the appropriate authorities and will assist them in any way possible. . . ."

Quinlin groaned.

"What's the matter?" Madeline asked from across the table. "You don't sound happy."

"The editor of the *Register and News* has just pledged to help us in the Carlisle case 'in any way possible,' " Quinlin said. "That means his pecker tracks are going to be all over this investigation."

"But Harper's your buddy," she said. "You trust him, don't you?"

"Harper's not the problem. His boss is the problem. Brewster's going to be a political pain in the ass and is going to keep the heat turned up. Harper won't be able to call his own shots. And we're in the grease on this one already."

Quinlin went back to the story. The executive editor's influence was already obvious. There were several effusive quotes from Brewster about Carlisle's "meticulous reporting" and his "literary grace on deadline." He could tell the martyrdom wasn't from Harper. The late reporter's accomplishments, Quinlin noted, were all academic and none professional, and they filled four graphs. There was even a quote from a professor at Yale who applauded Carlisle's "dedication to intellectualism," which, the academician noted, had resulted in a Phi Beta Kappa and a yearlong honors postgraduate program at some British university that Quinlin had never heard of.

Conspicuously absent in the story was any hint at a motive, other than the fact that Brewster had declined to comment on Carlisle's current assignment, inferring the murder stemmed from the reporter's aggressive pursuit of truth, rather than, say, from an act of violence by someone who hated his guts for a multitude of personal reasons. High drama on page one.

"When I get to town, Harper and I are going to have to have an understanding. Brewster and his paper are not going to run this goddamned investigation."

. . .

The AAA-Free As a Bird Bail Bond Agency was located, conveniently, across from the Lew Sterrett Criminal Justice Center, beneath a blinking purple-and-green neon arrow that pointed to a portable building perched on cement blocks. A four-foot sign across the front said in green letters with a purple outline, HOME OF THE GET-OUT-OF-JAIL CARD. Smaller lettering below noted that the firm specialized in *Felonies, State & Federal*. The building was located in the parking lot of an abandoned, boarded-up Exxon service station that still stood in the background. There were five parking spaces in the lot labeled AUTHORIZED PERSONNEL ONLY. A white Lincoln Continental with blacked-out windows was parked in the space closest to the portable building, and Quinlin figured it had to belong to Bumpy Rhodes. He couldn't see the chief proprietor trekking his fat ass all the way across the parking lot to the building.

Quinlin was looking at the right-front tire on the Lincoln when he heard the voice behind him.

"You're not thinking about stealing the tires off a man's car, are you? Surely they're paying you enough to afford your own wheels."

Skate Runnels was a wiseass when he was a cop; he obviously hadn't changed since he was drummed off the force for picking the wallets of the suspects he arrested.

"Which one of these high-dollar vehicles would be yours, Skate?" Quinlin asked. "You bail bondsmen must be making good money. There're some nice vehicles in these spaces. That your four-by-four Ford over there?"

Quinlin kept walking, heading toward the red Ford pickup, with the ex-cop following him. He made no secret of checking the front tires on each of the agency's vehicles along the way.

"So what the fuck you doin', Quinlin," Runnels asked, "inspecting our tires, for God sakes? Bumpy don't like people prowling in his lot."

"I figured Bumpy'd be worried about other things after that reporter kicked his ass on the front page. How much did that cost y'all? Half million, wasn't it?

"Y'all get new tires at the same time?" Quinlin said. "All these tires look brand-new."

"You need to get a fuckin' life, Quinlin."

"How's Bumpy's demeanor this morning? Think he'd buy me a cup of coffee?"

"Well, I reckon that ol' dog won't hunt," Bumpy Rhodes said, barely glancing up from the sports section. "I figured when I saw the paper that it'd just be a matter of time till you'd be here asking about that pop-dick reporter. See, what I do is make money, and you don't make money pullin' shit that's gonna keep you in the flood-lights. Me, I'm just a bidnessman providing a public service. And frankly, whoever done it, they provided a *gen-u-ine* public service. Carlisle was an asshole. Meddled in my bidness, that's a goddamned fact, but I didn't have time to kill him. Too busy, know what I mean?"

Bumpy Rhodes, Quinlin knew, didn't have to have time to kill someone. He had the unique ability to have someone killed without getting his own hands dirty. Untold numbers of his so-called clients were free on bonds, having been charged and indicted for some of the most violent crimes in Dallas County. Bumpy, by virtue of his signature on their bonds, controlled their freedom and their des-tinies. On whim, he and his bounty hunters could kick in their doors, handcuff them, and return them to county jail, no questions asked. In the perverse world of bail bonding, all Bumpy had to do was mention to the right client that Richmond Carlisle needed to pay for doing him dirty. It was the way debts were routinely settled in the netherworld of defendants and bondsmen.

"Just for the record, where were you Monday night and early Tuesday morning?" Quinlin asked.

The fat bondsman continued to peruse the sports page as if he hadn't heard.

"S'pose the Rangers got a chance at the play-offs without no decent pitchin'?" Bumpy asked. "Hell, they ain't got nobody who can get the ball over the plate. I'm over the hill, but I could hit their pitchin'."

"So where were you?"

"Where you'd like to been," Bumpy said, folding the sports sec-tion carefully and placing it in front of him on the desk. He looked Quinlin in the eyes and grinned, exposing a mouthful of crooked teeth the color of buttered popcorn. "I was hosing a client's ol' lady, but I don't s'pose she'd be proud to admit that to a *police*. On the other hand, ol' Bumpy does what he does pretty well. She might be *real* proud to be my alibi. Workin' in the justice system has certain fringe benefits, if you know what I mean, and I think you do. When's the last time some skank wanted to trade you a blow job for a free ride?"

The bondsman laughed deep from his gut and reached for the slobbery stub of a cigar in the ashtray.

"I'll need her name before I leave," Quinlin said. "Richmond Carlisle cost you a lot of money, Bumpy. You don't look like the kind of guy to part with a buck all that easily. I hear you threatened to kill Carlisle."

It was a fail-safe bluff, based on Bumpy's legacy.

"Damned right," the bondsman said. "Sumbitch came in here sayin' I didn't have enough collateral to be writin' all those bonds. Well, that's up to the sheriff's department, not some pop-dick with a press card."

"Yeah, your man in the sheriff's department got fired over those stories, didn't he?"

"That man had a wife and four kids, and now he ain't got no retirement," Bumpy said, phony and righteous indignation taking over. "Now, you want to talk about victims, how 'bout that pitiful sheriff's deputy? I got to make a place for him in my bidness now 'cause that reporter meddled around. That's more overhead to me, but I'll do it, 'cause it's the right thing to do. I'm a believer in doin' the right thing, know what I mean?"

All of Bumpy's runners and bounty hunters were defrocked cops. Quinlin figured the deputy was raking a point or two off every bond he steered Bumpy's way. And from a dated Department of Public Safety intelligence report, Quinlin knew Bumpy Rhodes could afford to do the right thing for a pivotal person in the sheriff's bonding division. According to DPS intelligence, Bumpy was a front man for Roderick "Roddy" Devereaux, who moved his illicit gambling operation from Dallas to Louisiana in the 1950s. When Bayou State politicians legalized casino gambling in the early nineties, Devereaux opened two "resorts," one each in Shreveport and Bossier City, and had more money than Ross Perot. Rumored in law enforcement—but not documented by hard evidence—was that Devereaux was mobbed up with a Cleveland crime boss who didn't believe in taxes. Bumpy's bonding business, like countless other marginally legitimate businesses, including Devereaux's casinos, supposedly laundered money for the Cleveland mob.

On Quinlin's scale, bail bondsmen wallowed like bottom feeders at the depths of the food chain. And those were the so-called legitimate bondsmen, who charged 15 percent of the bond up front for a man's freedom, then beat him near death if he tried to enjoy too much of it. Bumpy and others like him were lower than whale shit. Privately, Quinlin saw justice in the occasional defendants who no-showed for trial, making their bondsmen pony up the entire $100,000 or $200,000 bond. Paying off the bond was a major hickey for the bondsmen, but only a minor inconvenience for law enforcement. Ultimately, the kinds of people who get charged with crimes, make bonds, and run also return to their old habits and end up again in the backseats of squad cars. Just a matter of time.

"Bumpy, write that woman's name and number down for me," Quinlin said. "I'm going to be checking you out. It may be that I need to come back and we'll need to talk some more. Know what I mean?"

Bumpy's ham hand engulfed a pencil and he scrawled on a scrap of paper while looking at a card in his Rolodex.

"She'd be the one with the grin pasted on her face," Bumpy said, laughing at his own attempt at humor.

The bondsman's eyes turned serious. He shoved his business card across the debris on the desk and dropped it in front of Quinlin.

"Like I said, you wasting your time with me on this Carlisle deal," he said, "but when you get the ol' boy who done it, give him my card for me. Tell him I said he done the public a service and I'll post his bond for five percent, what with him being such a good citizen and all."

6

Clint Harper hated meetings. In the old days, before editors had MBAs after their names and before newspaper city rooms resembled stock brokerages, editors merely gave reporters their assignments, issued them a story length and a deadline, and expected to see the stories when they were finished. Over the last five years, though, things had changed dramatically in the profession and at the *Register & News,* and none of it, near as Harper could tell, had been for the better. Nothing could get done without meetings. Supposedly, meetings made reporters feel inclusive, as if their opinions mattered. In actuality, the meetings were inquisitions, during which reporters found themselves defending a story assignment, lobbying for the right to do it, and answering inane, premature questions like "What would the top of the story say?"

"My crystal ball is all fucked up," Harper once told Brewster in one of the so-called story sessions. "I don't know what the lead is because I haven't reported the story yet. Give me some time for research, and you'll be the second to know."

Hugh Arrington had been Harper's rabbi in the old days, shortly after the morning *Register* and the afternoon *News* merged—and before Arrington got tired of playing Brewster's head games and resigned to go to ABC's *20/20* news magazine as a producer.

"Never tell an editor more than he needs to know," Arrington had cautioned. "They've got the attention span of a thirteen-year-old speed freak."

It was Arrington's doctrine, one later embraced as a paradigm by Harper, that editors wanted to know only enough to take credit when the project won awards, but never enough to accept the blame when the stories got someone sued.

"Prior knowledge to an editor is Russian roulette," the old pro used to say. "See, they've got to maintain plausible deniability. Just in case they get shit in their beard."

This meeting would be worse. Brewster would be there, along with Ben Mason, the managing editor, Mark Silverman, the deputy managing editor for news, and Carlisle's parents. Ostensibly, it was an update, an opportunity to hear from Harper everything the medical examiner and the police had learned.

Harper knew he couldn't get by with his customary faded jeans, and he appeared in a coat and tie. Brewster sat at the head of the conference table, with the Carlisles on his left and Mason and Silverman on his right. Their faces were somber, and the room felt like a meat locker. Harper slid into the chair at the other end of the table from Brewster and put his notebook in front of him. It was the executive editor's show, and he waited for his cue.

"I'm certain none of us want to be here under these unfortunate circumstances," Brewster said in his affected Brit accent. "Nonetheless, it's incumbent on us to try to learn as much as possible about Richmond's, ah, unfortunate demise, to ensure we do everything possible to bring his attackers to justice."

Typical Brewster drivel, Harper thought. It was a feel-good session for Carlisle's parents, an opportunity to demonstrate the level of Brewster's concern and cooperation. And, Harper figured, probably an opportunity for everyone in the room to work out on him.

"In that vein, Harper, we expect a full briefing on even the slightest nuggets of information you've been able to glean about the investigation."

"Well, actually, virtually everything I know was in the story this morning," Harper said, "which, admittedly, at this point, isn't all that much."

"Oh, don't be so modest, Harper," Silverman said. "I'm sure your good ol' boy sources have told you everything they know. Good reporters always know more than they write, isn't that right?"

Mark Silverman, MBA, the executive in charge of all news gathering, had never been a street reporter. He was a graduate of Stanford and the *Register & News*'s management-training program. He was also an obsequious head-nodder and handwringer who had wormed his way to the deputy managing editor's job by perpetually testing the wind and following without question his superiors' orders. Typically, Harper thought, when senior management ordered the newsroom budget cut by 15 percent, Silverman lopped off another 5 percent, further ingratiating himself with the suits. It didn't matter that there wasn't enough money left in the travel budget to cover a 737 crash if it happened in the back parking lot. He probably wouldn't have recognized it as news anyway.

"The fact is," Harper said coolly, "the medical examiner is awaiting toxicology reports, and the cops don't know anything at this point. You've got to understand they just now discovered it's a homicide."

"Well, surely the Colters have to be suspects," Silverman said. "As you *well* know, Richmond was investigating them when he was killed."

Silverman would nibble you to death like a duck. His inflection was calculated to be snide, and it worked.

"What we *know* is that Richmond was poking around, asking questions about the Colters," Harper said. "What we don't know— at least I don't—is what his information was or where it came from. Or even if it was valid. And we don't know if the Colters even knew that Richmond was interested in them. If they didn't know Richmond was out there, there's hardly a motive on their part.

"On the other hand, Richmond had written about Bumpy Rhodes's bail bond business, and everyone knows that Bumpy's not someone you mess with. The point is, we don't know how many other people might have had reason to be mad at Richmond."

"Is it true, Mr. Harper, that you refused to work with my son on the Colter story?" Everett Carlisle asked. It was more an accusation than a question, and the senior Carlisle delivered it with iciness. His eyes never left Harper's.

"I'm not sure where you got your information, Mr. Carlisle," Harper said, scanning the three editors in the room, "but the situation was a little more complex than that. I had some questions. Richmond was, uh, reluctant to tell me specifically what his information was or where it came from. I didn't work—"

"Isn't there safety in numbers when you do this kind of work?" Annette Carlisle asked. She wasn't a bad-looking woman, but about thirty pounds past prime, the burden of living the good life, Harper assumed. Watching her seated next to her well-tanned, manicured, graying-around-the-temples husband, Harper figured she was too caught up in her own social circles to give a damn that her spouse was probably screwing around on her. Harper'd bet money on it. Fifty-year-old men obsessed with their appearances were either overcompensating or plugging their twenty-year-old secretaries.

The meeting was a put-up deal. Brewster, or maybe Silverman, had laid their son's death squarely at Harper's feet.

"To a degree, I guess, but—"

"I never wanted Richmond to come here in the first place." It was his mother again. "This place is so alien to his upbringing, just so different. Rattlesnake venom, for God sakes. Who'd ever hear of such a thing in New York City?"

Harper bit his tongue. No, he thought. In the Big Apple, cops just jammed broom handles up suspects' asses or shot them forty-one times. And perps, for no discernible reason, shot people sitting in cars with .44 Magnums.

"Who *are* these people, and what are they thinking?" she asked. "I told him it would be different here. I tried to prepare him. These people here, they're just not what he was used to. Not the way he was reared. What could prepare him for a heathen who would capture rattlesnakes?"

Annette Carlisle shook at the picture she had painted.

"But Richmond insisted it was a great place to get his start in writing," she said. "Get the experience, he said, and he'd go to the top. He wanted to come home at some point to the *Times*, which, of course, is an excellent newspaper. He graduated from Yale with honors, and you'd think that would suffice."

Harper had worked hard to get to the top at the *Register & News*. The paper wasn't a stepping-stone to him; it was a destination. At least he had thought so at one time. The Carlisles clearly regarded

Dallas as the last frontier, a backwater wide spot that civilization had skipped.

Brewster coughed, a signal that he was taking back the meeting.

"If this is, in fact, all you know about the investigation," the executive editor told Harper haughtily, "I suggest your time might be better spent working your sources to find out what's going on. Then you can report back to us when you actually know something."

"That might take awhile. I tried to tell you—"

"Well, go try."

Brewster dismissed Harper with a wave of his hand, like a impatient father would redirect a bothersome four-year-old. Harper was embarrassed in front of the Carlisles and felt his face redden.

"Silverman," Harper said, "I need to ask you a question outside, please."

The deputy managing editor appeared genuinely puzzled, then followed Harper through the door, which the reporter shut behind them.

"You ever pull some cheap shit like that again," Harper said, leaning into Silverman, "I'll stick that fuckin' Mont Blanc pen of yours up your ass and you'll shit ink for a week. I told you Carlisle couldn't do the story alone. You let him carry the ball by himself anyway. That was your call, asshole."

"You're not helping yourself with me," the editor said, sniffing as if he was bored. But Harper could see fear in his eyes.

"I could give a shit what you think of me," Harper said. "You don't fuckin' register on my radar."

"The Colter story was an important assignment and it had to be done," Silverman said. "You left everything to him—"

"I said I wasn't going anywhere, particularly Sul Ross County, unless I could judge the information and source for myself. This arrogant little shit comes in here fat-catting, claiming that one of the most influential families in Texas is somehow violating the law. Well, just fuckin' great. How? Says who? Some phantom asshole your man won't reveal? Well, Silverman, if you'd ever been a reporter, you'd know it doesn't work that way. If he didn't trust me to know the source, I didn't trust him to work the assignment."

"It was just a preliminary planning session," Silverman said, backing up a step to put some distance between them. "He would have told us at some point. You backed out because you didn't want to go to Sul Ross County and mess with the big boys. And now he's dead."

"Bullshit!" Harper shouted. "You pulled the trigger on the assignment, chose to let him go it alone. And you did it because you didn't have the balls to tell Brewster's fair-haired buddy no. Because you knew Brewster would be on your ass. It wasn't my job to baby-sit him."

"The story had phenomenal potential," the editor said. "The Colters are the crème de la crème of Texas society, real movers and—"

"Don't tell me who the Colters are. I'm probably the only one in the room who knows them. The fact is, your little turd of a reporter saw a front-page copyright, an award, and his ticket to his beloved *New York Times,*" Harper said. "Well, I'm not carrying him on my back. He should have been writing feature stories, god damn it. The problem is that neither one of you no-talent bastards knew what you were doing and things got out of hand."

The conference room door creaked behind them and Brewster appeared in the hallway. Not until the interruption did Harper realize how loud he had gotten.

"I think you've done quite enough already," the executive editor said to Harper. "Get out of here and do your job while you still have one."

Harper escaped into the cavernous newsroom. He could feel his pulse racing and his breathing was heavy. Only a few reporters had settled in at the bay of desks, all of which were shoved together in clusters of four. Harper's watch said it was only 8:50 A.M. He was surprised that the ordeal in the conference room had taken only fifteen minutes. It had seemed longer.

The *Register & News* was a morning newspaper, and the bulk of its reporters worked from 10:00 A.M. to 7:00 P.M. In an hour, there would be fifty or sixty reporters at their desks, reading papers, drinking coffee, and working the phones. Another twenty or so would be showing up in pressrooms at courthouses, city hall, and the police station, starting the daily news ritual all over again.

The few in the newsroom glanced his way. Any reporter emerging from the glass offices drew scrutiny, particularly if it was common knowledge there was a crisis. And any crisis became a matter of public record within minutes. Save maybe for prisons and hair salons, newspapers possessed society's most efficient grapevine. It was a logical phenomenon. The room was filled with people paid for their professional curiosity and their ability to tell good stories. But the stories on the newsroom grapevine were inevitably cynical. Bound professionally by the facts they wrote for the newspaper, reporters nonetheless took major liberties with the newsroom grapevine, always perverting the facts into the most ominous scenario they could conjure. Harper figured the cynicism was the natural outgrowth of a profession that saw too much death and destruction; good news was a waste of time. Generally, it didn't take much conjuring to figure out that any reporter summoned to the glass offices had his butt in a sling.

There were ambitious bastards among them, too, who thrived on their colleagues' misfortunes. The pleasure was all the greater if the target of management's wrath occupied a position to which they aspired. Through the years, Harper had accumulated more than a few colleagues who would pass up their Christmas bonuses to see him take a shot in the shorts and, maybe, get a shot at his job. Harper was a good ol' boy, Texas born and bred, in a newsroom that, like management, had increasingly become filled with imports from the Northeast. A few of the carpetbaggers, he knew, claimed behind his back that his Pulitzer was a fluke. The ongoing story was that he wasn't worth a damn since he'd sobered up. He knew his attitude hadn't salved any misgivings people had about him. Except for a few old-timers, he generally ignored the rest. They interpreted the snub as aloofness; Harper simply thought it was the most beneficial use of his time.

Today, though, he saw William Levenson eyeing him from his desk. Levenson was one of Richmond Carlisle's elitist running buddies, a graduate of Brown or Harvard—Harper couldn't remember which. Levenson had a smirk on his face as Harper approached.

"Any particular reason you keep staring at me?" Harper asked.

"Yeah," he said, loudly enough for the woman at the next desk to hear. "Don't guess Richmond's folks were exactly asking you to deliver the eulogy, huh?"

"You know, Levenson, if brains were cotton, you wouldn't have enough to make a Kotex for a pissant."

"You've been quiet the last few days," Madeline said. She was staying over on one of her midweek visits to the ranch. Putting chicken divan and asparagus hollandaise on the table, she asked, "What's going on behind those blue eyes?"

"Nothing, really," Quinlin said.

"Know what I think?" she said, not waiting for a reply. "I think you're depressed. It's been almost a year since Sarah died, and I think it's working on you. I think you're feeling guilt about her getting killed, and I think you're holding yourself needlessly responsible for it. And I'll tell you something else, Jeb. I think you ought to see someone who could help you."

"Naw, that's not it," he said. "I don't need a shrink. I think I'm just caught up in this Carlisle case. It's not only bizarre but it's a priority, too. The chief's office follows it by the hour. This case is weird enough without having the media pulling strings with the head shed. Just makes the pressure worse on a case that's already got its own warts and wrinkles. I mean, the mechanism of death is rattlesnake venom? Gimme a break. No ballistics to run, no drug to trace, not even a murder *weapon*. There're people with motive, sure. But shake it all out and the only thing I know for sure is that I'm looking for someone who likes to play with snakes."

"I'm sure there is some pressure," Madeline said, motioning him to the table. "But I also wonder about Sarah. I think you may be oversimplifying. You know what they say in AA."

"And which cliché would that be, O Omnipotent One?"

"Pain is optional."

"God, Madeline," he said, shaking his head.

"What?"

"Hell, listening to you is like being back in the jitter joint," he said. "Some things are just what they are. This isn't some deep-seated psychological mystery that goes back to my potty training. It's stress. It's a tough, high-profile case, with the big guys looking at me. I need a goddamned suspect, not a psychologist, if that's what you're saying."

"And the last time you had this kind of stress, you ended up in alcohol rehab," Madeline said. "It makes you vulnerable for the bottle, and you can deny this, but I smelled cigarette smoke on you yesterday. I don't like what this could do to you. All I'm suggesting, Jeb, is that you don't have to do this alone. Go see—"

"Oh, Madeline, just lighten up. I don't need this."

"Fine," she said, putting her fork on the plate and sliding back her chair. "We'll add this to the list of things we can't talk about."

7

Quinlin hated stakeouts. Just once he'd like to see a cop movie in which the hero had to piss like a racehorse and couldn't find a rest room. It was a fact in a detective's life, just as certain as the ninety-nine-cent heartburn from a fast-food drive-through. He stared at the four Styrofoam coffee cups on the floorboard of the Dodge and imagined his bladder the size of a football.

He'd had a tip one time that a man wanted on two murder warrants from Atlanta was holed up in a duplex in East Dallas. Quinlin had sat on the place for four hours when the coffee kicked in. It was almost dusk, and people were beginning to show up from work. When he couldn't contain himself any longer, he spotted a row of waist-high holly bushes beside a house and headed for it, keeping his eyes peeled on the driveway across the street.

He was in midstream when a light went on in a window two feet from him. Just as a woman screamed, he heard a car door slam across the street. He finished on the run, but the murder suspect was already in the house before he could get there. He kicked his way through the door, a battle ensued, and the bastard slammed him in the chin with brass knuckles, opening a gaping wound in his chin. Quinlin finally got him cuffed and outside, where a uniformed cop and an irate woman confronted him. "That's him!" she yelled, pointing at Quinlin, who realized his fly was still down. "He's the one who exposed himself. You sicko!" The suspect got the death penalty in Georgia, and Quinlin fared almost as badly:

He was the brunt of weenie-wagger jokes for months in the squad room.

Three hours of boredom were even worse now. He had to piss *and* he craved a Marlboro Lights. There weren't any convenience stores or rows of holly bushes at Landmark Center, the nondescript five-story building that housed the Dallas headquarters of the FBI. The building was four blocks from Planet Hollywood, on the fringe of the West End, a renovated historical district that includes the old School Book Depository, from which Lee Harvey Oswald wrote his startling chapter in American history. The eclectic mix of renovated and decrepit buildings and their tenants in the West End had become the center of Dallas's tourist business.

Pedestrian traffic had been relatively brisk, forcing Quinlin to focus his attention on the main glass doors of Landmark Center instead of on his painfully swollen bladder. Amazing, he thought as he watched two clean-shaven guys in gray suits and white shirts, how FBI agents came out of the same cookie cutter. There must be a bureau directive that agents have to shop at Brooks Brothers and visit their hairstylists every week for the Choirboy Special.

Just as Quinlin debated trying to find a men's room on Landmark's first floor, a stocky man in his thirties, wearing a dark suit and carrying a briefcase, emerged from the glass door at Landmark. Quinlin scanned the driver's license photo from DPS; it looked close enough. And the physical information—six foot three, 225 pounds—was a fit. He followed the man down Lamar and across the street to an open parking lot. He wanted to let David Cartwright get as far as possible from the building, where his colleagues would be less likely to see them. Experience had taught him that people didn't talk candidly in front of those they knew. Probably even less chance with an FBI agent. And people were even less likely to talk on the phone about things they didn't want to talk about. Plus, Quinlin couldn't watch their faces for reactions when he asked the questions. Asking questions in person was the only way to go. Which was why Quinlin had risked his bladder.

David Cartwright appeared perturbed when Quinlin yelled his name, and his attitude didn't change when Quinlin caught up to him and showed him his badge. The young FBI agent wore his blond hair short and was built like a fire hydrant.

"Bet you were a linebacker, right?" Quinlin said, looking him over.

"Lacrosse," Cartwright said tersely. "What you need?"

So much for small talk; Quinlin cut to the chase.

"I'm investigating the homicide of Richmond Carlisle, and I'd like to talk to you. There's a coffee shop about—"

"I've got to be somewhere," the agent said, checking his watch. "Why me?"

Quinlin ran down the story about the calls on Carlisle's caller ID from Cartwright's phone.

"Yeah, so? Sure, I knew Richmond. Socially. We were friends. That's about it. I don't know anything about his murder except what I read in the paper. We weren't all that close."

"You were close enough to call him six times in nine days."

The big agent shrugged. He opened the door to a blue government-issue Taurus and pitched his briefcase across the seat, glancing at his watch again.

"Look, I don't have time for this, either. I've got to take a leak," Quinlin said. "You were close enough to tell him, 'I've got something else you'd be interested in.' What was that about?"

"You ever hear of the First Amendment?" Cartwright said. "It gives citizens the right to call anybody they want and say whatever they want."

"Guess you've heard of the Fifth Amendment? It says you don't have to make incriminating statements about yourself. And since you're talking law," Quinlin said, "there's also this deal called the Privacy Act, which says a federal agent could go to the pen for leaking shit to a reporter. Ring a bell, hoss?"

"You got proof of that, you'd be here with a subpoena. You're here without jack," he said, bending into the Taurus. "I don't have time for this."

The Taurus started rolling off.

"Remember this handsome face, *Agent* Cartwright," Quinlin yelled. "You're gonna see it again real soon." The car was picking up speed, moving out of earshot, and the FBI agent couldn't hear the cop cursing him. But if he'd looked in the rearview mirror, he would have seen the Dallas detective walking quickly and ever so gingerly across Lamar, holding his crotch and dodging traffic to get to the alley behind FBI headquarters.

8

Harper was already at Gonzalez's, and Quinlin spotted him in a booth at the back. The business district of Jefferson Boulevard had seen its better days three decades earlier, but it was still one of Quinlin's favorite places. Hispanics had replaced Anglos as the primary business owners, and half the signs were in Spanish, advertising everything from wedding dresses and rent-to-own furniture to fruit drinks imported from Mexico. Around the corner on a side street, there was even a rent-to-own tire store where, Quinlin figured, people rented tires for their clunkers just long enough to pass the state vehicle inspection.

Gonzalez's was a hole-in-the-wall, down from a pawnshop that had a sign on the door that read ALL GUNS MUST BE UNLOADED, and just a block from the infamous and now-vacant Texas Theater, where Oswald was arrested after shooting Officer J. D. Tippit to death in 1963. But Gonzalez's food was great, just like the people. Judging from the half-full bowl of salsa and the crumbs left in the chip plate, Harper had been there awhile.

Mendalina spotted Quinlin and headed his way with a fresh bowl of chips and salsa fresco.

"Your friend here wanted to order without you, but I told him that'd be rude." She grinned. "I wouldn't take his order."

Quinlin chose *guiso*, his regular, a Mexican stew with beef and vegetables and cilantro, and Harper opted for chicken enchiladas with *salsa verde* and a side of *pico de gallo*. Mendalina returned with a huge glass of tea for Quinlin, then headed for the kitchen to turn in their order. Harper reached down on the seat and produced a stack of computer printouts the size of a Dallas phone book and pushed them onto the table, almost knocking the sugar shaker off.

"Man, you name it," the reporter said, "and the Colters are into it. And in a big way. The bastards own half the state."

"Jesus," Quinlin said, pulling the stack to his side of the table. "This is just the Colters' holdings?"

"Yeah, and incorporation papers, background checks, financials, lawsuits, marriage records, campaign contributions, everything you asked for."

"You know, I'm the cop here. Why don't I have all this stuff at my fingertips?"

"You could, if you'd learn to use a computer and spend some of the city's money on databases," Harper said. "But what you've got is better. It's called a search warrant."

"Yeah, but I've got to have four witnesses, ten fingerprints, DNA, and damned near a confession written in blood to get one," Quinlin said, flipping through the pages. "This is incredible stuff. I'm impressed."

"I'll tell you what's incredible," Harper said. "And that's the pressure I'm getting to write something. Brewster's all over my ass. Looks like I'm going to have to go through all these printouts, too, and see what I can come up with. Maybe I can write about the Colters without identifying them as suspects in Carlisle's murder. Start the stories out as in-depth profiles, maybe find a questionable business deal; then I'll be primed if we find something to link them to Carlisle's murder.

"So tell me, what's Comanche Gap like, anyway?"

"Don't even think about it," Quinlin said. "For one thing, the Gap's small enough that people would snap immediately that you're from out of town. And that automatically would make you suspect. If, in fact, they've already killed one reporter, what makes you think they'd be morally opposed to killing another one?"

"I'd be careful," the reporter said. "I may not be an Ivy League grad like Carlisle, but I'm smart enough to be scared."

. . .

It was a long day by the time Quinlin finally pulled into the circular drive in front of the log house. The glare of the pickup's headlights froze three deer grazing east of the house, and the lights and noise awakened Bingo, who had gone from dozing on the porch to springing up and down in place, begging to have his ears rubbed. Quinlin wasn't surprised that Madeline wasn't there. She had left that morning in icy silence, carrying more clothes than usual to her BMW. He'd tried to apologize, but she wasn't having any of it. She said she'd call, but he doubted it. He stared at the phone as he put on a pot of coffee, but he talked himself out of calling.

It was after nine, and Quinlin felt himself fading. If stress had caused their argument, as he'd claimed, a call tonight would only make things worse. His stress was off the chart, and he was tired to boot. Also, he knew Madeline was already mildly frantic about a research paper she was trying to finish for her master of fine arts degree at SMU. But the stack of computer printouts on the kitchen table intrigued him, and he knew he had to force himself to go through them before he could sleep.

While the coffee brewed, he called information in Comanche Gap and got Clay Moore's number. He felt bad as he jotted down the number. Growing up, Clay had been as good a friend as he'd had. They'd played football together, double-dated, and confided their deepest fears and wildest hopes. When Clay's dad keeled over in the barn with a heart attack, Jeb had been a pallbearer. Six months later, Clay, Jeb, and the other third of the triumvirate, Will Stevens, left for war together. He'd thought of Clay often through the years, particularly after hearing that he'd had some "adjustment problems" after being badly wounded in Vietnam, but he hadn't talked to him. Now Jeb was calling because he needed something.

Clay Moore sounded genuinely glad to hear from his old high school buddy. He passed on gossip he picked up in Comanche Gap when he went in for supplies—teachers who had died, friends who had divorced, people who had moved, and how Comanche Gap, in general, was withering like an oak tree with blight.

"You going to the cemetery workin' next weekend?" Quinlin asked him.

"Haven't gone in years," Moore said. "Why? You coming down?"

At one time, the annual gatherings of folks to clean up the country cemeteries were as much a Texas ritual as rodeos. Comanche Gap was one of the communities that still clung to its tradition. Quinlin had avoided the annual meetings after his father's death. He didn't want to run into the Quinlin family, which had disowned him when he hadn't shown up for the funeral. He figured he'd let sleeping dogs lie.

Then after he helped sell his mother's hundred acres seven miles west of town and moved her to Dallas, he felt disinherited from the land anyway. There wasn't a compelling reason to dredge up old, bitter memories. That is, until the last few years, when his mother increasingly reminisced about the old days. Not surprisingly the older she got, the more she missed her roots. She'd started on him in earnest two months earlier, finally telling him point-blank she wanted him to take her. Geneva Quinlin had worked the overnight shift at a rest home, emptying bedpans and scrubbing floors for twenty-five dollars a week to support him, and she asked precious little of her only child. He couldn't tell her no.

"Yeah, Mother wants to go real bad," Quinlin said.

"Well then, just might see you there," Moore said.

"So tell me, Clay," Quinlin said, trying to sound casual, "the Colters still running everything down there?"

"That ain't gonna change, not long as they still own the county," Moore said. "Way I hear it, the ol' man's turning over everything more and more to Buck and Wade. Guess he's getting old and wants to slow down some. You 'magine Buck and Wade being in charge of anything?"

He laughed. "Bet you neither one of them boys has ever worked up a sweat," he said. "Least not out of bed."

"Good thing Buck was born with money," Quinlin said. "He had to work, he'd starve to death, lazy as he is. You hear anything about him?"

"The barber told me last week that Buck's only son showed up at the emergency room with a busted jaw and welts all over him. He said if the Colters didn't own every cop in the country, ol' Buck'd probably be in jail for child abuse. Rotten bastard."

Quinlin jotted a note on the back of an envelope.

"Betcha Rebecca ain't just real happy about it, either," Moore continued. "Even with all Buck's money, she's probably thinking she made the wrong choice. You ever wonder what would have happened if you and Rebecca had—"

"It wasn't even close to that kind of deal," Quinlin said, interrupting. "We dated a few times. That's it. She was a sweet girl, no question, and gorgeous. But I didn't have two quarters to rub together, and I had enough sense to know it. With Buck lurking around in the picture, hell, there was always gonna be competition, and there was no way I'd keep up."

"People in town still like her, even if she is a Colter," Moore said. "I saw her the other day and, hey, she's still the prettiest woman in the county."

"Say," Quinlin said, changing the subject, "you try to make it to the cemetery workin' next weekend. I'd like to see you."

Quinlin began reading the computer printouts listing the Colters' business holdings. Dun & Bradstreet, according to one of the sheets, estimated Clendon Colter's net worth around $700 million, easily putting him among Texas's wealthiest residents, along with the Bass brothers from Forth Worth, a couple of Austin-based computer moguls, a Wal-Mart heiress, and Ross Perot.

Quinlin used a yellow Hi-Liter to outline facts he found interesting and wrote notes on a legal pad. On paper at least, Clendon Colter was a modern-day Horatio Alger, a by-the-bootstraps wildcatter who gambled wildly in the oil patch, yet wisely scattered his proceeds diversely, making him a poster boy for American free enterprise. The vast Pan Permian empire—every facet of it branded with the legendary gold outline of Texas with a superimposed soaring black eagle—included oil and gas production, pipelines, a refinery, a freight airline, a trucking company, banks, mortgage companies, livestock holdings, ranches, and land development. Quinlin remembered seeing *Giant* as a kid, sitting in the balcony of the Texan Theater in Comanche Gap and marveling at the wealth of Rock Hudson's ranching family. The Colter spread made Riata look like a sharecropper operation.

The nuts and bolts of the Colters' Pan Permian empire were there, but a lot of details were missing. Pan Permian was individually owned, and therefore not subject to the intricate reporting requirements demanded of public companies by the Securities and Exchange Commission. Still, Quinlin thought he detected a pattern. By design, it seemed, the Colters avoided any business activity that would place them under federal regulation or control; they appeared to be deliberately staying within Texas's boundaries. Pan Permian Air, even though its prime freight routes extended into Mexico, was regulated by the Texas Aeronautics Commission through a loophole in the North American Free Trade Agreement. Pan Permian Trucking, another big player in NAFTA, operated at the pleasure of the Texas Railroad Commission, instead of the U.S. Department of Transportation. The thirteen Pan Permian banks scattered across Texas were state banks instead of national, chartered by the Texas Banking Commission.

As successful as the ventures appeared on paper, particularly in a merger-acquisition free-for-all, the logical business decision, Quinlin surmised, would have been to expand throughout the Southwest, maybe even the nation. But everything that bore the Colters' Pan Permian logo seemed to operate only in Texas.

According to incorporation papers, old man Colter's heyday must have come during the early sixties. His first three corporations were registered in 1962 by lawyer Les Westgrove, who, if Quinlin wasn't mistaken, was currently the district attorney of Sul Ross County. The records showed that Westgrove had incorporated sixteen more businesses for Clendon Colter between 1963 and 1970.

Yeah, he thought, he could just see District Attorney Les Westgrove aggressively pursuing the grand jury to return an indictment accusing Buck Colter of child abuse.

Quinlin had gone through three-fourths of the stack by midnight. Just as he promised himself he would stop and go to bed, he happened on the computerized report from the Texas secretary of state's office on campaign contributions. Clendon Colter and sons Buck and Wade had each contributed the maximum ten thousand dollars to sixteen state representatives and nine state senators. Their political action committee, Pan Permian PAC, had also contributed the maximum donations to the same lawmakers, along with another twenty-two. The legislators and senators were among the biggest names in Texas, heading influential committees from Public Safety and Banking to Commerce and Regulation, in addition to controlling political appointments to a multitude of other state agencies and committees.

And those contributions were just those that were reported. Given the legitimate figures, Quinlin could only imagine the amount of money that the Colters scattered to politicians under the table. Hell, he figured, the family probably owns half the politicians in the statehouse outright, and the other half are probably scared of them or, equally likely, want to feed at the same illegal trough.

The Colters kept their business on Texas soil because they controlled it, pure and simple. With their wealth and political grease, Quinlin figured, they ought to change the state seal, replacing the five-pointed star and olive and live-oak branches with the Pan Permian logo.

Quinlin was exhausted as he turned out the lights, but he tossed and turned, wrestling with a familiar old nemesis—motive. Why would an influential family worth nearly a billion dollars kill a newspaper reporter?

Quinlin went straight for the stack of computer printouts even before he put on the coffee. It was 4:30 A.M. and he was as tired as if he'd hadn't been to bed at all. But he remembered something curious from the night before, something that hadn't snapped at the time. He thumbed through the ream of documents until he came to the stack from the Texas Railroad Commission. The commission's name was actually a misnomer based on its early history. In modern days, the Railroad Commission regulated not railroads but trucking and oil and gas production. It monitored not only oil wells but also oil leases purchased by drillers and developers. It didn't take Quinlin long to find what he was looking for.

According to the Railroad Commission records, Clendon Colter didn't record his first oil lease until late 1965. And production from the well, which wasn't a particularly big discovery by West Texas standards, didn't begin until January 1966. Yet Clendon Colter had painted himself as a wildcatter who'd struck it rich in the Permian Basin *before* arriving in Comanche Gap. The proliferation of corporations bearing the Pan Permian logo, Quinlin recalled from the computer records, had begun a full three years earlier—in 1962.

Contrary to the tales he told around Comanche Gap, Colter's early wealth came from somewhere beyond West Texas and the crude that flowed beneath its red dirt.

9

Jeb Quinlin hated the prairie, and early on, he figured that was the reason he hated Dallas. He'd grown up one hundred miles south, in the midst of thickets of oaks and cedars that thrived along the sides of rolling hills with arroyos and canyons. Dallas was surrounded by monotonous flatness the way a wild lily is engulfed by horehound. But if Dallas was a lily, Quinlin discovered, it was a gilded one.

Terrain, he learned, was only one of the reasons he despised Dallas. He couldn't imagine a more materialistic city in the country, and he thanked God that he worked homicide instead of fraud. Dallas prided itself on being the "buckle of the Sunbelt," a vibrant, aggressive financial hub whose influence was felt from Brussels to Rio. But when Quinlin looked up at the penthouses of Dallas's tallest towers, he saw faceless hordes in thousand-dollar suits who'd do anything easy for a buck. And the Mercedes they parked in the underground stalls bore testament to their stunning success.

Dallas had been ground zero in the savings and loan debacle, and it was here in this mecca on the prairie where they'd perfected the inflated appraisal for collateral you couldn't give away, then used the phony appraisals as the basis for multimillion-dollar loans. In the aftermath of the S&L scandal, Roger Wilmon once told Quinlin, seriously, that con men in Dallas could go untouched by the FBI if they just didn't get too greedy. "This is the white-collar crime capital of the nation," the special agent said. "We've got million-dollar cases backlogged. If the scammers keep their deals down to about seven hundred and fifty thousand, we don't have time to mess with them."

Old-time cops say it's tough to con an honest man. But with Dallas' penchant for quick money, the city became a magnet for every con man who could charge a Brooks Brother suit on MasterCard and lease a Lincoln. Dallas was willing to speculate a dollar on getting back ten, no matter how ludicrous the scam, from earning 40 percent interest on investment money to drilling slant oil wells in the Mexican desert. And when the inevitable sting un-reeled, nobody screamed louder or more indignantly than a righteous Dallasite parted from his dollar.

In extreme cases, the fraud slopped over into Quinlin's domain. Three times in less than ten years, Quinlin had investigated murders that had connections to the same downtown office building, NorTex Tower, which was notorious among fraud detectives as a haven for nickel-and-dime con men and their boiler-room telephone investment schemes. In one case, an investor in a supposed shopping center syndication killed a con man, and in the other two, the swindlers had turned on each other. The common thread, of course, was greed—easily more than a million dollars in each case. Dallas juries didn't flinch at sending a black man to death row for killing a convenience clerk over forty-five dollars, but the juries nonetheless acquitted one of the white-collar killers and gave the other two twenty years or less. Apparently, the more money there was on the table, Quinlin quipped to a prosecutor, the more justifiable and defensible the homicide. Justice may be blind, but it's also deaf and dumb.

Forty-five minutes south on U.S. 67, the prairie and Dallas both disappeared in the rearview mirror of Quinlin's Dodge. By Glen Rose, the flat land had turned to rolling hills that were heavy in mountain cedar. Comanche Gap was another forty-five minutes southwest, and Quinlin enjoyed the reprieve from asphalt and mirrored buildings.

The detective dreaded walking into the Sul Ross County Courthouse. Getting out without being recognized was an impossibility, he knew. Still, he had a high-profile murder investigation that was going nowhere fast. He didn't even have a hint of a motive. Whatever had lured Richmond Carlisle to the Colters could be buried in the records in the courthouse. It was a low-percentage lead, but it was all Quinlin had.

The detective had spent a half hour earlier in the morning backgrounding his lieutenant, Coy Matthews, on the Colters. He had spent the weekend analyzing the vast pile of records on the Colters and making a timeline that itemized their business dealings. "It's a long shot that you're going to find anything in the official records," Matthews had said. However reluctantly, the lieutenant finally had given his approval for the trip to Comanche Gap. "It's not like you've got anything anyhow." What the lieutenant didn't say was that he had the chief of detectives on his back twenty-four/seven over the Carlisle case.

Generally, the only way a commissioned peace officer goes into another jurisdiction is in "hot pursuit," as in chasing a speeder across a city limits. Quinlin was a Dallas homicide detective who would be a hundred miles beyond his jurisdiction. The normal procedure, based more on time-honored courtesy than legality, would have been to notify the Texas Ranger or the local county sheriff, who presumably would offer Quinlin assistance.

But since Quinlin had reason to believe that the Colters owned the local prosecutor, it wasn't a leap in logic to assume they also had their hooks in the Ranger and the sheriff.

Quinlin remembered Red O'Neal. O'Neal's dad had been sheriff of Sul Ross County more than twenty years, and Red had never had another job outside the department. When Red was a kid, he helped cook meals for the inmates and rolled the food cart from cell to cell. When he turned twenty-one, he got a deputy's badge. And finally, when his daddy got too drunk and too fat to get into and out of a patrol car, Red put his own name on the ballot and the power of incumbency passed down a generation. Quinlin wouldn't trust either of the O'Neals as far as he could throw the courthouse.

"You get jammed up down there with local law enforcement," the lieutenant had cautioned, "and it's going to be their word against yours. In their own backyard. And you can see how that's gonna shake out. You wouldn't have a chance, not if the Colters really do own the cops. And that's the best-case scenario. What if it gets really dirty?"

Matthews suggested sending Paul McCarren, Quinlin's partner, along, but Quinlin talked him out of it.

"Two people are more conspicuous than one," he argued, "and besides, I know Sul Ross County. It's where I grew up. I know how to handle myself there."

There was a seventy-mile-an-hour speed limit posted at the Sul Ross County line, and Quinlin turned on his cruise control and set it at sixty-five. He didn't intend to be stupid enough to give them probable cause to stop him. Six miles from the town square, he slowed to fifty and rolled down his tinted window.

To his left was a paved road that headed off in the distance and disappeared over a chalky hill. The entrance to the pavement was imposing, made of white native rock on either side, with a black ornamental iron arch overhead that read PAN PERMIAN RANCH HEADQUARTERS. In the middle was the Colter logo of the Texas outline and soaring eagle. Signs at the gate threatened trespassers with prosecution and warned that the premises were patrolled by armed guards. The iron gate was electronically controlled, apparently from a magnetic card reader mounted on a pedestal beside the drive. Twenty yards beyond the gate was a guard shack.

The headquarters ranch supposedly spanned forty thousand acres, far and away the largest spread in Sul Ross County, but there were also five other Colter ranches in Sul Ross and adjoining counties.

Quinlin sped up and watched the white cement fence posts of the Pan Permian out his windshield for as far as his eyes could see. He had priced fence posts like that for his little ranch—four dollars apiece. Dun & Bradstreet had its own criteria for estimating wealth; Quinlin had his. The Colters had a buttload of money. Few people in Sul Ross County could even afford their fence.

Quinlin slowed to thirty behind a goose-neck trailer loaded with about twenty red Santa Gertrudis calves. It had to be auction day at the commission barn. He sped up as he pulled out of the curve and passed the old Ford half-ton. Its driver waved from beneath a

crumpled straw hat, and Quinlin saw the brown trail of Copen-
hagen down the side of the door.

On the outskirts of Comanche Gap, he slowed to five miles under the speed limit. The Cross Timbers Drive-In Theater, off to his
right, had been abandoned for a decade, and years of gusting winds
had finally peeled its galvanized-tin covering, littering the ground
around the screen with rusty panels of metal. He had taken his first
date to the Cross Timbers, risked a kiss during the closing credits,
and was so euphoric when Dixie McCowan hadn't resisted that he
drove off with the speaker still stuck on the window of his pickup.

Four thousand people lived in Comanche Gap then, and Quinlin
had been one of sixty-eight graduating seniors. Now the population
sign showed barely three thousand. The town had been boring then,
and he figured it had to be worse for teenagers now. Outside of
the drive-in movie, a pool hall, a Kiwanis teen center for dances
and parties, and the Dairy Deluxe, there wasn't anything to do.
One night, Jeb had won twenty dollars, betting that he could drive
around the courthouse square fifty times without Red O'Neal's
daddy stopping him. Friday nights were football and basketball in
small-town Texas, but if you had dates on Saturday—and enough
gas money—most kids headed for Stephenville or Lampasas.

A mile before he got to the town square, Quinlin noticed the
old Goodson Farmall shop was boarded up with plywood. A single
rusted tractor and plow sat in the yard where new red International
Harvesters had been parked when he was a kid. Goodson had probably been the last link to snap in the intricate chain of high finance,
corporate mergers, and plummeting global farm prices. The so-
called trickle-down economy always swamped the little man. Quinlin remembered Henry Goodson and had gone to school with his
daughter, Peggy. He wondered what had become of the Goodsons
and how they made ends meet. A few doors down, the old Central
Freight depot had gone the same route, just like the garment-sewing
business across the highway and the old Magnolia service station
and mechanic's shop beside it.

The only building with any cars around it on the North Side
was the VFW post. Sul Ross County was dry, which meant you
couldn't buy beer or liquor there. The VFW post had a private club

license, which made it the only place in town to drink. Comanche Gap was a staunch Baptist town, and as his uncle Howard had once said, "The Baptists'll vote dry as long as they can stagger to the polls."

Quinlin wondered how many kids were like he'd been, loving the country, appreciating small-town values and the lifestyle, and wanting to stay, but not finding any way to make a decent living. They'd had to leave. He thought of a line from a Hal Ketchum song: "Bobby told Lucy, 'The world ain't round . . . Drops off sharp at the edge of town. Lucy, you know the world must be flat, 'cause when people leave town, they never come back.' " And so the enrollment in school dried up like oats in a drought and the population of the town's six nursing homes blossomed like thistle.

The only ones making it were those lucky enough to have inherited acreage in the country and who could land minimum-wage jobs in town. And even those jobs were at a premium. The best ones were county jobs, and the Colters controlled them even back when Quinlin was a kid. Those who eked out a modest living earned it. They worked forty hours a week in town, plowed their crops at night, and fed their stock on weekends. And they did it because they wanted to stay on the land.

He saw Trey Sullivan standing beneath the Sullivan Pharmacy sign as he pulled into the town square. Sullivan was talking to Rabbit Wilcox, the postman, who, in Quinlin's day, had been the fastest flanker for the Comanche Gap Warriors. Trey Sullivan was the fourth of his clan to dispense pills and mix concoctions for the town's sick. The Sullivans were part of the natural order in small towns where kids are raised in apprenticeships by fathers who inherited the trade from their fathers. Ranching, farming, welding, lawyering, and, in Red O'Neal's case, even policing. The only mentoring Quinlin figured he could have gotten from his old man was boozing.

Norman Rockwell couldn't have conjured up a more bucolic setting for the cover of *The Saturday Evening Post*. The imposing three-storied Texas granite courthouse stood alone in the middle of the town square, nestled among hundred-year-old pecan trees that rose to the roof. Two variety stores, a pair of drugstores, a café, a mail-order Sears, a furniture store, a Western Auto, a jewelry store, an antique shop, a grocery, an insurance agency, a western-wear mercantile, three lawyers' offices, and a growing number of vacant buildings lined the four streets facing the courthouse. In front of every business, the chamber of commerce had planted watermelon-colored crepe myrtles in huge white pots.

Beneath the pecans on the courthouse square, a group of old codgers, "the spit-and-whittle club," had spread a green felt cloth over a cement picnic table and were deep into their domino game, just like the generations before them. Towering above them a few feet away was a statue of Lawrence "Sul" Ross, the county's name-sake, standing with his hands on his hips, wearing a Stetson and a hog-legged revolver on his gun belt, his pants tucked into his cow-boy boots. Ol' Sul Ross was Quinlin's favorite character in Texas history, a true renaissance man if there ever was. Sul Ross had been appointed a Texas Ranger by the governor back when the Rangers' chief job was protecting settlers from Comanches. He was already a legend when the Civil War broke out and he enlisted in the Con-federate army as a private. One hundred thirty battles later, he was a battlefield-commissioned officer. After the war, he became a sher-iff in Waco, was elected governor, and ended his career as the pres-ident of Texas A&M University, the state's land-grant college.

The parking spaces around the courthouse were filled with pickup trucks. Quinlin drove around the square slowly, eyeing three patrol cars with silver badge decals on their doors parked near the basement entrance to the sheriff's department. In five minutes, he'd stand out like a twenty-dollar whore at Communion. Another fif-teen minutes and word would spread through all the floors of the courthouse and, Quinlin knew, certainly down to Red O'Neal's of-fice in the basement.

Small-town bureaucracies were as incestuous as they were cliqu-ish. A deputy district clerk would have a cousin who worked as a deputy sheriff. The lawman would have a brother-in-law in the county judge's office. And in this case, the county judge would owe his existence to the power brokers who got him elected—the Col-ters. In an hour, everyone around the square would know that Jeb Quinlin, a onetime local boy who had become a big-city detective, was asking questions about the county's most influential family.

And inevitably, the Colters themselves would know he was there even before he could get beyond the city limits.

Quinlin found an angle parking space a block off the square, behind Rafferty's Grocery. He spotted the Gap Rexall Pharmacy ahead of him and detoured through its door to the tiny coffee bar–soda fountain in the back. The worn hardwood floor creaked beneath his weight, just as it had when he was a kid stopping off every day after football practice for cherry Cokes, and the old familiar smell of tung oil rose up from the weathered boards. He had just given the elderly woman clerk a dollar for the Styrofoam cup of coffee and was waiting for his change when he heard the voice. He looked over his shoulder but didn't see anyone. The voice, vaguely familiar but not immediately identifiable, came from the other side of the aisle, by the prescription counter.

"Yeah, I worry about him a lot, but he seems to hold on," the woman said. "I guess you've got to be pretty tough if you've made a habit out of riding bulls all your life."

Rebecca Colter?

"Well, keep in mind, Rebecca, we can send this up to the rest home," a woman said. "You don't have to come down here all the time to refill it."

The elderly clerk gave Quinlin his change, actually counting out thirty-four cents in change instead of dumping the coins in his hand the way they did in Dallas. He thanked her and headed halfway up the aisle, stopping off at a display of sunglasses, where he could watch the door. He heard the floor creaking an aisle over and caught the profile of a petite woman on her way out of the glass door. She wore tight Wrangler jeans, a faded denim vest over a red long-sleeved shirt, and red Tony Lama ropers, and her auburn hair was tied in a ponytail with a red bandanna. The years had been benevolent to Rebecca Harrison Colter. He would have spotted her anywhere.

Quinlin followed her down the sidewalk and watched her step down to the pavement and around a black Chevrolet Suburban. A sign on the doors bore the Pan Permian logo and read HEAD-QUARTERS RANCH/REGISTERED SANTA GERTRUDIS CATTLE. He approached from behind just as she was about to get behind the wheel.

"So this is what homecoming queens grow up to be?"

She turned toward his voice, and he watched the puzzlement on her face change to a reassuring smile.

"Jeb Quinlin!" Rebecca said, spreading her arms. "Damned if you're not still the handsomest boy I've ever seen."

They hugged tightly with the car door open, and out of the corner of his eye, Quinlin saw a pickup make a lazy loop around them.

"Yeah," he said, "and standing here like a couple of drunk sophomores is about to get us both killed."

She slammed the door to the Suburban and pulled him by the hand up two steps to the sidewalk.

"I see you've already got some coffee," she said, "but let's go over to Fred's, where we can talk. It's absolutely great to see you again, Jeb. We can catch up."

They walked half a block to Fred's Café, she holding his hand the whole way, and headed for the first open booth. Rebecca yelled across the counter at Fred Petty, ordering two cups of coffee and pointing toward the booth. The old man nodded with a grin.

The old high school sweethearts gossiped about former classmates. "Can you believe that Dwayne Miller, of all people, became a Ph.D. and is teaching English lit at Florida State?" she said. And they complimented each other on how they looked. Clay Moore was right; Rebecca was still the prettiest woman in Sul Ross County.

"I was so sorry to read about your wife's death in the paper," she said, turning serious. "The way it happened and all, I know it must have been devastating for you. I guess I'm kinda surprised that you're still a cop, though I would never have figured you for a cop in the first place, not with your temperament. More like a social worker or a vet."

Quinlin looked off. "Life takes some strange twists, doesn't it?" he said. "Being a cop's the only thing I know. All and all, it has its moments."

She reached across the table and rubbed her fingers along the three-inch scar on his chin. It was spontaneous and surprisingly endearing, and it momentarily embarrassed him.

"Did that come from one of those strange twists?" she asked.

"That's what you could call an occupational hazard, I guess. A gentleman and I had differing views on an arrest warrant, and he, ah, expressed his opinion."

"Well, it makes you even more handsome, in a roguish kind of way," she said, taking a sip of coffee. An awkward silence fell on the booth.

"Obviously life's treated you well," Quinlin said, taking the opportunity to shift the focus. "Guess you stay busy. You've got a son, right? How—"

"So, what brings you back home?" she said abruptly.

"Just, uh, trying to check on some things for Mother. We sold her place and I just wanted to make sure all the paperwork was filed right. She got a tax bill from the county, which makes me wonder if the deed got filed at all. No big deal, just a loose end."

Rebecca held her cup in both hands, looking him squarely in his eyes.

"The last time we talked, really talked, you told me that you wouldn't be seeing me anymore because you had too much to do at the ranch and because you knew you'd be enlisting," she said. "You remember that, Jeb?"

"Well, sort of. But—"

"I've thought about that conversation a thousand times," she said. "You were lying to me. I think I know why. You were too proud and too insecure to tell me the truth. It was about Buck, wasn't it?"

Quinlin sipped deliberately from his cup.

"I knew you didn't have money, but it didn't matter," she said, never taking her green eyes off his face. "It hurt me that you could have thought I was that shallow. You know, the irony is that Buck didn't mean a thing to me back then. Whatever I came to feel about Buck came after you left. At first, I was hurt. Later, I was angry. It was like you gave up on me without fighting. And that wasn't like you. It made me feel like I never really mattered to you, but I don't think that's true, either."

Quinlin didn't know what to say. He took another sip of coffee to dodge her eyes.

"I think you're lying to me again," she said. It was a statement of fact, devoid of animosity. "You're not here taking care of business for your mother, are you, Jeb?"

"Not really, no," he said. "I'm, uh, just doing some preliminary legwork at this point. I've got a case that may or may not involve Sul Ross County. Probably won't pan out. You get a lot of leads in this business that just die on you."

"This is about Gary Bettman, isn't it?" she asked, her voice turning stern.

"I can honestly tell you, Rebecca, I don't have a clue who Gary Bettman is," he said. "Never even heard the name. Somebody we went to school with? I mean, I really—"

"No, he married a girl from Panther Junction and they have a small place out there," she said. "He used to work for my husband."

It wasn't just "Buck" anymore; it was "my husband." Was she defensive now, or did the thought of Gary Bettman, whoever he was, strike a raw nerve? Quinlin couldn't tell. She had dragged him into no-man's-land.

"What about Gary Bettman?"

"If you really don't know, I'm not going to tell you. I may have put two and two together and gotten six."

She glanced at her watch and was about to say something, but Quinlin cut her off. He knew she was about to leave.

"I couldn't help but overhear you at the Rexall about a prescription," he said. "Is Buck ill?"

"No, that's for Charley Blake," Rebecca said. "He's an old cowboy who used to work for the Colters. He's in a rest home, and I've kinda adopted him. Doesn't have any family. He's dying. Bad heart."

"Sorry to hear it," Quinlin said. "How *is* Buck doing?"

"You asking personally or professionally?" He could feel her watching his face.

"I don't know. And that's honest."

Rebecca reached across the seat for her purse and put on her sunglasses. Her car keys were in her hand.

"Uh, Rebecca," he said, grabbing her hand as she slid out of the booth. "There may be some point, I don't know, where I'll need to talk to you again."

"That'll be fine, Jeb," she said evenly. "But make up your mind before you call. If it's personal, I'd be thrilled to hear from you. I really would. I've thought of you a lot over the years. But if it's professional, don't bother. It wouldn't do any good. Buck's still the father of my son."

"I'm getting lost here," Quinlin said. "I didn't mention that I would want to talk about Buck. Just that I might want to talk to you again at some point. What are you worried about? Do you have some reason to think Buck's in trouble with the law? Maybe you ought to tell—"

"I don't feel comfortable talking to you about my family," she said, pulling her hand from his. "I think the world of you, always have. But there're some things I just won't talk to you about."

"Rebecca, do you understand how you sound? Like you're upset or trying to hide something? I talk to people for a living, and frankly, you're coming across as defensive, like—"

She was standing now and looking down at him in the booth. "I'm sorry, Jeb," she said, sarcasm creeping into her voice. "When I saw you on the street, I thought I was seeing a dear old friend after all these years. I was excited. I guess I was really seeing a cop who was conducting just another interview. I set myself up for a fall."

He heard the door open behind him and took the last swallow of coffee, which was cold. He pulled his cell phone from his breast pocket and dialed. He got his partner's answering machine.

"McCarren," he said, "pull state and federal warrants to see if you can find anything on a Gary Bettman, traditional spelling, I'm guessing, and probably with a Panther Junction address. Assuming a white male, DOB unknown. Apparently worked for the Colters in some way. Could be important. Call me or beep me if you find anything."

Nothing about his talk with Rebecca Colter had gone the way he'd planned. He had forgotten how strong and straightforward she could be. Not only didn't he have the chance to ask about Buck beating their son—a potential lever to get her talking about Buck—he was left feeling guilty, as if he had somehow betrayed a good woman. Again.

Quinlin winced when he saw the thirty-pound index book that contained Sul Ross County's property deeds. He had held out a slim hope that the county's commissioners had footed the bill to computerize their property records. With computerized records, he could have been out of the courthouse in an hour or two. Now, staring at the ten-inch-thick index, he knew he'd be lucky if he finished by the time the courthouse closed at five. The alphabetical index would refer him to two hundred or so smaller books lining the walls of the county clerk's office, arranged in chronological order, that contained the actual warranty deeds.

Property searches, like some homicide investigations, were tedious, intricate, and complex. Quinlin followed an axiom that he'd gotten from veteran homicide investigators when he was just a rookie: When passion, retaliation, or vindication wasn't obvious, follow the money. A good seven times out of ten, he discovered over the years, money was, in fact, the motive. Sometimes, it was easy to spot: a convenience store clerk lying in a puddle of blood next to an empty cash drawer, for example. Those cases took care of themselves, and even the laziest homicide detective could end a career with a decent clearance rate. Stickup men had an IQ that matched their shoe size. They left prints or other physical evidence and, most of the time, they killed while a surveillance camera in plain sight recorded their brutality and stupidity for posterity.

The more sophisticated the killing, though, the more difficult to follow the money. On occasion, the money motive was buried in a public document, a contested will, an acrimonious divorce, a fraud lawsuit, or a land deal in which someone had gotten screwed. Finding the motive was like searching for a slug in a weed-infested vacant lot; it could be there and you still might not find it. A motive woven into a public record, though, was almost as good as a confession. Records, however sterile and stilted in legalese, were factually irrefutable, and they were exhibits that jurors could haul back behind doors while they deliberated.

"Tell me what you're looking for," the deputy clerk said, "and I'd be glad to help you locate it."

"No, ma'am," Quinlin said, "that won't be necessary."

He knew what would happen if he mentioned the Colter name. Already, he could feel the people watching him, probably just because his face was unfamiliar. At least no one had recognized him. At some point, when he finished chasing down the property deeds and paper-clipping those he needed to copy, he'd have to show them what he was researching. But he wanted to wait until he was ready to leave. No need to make a bad situation worse.

"How far back does this index go?" he asked. "Does it cover 1960?"

"All the way back to 1950," the clerk said. "You with a title-search company or a lawyer's office?"

"Neither one," Quinlin said, lifting the book and heading off before she asked him point-blank. "Just some personal business. But thanks. I appreciate your offer."

The grantee section listed purchasers of property, and the Colters' ledger filled almost six pages in the huge index, accounting for more than four hundred real estate transactions in which the family or its holding companies had assumed ownership of land in the county. Scanning the entries, it wasn't hard to imagine the Colters' grip on Sul Ross County. Though Sul Ross wasn't one of the largest counties in Texas, it still accounted for about one thousand square miles, an area roughly the size of Rhode Island. According to deed records, the Colters held title to about a quarter of it.

The list was daunting, and Quinlin scanned it, not knowing where to begin. He pulled the deeds on the ten most recent transactions, all more than three years old, and eight of the ten listed the Colters' attorney of record as Les Westgrove, more recently the local district attorney. He had seen Westgrove's name on the DA's door on the first floor.

The deals were sweet, Quinlin thought: The Colters were a turn-key operation and they didn't need anyone handling anything for them. In each land transaction, the deal was brokered by Pan Permian Land and Cattle, financed by Pan Permian Mortgage, and closed at Pan Permian Title.

As he paper-clipped the deeds for copying, Quinlin sensed someone behind him. Turning, he saw the deputy district clerk standing over him. Her eyes were on the index in front of him, which listed Colter after Colter on the ledger page.

"You finding everything you need?" she asked, obviously embarrassed that he'd caught her looking at the documents.

"No problem here," Quinlin said, moving his hand to cover his notebook. "Appreciate your asking, though."

He waited until she had wandered off before he went back to the index. He looked at his watch. Barely after 10:00 A.M., and already word was going to be out that someone was asking questions about the Colters. The grapevine would spread like kudzu.

The biggest flurry in transactions, the detective noticed, had occurred between November 1959 and September 1961. It took him two hours to pull the books containing the deeds; he went through them in chronological order, searching for patterns and trends.

The pattern would have been obvious to anyone who knew Clendon Colter's obsession with using the Pan Permian name. Though Clendon Colter's name appeared nowhere on the documents, a private entity called PanPerm Joint Venture was listed as the new owner on all of the transactions. Texas law, blatantly manipulated by land promoters and the politicians they owned, made it virtually impossible to identify joint-venture partners from public record. Joint ventures were subterfuges to conceal ownership.

But notations on all of the deeds specified that property tax bills be sent to PanPerm Joint Venture, in care of two trustees. Charley Blake's address was listed as a post office box in Comanche Gap. Wasn't Charley Blake the old man Rebecca Colter had mentioned not an hour earlier? Quinlin jotted the name and box number in his notebook. Blake, he would bet, was a Colter functionary, and the postal box probably belonged to Clendon Colter.

More curious was the second trustee, Hoyt Garvin, a high-profile Austin lawyer who was one of the biggest Democratic power brokers in the state. Garvin's claim to fame, and the catalyst for his meteoric rise to political prominence, was that he had been chief of staff for the late Lanson McLain. Before he became president, McLain had been Speaker of the U.S. House of Representatives, where he was far more feared than respected. Historians in recent years hadn't been kind to the former West Texas rancher, noting that McLain had spent more on private investigators than he had on legitimate aides. As a result, political opponents with skeletons in their closets found themselves voting with McLain or paying the public consequence in humiliation. If Quinlin's recollection of history was correct, McLain would have been in Congress between 1959 and 1961, when the flurry of Sul Ross land changed hands.

In less than two years, PanPerm Joint Venture had bought sixty thousand acres in northwest Sul Ross County from fifty-one different property owners. According to the deeds, some of the parcels were as small as twenty acres; the largest was twelve thousand acres. The abstracts meant nothing to Quinlin, but he suspected that all the parcels were adjacent to one another and formed a huge block. Careful to close the deed books so no one could see what he had been looking at, he went around the corner to the office marked MAP AND PLAT. He located the legal descriptions for the property on a huge map hanging on the wall.

He didn't have to go through each of the fifty-one transactions to see the trend. The first fifteen he checked had been marked "Condemnation, 12/12/63; Comanche River Authority." He matched up the last five and they carried identical notations.

Returning to the county clerk's office, Quinlin pulled the grantor index, the book that contained the list of property sellers. After owning the land for barely more than two years, according to deeds, PanPerm Joint Venture had sold all fifty-one parcels of land to the Comanche River Authority on December 11, 1963. A day later, the river authority publicly condemned all sixty thousand acres and, on December 13, deeded it to the U.S. Army Corps of Engineers.

Quinlin's pulse was racing by the time he got back to Map and Plat. He asked the clerk, an elderly woman in a print dress, her gray hair gathered in a bun, for an up-to-date topographical map of Sul Ross County. When the clerk reappeared from the map room, he had to force himself from grabbing the map out of her hand. He grinned and nodded as he scanned the map.

"I'll be goddamned," he said. Quinlin looked up and saw the

old woman's expression. "I'm sorry. I, uh, just got carried away there for a second. Forgive me."

The entire acreage that PanPerm Joint Venture had bought up lay beneath the Comanche Bend Lake and Reservoir. And according to the map, another huge block of land in two adjoining counties had also been flooded to create the man-made lake. Quinlin knew if he checked records in Bosque and Erath Counties, he'd find PanPerm's tracks there, too.

He jotted the financing information off one of the deeds and carefully closed each of the deed books on the table. He fought the urge to jog, walking briskly instead to his Dodge, stopping off at Rafferty's Grocery for a pack of Marlboro Lights. He cursed himself for his weakness. It was better to celebrate his success with a cigarette than a bottle of Bud Light, right? Dialing Clint Harper's number at the *Register & News,* he lighted a Marlboro and talked while he sorted through his notes in the front seat of the pickup.

Five minutes and three Marlboros later, Harper hit paydirt in the newspaper's electronic library. "The first public mention I can find of the Comanche Bend project," Harper said, "was in a 1964 press conference—on May fifteenth. It was—"

"Well, I'll be goddamned," Quinlin interrupted. "Does the story have any figures in it? How much the government paid? Who announced it?"

"Our story ran May sixteenth, with a Washington dateline," Harper said quickly, sensing Quinlin's urgency.

The project wasn't even made public until five months *after* PanPerm had cornered the property and deeded it to the Corps of Engineers.

"Let me see—I'm reading it now," Harper said. "Here it is. It was introduced by Texas congressman Jimmy Joe Taggert. Um, he called it a 'conservation' project to help preserve the Comanche River. Here it is. The House Conservation Committee authorized seven hundred and fifty dollars an acre for condemned land, for a total of forty-five million in fed—"

"That's all I need," Quinlin said. "That's it."

"Yo, don't you think now would be a good time to let me in on what's going on?" Harper asked. "I mean, you're obviously excited about something. But this is ancient history, happened thirty years ago."

"I'm not saying it's a motive for killing Richmond Carlisle," Quinlin said. "This may or may not be what Carlisle was looking into. And I sure as hell don't know if this is what got him killed. But it's intriguing because it answers some questions about the Colters. Also shows Clendon Colter is a lying son of a bitch. He didn't make his money wildcatting in the Permian Basin, not according to Railroad Commission records anyway. According to property deeds, he made millions by screwing everyone in three counties.

"Bottom line is that two of Texas's finest used insider knowledge to rake off a kajillion dollars in federal tax money," Quinlin said.

He outlined the scenario for Harper: McLain used his muscle as Speaker of the House to wrangle funding for the so-called conservation project on the Comanche River. Then he drafted Taggert, a political hack and crony, to shepherd the project through committee, probably a quid pro quo for past favors. McLain got his old political buddy back home, Clendon Colter, to do the legwork. McLain's lawyer, Hoyt Garvin, created the blind joint venture to protect McLain's and Colter's identities. The joint venture bought up land from ranchers for four hundred dollars an acre, then sold it to the government for seven hundred-fifty dollars an acre. McLain and Colter paid $24 million for the land, according to Harper's rough figures, then flipped it to the federal government for a cool $45 million dollars—splitting a tidy $21 million in profits.

"McLain's share probably helped get him elected president," Quinlin said. "And we're getting a pretty good idea of what Colter did with his."

"There's a hell of a story there, whether it's tied to Carlisle's murder or not," the reporter said. "You know, an in-depth profile piece that could set up the major story if, in fact, the Colters really turn out to be suspects. It'd be a great behind-the-scenes read. The Colters are six-hundred-pound gorillas in Texas. And speaking of

six-hundred-pound gorillas, a story would also get the editors off
my ass for a while."

Detective Paul McCarren returned Quinlin's call as the senior detective was halfway back up the steps to the courthouse. Quinlin
had to pick up photocopies of the Colter deeds, some of which he
hadn't even had time to study. He'd had to rely on the clerk's staff
to copy them, which meant they would have shoved deed after deed
through the copier with the Colters' names on them. There
wouldn't be any secret about what he was up to. And he still had
one piece of unfinished business: Who was Gary Bettman and why
had Rebecca Colter been so cryptic and paranoid about him?

"Don't know where you came up with Bettman," McCarren told
his partner, "but you may be onto something. Bettman's apparently
a pilot, and I found a federal indictment against him for conspiracy
to smuggle drugs. He was arrested about two months ago at Addison Airport."

"Addison?" Quinlin repeated. The cell phone connection was
filled with static. Addison Airport was a commercial field ten miles
north of downtown and home to corporate jets owned by Dallas
companies. "Well, supposedly he lives in Panther Junction, which
is just a few miles from here. What was he—"

"You didn't let me get to the punch line, and you're gonna like
it," McCarren said. "Guess what he was arrested in?"

"The fuck do I know? A glider? What are you trying to tell me?"

"Gary Bettman was popped in one of Pan Permian Air's planes.
He was on the Colters' payroll. The feds confiscated the plane, some
kind of converted military cargo plane or something."

Quinlin didn't want to be seen on the steps, and he walked
around the corner of the courthouse to a concrete bench beneath
a pecan tree. He was lighting a Marlboro even before he realized
it. He took a deep drag, cursed under his breath, and crunched the
cigarette beneath his boot.

"Is there any indictment against Pan Permian Air or any of the
Colters?"

"Nope, not that I can find," McCarren said.

"Shit."

"But it's not all bad news, Jeb," McCarren said. "Check this. The feds filed an affidavit in support of a warrant to search the aircraft. But it wasn't the DEA. It was the Public Integrity Division of the FBI, which tells me they're looking at something a little more exotic than your garden-variety drug smuggling. Like maybe there's bigger fish here."

"Interesting," Quinlin agreed. "But a fed's a fed. They're gonna want to work with us about like Merle Haggard teaming up with Snoop Doggy Dogg. It ain't gonna happen."

"I'm not so sure," McCarren said. "Think we might have some new leverage. The agent who signed the affidavit was our friend, FBI Special Agent David Cartwright."

"Whoa," Quinlin said just as something fell on his shoulder. He looked up into the pecan tree, then to the shoulder of his corduroy coat.

"Fuuuck," he said. "God damn it!"

"What's the matter? I thought you'd be hap—"

"Why can't you ever tell me something straight out?" Quinlin yelled. "You turned a two-minute conversation into ten minutes, and a fucking grackle just shit on my shoulder."

After a brief stopover in the basement men's room of the antiquated courthouse to scrub bird shit off his coat, it took Quinlin only fifteen minutes to find what he was looking for. A property deed showed that Gary Bettman and his wife, Susan, owned 187 acres just outside of Panther Junction. The deed also showed that the Bettmans still owed the Pan Permian State Bank in Comanche Gap $278,000 on the note. A notation filed two days earlier claimed that the Bettmans were sixty days late on their monthly mortgage payments of $2,150 dollars. Pan Permian was foreclosing.

Quinlin was tired, although bolstered. He had come to his hometown without a lead in the Carlisle murder, but at least he was leaving with a shred of hope, however thin. A plane belonging to Pan Permian Air involved in a drug deal normally would have involved the DEA or maybe even Customs, but not the FBI's Public Integrity Division. One way or the other, Special Agent David Cartwright was going to talk.

Quinlin eyed the cell phone in the passenger seat and thought of Madeline. He normally did when he had good news to share or when he needed her to listen when the news wasn't so good. But he didn't know what he'd say. It might only make things worse.

Quinlin cranked up Merle Haggard when the tape hit "Fightin' Side of Me," and he was running the Dodge on cruise control five miles under the speed limit when he spotted the sheriff's unit at the roadside park. He watched in the rearview mirror as the white Ford Bronco pulled onto U.S. 281 behind him. Judging from the way the Bronco was closing the distance, it had to be accelerating quickly. A mile from the Erath County line, he saw the alternating red and blue lights in his mirror and heard the siren. He put on his right-turn indicator and slowly headed off onto the shoulder. He also dialed McCarren on the cell phone and laid the phone on the dashboard near the driver's window.

Sheriff Red O'Neal approached the pickup with his right hand on the butt of his .357 Magnum. Quinlin shifted the holster on his belt farther toward his back so it wouldn't be obvious to the sheriff. He didn't want to give him any grounds for provocation. Quinlin had forgotten how huge O'Neal was. Fatter than a holstein, yeah, but big-boned, too, and maybe six foot four. He figured the sheriff's neck for the size of his waist.

"Guess you better let me see your driver's license and proof of insurance, hoss," the sheriff said, stooping down to look in Quinlin's window. Quinlin had reached for his license and insurance card even before he'd stopped, and he handed them through the window.

"Well, I'll be goddamned," O'Neal said, staring at Quinlin's license as if genuinely surprised. "With them sunglasses on, I'd never recognized you, Jeb. Hell, it's been a lot of years, hadn't it, hoss?"

"A lot of years, that's for sure. Why you stopping me, Red?"

"Just wanted to talk to you a second. Say, what you doing in Sul Ross County?"

"I had some business I had to tend to."

"Well, I know it wasn't *official* business; elsewise, you'da stopped off at my office, am I right? I mean, you're still Dallas *po*lice, right?"

"You still haven't told me why you pulled me over."

"Well, if I'd known it was you, I'd never've done it, Jeb. But the fact of the matter is, you was sure hugging that center stripe when you came out of that curve back yonder. Figured I might have me a drunk driver."

It was bullshit. Quinlin knew he hadn't crowded the yellow stripe.

"See, what I try to do is what I call 'preventive *po*licing,'" O'Neal said. "I see somebody about to get hurt, why, I stop 'im, talk to 'im, see if I can't help 'im out a little. I just hate to see anybody get hurt when he doesn't have to, know what I mean, Jeb?"

The phony smile was gone and the sheriff's eyes were narrow and hard.

"You telling me I'm about to get hurt?" Quinlin asked. "Because I think you're trying to threaten me."

"What I'm sayin' is that you was driving too close to the edge of that center stripe and that sure nuff can get a fella hurt. You know, being too close to the edge."

"Look, Red, you gonna give me a ticket, give me a ticket," Quinlin said. "I don't have time for a reunion."

"You always had a wise—"

"Look, you and I both know you don't do patrol. So you figure you can jam me up?"

The cell phone on Quinlin's dash squelched.

"What's the deal with the phone?"

"I got my partner listening on the other end just because I trust you so much, Red. I just want a record of things."

Red O'Neal clenched his jaw, and Quinlin could see a twitch in the corner of his lip.

"Tell you what, Quinlin, you get your sorry fuckin' ass out of my county," the sheriff said. "Next time, you won't find me so hospitable when you're sneaking around in other people's bidness."

"If there is a next time, Red, things are going to be different. You need to know that."

10

At four o'clock on a Friday afternoon, the Blue Armadillo Café was almost deserted. It was a workingman's hangout with a heavy lunch crowd, a place where cattle-truck drivers, plumbers, an occasional cowboy, and cops routinely pitted their stomachs against whatever Truck determined to be the day's Armadillo Special. And most every working day, Truck decided on chicken-fried steak, a half-inch pounded slab of Angus beef swimming in white gravy loaded with pepper and a hint of bacon drippings. It was an artery-clogger, no question, but it was also the one dish, by virtually all accounts, at which Truck excelled. (By unanimity, his chili would unstop a sewer line quicker than Drano, and his sauerkraut and sausage guaranteed a ride on the porcelain pony.) Those same accounts deemed it a felony to eat Truck's chicken-fried steak without finishing with an oversize slice of Big Sue's coconut meringue pie.

A statewide magazine somehow stumbled onto the Granbury café and wrote it into regional history: "Regular people can't imagine the heavenly smells coming from such a peculiar place. Then again, regular people probably wouldn't venture through the front door without a tetanus booster."

During lunch hours, eighteen-wheelers sat bumper-to-bumper on the shoulder of the highway, and the gravel parking lot was packed with pickup trucks. Lines for lunch sprawled out onto the distressed wooden porch, which was decorated with everything antique that Truck and Big Sue could buy cheaply—old gas company signs, kerosene lanterns, plows, a gas pump, and, in the middle of the porch, beside the front door, a bigger-than-life concrete-molded replica of an armadillo, which Truck had painted blue, probably because blue was the only spare paint he'd been able to find.

Jeb Quinlin was always at work in Dallas during weekday lunch hours, but on days that Madeline didn't sleep over, the Dallas detective made it a ritual to stop off at six every morning for Truck's Side-Splitter. The Side-Splitter took Big Sue two trips to the table, hauling three fried eggs, a slab of sugar-cured ham, four biscuits, and flour gravy on one trip, and homemade apricot preserves and a pot of coffee on the next. Jeb was such a regular, he never saw a menu; Big Sue just showed up with her arms loaded.

The Blue Armadillo was the kind of place Quinlin figured a Yankee transplant like David Cartwright would absolutely despise. Which was why he chose it.

Quinlin had made a discreet inquiry about Cartwright with Roger Wilmon, the only fed he trusted. Quinlin trusted Wilmon not because he was an FBI agent, but in spite of it. They had met on common ground, an AA meeting, which had nothing to do with law enforcement and jurisdictional jealousy. But their bonds went deeper than badges and their susceptibility to booze. Their backgrounds were interwoven with Vietnam, Purple Hearts, busted marriages, overachievement, cynicism, and starting over.

The book on Cartwright, according to Wilmon, was pretty thin: decent kid, Dartmouth grad, Boston native, single, tries too hard, and intelligent, but devoid of common sense. He had once been assigned to an undercover role buying drugs and, according to Wilmon, he had been a disaster. "You could send him to the 7-Eleven with a hundred dollars and he couldn't buy a loaf of bread," Wilmon had said. For the last year, Cartwright had been assigned to the Public Integrity desk. "Still no savvy," Wilmon explained, "but you don't need common sense to deal with corrupt bureaucrats."

Cartwright was in a booth at the far end of the restaurant, looking out of place and preppy in a green-red-and-white Hilfiger long-sleeve pullover, freshly pressed khakis, and tassled loafers. The big agent was running a spoon disinterestedly through his coffee, clearly biding time. He glanced nervously at his watch. Quinlin was intentionally fifteen minutes late. It was part of his misdemeanor mind fuck, like the meeting place he had picked, because Quinlin's experience proved that nervous, out-of-place people only got more wormy as the clock ticked. And sometimes, that made them more vulnerable to telling the truth.

On the phone earlier in the morning, Cartwright had sung the same verse as he had in the parking lot, claiming he didn't know anything that could have gotten his buddy Carlisle killed. And if Quinlin didn't buy that, the agent had suggested smugly, he could pursue "official channels."

Quinlin was pissed enough, no question, to get his deputy chief and go to the agent in charge with his information. But he figured he'd still end up empty-handed. Cartwright's boss would probably turn over the information to the FBI's internal security squad, Cartwright would be severely disciplined or booted out of the Bureau entirely, and Quinlin still wouldn't have the information he needed.

"I got no problems with official channels," Quinlin had replied. "I'm an official kind of guy myself. I was just trying to accommodate you. I figured you might not want your official channels knowing about your calls to Richmond Carlisle's home phone just a few days before he showed up dead.

"And now there's something else, Cartwright. See, I know about Gary Bettman and the dudes who owned the plane he was flying."

The detective's challenge had produced only icy silence.

"Here's the real deal, Cartwright," Quinlin said. "I've got evidence that you've already violated FBI policy and the Federal Privacy Act by passing confidential information to a newspaper reporter. So if you're telling me I need to go through official channels, no sweat, I'll just run all this by the agent in charge and wish you luck in your new life. Because you're about to shit like a crippled turkey and fall back in it."

Reluctantly, Cartwright had agreed to meet, but it was imperative, he said, that it be at a place where he wouldn't be seen. No problem, Quinlin thought. Quinlin tried never to meet anyone on their home turf, where they'd have a comfort factor. Apparently, the agent still held out hope that Quinlin's investigative reports wouldn't include him or his relationship with the late Richmond Carlisle.

"Have a nice drive over?" Quinlin asked, sliding into the booth opposite the FBI agent.

Cartwright gave him the once-over, taking in his brown Lucchese kangaroo boots, faded Wrangler jeans, and denim shirt.

"You sure you're not a Texas Ranger?" Cartwright said with a derisive tone of disapproval. "You look like you just rode in with a posse."

"I like to be comfortable," Quinlin said. He made eye contact with Big Sue, who was leaning against the counter, and made a pouring motion for a cup of coffee.

"I won't be intimidated or blackmailed," Cartwright said. "You made certain misrepresentations on the phone, and the only reason I'm here is to clarify the facts."

"I'm not sandbagging anybody," Quinlin said. "The facts speak for themselves. I have evidence that you knew Carlisle well enough to phone him at home and say that you had more information for him. Which infers to a reasonable person that you gave him information previously. I want to know specifically what kinds of information you were passing on to him. It's part of my homicide investigation."

The agent sat silently, staring at his lukewarm coffee.

"Look, I see two roads here," Quinlin said. "One, you tell me everything you know and we'll keep it between ourselves at this point. Or, if that doesn't appeal to you, I'll go through the official hoops. And the latter route is going to generate some paper, both in my shop and in yours. Your name's going out front. You're gonna lose your badge and maybe even do some time for violating the Privacy Act. Seems to me that even Ray Charles could see there's only one way to go here."

Cartwright motioned toward the men's room and said, "Come with me." Big Sue was en route to the booth with Quinlin's coffee, and a quizzical look spread over her ample face when she saw both of them headed for the rest room.

The men's room was tiny and empty. Truck, who had transformed the Blue Armadillo from a feed store, clearly needed to spend more time cleaning. Investing in industrial-strength air freshener wouldn't hurt, either.

"So you want me to assume the position," Quinlin said, "or just take my word? You've been watching too many movies. I'm not wearing a wire."

Cartwright pointed toward the wall and patted the detective down anyway.

"No piece?"

"You don't pat down too many cowboys, do you? Left boot. Twenty-five automatic."

Big Sue was on idle at the booth when they returned.

"Your friend here too little to go by hisself or so big he needs help holdin' it?" she said loudly. "You boys was just bondin' in there, am I right?"

Big Sue grinned widely, did an about-face, and headed back to the counter. The place was deserted except for a truck driver in a black Harley T-shirt and a crumpled straw hat. He was feeding quarters into the jukebox, punching "Big City!" Merle Haggard's whiskey voice took over the Armadillo.

The sizing up was over, and Quinlin got to the bottom line. "Look, Cartwright," he said, "I'm not here to screw over you, and I don't plan on being screwed, either. It's pretty obvious we're not gonna spend the holidays together. That's all right, too. But Carlisle walked straight in on a stone-cold killer, and both of us have to do what we can to make this right. I sure as hell don't feel good about what happened to him. I doubt you do, either. I'd prefer the easy road. We gonna make this work or what? Your call."

Guilt and fear, Harper knew, were the world's greatest motivators. The detective sensed Cartwright was burdened by both.

"I don't have a choice," the young agent finally said, "morally or professionally."

"Not really," Quinlin said. He knew they'd be there awhile, and he yelled over the jukebox for Big Sue to bring the coffeepot.

"You think I got Rich killed, don't you?"

"I don't know the story," Quinlin said. "There might have been a couple of things that could have gotten your friend killed."

Rich Carlisle, according to Cartwright, was a fraternity brother, and they got acquainted at a regional frat smoker hosted by the SMU chapter. Beyond the fraternity connection, they had other things in common that bred friendship: They had grown up in the Northeast, attended exclusive universities, and were transplants in an alien region that they neither fully enjoyed nor embraced. Over time, they began spending off hours together, and two months before Carlisle's murder, they had gone snorkeling in the Bahamas for ten days. Familiarity bred a comfort zone—not unlike his own friendship with Harper, Quinlin assumed—and the young reporter and FBI agent began revealing their business to each other. Between the lines, Quinlin suspected, they were both ambitious and probably planned to use each other to make it up their respective career ladders. Leaks and exclusives—it was the way the parasitic game had been played since the invention of badges and press cards.

"Was Richmond being threatened?" Quinlin asked, trying to offer Cartwright an easy entry point into a conversation he knew the agent wanted to avoid.

"No . . . well, yeah," Cartwright said. "I mean, there was a bail bondsman he'd written about who was messing with him. But I don't think that's what got him killed."

The agent's eyes went back to his coffee cup. "I just mentioned some things casually and Rich became obsessed with them," the agent said. "I didn't start out to leak information; we were just talking over beers. You know, bullshitting about what we were working on. The next thing I knew, he saw it as the story of his career. I told him it was dangerous, but he was convinced he could handle it. He was sure the story would establish him as an investigative reporter. He said he'd never have to fight for credibility again."

"The story?" Quinlin asked. "You talking about Clendon Colter and his boys?"

Cartwright merely nodded, his eyes locked on the coffee cup in front of him.

The FBI agent's story was long and intricate. Unobtrusively, Quinlin took out his notebook and jotted notes. He tried not to interrupt with questions, letting Cartwright freewheel. There'd be a chance for follow-up later.

"Understand, we weren't investigating the Colters," Cartwright said, "at least not per se. We got all sideways with the state cops over the Colters, but that's another story. I can't prove it as we sit here right now, but there's no question in my mind that they're the big money behind a major cocaine-smuggling operation. . . ."

"You're shitting me," Quinlin said, unable to keep his silence. "The Colters? Drug kingpins?"

"Yeah, but that's not our focus. I'm assigned to the Public Integrity Division, and that's how I ran across the information I, uh, discussed with Richmond."

Cartwright rambled, taking a detour here and turning around there, but he presented a pitiful documentary on how bureaucratic lines in law enforcement get blurred, even erased by politics and public relations. The actual targets of the FBI's preliminary investigation, Quinlin finally surmised, were District Attorney Les Westgrove and Texas Ranger Mervin "Hoot" Gibson. Westgrove and Gibson were "circuit riders" whose jurisdictions spanned three sparsely populated counties in the northern Hill Country—Sul Ross, Bosque, and Erath. The counties were Clendon Colter's playground, the same place he'd worked the insider land scam thirty years earlier.

According to the FBI agent, the saga had begun a few months earlier when U.S. Customs arrested Gary Bettman. Bettman had veered from his flight plan from the interior of Mexico and disappeared from FAA radar at some point between Eagle Pass and Uvalde, just north of the Mexican border. The Customs Air Wing scrambled a plane, but Bettman was already airborne again on FAA radar by the time customs officials arrived.

An hour later, though, a customs task force ground unit seized a refrigerated meat-packing truck south of Uvalde. Concealed in a fake wall behind beef carcasses were one thousand kilos of cocaine, worth about $3 million on the street. The two Hispanic-speaking men in the truck claimed they'd been paid five hundred dollars each to drive the load to a truck stop in Junction on Interstate 10, where they were to receive another five hundred apiece and await further directions. An hour after the truck was busted, Bettman landed at Addison Airport, north of Dalla, and taxied to an airfreight terminal. Customs agents surrounded the plane and arrested him.

"And the connection to the Colters was the plane, right?" Quinlin asked.

"I'm getting to that," Cartwright said. "The plane was a C-123 bought from government surplus and registered to Pan Permian Air, the freight hangar was leased by Pan Permian Air, and Bettman was carrying a Pan Permian Air ID. And you know who owns Pan Permian Air?"

"The Colters."

"Exactly," the FBI agent said. "But the plane and hangar were clean. So here's customs with a no-dope case on the plane and holding its pilot. Even if they can tie the dope on the truck with the plane, it's conceivable at this point that Bettman is freelancing, right, that he's using company property to haul dope without Pan Permian's knowledge? Well, Bettman's got no priors and he's scared shitless. He makes bond on a conspiracy charge that customs knows won't fly and hires himself a lawyer. The U.S. attorney's throwing a bunch of stuff against the wall, hoping something will stick. The U.S. attorney tells Bettman that he'll get the FAA to jerk his ticket and he'll never fly again and that he'll end up doing forty years in prison.

"Lo and behold, Bettman and his lawyer want to do the right thing and try to cut a deal for complete immunity. Bettman's lawyer claims his client can take down 'powerful people in high places.' The inference, of course, is that he's talking the Colters. Bettman doesn't balk at taking a polygraph or wearing a wire."

"Sounds like a deal even the feds couldn't screw up," Quinlin said. "No disrespect intended. A nobody for kingpins. So where's the rub?"

The hitch, Cartwright explained, was that the bust on the border was a task force operation. While the task force was controlled by customs, there were also agents of the Drug Enforcement Administration, the Bureau of Alcohol, Tobacco and Firearms, and the Texas Department of Public Safety.

"When the head of the DPS hears that this is more than a one-shot drug case and potentially involves an investigation of Pan Permian, he claims the case should go to his agency," the FBI agent said. "The colonel does his dance about how the locals always get shoved around by the feds on big cases and how his guys are better equipped to handle a Texas investigation."

The head of the Public Safety Commission in Austin called the governor, who called congressmen and senators in Washington, who called the Department of Justice, which called the FBI.

Quinlin was confused. "So if the deal is greased by politicians and the FBI bows out," he said, "how does your Public Integrity Division still end up with an investigation?"

Considering the players and proximity, Cartwright's explanation was more than a little plausible. After the feds turned the Colter–Pan Permian investigation over to DPS, the U.S. attorney told Bettman and his lawyer that they had to take their offer to Les Westgrove, the Sul Ross County prosecutor. There was a meeting in Comanche Gap with Westgrove and Hoot Gibson, the Ranger. Bettman's lawyer renewed his offer to allow his client to take a polygraph and wear a wire in conversations with Pan Permian Air's chief pilot—the man Bettman claimed ordered the drug drop-off. Strangely enough, the prosecutor and Ranger declined each time.

Over weeks, and after they had pumped Bettman for everything he had, Westgrove told the feds that the pilot had concocted a grandiose conspiracy that implicated Pan Permian to cover his own ass. Bettman, according to the state prosecutor and Texas Ranger, was merely a freelance drug smuggler who got popped. End of story. End of investigation. The feds could do whatever they wanted to with Bettman, who still faced the lame conspiracy charge.

Bettman's lawyer, a wily, raw-boned Texan who wore two-thousand-dollar hand-tooled alligator boots, apparently had figured out the state investigation wasn't going anywhere. And further, attorney Jim Ed Mangus suspected he knew why. So he had suggested a final meeting between Bettman and Gibson. This time, the Fort

Worth lawyer instructed his client to stick a voice-activated tape recorder inside the breast pocket of his coat for his meeting with the Ranger.

"Mangus brought us the tape, and it was a slam dunk," Cartwright said. "It was also the basis of our Public Integrity investigation. When we heard it, we opened a case on Westgrove, the prosecutor, and the Ranger, Gibson. They were dirty, and Bettman had Gibson implicating both of them on tape. The next step up for us was the Colters."

The surreptitious tape, according to Cartwright, had Gibson telling Bettman that he'd known the Colter family more than twenty years and had even moonlighted for them periodically as a security consultant in their various businesses. Westgrove, according to Gibson, had been the Colters' local lawyer before running for district attorney, a campaign underwritten solely by Colter contributions.

"The Colters owned the prosecutor and the Ranger lock, stock, and barrel," the agent said.

"That's interesting," Quinlin said, "but it's a circumstantial case. You'd have to prove quid pro quo, wouldn't you? That the Colters got something in exchange for taking care of Westgrove and Gibson?"

"We'd just gotten the tape and opened the file when Carlisle got burned," the FBI agent said. "When you hear the tape, you'll hear Gibson getting bolder the more he talks. At some point toward the end, he's trying to scare Bettman. And so the Ranger says something like 'You better quit running your mouth about the Colters. You tell the feds anything else, and something bad's gonna happen to you.' Can you believe it—this is a Texas Ranger? And he's talking like he's bulletproof.

"Then Gibson tells the pilot, 'Take the hickey, say it was your deal, and do the time. If you had a real lawyer, he'd get the bullshit fed charge tossed. But even if you do time, I wouldn't be surprised if your family was provided for. But keep talking, and you'll end up on the wrong end of the thirty-eight-cent solution.' "

Quinlin had heard the term before from a crooked cop who confessed to killing an unarmed suspect in an alley. It was cop slang; thirty-eight cents supposedly was the cost of a single round of .38 ammo. As death threats go, it wasn't veiled. Equally important, the Ranger had also talked himself into potential charges of official oppression, obstruction of justice, and tampering with a witness. The tape, Quinlin figured, was a throw-down conviction on Hoot Gibson, hearsay at best, on Westgrove, and a major leap to the Colters.

"What were you guys doing with the tape?"

"We were having to get permission from the deputy attorney general in Washington to pursue it," Cartwright said, shaking his head. "Supposedly standard operating procedure on bigwigs. Colter's apparently big in Democratic politics, and we've got a Democratic administration. At least that's what I figure."

"Anybody in your shop know what Carlisle was doing when he died?" Quinlin asked.

"No," Cartwright said, barely audible.

"Specifically, what was Carlisle doing with the information you gave him?"

"I know he'd already contacted Bettman on the phone," the FBI agent said. "He told me he was going to Sul Ross County to see him in a day or so."

"When was that?"

"The day before his body was found."

"Think he told anybody else about what he was doing?"

"No way," Cartwright said. "This was going to be his big coup. He was paranoid about it, very proprietary."

The young agent sighed heavily and was silent for a long moment.

"Look," Cartwright said solemnly, "I need to correct the record. The fact of the matter is, I guess I primed Carlisle to pursue the Colters. The investigation had already been taken away from us once, and when we got a thread of it back, I figured the best we'd be able to do is put the Ranger and maybe the district attorney down for a few years. I didn't really have a lot of faith that we'd nail the Colters, not with all the politics and money involved. I guess I thought the only justice they'd get would be on the front page."

"What are you going to do now?" Quinlin asked. The combativeness was long gone from his voice. The big man was clearly hurting, and the detective didn't want to make it worse.

"Well, Richmond's death has become part of the investigation," the agent said. "I've got to put it on paper and submit it to the file. And obviously I can't do that without acknowledging my culpability. I screwed things up big-time."

Quinlin folded a twenty for Big Sue, tucked it under his coffee cup, and led the way to the parking lot. The two men stood a few minutes beside Quinlin's pickup before the cop broke the silence.

"David," he said, surprised that he had reverted to the agent's first name, "you may have played a little loose and fast, but you didn't kill Carlisle. He was old enough to vote. And from what I hear, he wasn't really prepared to listen to reason about this case anyway.

"Go ahead and write your report, but I wouldn't turn it in just yet. Things are fresh now and they look pretty bad, but they could change in a hurry. Right now, we're the only ones who know your voice is on Carlisle's machine. Frankly, your culpability isn't as important as finding the bastard who killed him. And I don't know how jamming yourself up with your bosses helps catch him. I'd like to keep it so that you and I could talk every once in awhile, maybe cut up our business a little bit."

Quinlin could see Cartwright's angst.

"Tell you what," Quinlin said, patting the agent on his shoulder, "why don't you drop by and visit with Roger Wilmon?"

Cartwright appeared surprised that Quinlin knew the veteran FBI agent.

"Roger's got a lot of miles on his odometer," Quinlin said, "and he'll know what to do. He's good people, and you need a rabbi.

"But don't drop your ass in the grease until you hear from me."

11

The Comanche Gap Cemetery was four miles west of town, nestled in a valley surrounded by rolling hills. The tallest of the hills, the one that always cast early-morning shadows over the little graveyard, was once a Comanche ceremonial ground. As a kid, Quinlin had scoured the hill inch by inch, finding a mother lode of arrowheads and spear points. He'd heard stories from old-timers about how the Comanches had buried their chiefs up there in the rocks, oftentimes with ornate artifacts and headdresses. When he was six, and while most of the adults were down in the graveyard pulling weeds and putting flowers on the mounded graves of their ancestors, his mother had caught him digging with a shovel. She ordered him to fill in the two feet of dirt he'd already dug, telling him that the Indian graves were sacred. He figured that even if the Comanches had nearly scalped his great-great-grandfather, the founder of Comanche Gap, that heathens, too, must command some respect in death.

As an adult, Quinlin learned on his own that there were exceptions to his mother's rule about respecting the dead. When his own father drank himself to death, Jeb, in his early twenties at the time, had refused to attend the funeral, even after a fundamentalist Baptist preacher had quoted him the verse about "honoring thy father." The ensuing argument was so heated that the only time Quinlin had set foot in churches since was to attend funerals and weddings. Parents, he figured, had to earn their kid's respect, just as his mother had. Being a real parent had to involve more than sperm and egg. Deep down, he knew that's why he'd never had children. He couldn't guarantee that he'd be a decent dad. There weren't any guarantees, particularly if you drank.

But if he hadn't respected his father in life—when the bastard was beating his mother and him in drunken rages—then how could he have any respect for him in death? Young Jeb knew he'd be a hypocrite if he showed up for his father's funeral. Today, his father's grave was on the north end of the cemetery, in the midst of the Quinlin family plot. Jeb's uncle, a drunk like his father, had bought a headstone right after his dad died. Over the years, Johnsongrass and bull nettle had grown over the mound that was his father's grave, and no one, not even his brother, placed plastic flowers at the marker.

The cemetery workings, a tradition in rural Texas in the old days, had changed since he'd last visited the old graveyard. No one actually worked anymore. The cemetery association paid "wetbacks," illegal Mexican aliens, to mow the grounds, fill in the armadillo holes, and rebuild the sunken, rain-gorged graves into mounds. Now the gatherings were just convenient excuses for old-timers to spread their fried chicken, squash casseroles, and potato salads on the big picnic tables and relive history.

As he looked around, Quinlin envisioned an earlier, simpler time. The women wore old-fashioned flower-printed bonnets and the men had big cowboy hats pulled down tightly to shield their heads from the sun. Quinlin also wondered if the Comanche Gap cemetery workings weren't about to go the route of the lightning rod. Most of the three hundred or so people were in their seventies or eighties, and their descendants had long ago moved out of the country. Another ten years, he figured, and the little cemetery would be grown over with Johnsongrass, just like most other country burial plots. On thing hadn't changed over the years, though. Quinlin was forty-four and six feet tall, but he was still "Little Jeb" or "Geneva's little boy" to virtually everyone his mother dragged him to meet.

Quinlin managed to disengage himself from his mother's grip and escaped to the coffeepot. Two old characters had made "cowboy coffee" as long as Quinlin could remember, dumping the coffee grounds and water into a hundred-pound iron pot that rested on a blazing mesquite fire. They dipped up the coffee, grounds and all, with metal ladles, and it was stronger than a stepped-on skunk. Their stories were a hell of a lot better than their coffee.

" 'Member back in the Depression, when everybody was so poor, the women made clothes outta old flour sacks?" Will Durban asked. "Well, I'll never forget it. Lissie McWhorter was sixteen, cute lil' ol' girl who, ah, had developed pretty well, and her momma had made her some underbritches out of an ol' Gladiola flour sack. Well, she bent over one day to water her pony, and right there across the butt of her underbritches, it said, 'Best in the West.' "

Dee Wilson hooted and ol' man Durban talked louder to get in his final line: "Yessir, and I figured her momma knew what she was talkin' about, too."

Quinlin was squatting on his knees, sipping coffee and laughing, when he felt the tap on his shoulder and heard an old familiar voice.

"Say, boy, you remember a trip on the Bus to Nowhere?"

It was Clay Moore, looking down at him with a crooked grin his right hand outstretched. Will Stephens was standing beside him, hands on his hips.

"Never saw anybody more scared than you was," Stephens said. " 'Cept maybe me. I don't think any of us had ever been out of Sul Ross County before."

It had been more than twenty-five years ago when the three inseparable high school buddies had boarded a Continental Trailways at Sullivan's Pharmacy on the square to head for Dallas's Love Field. Once there, the eighteen-year-olds had raised their right hands, pledged to defend the United States Constitution against all enemies, and gone their separate ways. Quinlin went to the navy, Moore into the marines, and Stephens ended up in the army—but they all wound up in Vietnam. They had kept up with one another through family and an occasional mutual friend, but they hadn't all been together since the airport.

Their talk had nothing in common with the old cowboys huddled around the coffee fire, and they moved their own reunion to the back of Clay's old GMC, parked beneath a spreading live oak on the edge of the cemetery. Jeb sat on the ground, leaning against the trunk of the oak, and Clay and Will dangled their legs off the tailgate. Early on, they dodged Vietnam, talking instead about their feats, miscues, and pranks in high school, some old mutual girlfriends, and wondering aloud about classmates they'd lost track of. Ultimately, Nam had to surface. It had changed all their young lives.

Clay Moore, an all-state, class AA linebacker in high school, had been gung ho all his life, and nobody was surprised when he'd opted for the marines. Nor had he surprised anyone when he volunteered for long-range recon, an elite bunch of soldiers whose job it was to penetrate enemy lines. He'd been in-country only three months when a Vietcong booby trap exploded beneath his feet, the shrapnel pulverizing his torso and legs like a slab of round steak run through a tenderizer. Navy doctors dug more than 120 metal shards from his right leg and torso, but there wasn't anything to save from his left knee down. Today, he walked with a pronounced limp, thanks to the prosthesis he wore on his left leg.

Quinlin could tell by listening that Clay had more serious damage than his leg. The detective had read about guys like Clay Moore, so-called trip-wire vets, who preferred to live alone, trusting their fate to no one. They were distinctly antigovernment and skeptical of anyone who wasn't a Vietnam vet. Moore's mother had died after he came home from Vietnam, leaving him 200 acres about twelve miles west of Comanche Gap. He had a 70 percent disability from the Veterans Administration and he raised a few cows and some grain sorghum to get by. He also mentioned several times hunting deer and other game, which he put in his freezer. He painted a picture of a simple life, one of self-sufficiency and living off the land, another hallmark of trip-wire vets. And while Clay didn't mention weapons, Quinlin figured it wasn't a stretch of the imagination to assume that Moore's small ranch was a fortified camp.

Will Stephens was probably the smartest of the three buddies—at least he'd made the best grades in high school, even though Quinlin never remembered him taking home a book. Stephens had become the youngest warrant officer helicopter pilot in the army. He'd started out flying Hueys, but then had worked his way up to Cobra gunships, accumulating a Distinguished Flying Cross and several other medals along the way. He loved flying, and after his discharge, he'd spent ten years flying engineers and crews to offshore drilling rigs in the Gulf of Mexico. Finally, he bought his own helicopter, a Bell Jet Ranger, which he leased to a country-music radio station in Austin for traffic reports.

The talk about Nam embarrassed Quinlin. He'd done his time all right, but nothing as dangerous or as glamorous as Moore and Stephens. He'd ended up on a gunship off the coast of North Vietnam. He was a "spook," who located enemy radio frequencies, tried to intercept their messages and decode them. For fourteen months, he and the crew of the USS *Oklahoma City*, "the Ghost of the Vietnam Coast," sneaked as close as they could to enemy targets and obliterated them in the darkness. Given the extent of Moore's injuries, Quinlin didn't even mention the minor shrapnel wound to his knee.

It was Stephens who brought up Clendon Colter:

"So here's ol' man Colter, right, who's the head of the local Selective Service Board. He's the one who made the choices about who went and who stayed. Man, I remember everybody who was on that bus. I looked around and I didn't see ol' Buck or his no-good little brother. Think there was a connection there?"

"Goddamned right there was a connection," Clay Moore said, bitterness dripping in his voice. "Nam wasn't no place for rich boys. Never saw one. Nam was fought by niggers, meskins, and poor white trash just like you and me."

Moore and Stephens joined Quinlin and his mother for lunch, and the three high school buddies vowed they'd stay in touch.

The day at the graveyard invigorated Geneva Quinlin. She rambled the entire way back to Dallas about seeing Bessie Anderson for the first time in fifty years. Gus Poer, she thought, didn't look too good, even though he was almost ninety; Grace Wilcoxson had the best potato salad at lunch; and Ruff Partin, except for a cheekbone crunched by a bull's hoof, was still the "best-looking boy ever to graduate from Comanche Gap."

"You know, Jeb," she said wistfully, "life's full of unpredictable things, isn't it? Things just happen over the years. We can't control any of them. The Good Lord's in charge of that. But don't ever forget where you come from. It's what we are, deep down, and that's one thing the years don't change."

He thought of Clay Moore and Will Stephens. He had wondered about them over the years, even if he had lost touch. However disparate their jobs, families, failures, and successes, the differences hadn't created a void that couldn't be filled in a couple of hours sitting on the back of a pickup under a live oak.

The country was his roots, and he was strangely proud of them as he watched the rough, rolling hills pass in the windshield. He thought of how artificial and flat Dallas was, and he dreaded going back, even long enough to drop off his mother.

"How come I'll never be as wise as you, Mamma?"

"You will," she said, staring through the windshield. "You just haven't lived long enough yet."

12

Panther Junction, according to the *Texas Almanac*, had a population of ninety-four, too small even for a fourth-class post office. Quinlin passed the school—a square two-story redbrick building with a dangerously stooped tin roof—that had closed not long after the Santa Fe pulled out its last freight train in the late fifties. It was an eyesore now, grown over in needle grass and mesquites. McPherson's General Store, the only occupied building left in the town, was on the other side of the farm-to-market road. Two ancient Magnolia gas pumps stood out front of the peeling white clapboard building, and tin signs nailed on the front advertised Mrs. Baird's bread, Amalie motor oil, and Clabber Girl baking powder. There were several pickups parked in front, and Quinlin continued on down the highway to the fork in the road. He took the left turn, a ranch road that ultimately linked with U.S. 281 on its way to San Antonio. Ten miles down the road, he knew he'd guessed wrong. He made a U-turn back to the fork, then took the unpaved county road, imagining what the splatter of loose gravel was doing to the paint on the undercarriage of his new pickup. As he topped a hill a quarter of a mile later, he met an oncoming sheriff's deputy, who looked at him curiously but waved without taking his hand off the wheel. Quinlin studied him in the rearview mirror and watched him vanish down the hill.

The fourth mailbox on the left, if the address on the federal indictment was correct, belonged to the Bettmans. He got out and unlatched the chain around the gate, climbed back in and drove a couple of car lengths into the rutted lane, and then returned to latch the gate behind him. The road ran a half a mile, twisting and turning around good-size hills, before he saw the house in front of him, setting on the edge of a breaking canyon. He saw a woman in a denim shirt and jeans running from the barn fifty yards to the house. By the time he killed the engine and was getting out of the truck, she was on the porch with a .12-gauge pump Remington pointed at his chest.

"I don't know who you are or what you want," she yelled, "but you can get back in that pickup and head out."

She was tall, thin, and attractive, maybe in her late thirties, and wore no makeup. She also appeared to know how to use the shotgun. Quinlin introduced himself and asked permission to reach for the ID in the back pocket of his Wranglers.

"Pull it out slowly," she said, moving off the porch toward him, "and put it on the hood. Then you move to the back of the pickup. Don't turn around. Just step backward."

He talked quickly as she examined the Dallas Police Department badge and credentials with his picture, mentioning that he'd grown up outside Comanche Gap.

"Bet if we talked a spell, we'd come up with some people we know in common," he said, noticing his country drawl had reappeared.

"Knowing people around here doesn't make them worth a damn," she said, pitching his credentials back on the hood. She moved back onto the porch and sat in a rocking chair, motioning him to another rocker about fifteen feet away. She kept the shotgun in the crook of her left arm, with her right hand near the trigger guard. He could see the safety wasn't on.

Quinlin told Sue Bettman he was a homicide detective investigating a death in Dallas County that her husband might have information about, and he acknowledged that he knew about her husband's claims of drug smuggling and political corruption. He simply wanted to talk to Gary Bettman and confirm what the FBI had already told him.

It took twenty minutes of conversation, but finally Sue Bettman put the safety on and leaned the shotgun against the wall. In a coincidence not uncommon in small towns, Quinlin had mentioned a teacher's name without realizing the woman was Sue Bettman's mother.

Finally, she invited him in, where she motioned him to the kitchen table and busied herself putting on a pot of coffee. Her husband wasn't there, nor were their two children, whom she drove to school herself, with the loaded shotgun leaning against the seat next to her.

Gary Bettman, after not working for three months, had finally landed a job with a small air courier service that delivered checks overnight from banks in the Rio Grande Valley to major bank clearing houses in Dallas. He was gone three days a week, and it paid half of what he had made from Pan Permian Air, but it was the only flying job he could find.

He'd worried about being gone from home, but he'd had no choice. Bills were piling up, and, in an irony that wasn't lost on Sue Bettman, the local bank—Pan Permian State in Comanche Gap—was threatening foreclosure. Her husband had insisted that she go nowhere without the loaded shotgun. The Bettmans' predicament reminded Quinlin of a Randolph Scott plot—a damsel in distress about to lose the family farm to foreclosure by the dirty banker who runs the town.

"Ever since that reporter got killed right before he came out here, we don't trust anyone," she said. "Can't afford to, not in this county."

She confirmed the surreptitious recording her husband had made with the Texas Ranger and produced a transcript. Richmond Carlisle had phoned her husband, and they had agreed to meet at the Bettman ranch.

"We were excited for the first time in months," she said. "Finally, we had someone trying to find the truth. But he never showed. At first, we just figured he'd been bought off like everyone else. Then Gary was getting some stuff at McPherson's the next day, some milk or bread, and Dermitt McPherson told him that a young guy in a convertible had asked directions to our place. We heard about the murder on the news the next day."

"So Carlisle actually made it to Panther Junction," Quinlin said, surprised, "but he never made it the three or four miles to your place, and his body ends up in Dallas County. He had to have been kidnapped, but by whom? Who else knew he was coming?"

Sue Bettman vowed she and her husband had told no one about the meeting, and they hadn't even mentioned it to their son or daughter, deliberately planning the meeting when the children would be at school. Quinlin remembered meeting the sheriff's deputy on his way out. The Bettmans could have been under surveillance, but even then, no one would have known that the man in the sports car was a reporter who posed a potential threat.

Quinlin knew the leak could have come from the other end, in Dallas, but he doubted it. No one at the *Register & News* would have known the Colters, not personally anyway, and from what Harper had said, Carlisle wasn't cutting up his business with anyone on the staff. Yet someone apparently knew to be waiting for Carlisle beside a deserted county road. And clearly, they hadn't wanted his body discovered in Sul Ross County. Someone had gone to a lot of trouble—and risked a lot of exposure—to haul his corpse back to Dallas.

"You don't still have those old party lines like we used to, do you?" Quinlin asked. "Where you can pick up on somebody's line and listen?"

"Those haven't been around in years," Sue said.

He got her permission to look around—for what, he wasn't certain. There were only two phones in the house, and they didn't appear to have been tampered with. Quinlin wasn't a bugging expert by any means, but he thought he could tell if something looked suspicious. Outside, the phone line was on a pole instead of running underground, and he followed the line to the corner of the house. Directly beneath the connection that linked the line with the house, behind a sage bush, he found a small metal alligator clip with a sliver of green insulation partially covered in the dirt. Insulation on the phone wires going into the house had been scarred, consistent with being clipped.

"Sue," he yelled, "have you had somebody out from the phone company recently?"

She hadn't. If someone had tapped the Bettman phone, they hadn't been sophisticated, which told Quinlin it hadn't been a court-approved federal Title III wire tap, the kind that the feds would have gotten.

Quinlin had had only one investigation that involved a court-approved wire tap, and that tap had been placed at Southwestern Bell's central switching station, where a reel-to-reel tape had recorded every conversation.

An exterior wire tap using an alligator clip was rudimentary and operated pretty much like a pair of jumper cables. When current flowed through the phone line, the clip intercepted it, duplicated it, and sent it somewhere else, probably to an energy-activated recording device that you could buy at any Radio Shack. The tap wouldn't have required its own energy source, but it would have been high-maintenance. The scenario made Quinlin shudder. The tap would have had to have been checked frequently, maybe even daily, which meant that someone, probably under the cover of darkness, had been routinely creeping right beneath a child's bedroom window. Clearly, the jury-rigged tap was how someone knew that Richmond Carlisle would be coming down the gravel road to the Bettmans. It was also how they knew he must die.

Quinlin went to his pickup, retrieved a camera, and took pictures of the alligator clip and the scarred telephone line. He'd make sure to give copies to David Cartwright when he got back to Dallas.

He doubted that whoever had checked the illegal tap would have risked coming down the lane from the main road. He went to the back of the house, where he spotted a narrow deer trail. He followed it down through an arroyo and up the side of a steep hill. At the top of the ridge, he had to crawl over a five-strand barbed-wire fence. From the top of the hill, he looked down on the Bettman ranch half a mile away.

The top of the hill looked as if it had been quarried for rock years earlier. There was a flat surface before it turned into a semicircle of gaping holes, and Quinlin could see relatively recent tire tracks. As he headed for the circular tracks, he noticed eleven cigarette butts, all of them unfiltered Camels, within two feet of one another. Somebody had had some time on their hands. He slid a business card beneath the butts and, finding nothing in which to store them, dumped them loose into his shirt pocket. The tire tracks led up the hill to the flat surface, looped around, and headed back down the hill. Wind and possibly some light rain earlier made them difficult to read, but Quinlin was certain of one thing: He'd seen these tracks before. The inside right-front tire was smoother than a baby's butt.

Before he left, he made plans with Sue Bettman to have her husband call him when he returned from work in two days. He still wanted to talk to the only potential witness he had. "Tell him to go to McPherson's and use the pay phone," he told her. "Just because there's no tap on your phone today doesn't mean there won't be tomorrow."

Before Quinlin turned onto the gravel country road outside the Bettmans' gate, he was on the cell phone to Crime Scene.

"I want your trace evidence people to start over on the Richmond Carlisle car," he said. "There's got to be a print or fiber or something somewhere in that car. Pull out the stops. Carlisle wasn't killed in Dallas County. He was driven there. And whoever drove that car was in it for at least an hour and a half with his body. There's got to be something there for us.

"Not only that. I'm bringing you some cigarette butts," Quinlin said, "that I'd like you to do some DNA on."

There was a long pause on the other end from Jeff Hill, the civilian who headed Crime Scene.

"And you want it compared with whose DNA?" Hill asked.

"I don't know yet. I'm working on it."

There was only one pickup at McPherson's Store, and Quinlin decided to risk it. He'd already been seen by a deputy sheriff, so it was a certainty that Red O'Neal knew he was in the county. If O'Neal was setting beside U.S. 281 waiting for him like last time, he was going to have a long wait. Quinlin had already decided to take a series of back roads back to Dallas, going through Dublin and Stephenville instead of the quickest, most logical route through Chalk Mountain and Cleburne.

McPherson's General Store was a throwback to the years of the Truman administration, and Quinlin was awed by the skip zone in time as he opened the door. Dermitt McPherson still sold licorice and hard candy by the piece out of glass jars on the counter, and there was an old glass-fronted meat case with forequarters and hindquarters that he sawed by hand. Nails, screws, and bolts were displayed loose in ten-pound open kegs, and the clock on the wall was encased in a red-blue-and-yellow neon sign advertising Grand Prize beer, a beer that hadn't been brewed since the 1950s.

Dermitt McPherson was behind the counter, and Quinlin assumed the lone pickup out front belonged to him. He wore a white apron that looped around his neck and tied in front. He was eighty if he was a day.

"You don't look the type to buy anything," the old man said. "The first direction's free. You'll have to buy something to get the next one. Where you tryin' to go?"

Quinlin introduced himself and shook the old man's hand, placing a photo of Richmond Carlisle on the counter.

"Yeah," Mr. McPherson said, "I saw him. Wouldn't likely forget him."

"Why's that?"

"First off, you could tell he wasn't from around here. He was a young man wearing suspenders. Only old people around here wear suspenders, and it's been that way for forty years. He wanted directions to the Bettman place, which I gave him."

"Do you recall exactly when that would have been?"

"Last Monday. The grocery truck comes once a week, on Mondays. I was out last Monday, ailin' with the creepin' crud. So it was Monday week."

Carlisle was probably killed that night. His body was discovered beside the road in Dallas the next morning.

"Anybody come in here asking questions about this man or acting strange?"

"Can't say that they did."

"You notice anything unusual about him?"

"He was a smart aleck. Made fun of my cash register."

The ornate machine looked turn of the century; it had three rows of ivory punch keys, a hand crank, and a solid oak cash drawer.

"I told him, I says, 'That's fine, but there's an antique dealer in here every week that offers me more for this cash register than you paid for that pitiful excuse of an automobile you're drivin'.' "

13

The nine-by-twelve-inch manila envelope was waiting on Quinlin's desk at headquarters when he came in. He glanced at it as he pulled his coat over the back of his chair, then headed for the coffee machine. He sipped at the coffee as he studied the printing on the envelope. It was a woman's hand, he'd bet, and it bore a Stephenville postmark but no return address. He tried to think of any woman he knew in Stephenville and came up dry. He slid a pair of scissors beneath the tab and opened it.

The unsigned computer-written note was only three paragraphs long:

> Dear Detective Quinlin:
> I saw the newspaper story about the reporter being killed with rattlesnake venom and I was horrified by the viciousness. I suspect more than I know, but I believe a man named Jerry Ray McCray may be involved in Richmond Carlisle's murder.
> McCray is an ex-convict who lives in Comanche Gap. He lives in a mobile home on several acres off the Old Stephenville Road. He's about six foot three and weighs about 250 pounds. He drives a brown Chevrolet pickup truck. He is an evil man who is certainly capable of killing. But you must be careful. McCray has friends who are *very* influential.
> I pray for your safety.

The note was paper-clipped to a dated copy of the *Comanche Gap Bulletin*. One of the stories on the front page had been highlighted in yellow and carried the headline THIRD TIME A CHARM FOR LOCAL MAN IN RATTLER ROUNDUP. According to the feature story, Jerry Ray McCray, described as a local rancher, had won the annual Sweetwater Rattlesnake Roundup for the third time in four years, capturing twenty-nine diamond-backed rattlesnakes in twelve hours. The largest snake measured nearly eight feet long and had thirteen rattlers.

The story quoted McCray as saying that people misunderstood rattlesnakes: "They sense fear. All you've got to do is act normal around them and they won't bother you." According to the story, McCray had "been bitten by rattlesnakes so many times that he claims he has an immunity to their venom." The story also pointed out that McCray wore handmade cowboy boots, belts, and hatbands made from the skins of rattlesnakes he'd trapped. He also grilled rattlesnake steaks over mesquite fires. "The meat tastes like tenderloin pork," he said, "and it melts in your mouth."

An accompanying photograph showed a grinning McCray squatting on his knees, holding a long rattlesnake just below its head and pointing it, fangs bared, toward the camera. The photo made Quinlin recoil. He may have grown up in the country, but he had never learned to tolerate rattlesnakes.

Quinlin went back to the envelope, studying the writing and the postmark, and then read the note again to make sure he hadn't missed anything. McCray had obviously made an enemy for whatever reason. After all his years in homicide, Quinlin was still amazed at the lengths to which people would go to get their enemies in trouble with the law. Spurned lovers, ex-wives wanting back child support, disgruntled business partners, and even motorists who'd been cut off in traffic had phoned or mailed in anonymous complaints. The leads had to be checked out, and Quinlin figured if he had a dollar for every phony grudge complaint he'd chased, he'd be able to afford cement fence posts.

He found himself studying McCray's photo again. What kind of person, he wondered, got off on playing with rattlesnakes? He'd known one in high school, a weird kid named Jim Pittman, who kept rattlers and copperheads in shoe boxes in his room. One of them got loose in the night, crawled up in bed with Jim, and sunk his fangs into his foot. The boy was taken by medevac helicopter to Harris Hospital in Fort Worth and ultimately had to have his leg amputated from the knee down. Judging from the photograph, McCray was a wing nut. But being a brick short of a load didn't make somebody a killer.

Quinlin headed for the computer that linked DPD with the National Crime Information Center and plugged in McCray's name. The anonymous tipster maintained McCray was an ex-con, and if so, his name had to be in NCIC. The computer lit up like a pinball machine: Jerry Ray McCray, DOB 11/20/49, POB Houston, Texas, had been arrested sixteen times since 1973 but, stunningly, had only been convicted two times. The conviction rate wasn't hard to figure, given the violence of his crimes. Anybody would be a fool to testify against McCray. He had been arrested for terroristic threat, aggravated assault, assault with intent to commit murder, two rapes, maiming, possession of an explosive device, carrying a prohibited weapon, drug possession, and extortion. The only two convictions were out of Laredo, in Webb County, on the Mexican border.

McCray was a for-real bad actor, and Quinlin's original misgivings about the anonymous tip were waning. The detective called the police liaison for the Texas Department of Criminal Justice to get the file on McCray's two stints in prison. McCray's first stretch, which began in February 1975, was for possession of an explosive device. He served seven years flat, with no time off for good behavior, at the Ellis I Unit, Texas's maximum-security equivalent of Leavenworth. Quinlin knew there must have been aggravating circumstances, because first-time convicts normally weren't sent to Ellis I, which at the time had also housed Texas's infamous death row. Beginning in April 1984, McCray spent his second stint, ten years, every day of it, at the Skyview Unit in Rusk for aggravated assault. Inmates in TDCJ knew Skyview as "the Lab." The compound sat on a hill above Rusk State Hospital, Texas's most secure mental institution for the criminally insane. Inside the double row of fourteen-foot razor-wired fences that surrounded Skyview, there were almost as many psychiatrists as guards. Its inmates were lip-dribblers and wackos who had committed bizarre, inexplicable crimes. Skyview was where Texas sent its most dangerous psychopaths.

Quinlin put in a call to the Webb County district attorney's office in Laredo for the prosecutor who had sent McCray down. He wanted specifics on the convictions. The prosecutor was in trial, but her secretary promised she'd return the call. The detective also checked McCray's driver's license and registration. He drove a '91 Chevrolet pickup truck with no lien, which meant it was paid off. The address on the registration and license was a rural route out of Comanche Gap. If Quinlin wasn't mistaken, the route covered the bottomland around the Leon River.

Quinlin picked up the phone, punched in another number. Clay Moore answered the phone just as he was about to hang up.

"Remember when I went to Ms. Todd and told her *I* was the one who'd hit her in the ass with the eraser, not you?"

"Yeah, you rotten bastard, *after* I spent two days in detention hall," Moore answered. "What's happening, Jeb?"

"Time to settle the score, Clay boy, so you won't owe me anymore."

Tomorrow, Quinlin would get on a plane for Laredo to check the record on Jerry Ray McCray and interview the prosecutor who had put him down for two sentences in the Texas Department of Criminal Justice. Clay Moore, it occurred to Jeb, was on the ground in McCray's backyard; he might have the answers that would make or break McCray as a suspect. Everything Quinlin knew about McCray was history. He needed something current.

"Know anything about a dude named Jerry Ray McCray?"

"Snake?" Moore replied. "Know enough to know he's crazy. And real bad news. Why you want to know?"

Quinlin gave his old high school buddy the shorthand version of Richmond Carlisle's murder and the anonymous letter and newspaper clipping he'd received about McCray.

"So, is McCray capable of killing somebody?" Quinlin asked.

"He is if you believe him," Moore said. "Claims to be a stone-cold killer."

Clay Moore acknowledged he didn't get out much. But occasionally, he said, when he had business in Comanche Gap, he stopped off at the VFW post for a couple of beers.

"They're mostly a bunch of drunks," Moore said, "old farts from World War Two and a few Nam vets, all of them reliving what badasses they were. You'd have to drink a case to ever hear the truth."

McCray, according to Moore, apparently was a regular, whose distinction was that he was drunker and louder than the rest of the drunks. McCray claimed to have been Special Forces, trained in demolition. Ironically, Moore said, McCray bragged that he'd been drummed out of the army on a Section Eight.

"Most people don't brag about being a mental case," Quinlin said. "He say why?"

"Said he went to Nam to kill slopes, not to play games with pussies," Moore said. "Said there were too many rules. Supposedly, he blew up a whole village. He claimed the people he killed were Vietcong. The army said they were friendlies in a no-fire zone. They wrote him off as crazy before they could court-martial him. Who knows? But, if you believe his shit, he's proud of a lot things most people wouldn't be."

"Like what?"

"Like being an ex-con. Don't know whether it's true or not, but he claims to have killed a black dude in the joint and gotten away with it. Also claims to be a mercenary. Or I guess that's what you'd call it. Way he put it was, he 'does things for people that ain't exactly law-abidin'.' No specifics. Just talk. So who knows?"

"He's told you all that?" Quinlin said. "He must trust you."

"Don't know about that, but he thinks I'm cool because I was marine recon."

"What's he do for a living?"

"He's got a place down on the Leon River bottoms. Claims he does a little ranchin', but I suspect he's all hat and no cows."

"Ever hear of him working for the Colters?"

"No, but, like I say, I don't get out much. Want me to ask around some?"

"No, it's probably best not to," Quinlin said. "Do me a favor?"

"No sweat."

"Just between you and me, I need to know if he's walking with a limp or if maybe his arm's in a sling or something, anything to indicate he's had an injury. And while you're at it, I need you to get a look at his front tires. See if there's anything unusual about them."

"His tires? What—"

"Don't want to influence you. Just take a quiet look, and if you see something interesting, just let me know. And if he smokes, find out what brand he smokes, okay? And listen to me. Don't go out of your way. If this is a problem, just—"

"Hey, I'll make it happen," Moore said, "but not because I owe you. You screwed me on that Todd deal. And for the record, I never gave *you* up for hiding Limburger cheese in the heating system. Not even when the smell forced 'em to evacuate the whole damned school."

"Just watch your ass and don't get caught."

Hanging up, Jeb turned again to the anonymous delivery. Jerry Ray McCray looked good. Only one thing didn't add up. What had the anonymous note said? "McCray has friends who are *very* influential." How does a violent scumbag with a record have influential friends?

Quinlin was intrigued by the writing on the envelope. It was distinctly feminine and, though there were no lines on the envelope, the printing was precisely aligned. What would a handwriting examiner say? Confident, intelligent maybe?

He would bet good money it had come from Rebecca Colter. But if his hunch was right, she would have had to have undergone a complete change of heart. If Rebecca was the anonymous source, she was drawing a map that ultimately could lead to her husband.

Rebecca Colter pulled the Suburban into the first parking space next to the sidewalk. Getting good parking at Cross Timbers Convalescent Home wasn't a problem. Despite their best intentions, once families put relatives in nursing homes, they seemed to visit less and less. Though Rebecca called him Uncle Charley, Charley Blake wasn't family. But she was still all the old man had in the world. She spread out her visits, generally visiting on Mondays, Wednesdays, and Fridays so he'd have company throughout the week. And because he complained so bitterly about the food, she always brought a picnic basket with fried chicken, meat loaf, or chicken-fried steak, even though it violated his rigid diet.

"There's not anything they can do for me anyways," Charley said frequently. "Why shouldn't I eat what I want if I'm dying anyway?"

But Charley Blake had stretched his logic and Rebecca's sense of benevolence last Christmas when he began asking for "a good shot of sippin' whiskey." Against her better judgment, she had finally acquiesced. She poured three fingers of Buck's Jack Daniel's into a thermos bottle and gave it to Charley on Christmas Eve. She felt so guilty and was so worried that she called early Christmas morning just to make sure he had survived the night.

"Best night I've had in years," Charley said heartily. "Drank the whole damned thing last night and slept like a newborn. I tell you, I think it's good for me."

He'd tried the ploy repeatedly over the next six months, but Rebecca hadn't fallen for it. The doctors were saying that it was just a matter of time before the muscles in his heart totally atrophied. The emphysema only compounded his medical problems. And at seventy-six, Charley Blake wasn't a great candidate for a heart transplant, the only procedure that could save him.

Rebecca Colter had trouble remembering that Charley Blake was gravely ill. He was a handsome old cowboy, whose blue eyes were as piercing as any twenty-year-old's. His mustache was meticulously trimmed, and he wore his gray hair longer than most men his age, giving him a distinguished look. His teeth were not only his own; they were straight and white enough for a Colgate commercial. He still sent out his white shirts and khaki Wranglers to the cleaners for heavy starch, and he wore his lizard boots every day, even if he had to walk with a cane. His medical problems had humbled him, no doubt, but he still carried his six feet four inches without a stoop.

She sat across from him, watching him enjoy his lunch, and imagined what a romantic character he must have been in his younger years.

Today, Charley ate the fried chicken to the bone and sopped up the juice from his black-eyed peas with a homemade biscuit. Half the ritual was over. Then they moved to the back porch for the other half. The "old farts," as Uncle Charley referred to them, migrated to the front. They had the back porch to themselves.

A stranger would assume they were father and daughter, the easy way they handled each other, he grinning proudly at her and she doting on his every move. In order for the equation to work, there'd have to be an assumption that she would have favored her mother. Rebecca Colter was barely over five feet, and if she owned a dress, no one at the nursing home had ever seen her in one. She always wore denim and boots, a rough contrast to her delicate auburn hair and her porcelain skin and green eyes. There were no lines at the corner of those eyes to give away the fact that she had just turned forty-four.

The old man and younger woman sat in rockers side by side on the back porch, looking out onto the Comanche Mountains. They weren't actual mountains, not by Colorado standards, but everyone in Sul Ross County called them mountains. It was rough country nonetheless, a peculiar part of Texas, where prairie yielded uncertainly to breaking rocky ravines and clumps of cedar. The country had its own distinctive majesty.

Rebecca reached over and patted his hand, which was on his leg. "Tell me something," she said. "I don't understand. The Colters abandoned you and yet I've never heard you say a bad word about any of them. How can you not be bitter at them?"

The old man collected his thoughts before he answered, and when he did, his eyes were still on the hills in front of him. "Things get clearer the older you get," he said. "I'm like an ol' quarter horse to them. Don't ride and rope no more, so not much good for anything anymore. I got put out to pasture, and they forgot about me. 'Sides sweetie, there's just not any room for hating somebody, even if you got good cause. Guess it's got something to do with getting ready to meet your Maker.

"Yeah, I was with ol' Clendon for almost forty years. And I did what he told me to do, helped make him a wealthy man. Fact is, I did some things that don't make me sleep all that well. But when you're young, you don't think about tomorrow; you just think about now. Well, tomorrow's here right now, and I'm damned sorry for some of the things I did. Can't take 'em back, just got to live with 'em. But I ain't gonna say anything bad about Clendon Colter. I was a grown man and I knew better. I'll have to answer for most of it, I know I will. Someday here pretty soon, I 'spect."

It was hard for her to believe Charley Blake had ever done anything bad. She had fallen in love with him the first time she met him, just before she and Buck married, twenty years earlier. His was always the quiet voice of reason and common sense and, though he was tough and sinewy, he was amazingly gentle in the way he viewed life. On occasion, when Buck had had too much to drink, it was always Uncle Charley who took him aside. She never heard precisely what Charley told him, but whatever it was toned him down and made him at least tolerable. Charley Blake was that way. If he told you something, you had to respect it, no matter who you were. So when it came time for Chad to be born, no one questioned her when she asked Charley Blake to be the godfather of her only child.

Rebecca figured they filled voids in each other's lives. Her father died while she was in junior high and her mother passed on shortly after she graduated. Charley Blake was either a bachelor or divorced while he was still a young man; he never said which. It didn't matter. Over time, the bond between the old man and the young woman grew.

The old man was uncharacteristically quiet, and they stared at the mountains. Clouds were rolling in, cloaking the sun and turning the sky bluish gray.

"There's some thunderheads over yonder," he said idly, "and the wind's pickin' up. 'Spect we'll get some rain tonight."

"Uncle Charley," she said, "I think the Colters have done something really bad and I don't know what to do. All I know is that I've got to do something. I can't sleep, either."

He held his silence the longest and she wondered if he had heard her.

"Nobody knows the Colters better than me," he finally said. "I've seen 'em born, I been to their weddings, and I've seen 'em die. This is what I see, sweetie. They're not like me and you, or anybody else, for that matter. They'll never be put in a situation that they won't do whatever they have to do to get by. And that means *anything*. That's just in their genes, I guess you could say. I'm not judging 'em for it. I'm just saying that's the way they are. And that makes 'em dangerous, like a gut-shot mountain lion."

The old man and young woman fell silent again. After a time, he saw her reach for her purse. He put his hand on her forearm and leaned toward her.

"You know, sweetie, I don't take anything you do for me for granted," he said gently. "And there's damned little I can do to repay you for all your goodness. 'Bout the only thing I can do is try to keep you safe. And Chad, too. It'd just kill me if any harm came to y'all. You need to let this thing with the Colters alone. No good can come of it. I've tried to tell you about them."

He paused for a minute. "I guess the reason I have trouble talking about them is because I'd have to admit some things about myself that'd make you think less of me, and I'd hate that." The old man's voice was breaking, but he pushed on. "I haven't always been the person you think I am."

The grip on her arm was strong.

"Rebecca, you got to promise me you'll leave this alone."

"I can't, Uncle Charley. I think they killed a man. I've already done something, but I don't think it's enough."

Charley Blake turned her face toward him and looked her in the eyes. "Well, it may be enough to get you hurt."

14

Quinlin took nearly an hour to brief Harper on Colter's insider land deal with Lanson McLain, the rough-edged Texas Democrat who became president, and the recent arrest of Gary Bettman on drug charges. The reporter was genuinely impressed, jotting down notes in his reporter's notebook.

By the time Mendalina brought their burritos to the back table at Gonzalez's, Quinlin had to rearrange the property documents on the table before she could serve them. And when a chunk of chorizo fell out of Harper's tortilla onto one of the deeds, Quinlin appeared wounded, as if someone had premeditatedly pissed on his leg.

"So are you going to write a story about this?" Quinlin asked as he swabbed the Mexican sausage off the document.

"Probably," Harper said, staring at the red stain. "The land deal's a great profile, and it has a nice political edge to it, too. Besides, it'd be a good set-up piece if we can ever prove that the Colters were behind the Bettman drug deal or Carlisle's murder."

"I've got a fresh lead, too," Quinlin said between bites of his chorizo, potato, and egg burrito, "but I haven't finished checking it out yet. I got an anonymous tip on a certified psycho with a history of playing with snakes and trying to kill people. He looks pretty good, but it's too early to know for sure."

"Sounds like he's what I need to make a story," Harper said. "What's the deal?"

"I'll run him down for you, but it's nothing you can use yet.

I've still got to put him with opportunity, give him some motive, and, most importantly, tie him to the Colters."

Quinlin ran down the lead he'd received in the unmarked envelope and told the reporter the results from the NCIC. He was careful not to mention his suspicion about Rebecca Colter being the anonymous source.

"Sounds like a real wacko," Harper said. "Uh, you forgot to mention his name. Are you not trusting me all of a sudden?"

"Doin' you a favor, hoss. You just don't know it. Way I see it, you're under the same pressure I'm facing. You're going to have to tell Brewster all of the stuff you've gathered on Colter's insider land deal. And I expect you to tell him about Snake Man. It'll make you look like you know what you're doing. But then, next thing you know, your editor's got your arm behind your back, forcing you to write a story. But you can't. You don't know Snake Man's name."

"I trust you," Quinlin said, trying to salve the hurt on his friend's face. "I just don't trust the assholes you work for. Or, for that matter, the assholes that I work for."

"Fact is, Jeb, we're both parasites. We just take turns riding each other. Looks like it's my turn."

Harper's eyes caught the manila folder leaning against the sugar shaker. "What's in the envelope?"

"Icing on the cake," Quinlin replied, opening the envelope and flipping through the two-inch stack of land deeds like a deck of cards.

"These are the last few land transactions by the Colters, covering the past three or four years," Quinlin said. "Think you'll recognize some of the names."

One by one, he plopped down the deeds on the table. Each one showed that the Colters had deeded property to other people, apparently free and clear. Two hundred acres had been transferred to Lee Roy Hudgkins, the county judge. Sheriff Red O'Neal got another 250 acres. Shad Culpepper, Sul Ross County's district judge, got four hundred acres from the Colters.

"Not hard to figure why the Colters own Sul Ross County, is it?" Quinlin said.

"That's arrogant as hell, leaving that in the public record."

"Not really," Quinlin said with a smug grin. "They weren't direct transfers. That'd be way too obvious. The Colters flipped the land through four or five different names—sometimes within a single week—before the land finally ended up in the officials' names. I about wore out the deed books running them down."

"Is Hoot Gibson or Les Westgrove in here?" Harper asked.

"No, that'd be too easy. They're probably paying them off another way, and probably bigger money. Just don't know what it is yet."

Quinlin handed a deed over the table to the reporter. It transferred 547 acres from the Colters to Bradford Merriweather. Quinlin had gone to school with Merriweather's younger brother, Bill. The older Merriweather was a lawyer and had become one of the top lobbyists in Austin.

"Five hundred acres would make a decent weekend place, don't you 'magine?" Quinlin said. "Bet you if we checked, Merriweather would be a member of Hoyt Garvin's law firm down in Austin. He was a local boy, and I'd bet your next paycheck that he carries water for the Colters in the capital. He's their fixer down in Austin."

Harper thumbed through the documents.

"Who's this? Jerry Ray McCray?" he asked.

Quinlin looked shocked and grabbed the documents. The last three pages were paper-clipped to the Merriweather deed. He hadn't seen them.

"I'll be goddamned," Quinlin said. "I didn't know this was in there. I must have missed it. This is Snake Man. Jerry Ray McCray. Colters gave this scumbag two hundred and fifty acres? What legitimate reason would there be for one of the most prominent families in the fuckin' state giving land to a punk ex-con?"

Quinlin saw Harper making notes in his notebook.

"McCray is still mine until I get this figured out, right?" Quinlin said. "I mean, I'm not going to read any of this shit in the paper, am I?"

"Come on, Jeb. It's a little late to be rewriting our rules, isn't it?"

"The Colters can't know that we've put McCray in the equation," Quinlin said. "I'm serious as a heart attack. Everything I'm trying to do will end up in the shitter."

"Chill, buddy. It ain't gonna happen."

• • •

Halfway to the house, White Deer bolted across the lane, followed by another buck, three does, and two fawns. Trapped momentarily in the headlights, the pelt on the huge white deer shimmered like neon. The other deer ran into a cover of post oaks, but White Deer stopped twenty-five yards short of the thicket, staring at the intrusion in his world. Quinlin slowed to a stop and watched him. The big buck wasn't scared, Quinlin surmised, just perturbed that a human had destroyed the peacefulness of his nightly routine. Quinlin might have a piece of paper that entitled him to the land, but he knew he didn't own it.

Once inside the house, Quinlin had his own ritual. He loaded the coffeepot—he wondered if he'd ever stop substituting caffeine for alcohol—and checked the answering machine. There was a hang-up call but no message, and he immediately thought of Madeline. The dull pain in his stomach quelled the urge to call her. He knew the problem; the solution was too complex.

He grabbed the half of a Sara Lee apple pie left in the refrigerator, tried to remember how old it was, filled a cup with coffee, and headed for the kitchen table. Funny the way Madeline influenced him. If she were there, he'd cut a slice of pie, put it on a dessert plate, and microwave it. Now he would eat it cold out of the throw away aluminum foil plate.

Still chewing the pie, he walked across the kitchen to his briefcase, retrieved a small rectangular box with the Smith & Wesson logo, and returned to the table, where he'd left his gun-cleaning kit a day earlier.

The SW 99 was brand-new, a joint effort between Smith & Wesson and gun designer Carl Walther. Quinlin hoped the dull black weapon was, in fact, as evil as it appeared. He'd bought it the day he got back from Comanche Gap. It was an event he had later minimized to Paul McCarren, but his encounter with Red O'Neal beside the highway had unnerved him. It was a confrontation that could have gone to hell in front of his eyes. A crooked cop with his hand on a .357 Magnum, in his own jurisdiction, no witnesses, stopping a motorist for probable cause, one who happened to be carrying a .357 Magnum of his own. O'Neal could have blow him out of the pickup, claiming after the fact that he hadn't recognized Quinlin as a cop and saying that for inexplicable reasons, Quinlin had just gone for his weapon. And with Les Westgrove running the grand jury, Quinlin's own killing would have been ruled a justifiable and unfortunate shooting of a cop who apparently had gone over the edge. And they could have made it look good, too, introducing medical records that he'd been treated for alcoholism. Big surprise that a drunk could be depressed and despondent enough to commit an act that defied logic. Dialing McCarren on the cell phone and leaving the line open, Quinlin knew, could have saved his life.

The .40-caliber SW 99 was seven and a quarter inches long and, because it was made out of polymer, weighed only twenty-five ounces, the size of a good steak. More significantly, it carried five more shells in its clip than Quinlin's old revolver held in its chamber, and with the spare clip he would carry in his pocket, it gave him twenty-two chances of surviving, instead of six. Quinlin hadn't been bullshitting O'Neal when he told him things would be different the next time they met.

Quinlin had surprised himself at the range. He was better with the automatic than his old standby, which he had carried since his rookie days on patrol. He had just finished cleaning the barrel and replacing the clip when Bingo launched his nonstop barking. Quinlin waited several minutes, thinking the Border collie would give it up. But Bingo wasn't showing any signs of shutting up. The incessant barking was unusual. Bingo accepted occasional armadillos, coons, and squirrels as everyday intruders on his turf, barking a few times or growling low in his throat to send them on their way. Whatever was out there now wasn't a nuisance, but threatening. Maybe a bobcat or a coyote. His neighbor had told him last week he had spotted a couple of coyotes on the prowl.

Just as Quinlin opened the front door, he heard a sharp *piiiing* and felt a tickling sensation behind his left ear. Instinctively, he dropped to his knees, running his hand behind his ear. He felt splinters. He looked up and saw the fresh burrow through the wood in the doorjamb. He rolled around the corner into the house and killed the lights in the great room. He ran for the SW 99 on the kitchen table, turning off the kitchen lights as he went. He made his way in the darkness to the back door and eased down the porch to the corner, the automatic raised upright in front of his nose. Peeking around the corner, he could see the Dodge's interior lights were on. Somebody had been inside the pickup.

It was as dark as the bottom of a well and the only sound he could hear came from his own feet as he crept along dried oak leaves. Whoever was out there would expect him to stay close to the house. He moved fifteen feet from the house and continued slowly toward the pickup. He needed to cut his profile, making sure he didn't give the shooter a large target. Twenty feet from the pickup, Quinlin bent to his knees, braced himself on one hand, and leaned onto the ground, gripping the .40-caliber auto in his right hand. Was the shooter still behind the pickup? He strained to see through the darkness. Probably not, not with the interior lights still on. Where, then? A shot of cold panic ran up his spine. Had he put himself between the intruder and the pickup? He had assumed there was one person. Were there more? He looked behind him.

He heard sounds of snapping twigs at the far end of the front porch. Was that a silhouette at the corner? *Concentrate, damn it.* It was black fog. He couldn't tell. He studied the black mass, concentrated on it. It didn't move. He brought the automatic around on his elbows, aiming it at the densest part of the dull black blob. If it wasn't the silhouette of a person, if it was his imagination, and if he fired, he was giving his position away, probably showing the shooter a muzzle blast that would pinpoint him as a target. Shooting was risky. He stared over the barrel of the automatic. He thought he saw a movement in the blob of concentrated dullness. He took a deep breath, excelled about half of it, and squeezed the trigger, feeling the recoil in his hand.

Uuugh.

Had he hit someone? Or had he made the sound as he exhaled? He eased to one knee, then ran stooped like an old man to the right-front corner of the Dodge. He dropped behind the tire and looked beneath the truck. He made his way to the opposite corner of the truck and waited. He *thought* he heard the rustle of feet running through dried leaves in the distance. He maintained his position. It seemed like an hour, but it was only ten minutes, according to his watch. Cautiously, he leaned through the open door of the Dodge and pulled a flashlight from the console. He didn't turn it on until he reached the corner of the house. He scanned the area beside the house and saw nothing. Slowly, he moved the flashlight back and fourth, flashing the beam farther and farther from the house, lighting up the brush on the south side of the house. Something moved quickly in the brush, probably a startled jackrabbit, and Bingo let out a low growl. Quinlin concentrated the beam of light on the ground in front of him, and he finally spotted several drops of blood on a clump of Johnsongrass. Not enough blood to have hit an internal organ, probably just a flesh wound. And judging from the sound of the quick steps in the dried leaves, whoever had lost the blood probably wasn't seriously wounded.

Quinlin went in the house for a clear plastic sandwich bag and knife. He stooped over the clump of Johnsongrass, carefully cutting the plant at ground level. There wasn't a lot of blood, but surely enough for the crime lab to get some DNA.

Whoever had been inside the Dodge had pulled the bundle of wiring from behind the dash, where it went into the steering column and led to the ignition. The wiring hadn't been cut, probably only because Bingo had interrupted the intruder before he could accomplish his goal. Car thieves, Quinlin knew, didn't operate in the boondocks, risking a quarter-mile walk down a private lane to hot-wire a pickup. His mind went to McCray, an ex-con whose peculiar rap sheet documented his familiarity with explosives. Quinlin backed away from the Dodge, careful not to touch anything, and pushed the door shut with his boot. Maybe Crime Scene could pull some evidence.

The cop bent on one knee and rubbed the Border collie behind his ears. "Bingo, my buddy, how 'bout a fat ol' steak for breakfast?"

15

Ten minutes before Quinlin had to leave for Love Field, he sat at his desk and waited for Paul McCarren to get off his phone.

"DPS shows McCray drives a '91 Chevy pickup," Quinlin told his partner. "Get somebody in Crime Scene to photograph the tail-lights of a '91 Chevy in the dark and throw in some others, like a Ford and Dodge, whatever. All at night. Then show the pictures to that RN who made the 911 call on Carlisle. See if she can ID the taillights she saw leaving from Carlisle's car. It won't be much, even if she picks the Chevy. But it'll give us another circumstantial piece, especially if we end up in a pissing match with the DA over whether we can file."

Quinlin picked up the phone and called Madeline. But he hung up when he got her machine.

Flying Air Rio Grande was like trying to ride a greased bronc. The skinny Fairchild Metroliner was an El Producto with wings, and it shimmied and shook like a belly dancer when it took off from San Antonio on its last ragged leg to Laredo. As the landing gear re-tracted back into its bowels, it sent a corresponding unnerving thud of metal on metal beneath the flooring, making the twelve wincing passengers glance uneasily at one another.

Once aloft, Quinlin fixated on the wings as they cut through the wispy clouds. For no good reason that he could discern, his mind went back fifteen years to a murder he had covered when he was still in uniforms. It hadn't been a premeditated homicide; he was certain of that. It was a burglary, one of maybe two hundred that had occurred that day in Dallas. A run-of-the-mill speed freak, carrying by happenstance a .38 he had stolen from a house only two hours earlier, was merely trying to support his habit by emptying a house while its owner was gone. He had stacked his loot beside the kitchen door and was just beginning to carry it to his car in the alley when the owner showed up. Startled and scared, and hyper and paranoid from the methamphetamine jitters, the burglar unloaded three rounds from the stolen gun into the homeowner's chest as he came through the utility room from the garage.

Quinlin and his partner stopped the killer a half a mile away for doing sixty in a thirty-mile-an-hour zone. The burglar was blithering like a three-year-old before Quinlin could even ask him for his driver's license. "I killed him! I killed him! I didn't mean to. Man, I was going to hock the damned gun. I hate guns. He scared me bad, man."

The "What-If Case," Quinlin called it. Fate, coincidence, destiny, crossed stars, full moon—whatever the catalyst, life was ironic. What if the burglar hadn't copped a gun at the previous house? What if the homeowner hadn't gotten sick at work and left early? Or what if he'd left five minutes later? Or earlier? Why couldn't the cheese-dick burglar or the sick salesman have gotten caught behind a DART bus like everyone else? Or had a flat? Two strangers, one minding his own business on a Tuesday afternoon, the other pilfering another man's belongings, and fate brings them face-to-face in a nanosecond. A forty-three-year-old husband, father of three, Little League coach who mouthed but never sang the hymns at church ends up passing his lifeblood through a penny-size hole in his carotid artery. A chicken-dick methhead with no ambition beyond his next score ends up facing a lethal needle on death row. Unexpected, needless death, Quinlin surmised, was the flip side of the lottery. No one was bulletproof.

Quinlin had showed up two hours later at the address listed on the salesman's driver's license, just in time to see a detective inform the victim's wife, fresh from work, that she was a widow. The salesman's wife was hysterical and, surprisingly, Quinlin thought, angry.

"Damn it, I knew it," she said over and over again. "We never go to bed or leave for work angry with each other. Never. Not in twelve years. We always kissed and hugged before we left. But this morning, we were mad. I don't even remember why. I watched him walk to the car and didn't say a word."

A paramedic had to give her a sedative.

The Air Rio Grande Metroliner was rocking and rolling in an air pocket, and its bulkheads were creaking like an old man's knees. Thirteen thousand feet below, all Quinlin could see through the window were mesquite bushes and scrub brush.

Something inside him felt the same way he'd felt beside the highway, looking into Red O'Neal's glass-shard eyes. He watched the vibration in the overhead bins and wondered how many times the Metroliner had taken off and landed. Or if the pilot on a not-ready-for-prime-time airline knew his ass from an autopilot.

He knew he'd try Madeline again from the car-rental counter. Life was too short.

16

L ook, I'm not trying to be a jerk," Quinlin told the woman, "but we're not getting anywhere like this. Get me somebody who can speak English. *No habla español.*"

A Hispanic guy behind the counter overheard the latest exchange and bellied in beside the uncomprehending woman.

"No need for a scene, señor," he said condescendingly. "What's the problem here?"

"This isn't a scene," Quinlin said. "I can show you a scene. The problem is that I expect to speak English in an American courthouse. Why do you hire people here who can't speak English?"

"Marita normally works in the files," he said. "She's filling in for someone who's sick. What is it that you want?"

Marita, Quinlin knew, was a symbol of an era long eclipsed in every place except the Rio Grande Valley. She was probably a county commissioner's or district clerk's niece, daughter-in-law, or maybe even the daughter of their maid. The *patrón* system was still alive and well in Laredo, where an influential power broker could deliver five or ten thousand votes to any political candidate with enough money. But the debt didn't end when the politician assumed office; the *patrón* reserved the right to control his machinery, primarily by dispensing government jobs and divvying up county contracts to family, friends, and allies.

Finally, Quinlin got directions to the basement, where the district attorney's criminal archives were kept.

Admittedly, Quinlin wasn't in the best of moods even before he arrived at the Webb County Courthouse. When he had tried Madeline's number from the airport, he'd gotten her machine again. Against his better judgment, he'd left a message this time, something like "I love you, Maddie. I'm in Laredo, but when I get back, we need to talk about our future. I, uh, love you." He knew he'd screwed up as soon as he'd said it. It sounded juvenile and knee-jerk, but it was already on the recorder.

His attitude hadn't gotten any better when he checked in with the district attorney's office. Zita Morales, the prosecutor who had handled both of McCray's convictions, was unexpectedly in court all day and couldn't meet him until after five. She left a message with her secretary that she'd meet him at White Willy's, which, according to the secretary, was a cop hangout three blocks from the DA's office. He'd have to pull the files on McCray by himself.

Laredo, he decided on his way to the courthouse, was where you'd stick the hose if you wanted to give Texas an enema. The place was broken out in poverty, and in one swath of town off the interstate, chickens and pigs ran wild in the front yards of lean-to houses, and abandoned cars on cement blocks were more prevalent than grass. Occasionally, Quinlin saw smoke from wood-burning cookstoves drifting from vents in the roofs, and he recognized the smell of tortillas. Washington giveaways had made their way to the border, and red-white-and-blue signs signaling federally subsidized programs like Headstart and WIN were more abundant than schools. Children played in vacant dirt lots and stared suspiciously at the new rental car as it passed. Hard living had left them wearing the kind of weary faces that Quinlin had seen only on adults. There were no 7-Elevens, no Albertson's, or any other chain stores, just small holes-in-the-wall where mom-and-pop entrepreneurs charged twice the price simply because residents had no way of driving across town to real stores.

Downtown Laredo was a street scene out of a cheap Mexican movie. Quinlin missed the courthouse on his first sweep through town and ended up at the international border, where he had to wait ten minutes for a procession of aging, decrepit, and overloaded Mexican trucks to pass before he could make a U-turn. He marveled at how Customs, DEA, and Border Patrol agents must persevere under the onslaught of Mexican trucks and how they could possibly intercept even a tenth of the drugs pouring into the country. Finally, he paralleled the Hertz Ford Taurus between a twenty-year-old GMC and a hailed-out Nissan pickup four blocks away from the courthouse.

A Mexican kid about twelve intercepted him before he could get to the sidewalk, offering to "protect your car, señor," for five American dollars.

"Tell you what, amigo, anything happens to that car," Quinlin said, "I'll look you up and put your little butt in jail. And how come it is that you're not in school, anyway?"

The kid ran across the street and vanished in an alley between two buildings.

By Dallas standards—and probably those of any other Texas city not on the border—Laredo was laissez-faire, if not Third World. Beaters with may-pop tires, cracked taillights, and baling wire holding their hoods down bore current vehicle inspection stickers on their windshields nonetheless. Quinlin figured you'd have to interview twenty people to find one with liability insurance, which was supposedly required by state law. And if the city had health codes, either they weren't enforced or merchants paid inspectors to look the other way. In a small plaza a block from the courthouse, Quinlin walked through an open-air meat market where a barbecued kid goat the color of rust hung stiffly from his hind hoofs, a landing strip for every fly in two countries. Vendors were hawking sandals with soles made out of tire treads, black-market Ray Bans, leather vests, sundresses, velvet Elvises, dashboard Jesuses, Mexican soda pop, and knockoff Nikes with the authentic checkmark logo, but spelled Nikee.

Take the drugs out of Laredo, Quinlin figured, and the economy would fall faster than a fat lady's tits.

Quinlin filled out the document retrieval form in the archives area and, in the blank marked "Reason for Query," he printed "Official Police Business," then flashed his Dallas Police Department detective's shield. It was still thirty minutes before a tired old man appeared with a two-foot stack of files and directed him to a well-used cubicle in a corner of the basement. Quinlin eyed the files and knew he'd have plenty to do before meeting Zita Morales at five.

He went through the records in chronological order, beginning in late 1974, when McCray was arrested by a joint task force of federal, state, and local officers for possession of an explosive device. While the task force caught him with two cases of dynamite stolen from a construction site in Eagle Pass, it was clear from the records that agents wanted him for an unsolved bombing four months earlier in a Laredo industrial park near the border. According to task force reports, four employees and a security guard had been killed when a bomb apparently concealed in a refrigerated van blew up at Tex-Mex Meat Packers. The motive, according to the report, was open warfare between two competing drug-smuggling rings, each of which used meat-packing plants as a front for smuggling cocaine.

Quinlin shook his head. It didn't take a great amount of imagination to figure out what could have happened had Bingo not alerted him to the man inside his Dodge. The next morning, he would have turned the key in the ignition and become buzzard bait.

He focused back on the file. Tex-Mex Meat Packers already had been under investigation by the task force after Border Patrol agents found nearly two kilos of coke concealed in beef carcasses in one of their transports. When agents of the U.S. Bureau of Alcohol, Tobacco and Firearms shoveled through the gutted remains of the Tex-Mex plant, they found heavy cocaine residue virtually throughout. The immediate suspects, according to the confidential reports, were members of a rival smuggling operation headed by Juan Carlos San Martín, a Mexican national known in drug circles as "El Gato."

A DEA intelligence summary, based on the agency's EPIC computerized list of known associates, diagrammed San Martín's organization down to its mules, listed tail numbers of aircraft in the smuggling enterprise, and noted a list of front companies, including

Trans-Rio Grande Beef Packers. But curiously, the intelligence apparently ended at the border. Under Domestic Associates, the notation read simply "Unknown."

According to an affidavit by a task force agent, a confidential informant had identified Jerry Ray McCray as an enforcer for the San Martín cartel and the man who had planted the explosives in the tractor-trailer rig at Tex-Mex. Offered full immunity on all charges, McCray had still refused to identify anyone for whom he might have worked.

Quinlin could tell from the documents that there wasn't enough evidence to charge McCray with the five murders, and he figured that task force agents were lucky as hell even to have caught him with the dynamite. Seven years was probably the best they could do. Meanwhile, McCray got a free pass from death row. The unsolved but undocumented murders, Quinlin knew, accounted for McCray's ticket to Ellis I Unit, an uncommon assignment for a first-time felon.

The file impressed Quinlin. Zita Morales was not only thorough; she was committed. Even after McCray had been transferred to Huntsville to serve his sentence, Morales had visited him twice, according to the file, trying to get him to roll over on his employers on smuggling and murder charges. Correspondence between her office and TDCJ showed she returned to Ellis I a third time, after McCray was implicated, but again not charged, in the gruesome racial killing of a black inmate. McCray, purportedly a member of the white-supremacist Aryan Brotherhood, was the only suspect in the murder, which apparently was triggered by the black convict's allegedly informing on the Aryans. The convict's throat was cut, but not before his eyes were gouged out and his ears and tongue had been cut off. Quinlin figured Morales had tried to use the convict's murder as leverage to bluff McCray into a confession on the packing-plant bombing. Whatever her ploy, it hadn't worked; McCray did his seven at Ellis I and walked on mandatory release.

The ex-con had lasted barely two years in the free world. The second file, opened in April 1984, documented one of the most violent criminal acts Quinlin had ever encountered. McCray apparently had reestablished his ties with the San Martín cartel as an enforcer. And from the file, it was a job he thoroughly enjoyed. Task force intelligence reports showed that San Martín apparently suspected Ivan Martinez, one of his drug captains and ostensibly president of Trans-Rio Grande Beef Packers, of skimming the proceeds. McCray appeared at Martinez's rambling estate on the outskirts of Laredo at 2:00 A.M. and, by means unknown to law enforcement, made his way past a seventy-five-pound pit bull and a state-of-the-art security system. Given that there were no prints linked to McCray, investigators theorized he'd worn latex gloves. Once inside, he stripped Martinez and tied him with nylon rope to a chair in the dining room. Producing a straight razor, McCray carved superficial cuts across the smuggler's throat, then lengthwise from his chest to his pubic hair.

Holding the straight razor against the throat of Martinez's thirty-two-year-old wife, Consuela, he shoved her on top of the dining room table and raped her while her bleeding and bound husband pled for their lives and screamed that he would lead McCray to the money. McCray untied Martinez and forced him and his wife at gunpoint to take him to the money. The bloody drug dealer led him into the master bedroom upstairs, where he moved a huge potted plant and retrieved $600,000 in cash from a floor safe. Downstairs, McCray tied Martinez back into the chair and forced his wife to perform oral sex. McCray then zipped up, walked ten feet to her bound husband, and slashed off his testicles with the straight razor. He went out the rear door to the patio and fed Martinez's balls to the pit bull.

McCray probably would have walked altogether had he not been a genuinely brazen sociopath who took too much pride in his work. As two doctors and three nurses hovered over Martinez in the emergency room of Our Lady of the Lake Hospital, trying to keep the mutilated smuggler from bleeding out, a "burly, disheveled" man shoved an attendant to her knees and sauntered into the room. Coolly and calculatedly, he pulled a straight razor from his pocket and opened it in front of the emergency crew, sending them cowering into a corner.

"I'm no doctor," McCray reportedly told them, "but I'd go a little heavier than normal on the penicillin. I soaked this bad muthafucker in hog shit for a week before I cut him."

Spotting Consuela Martinez in the ER, he turned to the man on the gurney and said, "You've got some damned good skank here, Ivan. Too bad you ain't built to handle it anymore."

Martinez later vanished from his hospital room in the middle of the night, taking Consuela with him, abandoning their belongings and the million-dollar estate. There were, therefore, no complaining witnesses to either attack.

Zita Morales, left with no physical evidence and no complainants, tried McCray on the testimony of the doctors and nurses, each of whom picked McCray's mug from a photo lineup.

Morales had been lu   to get ten years for McCray on the maiming of Ivan Martinez. She couldn't even file charges in the rape of Consuela Martinez.

Quinlin thumbed back to the front of the file, to a color book-in shot taken by the Webb County Sheriff's Department on April 4, 1984. The man in the photo, identified as Jerry Ray McCray, aka "Snake" and "JR Nasty," sneered at the camera. Quinlin wondered what kind of depraved human being was capable of injecting rattlesnake venom into another's sinus cavity. It wouldn't be a stretch for the psycho in the picture. The detective was mesmerized by the photo, taking in every minute detail: The hairline receded high into his scalp, like a heavy snow fronting an uphill forest, and the brown hair on the sides was long and forty-weight as it fell beside his ears. The eyes were flat and dull and leered out over a three-day beard. The mouth was an uneven hem that gathered heavily at its right corner, spawning the appearance of a permanently twisted grin. A mouse the color of a thundercloud protruded beneath his right eye, and dried blood was caked under his right nostril. The top third of his white T-shirt was tie-dyed with his own spattered blood, which told Quinlin that his arrest had not come easily.

But if the man in the photo had any trepidation about facing a future in cement and steel, it wasn't obvious by looking at him. The photo just as easily could have been snapped on payday in a mean beer joint. Just another fool on a stool, a little worse for wear, maybe, after a brawl in the parking lot, but nothing another brew wouldn't remedy.

Over the years, Quinlin had encountered a handful of cons like McCray, just them and him in the tiny crap green interview room on the third floor of headquarters, where he was close enough to smell yesterday's beer and nicotine. Even when he confronted them with the irrefutable evidence that spelled a one-way trip to Huntsville, they merely grinned, looking right through him with their flat eyes. It'd been under different circumstances, of course, but he'd seen eyes like theirs before. In Vietnam, they called it the "thousand-yard stare," and, for the men with the life-drained eyes, killing wasn't a choice, but a reflex, like scratching an itch.

"You killed three people," he once told a suspect in the box. "Don't you have any remorse?"

"Yeah. I got remorse. I left one for dead and she lived to testify against me," the killer said. "Three'll get you the needle. And four don't cost no more than three. I'm just real sorry I didn't kill the bitch, too."

Locking up cretins like McCray is society's only answer to crime. Prison is, pure and simple, punitive. But a hypocritical society kids itself that it's actually getting a twofer, that time in stir just might have a little rehabilitative value, too. Society predicates the punishment of its misfits on its own fears, and denial of freedom is the worst thing most people can contemplate. The thought of being locked for years on end in an eight-by-ten-foot cement and steel cubicle is more than most accountants and nurses can fathom. Society's error, Quinlin knew, is its assumption that the Jerry Ray McCrays of the world think like accountants and nurses.

The McCrays are flatliners. Morally, they languish at the bottom of the human food chain, their stone-cold demeanors never fluctuating two degrees either way. The McCrays don't fear doing time. Prison is just a layover,—albeit one without booze, drugs, or tail— on the expressway to inflicting society with more pain and death. No big deal. Stir to a con is like a residency to a doctor or boot camp to a soldier; it comes with the profession.

Quinlin's gullibility embarrassed him now, but it had taken him ten years of rounding up and questioning murderers before he begrudgingly accepted the validity of what old-time dicks told him from day one: One percent of the population needs a needle stuck in their arm—not necessarily to protect society, but just, by God, to balance the books.

The detective pulled the stapled mug shot from the flap of the folder and stuck it inside the breast pocket of his coat.

17

The panel light told him the landing gear was locked into place, and Gary Bettman checked his flaps and did his final scan of the instrument panel. The center line of runway 14/32 of the Aransas County Airport, meanwhile, was looming larger and larger in his windshield when he felt the belly gear and then the nose gear kiss the asphalt strip. He shoved down on the power to the Mooney 231, watched the rpm fall, and looked through the dusk for the first exit ramp.

Picking up bank checks in small burgs like Rockport was like driving for Greyhound. And probably paid about the same, which was a hell of a lot less than Bettman had made flying freight for Pan Permian Air. The hours were crap, and they never began until after banks closed and tabulated their checks, which meant virtually all-night flying. Worse, flying checks was like delivering the mail; neither rain, sleet, nor snow meant a damn. The bags of checks had to be at the correspondent banks in Dallas at the beginning of business the next day come hell or high water. If the on-board radar painted a major storm cell in your path, you went around it, over it, or under it, just as long as you ended up at Love Field by daybreak.

The only thing that made the job tolerable, actually even fun, was the Mooney 231. Guy Kerr, owner of Kerr Air Couriers, had four Mooneys, and the brown-and-orange '81 checked out to Bettman was the pick of the litter. It had just undergone an exhaustive overhaul and had only fifty hours on the new turbocharged engine when Bettman inherited it. It had a Stormscope, Northstar loran, and a King autopilot, though Bettman had to take off and land so often that the autopilot didn't get a lot of wear. No question, the Mooney was smoother than high-dollar whiskey.

As he taxied to the transient hangar in Rockport for fuel and the next bag of checks, Bettman double-checked the list of stops clipped to the sun visor. He'd already completed the "Border Strip" portion of the shuttle—Del Rio, Eagle Pass, Laredo, and Harlingen. After topping off his tanks, he would cover the "Home Run," with fifteen-minute stops at Victoria, San Marcos, Temple, and Waco. Unless the ground couriers screwed up and were running late, Bettman wouldn't even shut down, just taxi to the apron, where someone would hand him a receipt and toss the bags of checks into the back of the compartment.

He saw Jimmy waiting for him in the gray Chevron av-gas truck. Jimmy was probably only nineteen, but he was punctual and efficient, which was all that mattered to Bettman. Staying on schedule was critical, particularly if you hit a thunder cell and had to detour around it. Bettman yelled to Jimmy and headed into the transient hangar to sign the credit card for the gas and to check the weather. The pilot made his predictable chitchat with Marilyn, the night clerk, before he excused himself to go to the men's room.

Out on the tarmac, a white panel truck drove up behind the Chevron truck. A heavyset guy in cowboy boots and jeans unloaded a canvas bag and headed for the Mooney. He walked with a slight limp, favoring his left side.

"Where's Greg tonight?" Jimmy yelled.

"Sick, I guess. They didn't say. They just told me to fill in. Where's Greg put the receipt, you know?"

"On the left seat, so the pilot'll find it."

The courier in the Chevrolet van was gone in three minutes. Jimmy topped off the tank and headed the truck back to the hangar, waving at Bettman through the window.

Bettman idled the Mooney at the end of the strip, revved the engine, saw green across the board, and shoved the throttle forward.

The weather between the coast and Dallas looked good. Should be a milk run. With luck, he could be having breakfast with Susan and the kids before they left for school.

Captain Pete Sammons was about six miles due east of Rockport, just beyond the Intracoastal Waterway, when he heard the accelerating drone of the small aircraft. Sammons was winching in the aft nets on the *Mollie Bee,* and he looked over his shoulder at the sky. It was almost nightfall, and he saw the plane's revolving white lights. The plane was maybe five hundred feet up, and the old shrimper could tell by the pitch of the engine that it was accelerating for altitude. Sammons had seen them a thousand times, heading easterly into the Gulf, then banking sharply to the north to head inland at some point.

The old fisherman busied himself with the nets, looking through the floodlights to see if the catch was worth keeping. Increasingly, he was having to stay out longer to get the same haul. Sammons had been shrimping thirty years, and if the *Mollie Bee* hadn't been paid off, he knew he'd be as extinct as a lightning rod salesman.

Sammons was bent over the winch when his ears split with a horrendous explosion. Instinctively, he fell to his knees, scanning the surface of the water for the source of the god-awful noise. Finally, he noticed the yellowish reflection off the water and looked up, to see a red-and-orange ball directly over him. The fireball was like the Fourth of July fireworks he had taken his grandson to see, a bright red core, with orange and yellow streaks peeling off from the center like sparklers.

The shrimper heard the debris bouncing off the wooden deck before he ever saw it. Finally, he collected his wits and ran for the wheelhouse. Two steps from the winch, a chunk of seared brown metal the size of a car hood slammed onto the deck in front of him. As he moved around it, he felt his right shoulder go white-hot and saw the deck coming up at him. Up on one knee, he grabbed at his shoulder with his left hand, righted himself, and ran as best he could.

Inside the wheelhouse, the old man grabbed for the microphone on his ship-to-shore radio. His right arm was immobile, and when he reached with his left, his hand was covered in blood.

"SOS! SOS! This is the *Mollie Bee*! Come in. An airplane exploded on my boat. SOS! I need some help! SOS! Please . . ."

18

White Willy's was a hole in the brick wall tucked between AAA-Ace Bail Bonds and the Rio Pawnshop. A white Bluebird bus with a small blue insignia of the Texas Department of Criminal Justice was painted on a blacked-out window. Whoever the proprietor was had to have been a prison transport officer in a previous life, Quinlin figured. White Willy was convict slang for the prison chain buses that roamed Texas, gathering up freshly sentenced prisoners from county seats and hauling them to the prison's Diagnostic Unit in Huntsville. White Willy's unwilling passengers sat shackled to wooden benches that ran lengthwise down the sides of the bus. Heavy mesh screens separated the convicts from the driver, and another guard, a shotgun lying across his lap, sat backward in a chair, watching the chain gang.

When Quinlin's eyes finally adjusted to the blackness of the lobby, he was staring at a wall of prison memorabilia—a pair of belly chains with ankle cuffs, a lead-loaded blackjack, handcuffs, a riot gun, a handmade shank, a three-foot TDCJ insignia, and a six-foot black-and-white photograph of Ol' Sparky, Huntsville's legendary electric chair.

He walked around the partition into the bar and found a table for two. It was barely 5:00 P.M., and the narrow, deep bar was already filling up. Most of its patrons wore brown sheriff's uniforms or blue police ones or carried the telltale bulge of a weapon beneath their coats. It was hard to hear anything over the jukebox, which was locked on Dwight Yoakum's "Thousand Miles from Nowhere." Fitting, Quinlin thought.

Except for hauling a material witness out of a beer joint on South Lamar Street three months earlier, it was the first time in a year of sobriety that Quinlin had been in a bar. He'd dreaded it all day, after hearing that Zita Morales had chosen to meet him at the White Willy. A red-and-blue neon sign hung over the bar, advertising his old nemesis, Bud Light. He smelled beer; there had to be twenty-five drafts or open cans, and years of spilled brew had soaked into the upholstery and carpet.

His stomach tightened, and he wiped at the light sweat building on his forehead. What was it his counselor had called it—a BUD? Building Up to Drink. BUD. How ironic. His body was sending him a warning. He needed to think. Most of all, he needed to get the fuck out, before it was too late. He was a sailor on pay day in a discount whorehouse. The cool, dark environs that he'd always regarded as a refuge was a trap; he was too busy battling an anxiety attack for his brain to seize a clear channel. *What would Madeline think? God, he didn't even know if Madeline was still around.* He needed her.

Getting drunk was merely the unfortunate side effect, never the intent. Quinlin drank simply because he loved the taste of beer. The shrink in the treatment center had berated him: All drunks, he claimed, drank to get drunk.

Looking around the bar, watching people drinking and bullshitting after a rough day, he imagined the familiar old burn of the first slug of beer in his throat and the ensuing automatic urge to belch.

"What'll it be, cowboy?" She was young, maybe twenty-five, and impatient. He'd watched her scurrying from one table to the next. It was happy hour, and the cops and cheap booze were wearing her ass out. "Well?"

"Make it a Bud Light," he said impulsively.

"No, wait!" He caught her two steps from the table. She gave him a tired look.

"Make it an O'Doul's or Sharp's," Quinlin said. "Anything that's nonalcoholic."

She returned with a glass of ginger ale with a twist of lime. "We only have real beer. This work for you?" She didn't wait for an answer. She was in big demand at the next table, where an old bull in a deputy's brown uniform was making a circular motion for another round for him and his three buddies.

Quinlin was staring at the ginger ale when Zita Morales appeared at the tiny table.

"If you're not Jeb Quinlin, that's too damned bad. I'm gonna sit down anyway," she said. "You'll just have to excuse me. I've earned this Scotch, and I need it yesterday."

He stood up as she tossed her briefcase beneath the table and fell into the chair. He reached across and shook hands. The prosecutor was tall, maybe five-ten, and stunning in an ankle-length denim skirt with an ample slit up the side, a mostly red paisley blouse that buttoned at her throat, and a pair of black boots. Her hair was curly and fell around her shoulders and halfway down her back.

Zita was barely in her chair when the waitress automatically appeared with two Dewar's on the rocks. The assistant district attorney grabbed one, held it in the air in a silent toast, and downed it in one shot.

"You must be a regular," he said.

"I'm sorry," she said when the Scotch finally hit bottom. "I needed that."

"Rough day?"

"Regular day," she said, taking a sip from the second glass.

She looked at Quinlin's untouched ginger ale, grimaced, and said, "I just realized how this must look. You don't even drink, do you?"

"Not anymore."

"Oh, hell. I'm sorry. I, uh . . ."

"Don't worry about it," he said. "I still admire people who can handle it. I just don't happen to be one of them."

"I didn't say I could handle it. I just said I *needed* it. I imagine that's a big difference."

"I'm not a Jehovah's Witness about it," Quinlin said. "I'm not here to save your soul; I'm here to ask your help." He could see she felt awkward. "Fact is," he added, "I still don't trust people who don't drink. There's something wrong with them, uh, us, I guess. Besides that, I don't make value judgments. It's about the living in a glass house thing, okay? So if I have to carry you out of here at closing, it's still no big deal."

"You always this honest?"

"Try to be."

She looked at him dubiously, then grinned. "Detective Quinlin, you're a breath of fucking fresh air in this valley of sewage."

"Speaking of the valley," he said, "what's the attraction? I mean, no offense, but I didn't exactly mistake the valley for an oasis. You been putting people in prison for a long time. Looks like some high-dollar defense firms in San Antonio or Corpus would be camping on your doorstep. Especially, you, uh . . ."

"Especially me being a chick *and* a meskin?" she said.

"That's not—"

"It's all right," she said, grinning, "because it's true. I'd be a real catch for a white-guy firm, double points with the EEOC. Not to mention that I know a habeus from a hand job.

"I'm a local girl. I was a cop here for five years before going to law school. The thing is, I enjoy putting scumbags in the joint more than I'd like to see 'em living next door to my mamma. Not only that, but the Rio Grande Valley is ground zero in the drug war, and if you're a prosecutor, well, hey, it ain't gonna get any better than this. I might outgrow it, but I doubt it. Call it job satisfaction."

She caught him glancing at her ringless left hand, and he felt himself blush.

"Oh, I used to be," she said. "I guess you could say my marriage got written off as an occupational hazard."

Quinlin laughed: "You're good, Zita."

"You, too?" she asked, touching his ring finger.

"Something like that."

The waitress appeared, automatically again, with a fresh Dewar's.

"That's it for me, Wanda," Zita said, a little embarrassed. "Here's the tab and tip. We're outta here."

"Don't do that on my account."

"Unfortunately, old habits are hard to break," she said—sadly,

Quinlin thought. "I know a place we can talk without having to yell over shit-kicker music."

"Now you're the one who's blown it," Quinlin said in mock seriousness. "I am a shit-kicker, thank you very damned much, and this music here, well, it's my people's anthem."

Quinlin followed her out of downtown in his rented car, then through a series of diminishing streets, until they ended up on a narrow, pitted residential road in a lower-middle-class neighborhood. Zita Morales pulled into a driveway and Quinlin parked the Taurus in front. The house was the best-kept one on the street, a single-story tan adobe with arching Mexican windows and a red tile roof. Zita was waiting for him on the tiled porch.

"You've got a nice place here," he said.

"Not mine. It's my mamma's. You like homemade tamales with big chunks of pork and the best frijoles you've ever tasted? Follow me, my gringo friend. You're about to encounter heaven on earth."

If Yolanda Morales was upset that her daughter had appeared unannounced for dinner with a stranger, she never showed it. She was old-fashioned, serene, and gracious, and she spoke sparingly but genuinely in broken English. She loaded the middle of the small table with tamales, frijoles, corn tortillas, guacamole, and fresh *pico de gallo*. Then she reappeared with a platter of huge sliced tomatoes and onion, which, she announced proudly, were grown in her backyard.

"I'd like to see your garden, Mrs. Morales," Quinlin said.

The old woman was unabashedly thrilled, and she headed for the back door, turning on the patio lights as she went through the door. A string of red chili pepper lights lined the rear porch, and the lights from the porch illuminated the small yard. Manicured grass covered three-fourths of the yard and surrounded a small fountain that had a concrete Virgin Mary standing over it. The garden was in the corner by the stucco fence—tomatoes, bell peppers, onions, squash, cucumbers, jalapeños, banana peppers, and red chili peppers.

"You know, Mrs. Morales, I live out in the country on a ranch," Quinlin said, "and this is the kind of garden I intend to plant next year—if I can keep the deer out of it. I hope mine'll turn out half as good as yours."

"Don't plant the squash," the old woman said. "The squash bugs will ruin everything."

"Mine'll be a redneck garden," the detective said, grinning. "You know, blackeyed peas, okra, collard greens, some poke salad, maybe some turnips. Anything that'll compliment a chicken-fried steak. You know how we are."

Before they sat down to eat, Mrs. Morales offered her guest a Tecate.

"No ma'am, I don't drink." The old woman looked at her daughter and smiled approvingly.

Quinlin ate nearly a dozen tamales by himself, piling them high with the tomato, onion, cilantro, and jalapeño relish, and three tortillas, which he filled with frijoles and shredded Mancheho cheese.

Both generations of Morales women declined his offer to help with the dishes, ushering him into the living room. A while later, Zita appeared with a pot of coffee and two cups.

"We better get to the business at hand," she said, "before mother adopts you or tries to arrange a marriage. She's quite taken with you."

"I have that effect," he said. "Unfortunately, it only works on women seventy or older."

"Not necessarily," Zita said, opening her briefcase and rummaging for papers. It was a spur-of-the-moment comment, and she hated that it hung so long in the air. She dropped her eyes to the briefcase and rushed her next thought.

"You've, uh, seen the file on our boy, McCray, so you know he's wired wrong. But there're a couple of other things you need to know." She looked him squarely in the eyes. "He will kill you in a heartbeat and enjoy it. This is what he sent me from prison, his second time."

Zita handed him a photocopy of a meticulously printed letter on lined paper. The printing reminded Quinlin of a draftsman's. It had Jerry Ray McCray's return address at the Skyview Unit and his prison ID number in the upper-left-hand corner, and it began "Dearest Zita." The letter was succinct and surprisingly well written, however twisted its contents. McCray asserted that the reason Zita

Morales had prosecuted him so tenaciously was because she secretly lusted after him. "Over compensation," he termed it, "for the deep, erotic feelings you have for me." Though he professed to understand the reasoning for her relentless prosecution, he nonetheless vowed to "even the score at the appropriate minute—the minute you least suspect. You will pay dearly for your frustrations."

Then, in minute detail, McCray reconstructed Zita Morales's anatomy from memory and apparently assumed the portions he'd never seen.

"He was writing this to get off," Quinlin said. "Too much time on his hands."

"I don't think so. Read on."

McCray described an elaborate rape-torture in which he would hold her hostage for four days. He fantasized not only about forced sex but also about her pleas for forgiveness as he tortured her with cattle prods, sticks, and knives. "I'll save the climax, so to speak, for the next time I see you. Remember. You'll never know I'm there until I'm there. Then it'll be too late for you to apologize and far too late for me to forgive."

"What a sick bastard," Quinlin said. "Couldn't you prosecute this? Isn't it a terrorist threat or something? Surely to God—"

"TDCJ took all his good time away from him," Zita said. "I guess I could have done something else with it, but I didn't. It's hard to explain. See, I don't want to hit McCray with a glancing blow, some Mickey Mouse shit that'd add a year. He wouldn't appreciate the significance, and it wouldn't really matter. What I want to do is put the needle in his fuckin' arm. He changed the course of my life. He—"

"I understand. I really—"

"No, you don't. Let me finish. Every day that goes by, I'm surprised. I'm surprised that he didn't get me. There's a part in the letter, the part where he describes a quarter-size birthmark near my, uh, my pubic hair. Well, that's not imagination. He's seen me. He's stalked me. I was in counseling for months, but it didn't do any good."

Zita reached into the inside of her left boot and produced a .25 Ruger automatic from an ankle holster.

"This is always on my body," she said. "There's one just like it in my nightstand, one in my glove compartment, and one in the lap drawer of my desk. There's a Colt .45 in that briefcase. I know he'll come for me. It won't be pretty. Like he said, I just won't know when. Don't misunderstand me. I'm not a hysterical female. I'm just a realist."

Quinlin made a false start at saying something. He couldn't get it out because he didn't know what to say.

"It's okay," Zita said. "I didn't mean to get carried away. This man is certifiably evil. You have to know how sick he is. Or he'll kill you."

He's already tried, Quinlin thought.

Zita had reviewed her copy of the McCray file and made notes before Quinlin landed in Laredo. She studied them before she found her thought. She was coldly all business now.

"There's one other thing you might be interested in," she said. "I didn't make much of it at the time, but, given your interest in Comanche Gap, you might find something in it."

Both times she had prosecuted McCray, she said, he was represented by Hercules Banda, Laredo's top—and most expensive—criminal defense lawyer. Herc Banda was known all along the Rio Grande, primarily for defending drug smugglers. Zita had assumed that Banda's fee for defending McCray had been paid by Juan Carlos San Martín.

"But the last time, a lawyer showed up from your part of the state, and he sat in the second chair beside Banda," Zita said. "He didn't say much in court, but it was clear Banda was deferring to him. The guy clearly had stroke. I remember thinking at the time that there were a hell of a lot of other good lawyers closer to home—Jerry Goldstein in San Antonio and Racehorse Haynes and Dick DeGuerin in Houston. This guy's name was Jack Blevins. I'd never heard of him."

"Name sounds familiar, but I can't place it," Quinlin said. "What about him?"

"Well, I did some checking with the state Bar Association," she said. "He's dead now, but at the time he was down here, he was listed on their records as a name partner in Westgrove and Blevins in Comanche Gap."

Quinlin felt his pulse quicken. Les Westgrove had handled much of the Colters' civil law business before becoming district attorney. Now, Zita had his law partner four hundred miles south, defending McCray. Yet, McCray supposedly was a local enforcer for the San Martín cartel.

The prosecutor and detective were traveling the same route.

"Given that the DEA has never come up with San Martín's domestic connection," Zita was saying, "you have to won—"

"Wonder whether it's been Clendon Colter and his boys all along," Quinlin said. "Blevins, in the world of criminal defense, would have been a lightweight. He wasn't there to defend McCray. He was there to protect the Colters' interests, to make sure McCray kept his mouth shut. And probably to deliver Colter's share of the attorney's fees to Banda."

"That's the way I figure it," Zita said.

"It's not a smoking gun," Quinlin said, "but it certainly adds cred—"

Quinlin muttered as his beeper went off. He recognized the number; it was Clint Harper. When he attempted to go to the rental car to get his cell phone, Zita insisted he use her mother's.

"Yo, buddy," Quinlin said when he heard Harper's voice, "they've got you working late tonight. What's the occasion?"

"Your only witness in the Carlisle murder is at the bottom of the Gulf of Mexico," the reporter said.

"Bettman? What are you talking about?"

"His plane blew up a couple of hours ago," Harper said. "Saw it on the AP wire."

"Where?"

"Taking off from Rockport, down by Corpus Christi. But there's something else you should know. I just talked to the owner of the plane. He says Gary Bettman was the greatest thing since Chuck Yeager. The plane had just been reworked."

"Yeah?"

"The guy says it's got to be sabotage."

19

Quinlin had stopped off at the LaQuinta Inn on Interstate 35 on his way into Laredo, registered, and unloaded his bags into his first-floor room. It was an old habit, precipitated by his days in uniforms. Rent-a-cars, with their tiny Hertz logo on the back glass, stood out to car thieves like bumpkins to muggers. Generally, salesmen or tourists rented the cars, which frequently meant that their trunks were loaded with sample cases, suitcases, laptops, and souvenirs. The thieves would sell the cars across the border for seventy-five dollars; whatever was in the trunks was gravy. If someone hot-wired Quinlin's rental car, at least they wouldn't get his bags.

Bettman's crash in the Gulf meant that Quinlin would be checking out immediately and driving half the night, instead of getting a decent night's sleep and catching the first flight back to Dallas. He saw the blinking red light on the phone as soon as he opened the door to his room. He plugged his room number into the machine and heard Madeline's voice.

"You're so predictable, Jeb Quinlin. I knew you'd be at a La-Quinta. I just didn't know there'd be four of them in Laredo. You're right. I didn't answer the phone. I thought I needed time to work things out. I appreciate that you're willing to discuss our future when you get back. But don't stay up all night wondering if I'm leaving if we don't get married. I'm not.

"I've thought about it, to be honest. Because marrying you is my idea of a happy ending. I love you, Jeb, maybe even more than a ninety-dollar bottle of Chablis. That's why I'm willing to accept you on whatever terms you have to have. What I've figured out is that I can get over Chablis. And I know I can't get by without you.

"Pretty corny, huh? Well, too damned bad, Officer. Guess you're going to be stuck with me on whatever terms it ends up. By the way, I'm sitting on the back porch at the ranch. Twenty minutes ago, I saw White Deer in the backyard. He actually let a doe get within fifteen yards of him. Maybe it's an omen. Maybe there's hope for you."

He heard a beep; then Madeline sped up, knowing she was almost out of tape: "Be careful chasing the bad guys. I'm looking forward to making up. Love y—"

Quinlin was watching the exit signs off I-35 for the U.S. 59 cutoff when he saw the Circle K. Instinctively, he took the exit and pulled in front of the convenience store. A Hispanic guy was reading a book behind the counter and looked up long enough to nod. Quinlin headed for the coffee machine. He pulled the pot off the burner, held it under his nose, and winced. It was five-thousand-mile crankcase oil and bitter enough to cause chill bumps. He stuck the pot back on the burner. The first thing he saw when he turned was a wall locker of cold Bud Light. He opened the glass door, stuck his thumb and middle finger in the plastic handle holding the six-pack, and headed for the checkout counter.

What the fuck is going on? Why did I do that? A year on the wagon, a fucking year, and I'm about to blow it up. The Bud Light was a hand grenade. He closed his eyes tight and fought to get his bearings. *Put it up, dumb fuck. Just put it down and get the fuck out.*

He hadn't noticed it the first time, but the glass door buzzed when he opened it. He looked at the clerk, but his nose was still in the book. He shoved the six-pack back onto the stack and headed for the door.

"No beer?" the clerk asked.

"Uh, no," Quinlin said. "Just a pack of Marlboro Lights. And gimme one of those Bic lighters."

Back in the car, he let out a deep breath and leaned heavily against the seat. He needed sleep and he needed to eat—that's what his counselor would tell him. The antidotes to the urge to drink. He didn't have time for either. He peeled the cellophane off the pack of cigarettes, lit one, and dragged deeply. He felt the soothing effect of nicotine hitting his brain. Fuck it. Cigarettes were a misdemeanor compared to what he'd almost done. It was going to be a long night. At least he wouldn't have to spend it wondering if Madeline had written him off.

He turned on the ignition and spotted the cell phone on the seat beside him. He figured he'd run out of range for the mobile phone not long after he left Laredo, and he pulled his little spiral notebook from his coat pocket. He found Clay Moore's number and dialed it as he backed out of the lot.

"Clay boy," he said, "how's things in God's country?"

"Quiet, dude. The way I like it. Say, I checked out your guy McCray. We musta drunk a shitload of beer late last night at the Very Fucking Weird."

"Huh?"

"The VFW. Trust me, he ain't that hard to find," Moore said. "The guy likes me. Thinks I'm stronger than an acre of garlic. He even offered me a 'business proposition.' Don't know what it is yet, but he says it's worth five grand to back him up on some deal."

"What kind of deal?"

"Didn't say. Whatever it is, it's supposed to happen in a week or so. Said he'd tell me when he gets back."

"From where?"

"Didn't say. Just said he had business out of town, that'd he run it down for me when he got back. It's a shaky deal, whatever it is. Five grand is a substantial chunk of change for this ol' country boy."

"Damn, man, you sure you haven't worked undercover before? This deal, whatever it is, could be a biggie. Did you have a chance to check on the things I asked you about?"

"Oh, yeah," Moore said. "He was pissin' and moanin' about his hip. Said some son of a bitch had gotten lucky. That he'd take care of him when he had time. You know what he's talking about? Because I don't."

"I've got an idea," Quinlin said.

"Oh, I know what you meant now about checking the tires. The right-front one was a may-pop, all worn on the inside. That help you any?"

"Big-time," Quinlin said. "I wish I had a cast of that tread. Well, that's—"

"I can do better than that," Moore said, laughing. "How 'bout the tire its own self?"

"You took the fuckin' tire off his truck?"

"I left before he did, and checked his tire," Moore said. "I figured it must be pretty important to you. So I took the bumper jack out of his truck and pulled the tire. I left the jack under his bumper. I sat there in the damned parking lot nearly an hour waiting for him.

"Sure nuff, he comes stumbling out, drunker than a monkey. He's groping around for his keys, finally falls into the truck, and cranks it up. Puts that son of a bitch in reverse and guns it. Drives right off the jack and harelips himself on the fuckin' steering wheel. He baled out of that motherfucker madder than a slapped Jap."

20

The outline of Texas is an off-center profile of a man with a profound lifetime enjoyment of beer. The Texas Panhandle, from Dalhart down to Lubbock, is the head and neck, and the east-west part, the broadest, from Longview over to El Paso, is the beer-bloated gut. As if someone cinched a belt too tight around the navel, say somewhere around San Antonio, the tapering Rio Grande Valley, from San Antonio down to Brownsville, is his legs.

As the crow flies, it's about 120 miles east-northeast across the skinny boot of Texas from Laredo, on the Mexican border, to Rockport, on the Gulf of Mexico. But factor in the inexplicable twists and turns by Texas Highway Department engineers on the desolate flatland, a bumper-to-bumper wait at a Border Patrol checkpoint south of Freer, and a stop for coffee and a leak at an all-night truck stop, and the trip drags out to 185 miles and nearly four hours.

It was 2:30 in the morning when Quinlin saw the sign to the Aransas County Airport and turned into the gate. There was no control tower, and the only lights came from a mobile home that served as the operations base for Petroleum Helicopters and the transient hangar with a gas truck parked beside it. A woman at the FBO hangar told Quinlin that two investigators from the National Transportation Safety Board and the Coast Guard had formed a command post down on the wharf where the shrimpers tied up, and she gave him directions.

"We feel bad about that pilot, Gary," she said as Quinlin was walking out the door. "He was good people."

"Did you notice anything unusual about him or the plane?" Quinlin asked. "I mean, did he mention having any problems with it?"

"Not to me. He signed the voucher for the fuel and seemed tickled that the weather was good up toward Dallas. Just routine. But you might ask Jimmy. He refueled the plane."

Jimmy Eason was working a double shift, asleep in the back room. The woman roused him, and the red-haired, freckled gas man appeared momentarily at the counter, groggy and rubbing his eyes.

"No, there wasn't anything unusual that I noticed," he said after Quinlin showed him the badge. "Really didn't even talk to him, just waved, you know. You might check with Gr—Forgot. Greg wasn't here today."

"Who?"

"Greg Elliott," Jimmy said. "He's the regular bank courier, but he didn't make the run tonight. There was a substitute."

"What's his name?"

"Don't know. Never saw him before. Come to think of it, he wouldn't have talked to the pilot anyhow. He just pitched the bag in the plane and left."

Quinlin drove through the foggy darkness toward the wharf. From what he saw through the haze, Rockport was feast or famine. Off to his left and over a short high-span bridge was a community built along a series of canals. Each of the well-kept houses had its own marina, and judging from the few boats he could make out, they easily cost more than his ranch. On the right, as he approached the midpoint of Rockport, the houses turned to single-story wood-frame structures with unpaved driveways and fifteen-year-old pickup trucks parked out front. The same prevailing winds and salt water off the Gulf that had swayed the trees inland had sandblasted the paint off the houses, leaving them withered and decrepit. If there was any middle class in Rockport, he missed it in the dark.

He pulled his rented Taurus behind an Aransas County Sheriff's

Department vehicle and headed for a small building near the water, the only one with any lights. Looking through the window, he could see it was a general mercantile store, stocked heavily with canned goods, fishing supplies, and beer. Several men were gathered around a card table near the counter, drinking coffee out of throwaway cups. Quinlin spotted a man with graying hair who was wearing a blue windbreaker that had NTSB printed in yellow on the back, and he introduced himself.

Investigator Warren Wilson had flown in from Dallas on a Coast Guard jet, and he was planning the search, which would begin at daylight. He'd already been to the local hospital and interviewed Pete Sammons, the skipper of the *Mollie Bee,* shortly before he went into surgery.

"We've got a good statement from him on the explosion, and we've got the main location of the debris pinpointed," the NTSB investigator said. "There's not a lot of current tonight, so we should be in pretty good shape to find most of the plane. Some of the paper debris and a few pieces of flat metal have already floated to the top. We've got a Coast Guard cutter at the site, scooping everything up."

"Anyone here from the FBI or the Rangers?" Quinlin asked.

"Not that I've seen," Wilson said. "Should there be? I mean, what's the Dallas Police Department's interest in a plane crash off Rockport?"

Quinlin hit the high points, characterizing Gary Bettman, the plane's pilot, as a key witness in a homicide investigation, among other things.

"Excuse me," said a man standing behind them in civilian clothes. "I wasn't tryin' to listen in, but you investigatin' a homicide that's got some relation to this pilot?"

The guy was sturdy, like a cedar corner post, and he wore blue jeans, a red-and-black-checked flannel shirt, and bull-hide cowboy boots. A leather badge holder with a five-pointed star was tucked in his shirt pocket and he carried a long-barreled .38 on his right hip.

"I was interested in the pilot because of the players he knew,"

Quinlin said, "and I'd hoped he could give me a motive on a case I'm working."

The man identified himself as Marshall Towns, a detective captain with the Aransas County Sheriff's Department. He moved closer to Quinlin and the NTSB investigator before he spoke.

"Maybe y'all ought to know about something I'm working that may or may not be tied to this plane crash," he said. "I came out here to find out some things. Way I understand it, this plane was carryin' bank checks. Well, one of our deputies found an abandoned van earlier tonight that belonged to Rockport State Bank. The folks down at the bank tell us that it was used to haul checks to the airport, apparently to be picked up by your pilot."

"Well, the van wasn't hijacked, because I talked to somebody at the airport a little while ago and he said he saw the checks got delivered to the plane," Quinlin said.

"Well, here's the kicker," Captain Towns said. "The courier's name was Greg Elliott, and he definitely left the bank with the bag. Me and another guy from CID went back to the scene where the van was discovered and started looking around. It was dark as roofin' tar, but we found Elliott's body across a fence, out under some trees. Looks like somebody broke the ol' boy's neck."

Quinlin turned to Wilson, the NTSB investigator. "There's a possibility that whoever killed the courier could have put explosives in that plane. My suspect's got a history of explosives convictions. I know you don't know much yet, but could explosives be consistent with what you know?"

"Yeah—I mean, maybe," the crash investigator said. "The guy on the shrimp boat says the plane went off like a Roman candle. Good plane, from what I hear, and the shrimper says he heard the engine running strong. We've apparently got an experienced pilot. Yeah, it's possible. But I won't know—"

"Towns, I know somebody who can identify the courier who replaced the real one," Quinlin said. "And I've got a picture of my suspect. Let's go see if the guy at the airport can ID him."

Quinlin and the detective captain stopped off at Aransas County headquarters long enough to grab five book-in pictures to mix in with Jerry Ray McCray's for a photo lineup. Quinlin didn't want to get a positive ID on McCray, only to have it thrown out at an examining hearing by a shyster lawyer claiming it wasn't a fair identification.

Jimmy Eason had given up on sleep after Quinlin had awakened him earlier, and he was watching a *Mayberry, R.F.D.* rerun when the two detectives walked into the transient hangar. The kid didn't flinch; he picked McCray's photo the first time through.

"Maybe a little older, maybe a little heavier," the gas man said, "but that's him, no question."

Capt. Marshall Towns was elated when he and Quinlin returned to his cruiser.

"My victim hadn't even got rigor mortis yet, and now this bad boy's almost cleared," he said, edging his ample girth beneath the steering wheel. "And I was thinkin' I was gonna have some trouble on this one. Hell, we're gonna have time for a cold 'un. So where can I find this peckerwood McCray?"

"What you intend to do with him?"

"Get me an arrest warrant, haul his ass into the box, and make him crawl the walls," Towns said. "If he's got an alibi, we'll tear hell out of it. Make him do the chicken, know what I mean?"

Quinlin knew exactly what the small-town cop meant. The *Miranda* case and other "rubber hose" precedents hadn't trickled down to a lot of small Texas towns, despite being on the books for thirty years. And he knew a high-dollar lawyer like Hercules Banda would make a mockery of their case against McCray even before they could get it to a grand jury.

Quinlin instinctively liked Marshall Towns. The big captain was chicken-fried country, no doubt, but Quinlin liked his innate aggressiveness. What Towns lacked in current police procedure, Quinlin figured he made up in street savvy. The big-city detective eyed his new colleague across the front seat of the cruiser and decided he had to trust him.

"The deal is, Marshall, we might can make a case on your victim—if we can get some physical evidence—but mine's a lot shakier," Quinlin said. "And besides that, we jerk this dickwad off the sidewalk now and we're gonna lose our shot at a lot bigger fish."

The pair headed to the Surf Grill, Rockport's only all-night café, where Quinlin spent forty-five minutes outlining McCray's background and his ties to the Colters and, maybe, international drug smuggling. The Dallas cop also connected the dots on the public corruption case against Comanche Gap's district attorney and the Texas Ranger.

"Goddamned, bubba," Towns said, trying to make sense out of everything he'd heard, "you got your naked ass out on an awful thin limb here. You telling me the FBI don't give a shit and you can't trust the Rangers. And, friend, you're sitting here with barely a smell for jurisdiction."

"We can pull this off if you'll work with me," Quinlin said. "But with Bettman dead, McCray's the only long shot I got at tying my murder, the drug smuggling, and the public corruption together. You work with me, give me some time, and I'll make sure you get your charges filed on the courier. Not only that, we might can put him down for the pilot, too. That'd be a hell of a deal."

"Tell you what," Towns said. "I wouldn't have a clue about McCray if I hadn't bumped into you. I owe you for that. And, well, you ain't exactly what I expected out of a Dallas detective. What you think? Think we can run all this shit down in a month?"

"Maybe sooner," Quinlin said. "I got somebody close to him. And something may be going down pretty soon."

Towns mulled it over, then stuck his hand across the table.

He shook Quinlin's hand and said, "I 'magine we could be a pretty damned good team. Either that or we're gonna end up showing our asses big-time."

The rented white Explorer was idling in the shadows of the closed Phillips 66 station across from the Surf Grill. The man behind the wheel ran his hand across his two-day growth and reached onto the passenger seat for another hot Budweiser. He winced and cursed when his hip hit against the taunt seat belt. Across Main Street, he watched the two lawmen in the booth. He'd seen them go into the transient hangar at the airport and followed them. They were working the courier's death; that much was certain. But were they smart enough to link it to the plane crash?

Jerry Ray McCray cursed again, knowing he'd screwed up by not ditching the van and the body in one of the multitude of sloughs he'd seen near the airport. Hell, he'd had to take him in daylight, so what was he supposed to do? As it was, a Southwestern Bell repairman had driven right past him beside the road, when he had the little bastard begging for his life.

He could make a semicircle through the lot, pulling alongside the plate-glass window long enough to plug both the cops. He'd seen one waitress, and there was probably a cook back behind the partition, but it'd be over in three seconds and nobody would see a thing. He could be at the Corpus Christi airport in thirty minutes and back to Comanche Gap in another hour.

Better, though, to wait until the cops left the diner. Theirs was the only car on the lot, and he could do a drive-by, bracing the .44 Magnum on the window ledge and take them both out without even stopping. They'd never know what hit them. He cursed again, remembering what he'd been told: "Take care of Bettman. That's all. Then get your ass back here. *Nothing else unless I tell you to.*"

The cops were paying out. This was getting all fucked up.

The Explorer fell in without its lights behind the Aransas County squad car and followed it as it meandered to the wharf. The tall, wiry cop, the meddling asshole from Dallas, got out and walked around to the driver's side and talked for a minute through the open window to the shorter, fat one. Hadn't been for that god-damned barking dog, they'd still be picking chunks of him out of the trees. Quinlin walked to a Taurus, made a U-turn on the wharf, and headed back toward the Explorer, forcing McCray to duck beneath the dash to avoid being seen. McCray made a U-turn and followed the Taurus until it pulled into the SeaSpray Inn. In a perfect world, McCray would take an extra five minutes and put a .44 slug in the cop's temple. He was a pain in the ass, prowling around outside his jurisdiction. And there was the small matter of the cookie-size slab of skin he had blown out of McCray's hip, just below the pelvis bone.

Fuck Buck Colter. He was too damned cautious anyway. "*Nothing else unless I tell you to.*" Well, maybe he should have brought his fat ass along, let him see how these deals can get out of hand.

Reluctantly, the ex-con headed past the SeaSpray Inn, slowing to watch as the detective grabbed his bag from the trunk of the rental car. What a waste. Another living witness, just like the redheaded dude who'd pumped the gas into Bettman's plane. The kid was the only one who could put him with the plane before it disintegrated. If Quinlin and the fat cop hadn't shown up at the airport, the kid would be facedown in a slough somewhere, regardless of Buck Colter and his instructions.

Another week, maybe ten days, and Buck could stick it. He'd have enough cash to split. Head back to the valley, where people just wanted the job done, no questions asked. The anticipation made him grin.

"Helloooo, Zita. Come to Daddy."

21

The guy in Room 212 had checked in only four hours earlier, but already the skeletal overnight staff of the SeaSpray Inn knew he wasn't the ordinary late check-in. By 2:00 A.M., he had ordered two pots of coffee from room service, placed five phone calls to Dallas and one to Washington, had a return call from the FBI and three calls from the *Register & News* in Dallas. He had been upset that the gift shop, the only place at the motel that sold cigarettes, was closed, and he'd walked two blocks to a Circle K. Upon returning, he had quizzed the desk clerk about using the phone line for electronic transmissions, and he wasn't thrilled that the rooms didn't have voice mail. The clerk had had to remind him that there was no smoking in the lobby.

Clint Harper was under the gun: last Southwest flight of the night into Corpus Christi, frantic trip to Rockport in a rental car, bureaucratic bullshit from the National Transportation Safety Board, a drugged and aborted bedside interview with the only witness to the crash, an official "No comment" from the FBI (but an off-the-record confirmation from Quinlin's chief of detectives at DPD), and three arm-twisting calls from his executive editor, Garrett Anderson Brewster.

Harper scrolled to the top of his story and scrutinized it line by line. It hung together factually, he knew, but he was also "outing" the Colters and, indirectly, linking them to drug smuggling and, by inference at least, to murder. Normally, even the remote possibility of libel put skid marks in Brewster's pants, but now he was turning the screws: "Make it strong as you can and put everything you know in the story. I'll go over it here, make sure everything's okay."

Now there was a genuine comfort factor. Brewster, who'd never been a reporter, wouldn't know an inverted pyramid lead from a pipe wrench. He was an MBA country club hanger-on with a phony Brit accent who knew as much about journalism as he did widgets. Brewster just wanted something to show Richmond Carlisle's parents. As a journalist, Brewster had all the substance of a popcorn fart.

"Yeah, fine," Harper had told his boss. "But my byline goes on it. It'll be documented or it won't be in the story."

It was a bare-bones piece, one that he hoped to update before deadline.

By CLINT HARPER

STAFF WRITER OF THE *REGISTER & NEWS*

ROCKPORT, Texas—A pilot who perished in a puzzling midair explosion in the Gulf of Mexico Tuesday was an informant who had been feeding federal authorities information on the hierarchy of an alleged international drug-smuggling ring.

Gary Bettman, a forty-year-old Panther Junction pilot who until recently was a pilot for Pan Permian Air, became the second person this month to die on the fringes of an investigation into drug smuggling along the Texas-Mexico border. Two weeks ago, the body of Richmond Carlisle, a reporter for the Dallas *Register & News*, was found in his car in south Dallas County.

No cause has been determined for the explosive plane crash, according to investigators of the National Transportation Safety Board. However, sources close to the investigation say they cannot rule out the possibility of foul play.

A day before his body was discovered beside Houston

School Road, Carlisle was to have interviewed Bettman at the pilot's ranch near Panther Junction, according to his wife, Susan Bettman.

"He never showed up, and we didn't know what had happened until we heard that he had been killed," Ms. Bettman said. "Now this. I don't believe lightning strikes twice in the same place. They were killed for what they knew."

The FBI in Dallas declined to confirm or deny that Bettman had offered information on a smuggling operation, but other police officials close to the investigation said Bettman had given several statements.

The Dallas County Medical Examiner's Office ruled that Carlisle's death was a homicide. The reporter, who was researching the alleged narcotics connection, was struck by a blunt-force blow and injected with rattlesnake venom, according to Dr. Mark Berryman, the chief medical examiner.

Warren Wilson, an investigator for the NTSB, said it may take weeks to learn the cause of Bettman's crash, which occurred shortly after dusk on takeoff from Aransas County Airport.

Bettman, who was ferrying bank checks from the Rio Grande Valley to larger banks in Dallas, was a skilled pilot flying a recently overhauled airplane. Weather over the Gulf was uneventful, Wilson said.

The plane, a Mooney 231, exploded in a fiery ball of flames about six miles off the coast of Rockport, directly over a shrimp boat operated by Captain Pete Sammons.

"The plane was gaining altitude and it sounded fine, but then all of a sudden it just blew up," said Sammons, who was in serious but stable condition at Aransas General Hospital after falling debris from the plane severely injured his shoulder. "The engine sounded good to me, and he was on the same path that most of them boys take over the Gulf."

Bettman, according to federal court records, was indicted on drug-conspiracy charges after a federal task force arrested him earlier this year. According to the indictment, Bettman, then a pilot for Pan Permian Air, landed 1,000 kilos of cocaine, worth an estimated $3 million in street value, at an isolated airstrip near Uvalde.

"Gary Bettman was killed because of what he knew and who he was talking to," said his Fort Worth attorney, Jim Ed Mangus, late last night. "He was flying a Pan Permian aircraft at the time he was arrested. My client never had so much as a speeding ticket before that. He was not a drug smuggler. But as an employee, he followed orders.

"We believe we have conclusive proof of that, and we have made that information available to the appropriate authorities."

Clendon Colter, chairman of the board of the Comanche Gap–based Pan Permian Air, was not available for comment. However, the freight airline issued a written statement denying any knowledge of drug smuggling.

"We were shocked that one of our airplanes was used in this illicit operation," the release said. "The Colter family has a long and proud history of advocacy of good government in Texas and does not condone drugs. However, the airline has more than thirty pilots, and while we make attempts to hire honest, law-abiding employees, we obviously made a mistake with Gary Bettman. As soon as authorities made us aware of his arrest, he was terminated immediately from our employ.

"While we are saddened by his death, Pan Permian Air's good name has been victimized by Mr. Bettman's illicit and illegal use of our aircraft without our approval or knowledge."

The end of the story detailed the Coast Guard's plans for the search, an interview with the owner of Kerr Air Couriers, and public-record background on Pan Permian Air. Harper intentionally held out all the information about Clendon Colter's partnership with the late President Lanson McLain and their insider plot to build Comanche Bend Lake and Reservoir.

There would be plenty of time for a tough in-depth profile of the Colters and their murky empire. *If* the Colters didn't sue him first. Or worse.

22

Rebecca Colter was angry, and she ran her hand through her auburn hair as she stalked Buck in his recliner like a mountain lion on a hemmed-in jackrabbit.

"I'm going to get Chad," she said. "But I'll tell you this right now. If I ever come home and find another single red mark or black eye on that boy, I'll see you in hell. It's a shame when your own son is afraid to spend the night in his own house. And I don't blame him. You just better hope the Jensens didn't call the law when they saw the boy's face."

Buck Colter shrugged and sipped from his coffee mug.

"You drink too much," she said, "You fly off the handle. You—"

"And you need to shut the fuck up," he said. "You're about to work yourself to the point of no return. Saying a bunch of crap you'll regret. Chad's sixteen. He's not too damned old to do what he's told."

His eyes were as cold and lifeless as ball bearings; he could just as easily have been talking about a hired hand as about his only child.

"This is the second time, damn it," she said. "You don't discipline a child by hitting him in the face in a drunken rage."

"He's not a child; he's a teenager," Buck Colter said. "Which is his problem. I haven't done anything to him my own daddy hasn't done to me. You'll forgive me if I'm not in tears about a goddamned kid who'll probably inherit one of the biggest fortunes in the state. I imagine he can put up with—"

"*I* can't."

His brows furrowed, as if he'd heard something he'd never before contemplated.

"I said I can't put up with it anymore," she said.

"You're not going anywhere, not now. I've told you. I've got a deal going. It's important. I'm under a lot of stress. Maybe I've been a little too stressed, but it's about to be over. Then we'll all go to Colorado or the coast, or wherever you want to go. Don't make a damned bit of difference to me. But *nobody* is going anywhere right now," he said.

A voice from the wall intercom took over the den: "Mr. Colter, this is Massey at the front gate. Sheriff O'Neal is here and says he needs to see you on an important matter. All right to send him through?"

Colter walked across the room, depressed the microphone button, and said, "Send him on."

Rebecca had the keys to the Suburban in her hand. She stuck them in her pocket.

"I'll make y'all a pot of fresh coffee before I leave," she said, heading for the kitchen.

"That's a little better," Colter said. "I appreciate it."

Red O'Neal was at the front door in less than five minutes, rubbing the back of his fat neck as if he had slept wrong and holding a folded newspaper. Rebecca watched him through the glass in the door, shifting his weight from one foot to the other, taking a deep breath and staring at his boots. One of the things Rebecca Harrison Colter had learned to hate about money was how obsequious it made people, particularly around her husband. Buck Colter either didn't notice or he didn't care. As long as his will got done, it didn't matter. As he frequently put it to hired help, "It'll be my way or the highway."

No one understood that better than the sheriff of Sul Ross County. The gold star on his chest was like sticking tinsel on a dead mesquite. Red O'Neal was nothing but a step-and-fetch for the Colters. Rebecca used to believe Sheriff O'Neal was simply afraid of the Colters. More recently, she suspected they were paying him off, just like several other officials in town. It was probably both. Either way, O'Neal was a man who had sold his soul; that much she knew.

Twenty years earlier, when she was new to the Colter family, Rebecca had been pleasantly surprised at how people treated her— for no other apparent reason than she was a Colter. Local sales-people, doctors, lawyers, even Lanson McLain, the state's most powerful politician, granted special concessions to the Colters. Clendon Colter, his sons, and their wives had dinner at the Governor's Mansion in Austin, sat with the Carters at a White House luncheon, and chatted with Ethel Kennedy at the Robert F. Kennedy Memorial. Four senators and more congressmen than she could remember had been guests at Clendon Colter's mansion down the road.

But over time, Rebecca realized that it was only people who had something to gain, monetarily or politically, who made concessions. Among strong-willed, independent people, she detected silent contempt or, more infrequently, outright animosity.

If the Red O'Neals were parasites, her husband was an exploiter, not only of money but of people. Buck, much more so than his younger brother, Wade, was cut from the same cloth as his father. The trait accounted for Clendon turning over more and more of the Colter business to Buck. Buck understood the lay of the land: Money was power, and power was the oil that greased the Colter empire.

Buck bragged about being expedient. But after twenty years of seeing people's lives and careers broken, Rebecca knew her husband and father-in-law weren't merely expedient. They were ruthless. Even more so after Charley Blake had become too feeble to work his subtle influence on them.

Rebecca tersely directed Red O'Neal to the den, then continued on past him and her husband to the kitchen, which was separated by a counter that ran almost the width of the house. She busied herself with the coffeepot, trying to be quiet. O'Neal holding his Stetson in his hand, glanced at her several times, talking lower and lower. He handed the newspaper to Buck and fidgeted like a kid whose dad was reading his report card. Finally, he asked Buck out onto the porch.

The coffeepot was gurgling and wheezing, and she couldn't hear over the noise. She went to the door leading onto the porch and bent over a magazine stand as if she were sorting out old magazines. The glass door was barely ajar, but she could hear them plainly.

". . . like you said," O'Neal was saying. "But damn, I mean, it's in the paper and everthing. There could be some heat, you know?"

"Did you really think a fuckin' plane crash wasn't going to make the paper?" Buck snapped. "A reporter called here yesterday. I knew there'd be something."

He scanned the paper as O'Neal shifted his weight. "I am a little surprised at the way this Harper put the facts together," Buck said finally. "Makes us look like hell, don't it? Daddy'll sure be pissed."

"What if it gets the FBI in on us?"

"Give us another week or so and they can bring in the fuckin' CIA," Buck said. "I give a shit. Won't be able to show a goddamned thing."

"Jerry Ray says he ran into Jeb Quinlin down there on the coast," O'Neal said. "And he showed up down here after that reporter was whacked. Ol' Jeb, well, he's putting two and two together and—"

"And what? He can't do squat down here," Buck said. "He's a *Dallas* cop. He ain't got jack for jurisdiction. What's he gonna do, get the local Texas Ranger after us?"

Buck laughed heavily. On the other side of the wall, Rebecca stood up from the magazine stand, wincing at the creaking sound her knees made. Quietly, quickly, she made her way back to the kitchen and into the garage. She hit the garage door opener, backed the Suburban out, and drove off.

In the mirror, she saw both of them watching her. It made her skin crawl.

23

Residents of the Cross Timbers Convalescent Home were just beginning to rouse. Charley Blake was sitting in an easy chair in his room, already dressed in his starched white western shirt, khaki Riatas, and black cherry alligator boots. He was reading the newspaper while a nurse changed his bed linens. Rebecca Colter was already beside him before the old man noticed her. He knew something was horribly wrong.

"Sweetie, you look powerfully upset," he said. "What on earth is paining you this mornin'?"

Rebecca nodded toward the nurse and said, "Let's go sit on the porch, Uncle Charley. Get some fresh air."

"This about the story in the paper today?" he said, easing himself into a rocker. The air on the porch was crisp and damp from overnight drizzle.

"Yeah, and more. Buck's been drinking too much, and he beat Chad last night while I was up here," Rebecca said. "That's not the first time. He's stressed-out about some business deal that's about to happen.

"But the reason I'm upset is that I think they've killed somebody else, that pilot you read about this morning. Red O'Neal came out this morning and I overheard part of their conversation. They never said it specifically, but it was clear to me."

Charley Blake motioned her to the adjacent rocker. His brow was furrowed, and he was momentarily lost in thought.

"You got some place you could go for a spell?" he whispered. "Somewhere out of town or out of the state? Might be best for a while. Just until things settle down."

"You don't understand. I won't live with a killer. Or a man who beats my son. Whether it settles down or not, I just won't live that way."

"You know I'm afraid for you, sweetie," the old cowboy said. "I'd be worried if you stayed, and I'd be worried if you left. Buck's cold-hearted, like his daddy. Don't know that he'd handle your leaving all that well."

"I'm going to do more than leave," she said, reaching for his hand on the arm of the rocker. "I'm going to stop this madness before somebody else gets hurt. You never want to talk about the Colters, but I've got to know. I see something here, something else there, but I don't know what it all means. You know them better than anybody. Charley, I've got to know. You have to help me. Please. *Tell me.*"

He saw the determination in her eyes and knew she wouldn't be put off this time. She was as close to family as he had. She deserved the truth.

"Let me go to the room and get my hat," he said. "We're gonna take a little ride. I want to show you something. I'll talk while you drive."

Charley Blake's story was forty years old and one he'd figured he'd die without having to tell. Telling it to someone he cared about only made it more painful.

"Ain't no easy way to back into this story," the old cowboy told her. "I think too much of you to lie to you, and I 'spect you'd spot it right off if I did. You'll just have to think whatever you're gonna think about me by the time I get to the end."

He gave her directions and readjusted himself awkwardly in the passenger seat. "Been a spell since I've actually been in a truck," he said, trying to get comfortable. "This little trip's an awful big deal to me."

Rebecca had just turned off Texas 36 at the southwest corner of the square and gotten onto U.S. 281 when she saw Buck Colter's

red Land Rover headed toward her in the intersection, its left indicator blinking. The traffic light turned red at the northwest corner
before he could turn. They ended up facing each other across the
intersection.

"Damn," Rebecca said. "Wouldn't you know it?"

Buck was on his cell phone and apparently taking advantage of
the red light to rummage through something on the passenger's
seat. Rebecca eased the Suburban into a right turn around the
square and accelerated. At the next corner, she quickly turned left,
scanning the rearview mirror. The Land Rover was just turning off
281 a block behind her as she went around the corner. He had been
preoccupied, and she didn't think he'd seen her. She wasn't sure.

"He probably wouldn't think anything about it anyway," she
said. "He knows I visit you. All this stuff has made me paranoid,
I guess. I just don't want him knowing my business."

They detoured back to 281 North and drove a few minutes in
silence. When he thought Rebecca had calmed down, Charley Blake
plunged into his story.

He'd met Clendon Colter in the late fifties at a cattle auction,
shortly after Colter had moved to Sul Ross County from West
Texas.

"He was all hat and no cows, so the saying goes," Blake said.
"Didn't know a heifer from a horned toad. For what he paid for
those range cows that day at the auction, he could have bought a
good-size herd of registered Angus."

Charley Blake, at the time, was a past-prime rodeo cowboy, too
old and broken up to travel the circuit anymore. His bull-riding
days reluctantly behind him, he'd rolled his rodeo savings into a
450-acre ranch in the north part of the county and, for the last
couple of years, had made decent money ranching and brokering
cattle. Looking across the auction ring that day at the newcomer
in the starched Wrangler jeans, thousand-dollar boots, and new
Stetson, he knew that Colter was a potential client.

For the next two years, Blake traveled Texas, buying and selling
stock for Colter. Beef prices were up and the summers were wetter
than normal; he turned major profits for his new client and raked
off a 15 percent commission on everything he touched.

Though Colter left the impression around Comanche Gap that he was a self-made millionaire wildcatter, it soon became clear to Blake that Colter had actually married his money. His wife, Hope Shipman Colter, the quiet, reclusive daughter of a legendary West Texas wildcatter, had inherited her father's estate shortly before they relocated to the northern Hill Country.

"From everything I could see, Clendon didn't have two pennies to rub together before he married Hope," Blake said. "I 'spect that he didn't know any more about the oil bidness than he did the cattle bidness."

At some point, Hope Colter reined in her husband's wheeling and dealing. He'd already bought the main Pan Permian Ranch, built the biggest house in six or eight counties, bought an airplane, invested in his and hers Mercedeses, and purchased the local newspaper and AM radio station. The cattle operation, though it was showing substantial profits under Blake's supervision, fell victim to Hope's embargo on funds.

Colter explained the moratorium on spending as a "temporary cash-flow problem." His money, he said, was tied up in annuities and long-term investments, and even though his funds were vast, he couldn't touch them without paying major penalties.

"What I came to figure," Blake said, "was that Hope just flat cut him off. She never said much, but it was clear that she wore the pants in that family. And Clendon was madder than hell about it."

Blake remembered Colter showing up at his ranch one day not long after and telling him to pack two weeks' worth of clothes. By the end of the day, they were landing Colter's King-Aire on a long dirt airstrip in Mexico, in the shadows of the Sierra Madre. The place was desolate and isolated, about 150 miles southwest of Laredo, near Monclova. Supposedly, Colter had leased the five-thousand-acre ranch to raise Mexican range cattle for export to the States. Cattle and labor were dirt cheap in Mexico, and Colter's plan was to fatten the cattle and truck them to Laredo, where he would sell them at American prices.

The cowboy from Comanche Gap wasn't impressed. The only decent features of the ranch were the airstrip and an oppulent six-bedroom stucco hacienda at the foot of a picturesque valley. There wasn't vegetation on the land except scrub brush, greasewood, and cactus, and Blake told Colter he'd have to feed the stock virtually year-round. Hay and oats, even at Mexican prices, would more than offset any American prices, if, in fact, he could even get the cattle past the United States Department of Agriculture inspectors at the border. Colter wouldn't be dissuaded. The USDA wasn't going to be a problem. Blake's job was to buy a herd and train some *braceros* to manage it.

Blake figured out the first week that the ranch actually belonged to Juan Carlos San Martín, a handsome Mexican with graying hair. He wore elegant vested black suits, a black flat-brimmed hat, and black alligator cowboy boots and carried a black cane with a gold cat's head for a handle. Blake once saw him use the cane on the back of a hired hand's head.

"I was born at night," Blake said, "but not *last* night. I knew the guy was a drug smuggler the first time I laid eyes on him. I never saw him without six bodyguards round him, and ever one of 'em was carrying an arsenal. They called him El Gato, and he flew into the strip on a little black jet of some kind. He and Clendon Colter holed up in the hacienda for two or three days, with these body-guards watching 'em the whole time. Then he flew out. Tell you the truth, I was proud to see him leave."

Over the next twenty-five years, Blake would make maybe a hundred trips to Mexico at Colter's request, each time carrying an assortment of locked aluminum briefcases aboard the Beech King-Aire. The trips were circuitous, often requiring him to fly to Monterrey, Mexico City, or Guadalajara, only to double back to the ranch near Monclova. San Martín's lieutenants were always waiting, never allowing the King-Aire to take off until they gave the word three or four hours later.

"Clendon trusted me," Blake said, studying Rebecca for reaction out of the corner of his eye. "Buck and Wade were just kids back then. And, well, he paid me more than I'd ever make messin' around with cattle. He never used the word *drugs*, and neither did I. But I knew it, and he knew I knew it. It was just something we didn't talk about. Didn't have to.

"I guess I just figured I wasn't carryin' no drugs and I just looked the other way. Hell, I knew it was wrong. But fact was, sweetie, it was kinda fun, too. Oh, it wasn't like tryin' to stay on a bull for six seconds, but it wasn't far behind, neither. Flyin' all over the place in the middle of the night, knowin' I was carryin' hundreds of thousands, probably millions of dollars, eyeing these meskin *pistoleros.* I was carryin' an ol' hogleg in my belt, and I 'magine if I'd needed to, I'da used it. It'd get the ol' heart charged, I'll tell you that."

Blake was so deep into his story that he almost missed the turn off the dirt road.

"Turn right into that cattle guard," he said abruptly.

They drove a half mile down the caliche road, the Suburban's tires kicking up white dust, until they came to a stop in front of a well-kept single-story ranch house made of native white rock with green shutters. It was nestled in a grove of live oaks, and behind the house was an immaculate native-rock barn with a tin roof, a big corral made out of cedar posts, and an Aeromotor windmill.

"It's beautiful, Charley," Rebecca said, taking it in. "It's yours, isn't it?"

"Yep," he said. "It was home to me for a long time. Well, I 'spect we ought to just sit on that porch swing till I get this story out of the way. Then I'll show you around."

Just walking to the porch tired the old man, and he sat there catching his breath for a few minutes.

"Anyways," he said, "then money started comin' in agin, and we was blowin' and goin' in the cattle business agin. That's when Landon McLain showed up. He was a big deal even then, way before he became president. Him and Clendon somehow knew each other, and McLain would fly into Pan Permian Ranch and spend a week or so at a time. That's when we started buyin' up half the damned state. I 'spected that McLain and Clendon was partners on the land deal."

Blake recalled Clendon Colter showing him a map of Sul Ross, Bosque, and Erath counties, with a huge tract drawn where their boundaries met along the Comanche River. "That's about one hundred and eighty thousand acres there covering three counties," Colter told him, "and I want you to go out and buy it. Here's a list of the property owners. Buy it as cheap as you can, but you can't go over four hundred an acre."

"I told him that was a buttload of land for a ranch," Blake said, "considering he already owned a major chunk of Sul Ross County. He told me he'd formed some kinda partnership to handle investment property. Way he said it, I knew I wasn't s'posed to ask a lot of questions, just go get it done. I was to make the deals, then take them to Les Westgrove, who'd draw up the papers."

By his own admission, Charley Blake was something of a celebrity in the northern Hill Country. He'd been a world-champion bull rider four times, and he'd grown up riding at arenas throughout the area. He wore a championship belt buckle the size of a big man's fist, and it was nearly impossible for him to walk around the square in Comanche Gap without someone stopping him to talk. Most importantly, ranchers respected him.

"Clendon needed me," Blake said. "Most of the ranchers didn't know him, and if they did, they didn't care for him. He was a Coca-Cola cowboy, and it was plain he didn't know his backside from a salt lick. 'Sides, people in these parts didn't trust people from out of town."

Four hundred an acre was a decent price for grazing land in the early 1960s. In fact, it was more than fair for some of the land, which was rocky and wouldn't grow anything but mesquite and ground squirrels. Getting takers wasn't tough, but he ran into a few owners who taxed his good ol' boy negotiations; ultimately, Blake won them over.

Clarence Redford was a different story. Well into his seventies, Redford had lived on his three hundred acres all his life, just like his daddy and granddaddy before him. It was a hardscrable operation, with a decrepit old frame house, a lean-to barn, and a stock tank that leaked like a sieve. The small ranch was in the epicenter of the 180,000 acres Colter had drawn on the map. Redford lived there with his crippled wife, Gladys, and he still worked a few head of Angora goats. Mostly, though, the elderly couple subsisted on Social Security. Clarence Redford wasn't interested in selling, not even when Blake upped Colter's limit to five hundred an acre.

"I worked on Clarence for three months, and he wouldn't budge," Blake said. "I told Clendon that Clarence didn't think the money would be enough to take care of Gladys if she had to go to the rest home. Ol' Clendon got red in the face and stomped around in his boots, throwing crap around his office. Said no pissant farmer was gonna screw him around. I said, 'Let's offer the ol' boy some more money.' I felt sorry for Clarence. Clendon wouldn't have it. Said he'd take care of Clarence Redford, by God.

"All that drug stuff, I guess, told me a lot about what Clendon'd do to get his way. But what happened with Clarence, well, that's a different deal."

The next morning, Charley Blake saw Booger O'Neal drive up to Clendon's house in his sheriff's car, and both men left. A few hours later, they came back, and Blake could tell Clendon Colter was in a good mood. Colter told him that he and the sheriff had gone to talk to Clarence and, while they were talking to him out behind the barn, he just hit the ground dead.

"Told me that Clarence must had a heart attack or stroke," Blake said. "Well, that ol' dog wouldn't hunt. Not with me. Clarence was old, but he was stronger than a mule. Either Clendon or the sheriff—maybe both, for all I know—killed the old man. Now, could I ever prove that? Hell no. But I guaran-*damn*-tee you, they killed him."

"With the sheriff right there?" Rebecca asked, incredulous.

"Sweetie, ol' Clendon owned Booger outright. The O'Neals are so crooked, they have to screw on their pants."

A week or so later, Blake said, winding up his story, Colter gave him a check made out to Gladys Redford for ninety thousand dollars and told him to deliver it.

"He not only killed her husband; he took the damned land for a hundred dollars an acre less than what we was givin' everybody else. I drove the woman to the rest home myself."

The story left the old man drained. They rocked in the porch swing in silence for a while before he tried to resume. Rebecca saw tears in his eyes.

"I told Colter that I knew Clarence Redford didn't just die of no natural causes," Blake said, "and he just looked at me real cold. It was a little tense, and he says, 'Well, just go tell the sheriff.'

"Course, it was just a little while after that that I figured out what Colter had done about the land. The army flooded ever damned piece of property I bought and made a lake outta it. There ain't no tellin' how much him and ol' Landon McLain made off that. But I'll tell you this. They murdered an ol' man just to get it done."

"Do you think Clendon or Buck is the one killing these people now?"

"Well, I 'magine it's Buck," Blake said, "but I don't know for sure. Toward the end, before I left, things had changed. Ol' Clendon still knew what was goin' on, sure nuff. They had gotten some pretty rough characters workin' for them—called 'em cowboys, but course they weren't. Guys that'd do whatever they were told. I jumped Clendon about it one day, told him he had a goddamned cowboy mafia workin' for him. He was proud of that, repeated what I'd said, laughed about it. Took it as a compliment.

"More and more, ol' Colter was turnin' everthing over to Buck. See, Buck is his father's son, the apple that don't fall too far from the tree. Wade's different. He's go along to get along. Oh, Wade knows what's goin' on, but he's in the background. Now, Buck, he's a different story, and his daddy knew that. Buck's just as cold-hearted as his daddy. I 'spect worse.

"I was . . ."

"What is it?" Rebecca asked. "You were what?"

Charley Blake was embarrassed. "Well, I was a little surprised, knowin' you and all over the years, that you ever tied up with Buck."

"I was young and stupid," Rebecca said. "I knew Buck was arrogant and headstrong, but I just figured that was because he'd grown up with money. When you're twenty-four, you think you can change people. Well, I realized too late that I couldn't. And to be honest, I guess I was awed by all this money. I wasn't raised that way. You realize I've never had a budget? I couldn't imagine going to the grocery store and just buying whatever you wanted, no matter. Buck would fly me to Dallas, have a limo pick me up and take me to Neiman-Marcus. They treated me like royalty. 'Yes, Mrs. Colter. Try this on, Mrs. Colter. We'll just bill you.' Now I hate to admit it. I was young and stupid and greedy.

"Then Chad came along and I didn't feel like I could leave. I felt like I'd be robbing my son of his birthright. Now I'm scared to death that Clendon's and Buck's genes are flowing through his blood."

Charley Blake's house was big, by bachelor's standards—four bedrooms, two and a half baths, an overpowering den with a native-rock fireplace at its center, and a kitchen with two ovens. "When I built it, I actually thought I'd have me a family someday," he said wistfully. "That never came to pass."

The house was musty, having been closed up for nearly two years, and Rebecca spotted occasional dust balls under the furniture. The decor was predictably Spartan, Rebecca thought, but tasteful. Charley had tried his hand at photography for a while, and he'd blown up several black-and-white prints of windmills in the sunset, cows being branded, and lonely dirt roads winding over hilltops. He'd even taken some pictures at the hacienda at Monclova. The furniture had a western style to it, heavy with oak and laden in leather, and the rugs that covered the hardwood floors were contemporary western.

Blake had his back to her, prowling through a wall safe that had been hidden by a picture of a cow nursing her calf.

"I love this place, Uncle Charley," she said. "It's . . . well, peaceful. I can see why you love it so much."

"I'm proud you do, sweetie," he said, facing her. He handed her a thick folded document and eased himself into a leather recliner.

"I brought these papers out here about six months ago," he said, "and I got a copy in my room at the home. But I don't trust things to stay in my room."

Rebecca scanned the document, occasionally looking up at the old man. She was shaking her head.

"I, uh, can't. . . ." Her voice broke and she dabbed at her eyes with the back of her wrist. "I just wouldn't feel right about this, Uncle Charley. I mean . . ."

"You talked awhile ago about blood," he said. "Well, you don't have any of mine. But you're all I got in this world. I wouldn't be any prouder of you if you did have my blood.

"I knew this day would come. Had to. You can't live like this anymore. And you can't be beholden to the man you're tryin' to leave. Now you don't have to. This isn't what you're used to, I understand that. But there's more than four hundred acres of good, productive land here, free and clear, and this house'll last you for the rest of your life. And then you'll have something to leave Chad. You won't be beholden to anyone."

Rebecca slid into a heavy chair. Her head was in her hands, and she could feel tears on her fingers.

"This isn't just for you sweetie," he said. His voice was high and tenuous, like an overstretched rubber band. "It's for me, too. I've taken some wrong turns in the road. I don't figure I deserve a damned thing, much less everthing you've given me since I've known you."

The old cowboy's voice faded, and Rebecca could hear his chest wheezing from across the room. She went to the Suburban and came back with the portable oxygen tank he'd tried to leave at the rest home. She didn't ask him; she put the clear tube around his neck, fitted the breathing device into his nose, and turned on the oxygen. He didn't argue with her.

It was several minutes before he tried again.

"I want to give you this place. When I drew up the will, it made me feel good. Don't get me wrong. I've messed up pretty bad, no question about that. That's on me more than it is the Colters. But I've had my times, too. This ain't meant to be braggin'; it's just fact. I could hold on to a bull 'bout as well as Willie Nelson can play a guitar. And there was a string of awfully pretty women, I guess, that thought I was pretty impressive. And I . . ."

The wheezing was getting worse.

"And I always made enough money, even before I sold out to Colter, to have everthing I ever needed and some that I didn't, like good sippin' whiskey.

"Here's where I'm going with all this," he said. "The rubber's about to hit the road. You need to get that boy—and your own self—out of that house. Buck's doin' you dirty. That ain't gonna change. It ain't in him. You need to leave right now. Now you got a safe place to go.

"It'd make me proud if you came here," he said. "This don't mean nothing to me anymore anyways. Like ol' Willie says, 'Turn out the lights. The party's over.'"

The norther blew in about 3:00 A.M., its frigid wind stripping the leaves from the blackjack oaks like a thrasher through a wheat field. The old man peering through the window wore plaid pajamas and had a tiny clear hose stuck in each nostril. He put his hand palm down on the windowpane and felt the cold. The wind whistled and he watched through the dim porch light as it stripped the oaks, their red and yellow leaves swirling on the ground beneath them. Another hour and the trees would be bare.

He disconnected the oxygen and turned off the gauge on the steel bottle. He showered, shampooed his gray hair, shaved with a straight razor, and put on his best cologne. He dressed in a crisp pair of Riata khakis and his best white western-cut shirt, then put on his newest pair of Lucchese black cherry alligator boots. He reached into a zippered duffel bag at the bottom of his closet and produced a silver and gold World Champion Bull Rider belt buckle and a pair of sterling silver spurs. When he was finished, he put on his gray Stetson and stared at himself in the mirror. Everything he could see looked good, if he did say so himself. It was what he couldn't see, beneath his chest, that plagued him.

Even with his spurs, the woman at the circular nursing station didn't stir from her nap. It was the plight of the infirm, he figured, that they were left to depend on minimum-wagers. When he opened the back door, the wind stabbed his lungs like a knife, making him gasp for breath. Cautiously, he walked down the slope fifty feet to the biggest blackjack oak on the lawn. It was near freezing, and the cold made him light-headed. Gently, he lowered his back against the trunk and stretched his legs out in front of him, putting his hat onto his lap.

Nothers begin in Colorado and pick up speed over the flatlands in New Mexico and the Panhandle, with nothing to slow them until they land like a heavyweight's fist in the northern Hill Country. The old cowboy felt the punch in his chest, the cold air searing his passages and making him wheeze. He coughed deep from inside. It was so cold, he couldn't get his breath. Yet he breathed as deeply as he could. He felt himself getting woozy. A leaf brushed his cheek and he reflexively grabbed it. It was brown and stiff like parchment, and he crumpled it in his hand.

It was Charley Blake's final act on earth.

24

The preliminary report from Southwest Institute of Forensic Science came in while Quinlin was en route back to Dallas from the Gulf Coast. Paul McCarren called him on the cell phone and read him the results.

Quinlin was disappointed that Crime Scene analysts hadn't found any of Jerry Ray McCray's fingerprints—or those of any other stranger—on the Dodge. Whoever it was—and there wasn't a thread of a doubt in Quinlin's mind—who pulled the wiring from beneath his dash had worn latex gloves. And the cigarette butts Quinlin had collected near the Bettman ranch and the bloody John-songrass from the night of the shooting was still at the FBI lab in Washington awaiting DNA testing.

But the tire tracks taken at the scene when Richmond Carlisle's body was found in south Dallas County matched the tire Clay Moore had taken off McCray's pickup. And Jan Baynum, the nurse who had spotted a pickup pulling away from Carlisle's car that night, positively identified the taillights of a Chevrolet, just like the one McCray drove.

The information gave Quinlin a comfort factor, but the findings were useless in court. A photo lineup of taillights wasn't exactly scientifically foolproof, and a defense attorney would have a field day challenging the chain of custody in the tire evidence. The prosecution would put Clay Moore on the witness stand, and he would testify that he had delivered the tire halfway to Dallas, where he'd turned it over to Detective Paul McCarren. Yes, he would swear, the tire came off a pickup truck owned by Jerry Ray McCray. And then the defense attorney would ask, "So how did you come in possession of this tire?" Best-case scenario, the evidence would be tossed out; worst-case, Moore would get charged with theft.

"I'd still pay good money to have watched McCray drive off that jack," McCarren said.

"The thing about Clay is that you need to be terribly specific, I discovered," Quinlin said.

He was about ten minutes away from his ranch. He told McCarren he'd be in the office in two hours, but he wanted to stop off long enough to feed Bingo, check the mail, and put out some oats for a pregnant cow in the barn. Driving an hour from Love Field just to turn around and head back to Dallas would mean two blown hours, but he didn't mind. Spending three days in the Rio Grande Valley and the Gulf Coast had made him appreciate north Texas. It had been in the mid-seventies down south, and humid. It was barely above freezing when he got back to Dallas, and the cold air had taken care of the ozone. As he drove southwest, he noticed water standing in the ditches, and he hoped the rain had made it to Granbury.

Quinlin saw Madeline's BMW in the circular drive, and he pulled in behind it, swerving at the last minute to dodge Bingo. Depending on circumstances, Madeline might or might not be there when he got home. Bingo, well, he was different. He was always there, begging for affection. The Border collie loved him when his lieutenant was pissed at him, when Madeline wasn't speaking to him, and when defense attorneys attempted to disembowel him. And he had kept Jerry Ray McCray from planting a bomb that would have killed him. Man's best friend.

Quinlin was crouched down, rubbing Bingo's ears, when he heard the pecking on the window. He looked over his shoulder and saw Madeline standing on the inside windowsill, naked except for a pair of red cowboy boots. Bingo, God bless him, would have to wait.

Barely inside the front door, Madeline was unbuttoning his shirt and unzipping his pants.

"You have to go to the office today?" she whispered, nibbling on his ear.

"Yeah, but I can sure as hell be late."

Quinlin was dozing when he heard Madeline's voice. "I said, you put on some coffee and I'll walk down and get the mail."

Her blouse was unbuttoned and her breasts jiggled as she wiggled into a pair of tight jeans. He enjoyed the process, and rolled over on one elbow to watch.

"It's too cold to walk to the mailbox," he said. "Hang on while I get some clothes on and I'll drive you in the Scout. I need to charge the battery anyway."

"Good," she said. "It'll give you something to do besides leer at me."

There hadn't been time to talk about the latest turmoil in their relationship. That conversation undoubtedly would occur that night, probably after dinner. Quinlin actually found himself looking forward to it, instead of dodging serious discussions about their relationship like he normally did. He hated it when she was gone. The thought of her leaving again depressed him. In the hours on the road in a rental car, he knew he desperately wanted resolution. And he knew what he'd have to do to get it.

Paul McCarren had a semiserious theory about why men had trouble making commitments to women. He called it the "better deal axiom." Like it or not, the young detective claimed, commitment was subconsciously biological; it was rooted in sex, pure and simple. The theory, Quinlin suspected, also explained why his partner would probably die single. *And* why men justifiably were pigs.

Single men dodged commitments, according to McCarren, out of fear that they'd settle for less than the perfect hump. His theory also accounted for why men cheated on their wives. "They aren't tuned in enough to really know themselves, so they settle for less, later figure out what is missing—that being perfect sex—and start looking all over again for it."

"Sounds a lot like two dogs in a vacant lot," Quinlin had once said.

"Exactly," McCarren replied. "See, it's the natural order of all animals."

"So how you know when you find it?"

"Don't know yet." McCarren grinned. "Still conducting experiments."

Sex with Madeline was beyond Quinlin's imagination. But over the last year, he'd realized his formula for commitment was more encompassing than his partner's. Fact was, he had probably fallen in love with Madeline in the jitter joint, long before they ever had sex or even kissed. She was smart, had an insightful sense of humor, and, above all else, was decent and honest, even when it hurt her—tributes Quinlin would never relate to McCarren, for fear of being branded "warm and fuzzy." Besides, it was nobody's business except Quinlin's.

The wind was picking up out of the west and the clouds were turning gray. By nightfall, north Texas would get its first freeze of the year. Quinlin regretted not putting on his insulated vest.

"So, I was thinking, Officer," Madeline said, buckling herself into the Scout. "You think it's about time Lobo Mesa had a full-time foreman?"

"What are you talking about?" he said. "I do well to make the mortgage. How'd I pay a foreman?"

"You're looking at her. I was thinking I might just move my stuff out here and hang around full-time."

"You serious?"

"Could you handle it? Or would it be too much pressure?"

"I'd love to have you here when I come home. And when I get up. And everything in between."

"Good," Madeline grinned. "The movers are supposed to be here right after lunch. I took certain liberties, me being a part owner and all. I'm glad you approve."

She undid her seat belt, put her arm around him, and kissed him in his ear.

"So we're gonna live in sin?" he asked, pulling up beside the mailbox.

"Guess so, Officer. Whatever works."

She left the door open, and the frigid draft hit him like an ice pick.

"Well," he said loudly, "maybe we ought to just get—"

"*Heyeee!*"

Madeline's scream froze him. Her hand was on the lid to the mailbox and he saw her jump back, stumbling onto the asphalt pavement and landing on her butt, as if she had simply sat down.

Quinlin saw it when he bolted from the Scout: About two inches of the snake were protruding from the mailbox. He remembered a pair of welder's gloves he'd used to handle barbed wire, and now he retrieved them from the backseat.

He grabbed the rattlesnake behind its head and pulled it from the box, unreeling it like a garden hose. He swapped ends, grabbing it by its tail and popping it sideways like a whip. He snapped its neck and pitched it in the ditch.

Madeline was standing when he got to her, trying to catch her breath.

"Did he get you?" he asked, checking her right hand.

"No," she said, her voice breaking. "He just . . . just scared . . ."

"We're lucky it's cold," Quinlin said. "They're cold-blooded, and they're lethargic in this weather. Otherwise, he would have gotten you good."

He held her close to him. She was limp and trembling.

Or was it him?

25

Clay Moore went to the antique stove and poured two cups of coffee from the blue metal pot. It was fitting, Quinlin figured, that the severely wounded Vietnam vet wouldn't have an automatic coffeemaker. Just as fitting as Moore's house. It was almost one hundred years old, a white frame single-story with a native-rock chimney, and he'd inherited it from his parents, who, in turn, had inherited it from their folks.

Clay apparently was good with his hands; the improvements were obvious but simple and functional. He had put native rock belt-high around the exterior of the house, and rough-hewn cedar above it, painting it with water preservative, then added a tin roof, which gave it a rustic appearance. He had converted the front quarter of the house into basically a single huge room by knocking out the wall separating the living room from the kitchen. He had replaced it with a counter, which gave a feeling of openness. Two bedrooms and a bath lay behind the kitchen, and Quinlin assumed they, too, had gotten a renovation. The old house had changed dramatically from when Quinlin used to visit on weekends.

Clay motioned his old friend to a pair of cane-bottomed rocking chairs facing the potbellied iron stove at the corner of the room and handed him his cup. The wood fire felt good, and the smell reminded him of his childhood.

"That's quite a collection of guns, hoss," Quinlin said, nodding toward a wall that was covered with gun racks and rifles. He spotted a few automatic assault rifles. "They legal?"

"Some of 'em."

"We could have won if we'd had an arsenal like that."

"Naw," Moore said, "the chickenshit politicians wouldn't have let us use 'em."

Vietnam clearly was a part of Clay Moore's every day, beyond his having to walk on a prosthetic leg. He wore a camouflage T-shirt with his bleached-out jeans and a pair of leather and fabric jungle boots. Quinlin had spotted a cammie jacket on the coatrack when he came in.

"You still think about Nam a lot, don't you?" Quinlin asked, sipping his coffee.

"Only when I'm awake or trying to sleep," Moore said. "And sometimes when I dream."

"You think you've got PTSD?" Quinlin asked. "I mean, a lot of us do, even thirty years later."

"Beats the hell out of me. Tell you what, though. Nam's a life-changer, I know that. Let's just say that I don't consider it a re-warding, positive experience."

Moore's bitterness lay more in his face than in his words. Quinlin noticed the tightness around his buddy's eyes and the set of his jaw when he talked about Vietnam. It was understandable, considering what had happened to him, but Quinlin hated that the ghosts were still there.

Quinlin eyed the guns on the rack. "Does hunting help?"

"Sometimes," Moore said. "Sure does on the food bill. I got two freezers in the shed, one filled with venison and the other with fish. I enjoy being outside in the brush, aware of what's going on around me. Sometimes it gets too real and I think I'm back over there. A twig will snap or a jackrabbit will rattle the brush. Hell, man, I'm back in the mode. It'll fuck with your head."

Watching his buddy over the stove, Quinlin understood why Jerry Ray McCray would trust Moore. He still looked like what he had once been—a trained, sanctioned killer, the kind of guy you knew you could rely on. Except for bitterness, which was probably an attraction to McCray, Moore's face was coldly impassive. All these years later, he still had the thousand-yard stare, the steely, cold eyes that had seen destruction and could wreak it again if he had to. The bitterness and the stare created an air of volatility in the man, like the lethal potential of juggled nitro.

"You know," Quinlin said, "you sure as hell don't have to go through with this. You need to know up front that I shouldn't even be here. My jurisdiction on this case is about as phony as Mrs. Babson's tits used to be."

"I'd forgotten about her," Moore said of their former high school civics teacher. "She wore enough foam rubber to float a boat."

"So the deal is," Quinlin said, "if this plan goes to shit on us, we're out here by ourselves. They ain't gonna be no backup. Can't pop smoke and call in the Cobras."

"Hey, at least you're up front about it. That's better than I'm used to."

"You sure he won't shake you down for a wire?"

"Hell, I ain't sure the sun's gonna set tonight. But he's never made me think he doesn't trust me."

"What I want to do is be outside the VFW," Quinlin said. "I'll not only be listening to what McCray says but I'll also be recording it. If he says the right thing, then I can take the tape to the FBI or DEA, or both, and turn this over to somebody who does have jurisdiction. Then we'll ease you out."

"Frankly, I'd like to keep it with us," he said. "Your federal government has a way of turning simple shit into a cluster fuck. I trust you. I don't know these other bastards."

Moore was more right than Quinlin wanted to admit. The federal police bureaucrats would have to consult with the federal lawyer bureaucrats, and before it was over, there'd be a major policy analysis, a political assessment, and, ultimately, a federal circle jerk. They'd already screwed up the Colter investigation once with politics. And the bottom line, Quinlin had to acknowledge, was that the Colters would probably die rich and old, rather than in a federal prison they so richly deserved.

"At least one FBI agent's already called me a cowboy on this deal," Quinlin said. "I don't bring them in, they'd probably indict me for obstruction."

The detective wanted to get Moore off the federal government. No way he was going to change his buddy's paranoia. Quinlin didn't even believe his own argument.

"No question, McCray is the critical link," Quinlin said, his thoughts turning to the snake in the mailbox and the attempt to put a bomb in his pickup. "Fact is, I got some personal reasons for taking the bastard down. But in the grand scheme, he's just a grunt. We could probably jerk him off the street right now with what we've already got and put him away till the cows come home. He still wouldn't roll over on the people we really want— the Colters and their three whores, Westgrove, Gibson, and O'Neal. Not to mention the south end of their connection in Mexico."

"You're preaching to the choir," Moore said. "I'm in. You give the orders and I'll walk the point."

"You still think we're two days out?"

"McCray called me last night. Said he'd just gotten back in town but that he had some business to take care of. He wanted to know if I'd meet him in a couple of days to discuss our 'business proposition.' I told him I was interested. Make my phone ring."

They finalized a plan contingent on McCray's call. Quinlin would get to Moore's ranch as quickly as possible with the body transmitter. Moore had the numbers for Quinlin's office, home, mobile phone, and beeper.

Their business done, the two high school buddies sat around the fire, drinking coffee and chatting about beef prices, weather, families, and the merits of metal fences versus cedar posts. The talk turned to high school and what their classmates had done since graduation.

"You know something I never understood?" Moore said. "Rebecca Harrison, and why she married Buck Colter. I mean, I can imagine why. Money. But I would have never pictured them together."

It was a perplexing question, one that Quinlin had had since he'd started the investigation.

"I know what you mean," Quinlin said. "Didn't really add up.

Becky was as straight as anyone in school. Beautiful and smart. And a real Bible-thumper. Her family was in church every time they unlocked the doors at First Baptist. And even then, Buck was a turd. New cars, skiing on Christmas vacation, and a wad of cash to buy anything he wanted. A real spoiled asshole."

"You dated her. How come that didn't work out?"

"Don't guess I really know. Maybe I was too young. Too stupid, maybe. She was a sweetheart, too. Real nice. But I heard Buck was already on the scene, and I never asked her out again. Hell, when I found out about Buck, I knew I was out of my league."

"I've seen her in town a few times with a boy. Looks like he's a teenager. She's always real friendly, like she really hasn't changed all that much. Money hasn't gone to her head, I don't guess. And she's still a knockout. You know, I wonder if she knows what ol' Buck's up to. Looks like she'd have to, unless she's got her head in the sand."

Quinlin didn't mention he had talked to Rebecca.

"I've wondered, too," Quinlin said. "I'd be surprised if she knew. On the other hand, living with someone twenty years or so, you'd think she'd have to know. I know one thing from being a cop. Money corrupts. In some cases, money kills. I guess somewhere there're people with money who haven't been corrupted. I just never see 'em in my line of work."

When Moore opened the door for Quinlin to leave, the detective noticed a neatly lettered slogan in a frame on the wall. He hadn't heard the saying since Vietnam: *When I die, bury me facedown so the world can kiss my ass.*

Guilt swept him. His friend, through no choice of his own, was barely a marginal member of society. Pain from yesterday made it tough for him to live today, and the uncertainty of tomorrow made him dread trying another day. Moore was a trip wire. His body was in Sul Ross County, his mind was in Southeast Asia, and his soul was up for grabs. Quinlin knew it wasn't fair to bring him in on a dicey situation like this.

Drinking coffee while sitting around a couple of burning logs, he trusted Moore. Under stress, though, when Moore was alone, he just as easily could be a hand grenade without a pin. He'd proved that when he took McCray's tire.

"Hey, man," Moore said, hugging him. "You know you can trust me, right? You'll never have to watch your back with me around."

26

W hat do you mean, am I sure?" Quinlin asked. "About McCray? Hell yes. I mean, do we have enough physical evidence to put him away? Maybe, maybe not. But we know he was watching Bettman's ranch, and probably bugged it. The tire tracks put him at the scene with Richmond Carlisle's car, and I got a guy down on the coast who puts him with Bettman's plane minutes before it turned into a sparkler."

Quinlin searched his lieutenant's eyes, trying to read him. Coy Matthews shot a dubious glance at Paul McCarren.

"What's going on here?" Quinlin asked. "I mean, do we have the connect yet to get the Colters? No. But we're gonna have it real soon. That's what I've been doing. I got a guy—"

"I think you may be on the right track, Jeb," Matthews said. "But it may be that McCray is just a psycho wing nut. . . ."

"He *is* a psycho wing nut," Quinlin said, hearing the defensiveness in his own voice. "Look, this is a guy who cut a man's balls off and fed them to a dog. That qualifies for psycho. . . ."

"But it's a big leap from this cretin to the Colters," Matthews said. "You can't put him with the Colters. Maybe he's working his own deal."

"No fuckin' way," Quinlin said. "That's what they tried to say about Bettman. Look, I've gone through McCray's files. He's a freak, yeah, but his MO is that he gets paid to be sadistic. He's an enforcer. That's gonna be the connect with the Colters."

"McCarren here and I came across another wrinkle, that's all," Matthews said. "While you were down south. And we've got to take a hard look at it. Due diligence kind of deal. But Jeb, it looks good."

A couple of narcs caught a crack dealer with barely enough rock to score a felony. The guy, Demetrius Wheeler, was a small-time dealer who'd already done two stretches in TDCJ for drugs and was out on bail for another dope charge. When the narcs told him they were filing habitual criminal charges against him, Demetrius broke bad, breaking one narc's arm and superficially whacking up the other with a box cutter. Facing life on the bitch and flaky charges of assault with intent to commit capital murder on the narcs, Demetrius was looking to deal. He claimed to have information "on somebody damned big." Knowing the narcs had a boner for him, he refused to talk to anybody except Homicide.

"You remember our friend Skate Runnels?" McCarren asked.

"Yeah, sure," Quinlin said. "Badass ex-cop who works for Bumpy Rhodes. Talked to him awhile back about Carlisle."

"Demetrius's story is that his ol' lady put down five grand in cash with Bumpy to make bond for him on his latest gig," McCarren said. "Demetrius says that Skate offered to give it back if he was interested in popping somebody. He says he later found out that the target was Richmond Carlisle."

"That doesn't work for me," Quinlin said.

"He's not saying he did it, Jeb," Matthews said. "He's saying he was offered the hit for five thousand."

"Unless he's got something to grab hold of, it's a pissing match between Runnels and Demetrius," Quinlin said. "And to be perfectly honest, I wouldn't know which one to believe."

"Exactly," the lieutenant said. "But the deal is, Demetrius passed a polygraph. And last night, we sent him to see Skate Runnels with a wire."

Matthews went to his desk and returned with a tape recorder. "This is what he got," the lieutenant said, pressing the play button:

"I didn't mean to be hasty with you the other day, man."

Quinlin could tell by the dialect it was Demetrius.

"What you talkin' about, asshole?"

"Your, uh, you know, ah, the business proposition you discussed."

"Yeah, so?"

"So I was thinkin', you know, I could use the bread. I didn't think it through good. So . . ."

"You don't get out much, do you? Ever read the fuckin' paper, man?"

"What you mean?"

"That deal's dead and stinkin'. The newspaper dude's already been whacked, chump. You're just a little fuckin' late, know what I'm saying? . . ."

"Get an arrest warrant for Runnels," Matthews told the pair of detectives, "and charge him with solicitation of capital murder. Lean on him. Let's see what he's got to say."

27

I f his own butt weren't on the line, Clint Harper would have enjoyed the scenario in the third-floor conference room. Clendon Colter and his attorneys were fifteen minutes late, and the executive editor of the *Register & News* was pacing a rut in the carpeting, glancing at his watch every fifteen seconds.

"What do you think, Harper?" Garrett Anderson Brewster asked. "Is he gonna threaten us with libel or what?"

Harper noticed something remarkable. Agitated and scared, Brewster's phony Brit accent had vanished; he sounded like a native Texan. The reporter acted as if he hadn't heard the question. But no, when the executive editor repeated himself, he wasn't British anymore. What kind of man, Harper wondered, would go through life affecting an accent just for image? Looking at Brewster in his thousand-dollar double-breasted suit and lizard loafers, he saw a man who had politicked and brownnosed his way to a position far beyond his professional ability. And now that he faced uncertainty, the cracks in his image splintered like a broken mirror.

"No," Harper said. "If he was suing us, we'd get the message from a process server. He's coming here to intimidate. To make a statement."

"And that statement would be what?"

"To scare hell out of us," the reporter said. "Make sure we don't write anything else about him. He'll huff and puff and expect us to cower in the corner."

"Harper's probably right," said Paul Watling. "That story wasn't actionable. I'm sure Colter didn't like it, but his lawyers have told him he doesn't have a libel case. He wants to rattle the saber."

Watling's firm had represented the *Register & News* for as long as Harper had been on staff. Watling was a savvy lawyer, probably because he'd spent a brief tour before law school as a reporter, and he actually tried to help reporters get stories in the paper, instead of gutting them. Harper admired him.

Harper had sat through countless meetings like this, and they routinely turned into inquisitions in which he was attacked professionally and personally. One guy about whom he had written unflatteringly, an old hack congressman from an outlying area, had apparently hired a private investigator to dig into Harper's background. The congressman, who had left taxpayers holding the bag for $3 million in defaulted loans from a busted savings and loan, managed to work into his conversation Harper's favorite watering hole, a description of his Bronco, and the fact that Harper was divorced.

Spineless, unethical bastard that he was, Brewster acquiesced to the corrupt politician's pressure and pulled the plug on Harper's story before he could get it into the paper. But Harper had discovered early in his career that justice was neither neat nor tidy, and seldom pretty. He had bundled up all his records on the good congressman, put them in a FedEx box, and sent them to Brett McCaleb, his competitor at the *Fort Worth Light*. The exposé appeared a month later under McCaleb's byline, and he won a Texas Headliner Award for running the garbage congressman out of office.

"I'll tell you this," Brewster was saying, the Brit inflection returning with his confidence, "if this gentleman thinks I'm just going to wait—"

Gwendolyn, Brewster's stone-faced secretary, appeared in the doorway to the conference room, announcing too loudly the arrival of Clendon Colter and his entourage.

The old millionaire wasn't what Harper had expected. He was a big man, maybe six foot four and 225 solid pounds, erect for a man in his seventies, and icy in his stare. He moved through the door like a man on his own turf, leaving Brewster standing with his hand outstretched. He was dressed like a cowboy, with a blue western-cut oxford shirt, black jeans, handmade black kangaroo boots, and a black Stetson, which he hadn't removed indoors. His gray hair was stylish and long enough in the back to fall down the collar of his shirt. He walked to the head of the table, where Brewster had left his coffee cup, shoved it aside, plopped down his briefcase, and sat down. Two lawyers and the U.S. attorney trailed him into the room and took seats on either side.

Harper was at the other end of the long table, by himself, and he was the only one who hadn't gotten up. He was surprised to see Ronald Stokes, the U.S. attorney for the Northern District of Texas, and knew the ante was about to go up. What was the chief federal prosecutor doing in the company of Colter's legal henchmen? Colter and Stokes were both prominent Texas Democrats, and that was probably the tie. At least the obvious one. Having enough stroke to drag along the chief federal prosecutor was impressive, particularly to a confrontation with a newspaper. There was no telling how many markers Colter had out, or who held them. Harper had the feeling he was about to find out.

Clendon Colter didn't waste any time on perfunctories or introductions.

"I'm Clendon Colter," he said, even before Brewster could move his cup and legal pad to another seat, "and I've got other places I need to be. I assume you boys do, too. So let's talk turkey.

"My lawyers here tell me I could sue the hell out of you right now," Colter said, "and probably win. That's what I want my lawyers to tell me. I pay them damned good money to tell me that."

Brewster saw an opportunity and tried to take it: "Well, if I might—"

"You might in a minute," Colter said. "But I called this meeting, and I haven't finished saying my piece."

Harper was intrigued. The old man was a laser going through butter, and he wasn't going to take any shit from Brewster. It was like Russia and Red China. Harper hoped they pissed on each other. Money and power guaranteed Colter a certain amount of self-confidence. Begrudgingly, Harper gave him points for savoir faire.

"Am I saying something you think's funny, boy?"

Colter was looking squarely at Harper, who hadn't realized he was grinning.

"Not at all," the reporter said. "Please, go ahead. I'm all ears."

"Well, you had your say on the front page of the newspaper. I figure you can at least let me talk.

"No, I'm not going to sue you right now," Colter said. "But there was some bullshit stuff in that story, and if I see things like that again, I can guaran-damn-tee you, I'm coming after you hard."

He was looking at Brewster, who kept his eyes on the legal pad in front of him.

"You've made certain innuendos about this Bettman character flying dope for me," Colter said, his voice going cold. "Anybody who knows me—and several of them could buy and sell this damned place three or four times over—knows I'm hard against dope. Won't tolerate it.

"Now, I've asked Ron here, Ron Stokes, the U.S. attorney, to explain to you that I'm not now nor have I ever been a suspect in any goddamned smuggling operation. Am I right, Ron?"

"That's right, Clendon," the federal prosecutor said on cue. "There were some preliminary allegations forwarded to my office and I assigned some agents, but there wasn't anything to them. There was never any active file opened."

"So, all that crap about Bettman being an informant was total bullshit," Colter said. "And if I ran this rag, I'd want to know how in hell that landed on my front page."

Brewster made no attempt at an answer.

"That's it? Nobody knows? Nobody cares?"

Harper had seen the phenomenon before. Unchallenged, the complainant, particularly one as strong as Colter, likes the sound of his own rhetoric, works himself into righteous indignation, and escalates the battle into a frenzy. Unchecked, they sometimes left the newspaper and filed a libel suit.

The executive editor was avoiding eye contact with everyone.

"The story said Bettman was an informant because he *was* an informant," Harper said. He wouldn't mention that he got a copy of the tape from Bettman's lawyer of the pilot's conversation with law enforcement. That revelation would come in a courtroom if Colter sued.

"Bettman not only offered evidence to the federal government, which discounted it apparently for political reasons," Harper said, "but he took it to Comanche Gap and offered it to the local district attorney and Texas Ranger. It's not certain, at least to us right now, why they didn't act on it. We're still trying to find out."

"Let me get this straight, stud. Are you sitting there threatening me with another story? Because if that's what I'm hearing, I'll turn this goddamned place upside down with lawyers."

"We're certainly not threatening you, Mr. Colter," Brewster said. "And I, uh, won't even say that we'll have another story. Uh, we just don't know at this point."

Colter turned to the oldest gray suit in his entourage. "What'd you tell me this story had already cost me?"

"Easily fifty million in actual damages to your reputation," the silver-haired lawyer said, "and I estimate a jury would award you another fifty million in punitive damages. I also be—"

"So are you sons of bitches willing to take a hundred-million-dollar dice roll on that boy sitting down there?" Colter asked, pointing at Harper.

"You must understand that we're comfortable with the information Mr. Harper used to write the story or we wouldn't have published it," Paul Watling said. Brewster was incapable of voicing a defense, and Watling rose to the occasion. "We obviously believe we can defend ourselves in court."

"Yes or no," Colter asked, "is he working on another story about me or not?"

"I'm still doing research," Harper said, "and it could or could not develop into a story. We'll look at the facts objectively and determine if they merit another story. If they do, we'll contact you, give you an opportunity for fair comment before the story runs."

Damned right, there was another story—*if* Brewster had any balls left after the meeting. Harper was merely reading self-serving garbage into the record for the benefit of Colter's lawyers. Something that would look good in depositions if they did sue.

"You got any questions of me," Colter said, his face reddening, "you ask 'em right here and now in front of my lawyers."

"Well, I'd have several," Harper said. "Do you have time?"

"What you want to ask about?"

"The general topics, I guess, would be why the chief federal prosecutor is tagging along, vouching for you in a potential civil lawsuit, and, still along those ethical lines, whether Les Westgrove's former position as your personal lawyer influenced his decision on whether to investigate you criminally. Also, there's the whole question of how you knew to buy up sixty thousand acres just before the federal government decided to build a lake—"

"That's it, you motherfuckers!" Colter exploded, rising from his chair. The veins in his head turned purple. "You ain't gonna piss on my boots and tell me it's raining. You write my name in this fuckin' rag one more time, and the next time you see me, it's gonna be in a goddamned courtroom. And you can take that to the bank: You're gonna bleed like a hemorrhoid hog when I get finished with you."

Brewster was out of his chair and in the doorway before Colter could get there.

"I think there's been a misunderstanding," Brewster was saying. "If you'd—"

Momentarily, the two men were eye-to-eye, Colter dwarfing the fastidious editor in the Italian suit. Colter shoved Brewster out of the doorway, leaving him with a final thought. "Grab your ankles, bozo. I'm fixin' to drive a truck up your ass."

28

Divorce? You're crazier than I thought. Yeah, I'll give you a divorce. You want a divorce, you got it. But you'll walk out of here with the clothes on your back," Buck Colter said. "And you really think you'll get custody of Chad? Over my dead body."

"I've talked to the best lawyer in Fort Worth," Rebecca said, "and half of everything you own belongs to me. That's the law. And when the jury hears that you're a drunk who beats his son, child custody won't be a problem. I'm comfortable with Chad making his own decision."

"Where in the hell have you been living—Mars?" he asked. "Do you really believe your precious divorce would ever get to a jury in Sul Ross County? Yeah, and I'm enrolling in the seminary."

Buck Colter laughed loudly and put his coffee cup on the desk to keep from spilling it.

"Do you think people in town treat you like a queen because your name is Becky and you've got pretty hair, a fair ass, and you're friendly?" he said. "Shiiit. You're a Colter. That's it. The last name. That's all you got. Without it, you're just what you were when I found you, a piss-poor country girl and a fairly decent piece of ass. You—"

"I won't listen to that kind of talk," she said, heading for the door to his study. "I should have done this—"

"Just a goddamned minute," Buck said, grabbing her by the arm. "You ain't gonna do anything until I—"

"Get your damned hands—"

The phone rang on Buck's desk, and, surprisingly, he let her go immediately.

"You're not doing a goddamned thing until we talk," he said over his shoulder. "You understand that? I mean it, too. Now, get your ass out of here. This is important."

He waited until she left to pick up the receiver. She left the door to the study open, then stopped around the corner. Immediately, Buck's attitude changed. He was calm and deferential; he was talking to his father.

"Another one? Saying what?

"We've got to sue 'em, Daddy. We don't, they're just going to cause us more problems and maybe even get some feds down here. Stokes is strong in his backyard, but what if somebody in Washington calls the shots? Besides, he may not stay stupid forever."

There was a long pause while Buck listened to his father.

"We can't do that, not now. The product's on the ground. Gato says seventy-two hours or nothing. And we can't afford nothing. Not on this one. He's got everyone taken care of down there, but it's a fluid deal. It's taken me three months to set up everything on this end—people, planes, trucks, the whole deal. Hell, I mean, it's right here, not in the middle of some fuckin' desert. If this was a regular deal, fine, but this one . . ."

Rebecca saw Buck glance toward the doorway, and she moved just in time.

"Nothing I can't handle. I saw her with Charley before he croaked, and I suspect the old fart told her a bunch of crap. Yeah, but not until after the deal's done. We don't need that now."

Rebecca felt the panic in her chest. Quickly and quietly, she walked to the sunroom at the other end of the house. She saw her hands trembling as she collapsed into her favorite chair. Adrenaline was jumbling her thoughts. She had to get Chad off the ranch. Any day, the roof was coming down. Charley would have known what to do, damn him. His place would be the first place they'd look. She heard Buck's voice. He was off the phone.

"Rebecca, god damn it, where are you?"

• • •

Detective Sgt. Sarah Demerett was a legend at Dallas Police head-quarters. A year earlier, she'd won the International Chiefs of Police Association award as the best fingerprint expert in the nation. While a typical fingerprint specialist matched between one and two hundred fingerprints a year on the automated fingerprint identification system computer, Demerett had made positive IDs on 514 latent prints.

The megamicrochips in the AFIS fingerprint system, linked with the Texas Department of Public Safety headquarters in Austin, contains the ending ridges, bifurcation, and dots of nearly 4.5 million people, most of whom have been booked into the jails in the state's 254 counties over the years.

Demerett, tiny, understated, and modest, made national head-lines when she solved one of the biggest serial rape cases in Texas history. The so-called Bad Breath Rapist had sexually assaulted and tortured more than one hundred women in six years. When one of the victims told detectives that the rapist had drunk from a plastic cup on her kitchen counter, they retrieved a smudged partial print.

The first run through the computer spit out fifty-two possibilities of matches. Over two days, the diminutive sergeant pored over the ridge characteristics of each of them, finally winnowing the latents down to those of Arturo Rangel. Rangel had been handled only one time, in El Paso, six years earlier, for burglary. The rapes were stranger-on-stranger crimes, Rangel had no MO for sex offenses, he was a loner, and he wasn't even known to be in Dallas, making it virtually impossible to have caught him without Demerett and AFIS.

When Deputy Chief Jon Abrams heard that someone had put a rattlesnake in an officer's mailbox, he assigned the case to Demerett. Even though the partial print off Quinlin's mailbox was smudged, it only took the fingerprint expert two hours to pull Jerry Ray McCray's name out of the microchip.

"No question about it?" Quinlin asked.

"Nope," Demerett said. "We got a thumbprint off the handle. Mr. McCray scored seven thousand and one points out of a possible nine thousand nine hundred and ninety-nine. Plenty enough to put him away."

"I wish it were that simple," Quinlin said.

The computerized printout was in his chair when he returned from the Identification Section downstairs. DPD Communications had received it fifteen minutes earlier from the Aransas County Sheriff's Department. It was from Capt. Marshall Towns, Criminal Investigation Division, and it was marked "*URGENT.*"

> On this date, investigating officer received information from National Transportation Safety Board investigator Warren Wilson regarding a plane crash off the coast of Rockport. The preliminary investigation of the crash, based on NTSB and FBI lab–Washington analysis of metal aircraft debris recovered from a shrimp boat, indicates traces of pentaerythritol tetranitrate (PETN).
>
> PETN is a primary compound found in plastic charge explosives. NTSB advises that an explosive charge containing PETN could have been designed to detonate at a specific altitude or at a specific time. The presence of PETN indicates the strong possibility that the plane was tampered with before takeoff from Aransas County Airport.
>
> Crime Scene analysis on evidence recovered in a Chevrolet van used to deliver cargo to the aircraft and from which a messenger was abducted and killed indicates a partial left index print matched to Jerry Ray McCray (DPS#55172126).
>
> Please advise regarding the time frame previously discussed for clearing this case with the suspect identified above.

29

C redit where credit's due," Quinlin said, unlocking the handcuffs. "You were a sorry cop, but you're stupid, too."

Skate Runnels winced as he rubbed the depressed skin on his wrists. Uniforms had picked him up at his house in Pleasant Grove on the arrest warrant, and they told McCarren when they dragged him in that he was begging them to take a leak. For the last three hours, he had been locked alone and cuffed in Interview Room 3.

"I need to piss and to call my lawyer," Runnels said. "In that order."

"You've got a right to a lawyer," Quinlin said. "You remember that part, right? But our men's room . . . well, its backed up. I apologize. We'd have to take you down to two, but then we'd have to cuff you again. Let's just give you some time to get the blood flowing to those hands. They look a little purple to me."

"We want you to be comfortable," McCarren said from his chair against the wall. "We're sorry we couldn't get to you sooner, but, man, it's been crazy around here. A genuine crime wave."

Skate Runnels's legs were together at the knees and he was breathing shallowly. "Don't fuck with me, man," he said. "I've got to piss. I'm hurting here."

"Yeah, we'll get to it," Quinlin said, dragging up a chair next to the suspect's. "Coming right up."

"Some coffee, a soft drink?" McCarron asked, sipping coffee.

Runnels figeted, bouncing his legs nervously on the balls of his feet. "Fuck you," he said. "I ain't saying anything 'less I get to piss."

"Like I was saying," Quinlin continued, "you ain't too smart, Skate. We got three burglary detectives tossing your house right now, and you know what? They've only been there forty-five minutes and they've discovered a pickupload of stolen shit. I figure by day's end—"

"Don't know nothing about no stolen stuff," Runnels said. "I need—"

"And the big-screen TV?" Quinlin said. "You really screwed the pooch on the TV, Einstein. That came out of an assistant DA's house in North Dallas. Serial numbers match real good, don't they, Paul?"

"Yeah, I'm predicting a pretty vigorous prosecution here," McCarren said, pulling his chair across the table from Runnels and Quinlin.

"Wouldn't surprise me, Paul," Quinlin said. "What does surprise me is that ol' Skate here gave us a freebie. I mean, did we ever think he'd be stupid enough to fill his house like a pawnshop? I'm figuring the DA, seeing as how his TV set ends up in Skate's living room—right in the middle of football season—is probably gonna give him a dime on burglary alone. And, hey, we haven't even gotten to the solicitation of murder."

"See, Skate, you left out a key step in the traditional bail bond process," McCarren said. "You never take hot stuff from your dirt-bag clients, moron. What you do is make them fence it *first,* then they pay you in cash. See, what we've got here is receiving and concealing stolen property. The statute is called 'burglary of a habitation.' "

"What you've got is shit," Runnels said. "Let me piss an—"

"Paul, put the tape recorder up here," Quinlin said, patting the table. "I don't have a lot of time here. Skate, my friend, we're gonna run this down to you, and you can do whatever you want. You can call your lawyer, or maybe we can do something for you. It's your deal, but you're dead and stinking here. We got enough to put you away on burglary. That's a slam dunk. And here's the finale."

It was McCarren's cue to punch on the tape recorder. Demetrius Wheeler's voice took over the room.

" 'So Runnels,' he says, 'hey, all you got to do to get the five long is whack this newspaper dude.' I'm looking at his stupid white face—like, How the hell would I do that?—and he pulls this piece outta his coat and hands it to me."

"What's interesting here, Einstein, is that Demetrius gave us the piece," Quinlin said, turning off the tape. "And, yo, guess where it came from? The police property room. And the logs put you in the property room before your untimely resignation. You took the piece for a throw-down boot gun, something you could leave beside some unarmed puke's body sometime. Not smart."

"So let me catch up here," McCarren said. "We've got one burglary of a habitation and one theft from the property room. And, oh, did we forget to mention that we got your prints on the throw-down gun? Or that Demetrius passed the box?"

Skate Runnels was twitching like a run-over snake.

"Man, I read the paper," the ex-cop said painfully. "The reporter wasn't killed with no gun."

"Yeah," Quinlin said, "Richmond Carlisle was a popular guy. People were standing in line to pop him. You and the crack man moved too slow, and somebody beat you to him. That's why we're putting you down for *solicitation* of murder, not the actual deed. Makes a shit to us, one way or the other. Solicitation carries a life sentence, too."

Runnels was in agony, and his next words came out in a pitiful soprano. "If you'll deal here on this thing, I can take you to the next level, to who you're looking for. It ain't me, man."

"Ray Charles could see that," Quinlin said. "You're a twenty-watt bulb, Skate."

The suspect was holding his genitals with both hands, and his legs were bouncing uncontrollably.

"What I have to do?" the big man asked, barely audible now.

"Wear a wire on Bumpy," Quinlin said.

"I'll do it, if you'll talk to the DA."

"Sorry," Quinlin said. "You're fading out on me. I can't hear you."

"I'll do it," Runnels said loudly, tears welling in the corner of his eyes. "I've got to piss. God damn it, I beggin'. *Pleeease.*"

30

Quinlin had never been beyond the lobby and coffee shop of the Hyatt Regency, and the eastward view of downtown Dallas from the fourteenth-floor sitting room was impressive at dusk. He saw a couple of doors, which he assumed led to the bedroom and bath.

"This suite was all they had," Rebecca Colter said, sensing his silent question. "It's way more than I need just for me, but I didn't have reservations. Frankly, it was the first decent thing I came across driving in. I haven't done a lot of advance planning lately. I appreciate your coming."

He sat on the end of the couch, and she pulled a chair beside the coffee table.

"I wasn't sure you'd ever speak to me again after our last conversation," Quinlin said. "I need to apologize. Nothing about that went the way I wanted it to. I wasn't—"

"This is a pop quiz," she said, breaking the ice. "Where did we go on our last date?"

"Easy. We saw a James Bond movie in Stephenville, then ate hamburgers at Jake and Dorothy's. If you'd ordered chicken-fried steak instead of a hamburger, I would have had to wash dishes. I had exactly fifty cents left for a tip."

"I figured as much. That's why I ordered a hamburger with no fries, and a cherry Coke instead of a shake. Next question: Why didn't you ever ask me out again? I had a major crush on you. You broke my heart."

Quinlin hoped he wasn't turning red. "Well," he said, "I, uh, wasn't broken out in common sense in those days, but I had enough to know I couldn't compete with Buck Colter."

The mention of her husband's name took her smile away. She leaned forward in the chair, closer to Quinlin's face.

"He's the reason I'm here," Rebecca said, her forehead furrowing. "Big surprise, huh? I wasn't very honest when we talked in Comanche Gap. You don't need to apologize for the conversation. I do. I've suspected things over the years, but that's all I had when we talked, suspicions. I was torn. If my suspicions were true—and I'm pretty certain now that they are—the father of my only child has been responsible for some pretty unforgivable things."

"What's changed since we last talked? I mean, why now and not then?"

"Two things, I guess. First, he's been abusive to Chad. That's my son. He's beaten him pretty severely, the first time seriously enough I had to take him to the hospital. It happened again after I saw you. I can't explain how that makes me feel. The first time I thought it was a horrible, drunken fluke. Now, I think it's just the real Buck coming out. Which makes me believe he's capable of anything. So I started actively trying to find out who my husband really is.

"I sent you some things anonymously awhile back. Now I realize how cowardly that was. Maybe not cowardly. Maybe I wasn't really ready to risk everything. I don't know. But now I don't have a choice. To make a long story short, my husband is a drug smuggler and a killer, among other things."

She said it matter-of-factly, like mentioning that he was Baptist and a Rotarian. Quinlin admired her candor.

"He's got to be stopped," she said. "And there's some urgency, too. Something's about to happen."

"Rebecca, I probably know more about your husband and his family than you think," the detective said. "I took your mysterious information seriously, and—"

She got up in midsentence and walked through the door into

the bedroom. When she returned, she handed him an old-fashioned leather journal with bound blue-lined paper, and sat beside him on the couch.

"Charley Blake knew the Colters better than anyone," she said. "He, uh—how should I put this? He was a wonderful old gentleman, but over the years, he did certain things for Clendon that were criminal. In the end, when he was dying, he told me everything. Right before he died, he left this journal for me. It was in a sealed envelope that he had left with a nurse."

Quinlin scanned the small journal as he listened to Rebecca. The book was maybe four times bigger than a pack of cigarettes, and the leather was worn at the corners, probably from being pulled repeatedly from an inside coat pocket over thirty-five years. The detective noticed that the first entry, written in pencil and dated 10/22/58, logged the sale of 244 head of Angus cattle to Clendon Colter. He thumbed through the journal, noticing as the pages turned that the entries were in pencil and blue, black, and red ink, apparently whatever writing instrument Blake was carrying or could borrow at the time.

It was an amazing record of a man's professional life. Charley Blake's penmanship was good, but as Quinlin flipped the pages front to back, he noticed Charley missed the lines on several occasions, and the detective wondered if some of the entries might have been made at night. Quinlin also noticed the change in Blake's writing from the front of the book, where his penmanship was sure and steady, to the end, where it appeared palsied.

"You can take it with you," Rebecca said. "It'll take you quite awhile to go through it, but it's really a very revealing look at the Colters. If it didn't involve me, I'd think it was fascinating. Charley wrote down the names of drug dealers he met in Mexico, the identification numbers of planes that flew dope, where they landed in the States, and even the names of Mexican officials Clendon and his partner, this guy named San Martín, bribed. All that interspersed with 'To Do' lists, what looks like the combination to a lock someplace, his mother's birth date, and even a recipe for something called Budweiser beef stew."

Quinlin was distracted as he read the last entry:

"So, sweet Rebecca, I really hate leaving you this way. And I'm worried to death about you and the boy. But even alive, in the shape I'm in, there's not nothing much I can do. One thing I know is this. You are tough. Like a cactus blossom. Pretty and delicate, but try to pick one, it'll bite you bad. Just be awful careful.

I know you'll know what to do with this book. And knowing you, it'll be the right thing, too. You're going to be really put out with me for what I'm about to do, but I think the time's right for me. The old ticker and these lungs are just about gone. It feels like I got sandpaper inside me every time I take a breath. If I was an old bull, somebody would shoot me just to get me out of my misery. It's funny, ain't it, how we take more pity on an animal than we do on another human being?

I was sitting here thinking after you left. Six seconds on the back of a bucking bull is an awful long time, but seventy-six years don't seem like much. I sure wish I had done some things different, and I imagine I'll sure pay for that in the next little while. Never spent enough time in church, but I'm pretty sure now there's a heaven and a hell. I guess I'll know for sure if Clendon Colter and I show up at the same place. Be my luck.

Anyways, I hope I did the right thing in the end, telling you everything and giving you this book. And I think you and the boy will do just fine out at the ranch. Funny what you remember at the end. Something my old daddy once told me—you don't judge a man by where he is. You judge him by how far he's come."

"This old man obviously thought the world of you," Quinlin said. "When this is all over, I'll make sure you get this back. I know it's important to you."

"Will it help?"

"I've got to read it and see," Quinlin said. "Just thumbing through, it appears to confirm many of the things I've already come up with. But it looks like it also adds a tremendous amount of detail, too. At the very least, it'll sure fill in some blanks and establish some patterns."

Texas law had a provision for dying declarations. In all of Quinlin's years in homicide, he'd only had one case in which a witness on his deathbed had implicated his killer. But the testimony was powerful in a courtroom, and Quinlin could tell from the juror's faces as he testified that the killer was going to get the death penalty.

Charley Blake's death, the way Quinlin figured, posed a thorny legal-moral dilemma. Morally, maybe even legally, his death was suicide. Clearly, the old man premeditated the time, and he knew that his course of action would kill him. But he hadn't put the barrel of a shotgun in his mouth and pulled the trigger with his toe, or swallowed two hundred Tylenol, or slashed his carotid artery with a machete. The way Rebecca told it, he had merely gone out in the cold, as was his right, leaned against a tree, and folded his hands.

The journal he left behind was the remarkable road map, albeit dated, to a major international drug-smuggling operation. A jury would find it dramatic proof that one of the wealthiest families in Texas had reaped its fruit for years from a poison tree. But could dying declarations be written, instead of uttered, in the last few seconds of life? Quinlin didn't know. And could the damning statement of a third party's criminal culpability be made by someone who was actually on the brink of killing himself?

Rebecca ordered coffee from room service, and she spent an hour briefing Quinlin. She recounted everything Charley Blake had told her, along with what she had overheard in Buck Colter's conversations with the sheriff and his father. There was little doubt that her husband had arranged for Bettman's plane crash or that he was planning a major drug deal, apparently to take place on Pan Permian Headquarters Ranch.

"So whatever's happening, it's supposed to happen in a couple of days," Quinlin said. "That's not much time. Not to mention that we've got to come up with a plan that'll keep you and Chad safe until this thing's over."

The sixteen-year-old was safe, Rebecca believed, at least for the moment. He was staying with one of her cousins near San Antonio.

"As nervous as Buck is right now," she said, "I don't think he's got time to do anything to either of us."

"I'm not willing to bet your lives on it."

Quinlin went to the desk drawer and retrieved several pieces of paper with the Hyatt Regency letterhead. He gave Rebecca a sheet and moved to the coffee table. He directed her to sketch a rough layout of the Pan Permian property, pinpointing all its roads, the locations of Clendon's, Buck's, and Wade's houses, the barns, and the runway. As she drew the map, Quinlin asked questions about security, jotting notes.

There were only two entrances, the main one off U.S. 281, and the other, which was off County Road 2005, a marginally two-lane caliche road nine miles to the southeast. Both were manned by armed guards around the clock. A graded fire road ran inside the ranch's perimeter fence, and guards in Jeeps drove them continuously in opposite directions. The guards, according to Rebecca, were generally off-duty sheriff's deputies, game wardens, and state troopers who were well paid for their moonlighting, which, Quinlin knew, also made them deeply indebted to the Colters. All of the outposts and the three Colter houses, along with the main barn, the airplane hangar, and the Colters' vehicles, were linked by radio.

"I don't know any specifics," Rebecca said, "but there's also some kind of electronic intrusion detection on the fence line all the way around the ranch."

When Clay Moore first told him that McCray was hinting a drug deal could go down in Sul Ross County, Quinlin was skeptical, particularly of the Colters using their own ranch. Only a fool, he thought, would bring a load of dope into his own backyard. But as Rebecca ran through the extensive security of Pan Permian Headquarters Ranch, and knowing the Colters owned virtually everyone in the county who wore a badge, Quinlin realized the plan not only wasn't stupid; it was boldly brilliant. Buck Colter was controlling all the variables on the north end the same way Juan Carlos "El Gato" San Martín was manipulating the drop zone on the south end. Sul Ross County law enforcement, including the county's only Texas Ranger, was as corrupt as the infamous *federales* in Mexico's interior.

And the desolate terrain of the isolated Pan Permian Headquarters Ranch, Quinlin figured, would only enhance the Colters' plan. It was a nearly two-hour drive to any large city. The ranch was irregular in shape, and at its widest point, it was nearly thirteen miles fence post to fence post, bigger than at least a couple of Texas counties. A ridge of tall, rough hills rimmed the ranch on three sides like a horseshoe, and the rangeland below broke sporadically into arroyos deep enough to swallow large trucks. Throughout, a maze of white gravel roads ran like a spiderweb through the forty thousand acres, and there were at least two dirt landing strips in addition to the asphalt strip at the hangar. Surveillance would be virtually impossible.

Standing over Rebecca's shoulder as she sketched the layout, Quinlin realized he didn't even know how the drugs would be delivered—by truck or plane. Or when. Or even for sure *if* the main ranch was the drop point.

Rebecca was caught up in her drawing, and Quinlin fell heavily onto the couch, swept with futility. Interdicting a major drug operation called for a task force. He was one cop without real jurisdiction. A *homicide* cop, not a narc. He didn't know cocaine from cornstarch. He'd seen movies of where a cop would lick his finger, sticking it into a bag of white powder, and then into his mouth. He'd look knowingly and say, "Yep, that's coke." How'd the cop know? What was cocaine supposed to taste like?

He knew his only hope was Clay Moore. If Moore could get Jerry Ray McCray on tape—explicit and definite, without bullshit dope euphemisms—he would simply drop it in the hands of the FBI and go his own way. It wasn't his deal anyway.

"I *said*, do you have a plan?" Rebecca asked. "What are we going to do, Mr. Detective?"

Quinlin was jolted back into the present.

Yeah, he had a plan. The plan hinged on a trip-wire vet who saw slopes in coolie hats and black pajamas every time he fed the cows; his rural mail carrier was a federal bureaucrat, and his congressman owned stock in the chemical conglomerate that got rich off .155 shells and Agent Orange.

"We're in control, Rebecca," Quinlin said, grinning. "It's all a matter of timing, just waiting for our best shot."

In actuality, Quinlin had never felt more inadequate or uncertain in his life. He held her hand as she walked him to the door.

"You stay put until you hear from me," he said. "I've got some loose ends to tie up."

"I, uh . . ."

He glanced down and saw her tears.

"You gonna be all right?" he asked, hugging her.

"I know it sounds strange," she said, wiping at the tears with the back of her hand, "but I feel good about what I'm doing. Scared to death. But it feels right. It is, isn't it, Jeb?"

He took a deep breath and exhaled. "Yeah," he said. "No question about that."

31

At 4:00 A.M., the temperature was nineteen degrees, and a stiff, steady wind from the north made it wholly intolerable in the camouflaged deer stand. The fifteen-foot stand was barely in the tree line, overlooking a corn feeder fifty feet away at the edge of the pasture.

"We're two goddamned hours too early," said the tall, thin one, hunkered down beneath the bare window with his arms wrapped tightly around himself.

The shorter, heavyset one scanned the pasture with binoculars. There was a full moon, and he was surprised how well he could see.

"A total waste of fucking sleep," said the whiny one.

"I thought accountants were supposed to be patient. You're wound too tight."

"And you're Davy fuckin' Crockett? You didn't even have a hunting license until—"

"Holy shit. Will you look at this?"

"Damn, he's huge. Is it the moon or—hey, he's white! That son of a bitch is white! A fuckin' white deer, man!"

As he spoke, the shorter, heavy one propped the Remington .223 against the bottom of the window and squinted through the scope. The white deer was walking toward the deer feeder, straight into his sight.

"Get 'em in the shoulder," Slim said. "Don't ruin that rack. Man, can you see that son of a bitch over your mantel?"

Shorty clicked off the safety and lined up the crosshairs on the middle of the white deer's throat. The trophy was almost to the feeder. Any closer and this was going to be an embarrassing story. A thirteen-year-old could make this shot.

The shot shattered the meadow. At precisely the moment the lead slug struck his throat, the deer bit through his tongue and pissed himself. A smoky puff exploded from his mouth as the warmth of his last gasp hit the frigid air. Collapsed onto his front knees, he wobbled momentarily and fell dead in a patch of purple thistle.

Five hundred yards across the fence line in the log house, the muffled pop roused Madeline Meggers from her sleep. She wrinkled her brow but didn't open her eyes. She lay still, listening, then drifted off uneasily. The exhausted man beside her didn't rustle.

32

A lot of people can kill in war, but it's a different story when you know you could go to jail for it," he said. "What I'm bettin' is that you don't give a damn one way or the other. Am I right?"

"Killin' is killin'," Clay Moore said. "It don't make a man less dead if the government backs it. Dead's dead. A man needs a reason to pop a cap. In Nam, it was getting out alive. What I'm hearing you say is there's five grand for me in this deal. That would be a reason. I hear you talking money, but I ain't seen any. So I ain't got no reason at this point."

Quinlin grinned and nudged Paul McCarren in the front seat of the Dodge pickup, pointing at the recorder.

"Clay's good," Quinlin said. "He's going for the money. We bundle up some cash with this tape, and even the feds will have to get off their asses."

"If they don't find our asses frozen in this parking lot," McCarren said. The thermometer above the windshield showed it was twenty-three degrees.

The transmission quality could have been better, but the conversation between Moore and Jerry Ray McCray inside the VFW hall fifty feet away was easily distinguishable, even though they were talking in hushed tones.

"You'll see some money," McCray said. "Money ain't no problem in this deal. The people I work for, five grand's chump change. I'm just wantin' to make sure that the dude watchin' my ass has the stones to pull the trigger."

"That's something all the talking in the world ain't gonna answer," Moore said. "You ain't ever gonna know for sure until the time comes. You do some checking around, you'll hear I'm standup. I don't walk away from nothing."

The sound of ice cubes tinkling against glass came through the transmitter.

"God damn it," McCarren said, "just tell him what he wants to hear."

"He's cool," Quinlin said. "That's why McCray trusts him. Clay's not a bullshitter."

"So, tell me, this deal just me and you?" Moore resumed.

"Oh, hell no," McCray said, laughing. "We gonna be surrounded by all the law enforcement in Sul Ross County. Really. That's the beauty. Most of 'em won't have a clue in hell what's going down in front of them, but they'll make sure no real *police* show up without us knowin' it."

"Guess I'm not reading you," Moore said. "We *want* cops there?"

"See, we're gonna be getting two trailer loads of, uh, product, you know, in two or three days," McCray said. "Hear what I'm sayin'? The cops at the gate ain't gonna know what's in the trailers, see? I mean, there'll be some—the sheriff, the Ranger—who'll know what's happening, right, but the rest are just gonna let the trucks through and stop anybody that tries to come in after them. That way, see, all we got to worry about is the bad guys."

"You mean the dudes bringing the stuff?"

"Right, the meskins. See, I used to work for them before, down on the border. And El Gato, the main man, he's a sorry muthafucker. I've seen him rip off people before. Been part of it, in fact. Now on this deal, there's gonna be about ten million in cash in the barn. And that kinda cash makes people nervous and crazy. Our job is to make sure his meskins don't leave with the money *and* the dope. See what I'm sayin'? A rip-off."

"What kind of dope?"

"Let's just call it product. Does it really make a shit? It could be ten million in ball bearings, for all you need to know. My job, *our* job, is just to make sure the product changes hands and our guys don't get fucked. Makes a shit what it is, know what I mean? It could be ass wipe. Deal is, we don't trust these fucks."

"Am I looking to you or 'our guys' to pay me? That's all I need to know. 'Cause I don't plan on leaving empty-handed."

"I'm gonna take care of you on the front end tonight," McCray said. "When the deal goes down, you'll get the other half. And know this. You have to grease somebody, there'll be a bonus. I fuckin' guarantee you that."

"So what do I do, specifically?" Moore asked, deliberately sounding confused. He was remembering the checklist Quinlin had given him—get McCray to commit on money, time, dope, any details about the plan. "I mean, where and when do I show up? Do I bring my own piece? I mean, I don't want to screw this deal out of ignorance."

"Plenty of time for that, stud," McCray said. "The deal was s'posed to go down tomorrow night, but it's been backed off forty-eight hours on the Mexico end."

Quinlin breathed a sigh of relief in the cab of the Dodge. The deal was moving like an avalanche, and he needed another day to negotiate with the feds, who didn't exactly turn on a dime.

"Here, take these," McCray was saying. "Don't leave home without 'em."

"Beepers?"

"Yeah. One's a backup. When they go off, you got exactly thirty minutes to get into town and meet me on the square. You'll leave your pickup and go with me. I'll give you the final details on the way to the ranch."

"What ranch?"

McCray laughed. "You ask too many questions, hoss. 'Fraid you're gonna miss out on some action? Calm down. I already told you more than I was s'posed to."

In the truck outside, the two detectives cursed.

"Kill that drink," McCray said. "I got some stuff in the truck that'll make you real happy. Meet you at the door. Got to drain my lizard."

The transmitter was silent for fifteen seconds; then Clay Moore's voice came through loud and clear. "Y'all hear that? We're getting ready to go outside. Time to get small."

Quinlin surveyed the parking lot. There were twelve pickup trucks, not counting his own, and the only light came from the entrance to the VFW hall. McCray's Chevy was parked in front, near the corner of the building. Quinlin's Dodge was in front, on the other side of the lot, backed in between a couple of Fords.

"Looks like some money's going to change hands," McCarren said. "Nice."

"Real nice," Quinlin said. "We've got the dirtball saying dope on the tape, he ID's the Mexican connect, and looks like he's about to pass on some money. Still wish we had more specifics, but, hey, ol' Clay's going gangbusters. The dude's got cantaloupes for balls."

"Your friend's scary," McCarren said. "I'm not real sure he's acting."

"He is scary," Quinlin said. "That's why McCray trusts him."

McCarren grabbed the 35-mm camera with telephoto lens and crouched beside the pickup, gently shutting the door so the dome light would go off.

"There's not much light over there," he said. "This isn't a gimme."

McCray and Moore stepped out the front door, McCray carrying a bottle of beer. They walked to the passenger side of McCray's pickup, and its owner scanned the parking lot. The interior lights came on when he opened the door.

McCarren was crouched between two pickups with the camera. He tried to maneuver around the bed of a pickup, then stopped when he heard the crackle of gravel beneath his feet. He would have to raise up and shoot over the bed.

"You're gonna hurt my feelings if you count that in front of me," McCray said, handing Moore a thick white sealed envelope from the truck's glove compartment. "You'll get the other half after the deal's done. Put it in your pocket. I want to show you something."

Quinlin grimaced at the sound of the shutter, but McCray never hesitated. He handed Moore his beer and then pulled the rear of the pickup seat forward. Reaching behind, he produced a rifle, repositioned the seat, and handed the weapon to Moore.

"What the hell is it?" Moore was loud and clear on the transmitter.

"It's a goddamned work of art is what it is," McCray said. "This here's a Russian Dragunov SVD. It's a genuine by God sniper rifle. You gonna love it, if you know what I mean. These bad muthafuckers ain't that easy to come by. Tell you what it'll do. It'll blow a gnat's ass off at six hunnerd meters. Gottcha ten-round magazine and four spares there. There's two boxes of original Russki ammo there on the floorboard. You can spend tomorrow sightin' it in and gettin' used to it."

Moore bounced the black rifle in both palms. It was light—less than ten pounds even with the NSP-3 nightscope—with a twenty-four inch barrel and a detachable box magazine. He put it to his shoulder, looked through the scope, and panned the parking lot. At the opposite end, he saw Quinlin's partner duck his head beneath a pickup, and he grinned.

"Looks pretty decent," Moore said, taking the rifle off his shoulder. He ran his thumb back and forth over the bridge of the rifle where the serial number had once been; the numbers had been melted with an acetylene torch.

"Just a little safety precaution"—McCray grinned smugly—"in case you have to drop the damned thing in a hurry. Don't want nuthin' coming back to bite us in the ass, know what I mean?"

Moore put the sling over his right shoulder and grabbed the boxes of ammo off the floorboard.

"So beep me when you're ready," he said. "I'll be there."

"Just one small deal I hate to bring up," McCray said, grabbing Moore by the shoulder, "but something's got to be said. I trust you or you wouldn't be here. That's a damned fact. You're the real deal, I know that. But lookee here. People that's tried to fuck over me in the past, well now, they're all dead and stinkin' under a bunch of weeds and cow shit. Just so you know where I'm comin' from, hoss. Know what I'm sayin' here?"

Moore shrugged off McCray's hand.

"Understand me," Moore said. "Don't ever touch me again. That's the main thing. The other thing is this. People who like to listen to themselves talk bother me. Particularly when they're talkin' shit. When I tell a man I'll do somethin', I'll get it done. You talkin' shit don't affect me one way or the other, 'cept I don't appreciate it. You beep, I'll be there. Period. Just don't fuck with me."

Clay Moore, the rifle slung over his shoulder and his arms loaded with ammunition, turned his back on McCray and headed across the lot.

"Hey, man," McCray yelled. "No hard feelin's, right? Just bidness, you know? Hey, hoss."

The man in the camouflage jacket kept walking.

"Don't think I would confront that psycho, then turn my back on him," McCarren said, watching from the front seat of Quinlin's pickup.

"That, my friend, wasn't an act," Quinlin said. "And the best part is, McCray knows it wasn't an act."

33

Jeb Quinlin was preoccupied and in a hurry to get back to Dallas. He had to drop off McCarren at his car in the DPD parking lot and, according to a page and an insistent but brief, sketchy phone call from Clint Harper, meet the reporter no matter how late Quinlin got in. Quinlin knew there was no fat in the next few days. He still had to come up with a plan that would safeguard Rebecca Colter without running up warning flags with her husband. Catching Buck Colter, his brother, and father dirty in a dope deal, he knew, was his only hope of clearing the Richmond Carlisle case. He had to run down the evidence for his boss and then again for the feds. And he still had an hour's drive tonight from Dallas to Granbury before he could get some sleep.

He had to fight himself to keep the Dodge within the speed limit, catching himself several times doing eighty-five on the two-lane highway as it twisted its way through the foothills.

"So we just lay the tape and Rebecca's affidavit on the U.S. attorney's desk and walk away?" McCarren asked. "Sounds like our only shot. The feds ought to thank us."

"Yeah, right," Quinlin said. "Nothing's ever easy with the feds, but this is a slam—"

Quinlin instinctively lifted his foot off the accelerator and glanced at the speedometer, which was pegged at ninety. They were on the curve coming out of Chalk Mountain when on the right shoulder he saw the unmistakable reflection of his head-

lights in an animal's eyes. He veered into the oncoming lane, trying to straighten out the curve and cut his speed at the same
time, when the startled doe hurtled the hood. It was an amazing
leap, so close that he and McCarren flinched in their seats. Quinlin saw the deer's left-rear hoof in front of him, close enough
that he could have reached out and grabbed her had it not been
for the windshield.

When he was seventeen, he'd come up one night on a mangled
Ford pickup in a bar ditch beside a ranch road. It was back before
seat belts, air bags, and headrests were installed in cars, and through
the shattered windshield he saw a dead spike buck draped over the
driver. Prying open the driver's door, he saw the driver's head
lodged unnaturally against the back glass of the truck. The impact
of the deer had snapped the man's neck like a weathered twig.

By the time he dropped off McCarren and took the Knox-
Henderson exit off Central Expressway, it was after midnight. Clint
Harper was in a booth at the rear of Denny's, sipping coffee and
reading over a computer printout. Judging from the butts in the
ashtray, he'd been there awhile.

Harper was lower than a gutter drunk on Thunderbird. Garrett
Anderson Brewster, the same executive editor who had badgered
and threatened him for copy that would shed light on Richmond
Carlisle's murder, had summarily shit-canned his story on Clendon
Colter's insider land deal with a former president.

"That's a story that would run on the front page of every paper
in the country, regardless of Colter's involvement in drug smuggling," Harper said, lighting another cigarette. "A multimillionaire
Texas tycoon in bed with a former president to screw the taxpayers
out of millions on a needless federal project? Let me up, for Chris-
sakes."

"Gimme one of those, would you?" Quinlin asked. "So why's
Brewster getting cold feet?"

"Clendon Colter himself showed up, threatening to sue the shit
out of us if we ran anything else about him," the investigative
reporter said. "It was a bluff—the story's safe and based on public
record—but Brewster swallowed his balls. A high-profile lawsuit
wouldn't look good to the board of directors."

Caffeine and nicotine rejuvenated Quinlin, or maybe it was the excitement of telling Harper about the tape locked in his glove compartment that implicated the legendary Colters in an international drug-smuggling operation.

"Shiiit," Harper said. "So, like in a couple of days, you're gonna pop the bastards?"

The reporter's cynicism was gone, replaced by the scent of a bombshell story.

"It's not quite that easy," Quinlin said. "McCarren and I are meeting in the morning with Chief Abrams to outline the case. Then we're going to the U.S. attorney with the evidence. We're going to—"

"I wouldn't do that if I were you," Harper said. "The U.S. attorney's gonna shit on you and your case, and probably drop a dime on you with the Colters."

"What the fuck you talking about? We got—"

"It doesn't make a shit what you got, Jeb," Harper said. "You need to understand. The Honorable Ronald Stokes himself showed up with Colter's entourage at the paper. While Colter's talking about how he's not a suspect, never been a suspect, hates drugs and all that shit, the U.S. attorney is saying amen the whole time. Don't know what the deal is, but they're ace-boon-coon buddies."

Quinlin was shaking his head, shell-shocked. He sat silently in the booth and didn't notice the waitress refilling his cup. Finally, his mind returned to the table.

"Got any smokes left?" he asked.

Over the course of an hour the next morning, Deputy Chief Jon Abrams listened as Quinlin and McCarren outlined the case against Jerry Ray McCray and, by association, the Colters. Only occasionally did the chief of detectives interrupt to ask a question, though he frequently jotted notes on a legal pad. Quinlin studied the chief's expression as he listened to the recording of Moore and McCray, and the detective could tell his boss was impressed. And while the tape unfortunately was devoid of any direct mention of the Colters, Quinlin had shored up the family's culpability by using Charley

Blake's journal and a sworn affidavit from Rebecca Colter in which she detailed Sheriff Red O'Neal's visit with her husband and Buck's phone conversation, ostensibly with his father.

Jon Abrams's twenty-seven-year legacy to the Dallas Police Department was one of unquestioned integrity. He was tough but fair, and, by almost everyone's account, apolitical. Most importantly, in Quinlin's opinion, the chief of detectives was the smartest detective he'd ever known. As a young cop, Abrams had spent enough time on the bricks to be street-smart, and he had combined that savvy with what Quinlin suspected was a near-genius IQ. He was tall and, at fifty-four, taut and tough from jogging six miles before showing up at work by 7:00 A.M. every day.

"Let me say this, gentlemen," the chief said. "What I've seen here this morning is some extraordinary police work in the face of some very extenuating circumstances, and, of course, I'm referring to the political influence and public corruption in Sul Ross County. What your investigation accomplishes, it seems to me, is abundant probable cause, certainly enough for the federal people to get subpoenas, warrants, and maybe even a Title Three wire-tap order for a RICO investigation."

Quinlin had seen the case as a RICO investigation almost from the beginning. The RICO Act gave police broad discretion in using individual crimes, from drug smuggling and money laundering to extortion and murder, to establish a single ongoing criminal enterprise that carried mandatory life sentences.

"Of course, RICO investigations are exhaustive and time-consuming," the chief said, "and that's a luxury we don't have, not with this drug deal going down imminently. We'll turn over the investigation to the U.S. attorney, with his assurance, of course, that we'll be actively involved throughout."

"That's the rub I referred to earlier, Chief," Quinlin said.

The senior homicide detective then related Harper's story of U.S. Attorney Ronald Stokes speaking in Clendon Colter's behalf during the meeting at the *Register & News*.

Jon Abrams's brow furrowed as he listened, and Quinlin could tell the chief of detectives was angry.

"The U.S. attorney goes out of his way to involve himself in a civil situation?" the chief asked incredulously. "Why? I've never heard of that. I don't know why, but he's obviously overstepped the bounds of propriety. We present him with this evidence, he's going to have a conflict of interest, not that he hadn't previously. And worst case, he's looking at obstruction of justice."

The chief's office was silent as Abrams moved to a window and peered down three stories to Harwood Street.

"We could cast our lot with Aransas County and work McCray on the murders of Bettman and the bank courier," Abrams said, still looking out the window. "If the evidence is there on Bettman, we could work backward to get us to the Carlisle case. Under threat of the death penalty, McCray might give us the Colters."

"I don't think that's likely, Chief," Quinlin said. He explained Zita Morales's pair of cases in Laredo in which McCray had refused immunity and taken the sentences instead.

"Just trying to contrive a way that we could avoid federal involvement," Abrams said. "Or what about a different federal involvement?"

"I'm not following you, Chief," McCarren said.

"Stokes is in charge of the Northern District of Texas," Abrams said. "McCray says on the tape that the drugs are coming from Mexico, and he further states there're two truckloads. They have to get across the border some way. And the border, depending on which part, is either the Southern District or the Western District of Texas. Maybe we could take our information to the border and take the load down there."

"We don't have that much time," Quinlin said, "and besides, we catch them in Comanche Gap, we catch them on the Colters' ranch and we catch the Colters red-handed. *If*, in fact, the drop is on Pan Permian Ranch, like we think it is.

"As strong as the Colters are, I'm afraid that if we don't catch them dirty, we'll never make a case," Quinlin said. "A circumstantial case against these guys ain't gonna get the job done."

"Are we sure we can't just turn over our evidence directly to the FBI without them having to call in the U.S. attorney?" McCarren asked. "If they made the bust, Stokes would have to prosecute the Colters, whether he wanted to or not."

"That's not the way the federal system works," Chief Abrams said, "at least not on this level. With this kind of dope, this amount of money, and the political stroke of these suspects, no agent in charge is going to risk his career without getting the U.S. attorney's thumbprint up front. It'd be suicide."

The room fell silent again as the men immersed themselves in alternatives. Quinlin felt the frustration building.

"We can't just let them pull this off because of politics and bullshit," he blurted after several minutes. "I mean, my god, two truckloads of dope, multimillions of dollars, probably enough guns to arm a banana republic—we'd be negligent as hell if we let this happen. Not to men—"

"Hold on, Jeb," Chief Abrams said. "No one's suggesting a free pass. This is just a delicate situation, that's all. There's a solution; we just haven't stumbled onto it yet."

The chief picked up his phone and punched the intercom button. Within moments, he was asking the police department's liaison attorney with the DA's Office to research the law on jurisdiction.

"Specifically, I want to know the legal precedent, if any, for a local police officer to effect arrests outside his normally constituted jurisdiction," the chief said. "For example, a Dallas officer's ability to make arrests in, say, Corpus Christi. And I need to know soonest."

The chief looked at Quinlin. "You've got things to do. I'll find you when the attorney gets back to me."

"As a courtesy, I've got an obligation to brief a couple of FBI agents on our information," Quinlin said. "You have a problem with that?"

"Which ones are you talking to over there?"

"A young agent named David Cartwright. He's the one I mentioned earlier, the guy who leaked the aborted Public Integrity information to Richmond Carlisle. He's a decent kid who just fuc—uh, screwed up, Chief. The other guy is Roger Wilmon."

"You know Wilmon?"

"Yes, sir," Quinlin said, noticing a reaction from the chief. "He's an old acquaintance, more personal than professional. No direct knowledge of the case, but . . ."

"Roger Wilmon's a good man," the chief said. "We've worked together in the past. I trust him. Give him my regards."

"Stokes isn't corrupt. He's lightweight and stupid. He was a faceless pissant civil lawyer with a high-dollar downtown firm who happened to attend the right dinner parties and contribute to the right party. He's walking proof why U.S. attorneys shouldn't be politically appointed."

Special Agent Roger Wilmon didn't mince words. It was one of the reasons Jeb Quinlin liked him. That and the fact that the former Green Beret lieutenant would walk barefoot through broken glass to make a case, any case. The senior agent's reaction to Quinlin's rundown on the Colters appeared to surprise David Cartwright, who looked around the FBI coffee room to make sure no one was within earshot.

"So, what's going to happen here, bottom line?" Wilmon asked.

"Don't know yet," Quinlin said. "Abrams and I are meeting later, but it doesn't look good to me. Abrams is a stand-up cop. He'll do whatever he can, but we just don't have a lot of alternatives. We're local yokels. You can piss farther than our jurisdiction goes. DPS has a dog in the fight, so they're out. Stokes has some kind of tie to Colter, so you guys are out."

"Now ain't that a pisser?" Wilmon said. "Supposedly one of the top law-enforcement agencies in the world, and we're sitting here pulling our puds because the top federal prosecutor is some kind of numbnuts."

"What pisses me off is that Colter is so politically stout that he's gridlocked the whole fuckin' justice system," Quinlin said. "Throw some money here, throw some there, do a favor here, scratch somebody's ass there, and the arrogant son of a bitch becomes bulletproof."

The detective pushed a photostatic copy of Charley Blake's journal and a cassette copy of the McCray tape across the table to the two agents.

"Don't ever say DPD sandbagged you on this deal," the detective said. "Just wanted you to know up front what we had. Not that it makes a flyin' fuck of difference."

• • •

The heavyset man in snakeskin boots pulled to the back of the ranch house and retrieved a crowbar from the floorboard. There hadn't been any cars in front, and he scanned the back and the barn, but he didn't see any there, either. He wedged the flat end of the crowbar between the door and the jamb, just above the lock, and shoved his weight behind the handle. The wood splintered and the door popped like a .22 shot.

The house was musty, and there was a chill in the air. The refrigerator was empty and turned off. A fine coat of dust layered the flat surfaces of the cabinets, the kitchen table, and the coffee table. The trash can beneath the kitchen sink had a fresh white plastic bag, but it was empty. The edge of a yellowed envelope stuck out from a cushion in the couch. It was an insurance company statement addressed to Charley Blake and dated May 28, 1993. He checked every closet in the house but didn't find any clothes. He picked up the phone, but there was no dial tone. When he turned on a water faucet in the master bathroom, all he got was a gurgle.

Jerry Ray McCray made his way back to his pickup and reached in for the cell phone.

"Yo, it's me," he said momentarily. "Ain't nobody been here in months, maybe years. Know what I mean? I done looked around town and—"

"Keep looking. You find her and haul her ass back here *now*. No telling what she's doing, but her timing's piss-poor. You find her, hear me?" The man had a cold, no-bullshit voice.

"I'm not exactly sure just what it is I'm s'posed to do when I find her. I figure she's not gonna want me to drag her home. I mean, she's your wife and all. Do you really want me to—"

"You do whatever the hell you need to do. She can't be running her head to anybody, not now. If you need to knock her ass around, get it done. Whatever it takes. There's too much stuff going on right now to be fuckin' around. You understand me?"

McCray pitched the phone in the passenger's seat. Buck Colter, he figured, must have finally rented some balls.

• • •

McCoy v. Sullivan, according to the Texas Court of Criminal Appeals, upheld the night of the then Fort Bend County sheriff, Ben Sullivan' to go to San Augustine County, 150 miles to the north, to arrest a white man accused of killing two blacks. It was the most definitive Texas precedent in determining the jurisdictional bounds of a local police officer.

"There're several cases addressing 'hot pursuit' arrests," Chief Abrams said, "but *McCoy v. Sullivan* is the only case that directly addresses our situation. That should be good news. Except for the fact that the case occurred one hundred and twenty-seven years ago."

The case was rooted in Reconstruction Texas in May 1868. Sheriff Sullivan who'd been a Union sympathizer, had an arrest warrant for Willard Brockman, a former Confederate soldier who had stabbed and killed two former slaves in Fort Bend County. When Sullivan presented the warrants to San Augustine's Sheriff Micah McCoy, once a captain in the Confederate army, McCoy refused to arrest his former compatriot. Sullivan waited until nightfall, burst into Brockman's cabin, and spirited him away to Fort Bend County, where he was tried and hanged for murder.

Chief Abrams handed Quinlin a copy of the appeals court's opinion, one paragraph of which he'd highlighted in yellow:

> A duly commissioned peace officer from any locale has a lawful responsibility to effectuate an arrest even when authorities with local jurisdiction or more direct control refuse or otherwise abrogate their lawful responsibilities for whatever reason. To allow laws to go unenforced due to deliberate negligence or professional incompetence would interfere with citizens' rights to enjoy fair and equal application of laws and thereby create chaos and dangerousness among the constituency.

"Our lawyer says he'd hate to have to defend us on a onetime precedent that's over a century old," Abrams said.

The chief of detectives had also briefed the DA on the details of Quinlin's case.

"His attitude, frankly, was, 'Why rollerskate in a buffalo herd if you don't have to?'" the chief said. "Carlisle's homicide is our nexus, of course, but the DA thinks we're holding on by the thinnest of threads. Or, as he put it, 'We need to run backward from this one.'"

"So just throw Carlisle's homicide in the air and walk off?"

"Tell you what I'll do," Abrams said, dropping the tone of his voice. "This case angers me as much as it does you. I'm going to give you the widest latitude possible. You can take a couple more weeks and see what you can put together."

"Chief, I've got an idea," Quinlin said. "It's rough and, to be honest, flaky as hell, but it's something that might work. I'd like—"

"Like I said, Jeb," the chief said, a small smile appearing at the corners of his mouth, "you have the widest latitude possible. You're a resourceful, dedicated detective. I don't have to know the smallest details.

"Good luck."

Quinlin looked at his watch as he dialed information for the 512 area. It was 4:00 P.M., and he still had to meet with Rebecca Colter. He was already fifteen minutes late, but the Hyatt Regency was on the western edge of downtown, only about three minutes from headquarters. She knew not to leave without talking to him.

There were two listings in Austin for Will Stephens, a home number and a business phone at the airport. Quinlin took both. Knowing his old buddy flew a traffic helicopter for a radio station, he opted for the work number, hoping he could catch Stephens before he went airborne for rush hour. A receptionist answered the phone. Stephens was still on the heliport, running up the engine on the Jet Ranger; she patched Quinlin through to the cockpit.

"You sound like you're in a washing machine," Quinlin said. "Can you hear me? This is Jeb Quinlin."

There were pleasantries, but the sound of the whirring rotor forced both of them to yell.

"Tell you what," Quinlin said. "Can you call me tonight? I got a hell of a proposition for you."

"What kind of proposition?"

"I need you and your helicopter," Quinlin yelled. "It's a long, sad story. I'll brief you tonight. Bottom line is this, though: It's a chance to prove you're still a red-white-and-blue American. Oh, yeah, almost forgot. Did I mention I can't pay you and there's a remote possibility you might get shot at? So, sound like something you'd be interested in?"

Quinlin could hear the rpm increasing in the rotor, making it even tougher to hear.

"Either this line is truly fucked up," Stephens yelled, "or you been hitting the bottle again. Yeah, sure, I can't wait to get shot at. Something I miss every day. I'll check you tonight."

McCarren was fidgeting beside Quinlin's desk, biding time until his partner got off the phone. The young cop was animated and grinning, and he jumped in as soon as Quinlin hung up.

"I know you're busy, Jeb, but you got to see this. It's worth a week's pay, better than a blow job."

McCarren led Quinlin down the corridor toward the interview rooms. "Bumpy was way too busy to meet our guy Skate so we could catch him on the wire," McCarren said. "We had to set him up on the phone. So Bumpy's wanting off the phone real bad, and finally he says the magic words. Three uniforms and I go out to his house to pop him."

McCarren steered Quinlin to the one-way glass outside Interview Room 1. "Take a look," he said.

Bumpy Rhodes was sitting in a chair with his hands cuffed behind him. The fat bail bondsman was naked except for a pair of DPD prisoner-issue, badly overburdened Fruit of the Looms.

"What's that red shit all over him? That can't be blood or he'd be at Parkland."

"Marinara sauce"—McCarren grinned—"with just a hint of garlic and a touch of oregano, judging from the smell. I can't wait to talk to the grand jury. This is gonna be priceless."

McCarren and one patrolman had gone through the front of Bumpy's house, the other two cops through the back. They heard moaning and followed the sound to the master bathroom.

"This fat bastard's laying in the tub with a hard-on, a real diamond cutter, and some naked dirtyleg is on top of him, swabbing him down with marinara and linguini," McCarren said. "I shit you not. Well, we' trying to get them outta the tub—he's just laying there now all docile like an egg-suckin' dog, 'cept he ain't got no purple throbber anymore—and she's as big as he is, and she's got one of the patrol guys down between 'em, punchin' the shit outta him."

For the first time, Quinlin noticed his partner's shirt and pants. He looked like he'd been the loser in a paint-flinging fight.

"Pretty soon, the other cop's in the tub, and I'm on the side, tryin' to pull the bitch off all of 'em," McCarren said, breaking himself up with his own story.

"Anyhow, we don't get the full import of what's been going on until we get them up and separated. Falina has stuffed his fuckin' nose and ears with linguini."

"What kind of prevert is—"

"Oh, we're not finished yet. Well, one of the guys and I have Falina facedown on the floor—not a pretty sight, I assure you—and ol' Bumpy's snortin' and shakin', trying to clear his head of this shit. See, now he's nervous and understandably embarrassed and, all of a sudden, this fat fuck breaks wind. . . ."

"Oh, gawd."

"Shooting linguini all over the poor bastard trying to cuff 'im."

34

Rebecca Colter saw the gate guard go for the phone as soon as she drove through the cattle guard. Sure enough, Buck was pacing in the driveway and appeared at the driver's door of the Suburban before she could kill the engine.

"You want to explain where the fuck you've been?" he said. His face was redder than usual, and this time she knew it was more than the booze. "Goddamn it, you can't just fuckin' leave without sayin' something to somebody. I've had people out lookin' for you."

As casually as she could, Rebecca motioned toward the back of the Suburban. The third seat had been laid down, and the cargo compartment was loaded with boxes and shopping bags that bore logos from Neiman-Marcus, Foleys, Best Buy, and the Container Store.

"Dallas," she said simply. "I hate it when we argue. I needed to get away for a while. I spent the night in a nice hotel, had a massage and a makeover. And I, uh, went on a little binge with the credit cards. I feel better now. You want to give me a hand, or do we have to pick up the misery where we left it?"

Rebecca moved quickly to the rear of the Suburban and opened the doors. She stared impatiently at Buck Colter, who was still where she'd left him, speechless. "Well?" she said.

He got his second wind as he approached. "So this is it?" he asked as she loaded his arms with boxes and bags. "You fuckin' went shoppin' because you're pissed? Gaawd damn. And what'd you do with Chad?"

"He's with Mickey and his folks. I didn't want him to hear all the animosity and arguing. It's no big deal. We'll fly him back in a couple of days. He's in honors everything. He's not getting behind. He could use the vacation."

"This beats the shit outta me."

It was working. All she had to do, she reminded herself, was stay calm. Be casual. He was behind her, headed into the house.

"I'm better now," she said. "By the way, you've been moaning about the TV in the den. The Cowboys play the Redskins—when is it, next weekend? Well, you'll be watching the game on a new sixty-inch projection TV. It's going to be delivered.

"I know, I know," she said, extending her arm toward Buck, palm out. "I'll cut down. But sometimes you really make me crazy, the drinking and yelling. I really will cut down. But I needed to be away from you for a while."

"It's not the damned money," he said. "Just don't vanish like that again."

"If you'll help, we can get all the stuff in a couple more trips."

Her husband turned and left the room, still shaking his head. Rebecca Colter leaned both hands on the table, closed her eyes, and took a slow, deep breath. She prayed he hadn't seen the tremble in her hands.

Taking another deep breath, she checked the empty doorway and reached her right hand inside her bra, relieved that the spare ignition key was still pinned there. She had checked beneath the dash shortly after driving through the gate. The cell phone and walkie-talkie were still where Jeb had taped them.

Now all she had to do was wait.

Madeline leaned over the table and kissed Coal Tar squarely on his shaved head, eliciting a gutteral, embarrassed moan from the hulking black man.

"You know I was just teasing, don't you?" she said, laughing.

"What the hell I'm s'posed to think, you tellin' me my place looks like Mu'ammar Gadhafi's army trained there?" Winston Robishawn said, checking out the restaurant to see if anyone had witnessed his ordeal. "Shit, man, least you ain't living with no rattlesnakes no more."

"I take it there's a difference in housekeeping between millionairesses and bachelors?" Quinlin asked. "Couple of days, and she's already at your throat over the health code. I think she's telling you something here, Coal Tar."

"My *friends* call me Winston, pretty much 'cause that's my goddamned name, see?" the big man said. "You the onliest two I know who calls me Coal Tar."

"It's 'cause we love you more, man," Quinlin said.

"Uh-huh, I heard that."

The waitress appeared at their booth, carrying a tray that'd give Jesse Ventura a hernia. She balanced it on the edge of the table and began shoving the plates in front of Coal Tar, with him quickly rearranging them to give her more room—a huge rack of barbecued pork ribs, individual dishes of potato salad, coleslaw, collard greens, fried okra, and black-eyed peas, four rolls, and a plate piled high with sliced purple onion, jalapeño peppers, and homemade bread-and-butter pickles.

A man in a barbecue-stained white apron showed up behind the waitress with Quinlin and Madeline's tray. When the waitress had served them, she asked if they needed anything else.

Coal Tar, his forehead furrowed, had inventoried his order and was obviously disappointed. "Didn't you forget somethin' here?" he asked.

"Nawsir, I sure didn't," she retorted smartly. "I know you got a half a pound a sliced beef coming, but I didn't have no room to bring it."

She scanned the food in front of him haughtily, then added, "I 'spect you ain't gonna starve before I get back here with it."

"You eat here often?" Quinlin asked, grinning.

"Her brother runs the place, and they're both sour folks. But they know some stuff about barbecuin'. See, you white folks think you got to use mesquite. That ain't right, man. This here is real East Texas pit barbecue. Hardwoods, that's the deal, and you got to use a pit, not no cheap-ass metal barrel, and let 'em smoke all day long. See what I mean? You don't chew these ribs. They melt in your mouth, see?"

He ran a meaty rib through his mouth and produced a bare bone. "And see here now," he said, licking his lips, "I don't like to stereotype, but you white folks, you use too much tomato, see? You got to throw in some honey in the sauce and just a dab of vinegar. That sets it off."

Professionally, Winston Robishawn, aka Coal Tar, was an alcohol rehabilitation technician, and Quinlin and Madeline had made his acquaintance a year earlier when they committed themselves to the drunk ward at Cedar Ridge Hospital. Personally, the way Coal Tar put it, time and circumstance had made him and Quinlin "tight."

"Tight" meant they met at least twice a week to accomplish the two biggest goals in Coal Tar's life—eating and watching Monday-night football. In his previous incarnation, Coal Tar had been a third-round draft choice by the Cowboys out of Texas Southern University. Before he blew out his knee, he started four games as defensive tackle. Rehabilitation, he claimed, killed his career. While he acknowledged having dabbled occasionally in cocaine and booze back in those days, his biggest setback came at the table. When the six-foot-six Robishawn reported for training camp in Wichita Falls, he slammed the scales at 335 pounds—fifty pounds over his playing weight. He was waived the same day.

"Say, man," Coal Tar said to Quinlin, "I appreciate you talkin' to my class the other night. Won me some points with my thesis counselor."

The stack of ribs was picked clean beside his plate. He had moved on to the sliced brisket and vegetables and rolls.

"She's a honey, did ya notice?" Coal Tar asked.

"A real racehorse, not your typical Ph.D. pointy-head social worker."

"Hey, what, I'm not here?" Madeline asked in mock indignation.

"So when you finish your thesis, what you going to do?" Quinlin asked. "Still thinking alcohol counseling?"

"Not really," the big man said, sopping barbecue sauce with his roll. "I been thinkin' something kinda close to what you do. Thinkin' about being a PO. You know, parole officer."

"I can see it," Quinlin said. "That'd work."

"What I see is a walking case of excessive force here," Madeline said.

"Naw," Coal Tar said. "I ain't gonna touch nobody. Just convince 'em verbally—you know, give 'em a little talking-to."

Quinlin spotted Madeline's hand on the table and laid his on top. They'd both been finished with dinner for several minutes and were watching Coal Tar across the booth.

"I've missed you," he said quietly, squeezing her hand. "This case'll be history in a couple of days and we can go back to being laid-back ranchers. I got some vacation time coming. How about you teaching me to ski in Aspen or Vail or someplace like that?"

"You can't walk and chew gum, Jeb Quinlin. You'd come back in plaster of paris or in a box."

In the parking lot, Madeline tried again to get Quinlin to spend the night at Coal Tar's.

"Can't," he said lightly. "I've got people to see, places to go. Got to get a plan down for tomorrow."

He opened the passenger door, squeezed Madeline tightly, and kissed her neck, then helped her in. He walked to the other side of the car and waited until Coal Tar had started the engine, making a motion for him to roll the window down.

"You put up with her another coupla days?"

"If she'll keep her damned mouth shut about my housekeepin'. Maybe."

"You've been a good friend," Quinlin said, offering his hand through the window. "You do me one more big one?"

"Cost you another supper."

"Fair enough. My deal's about to go down. When I get this shit behind me, you figure you could find time to be my best man?"

Coal Tar grinned through the window, and Quinlin motioned him to leave.

"What?" Madeline asked, craning around the huge man behind the wheel. "What'd you just say? Did you say—"

Coal Tar put Madeline's BMW in gear and started rolling off, leaving Quinlin grinning in the parking lot.

"God damn it," she said, bending in the passenger seat to look at Coal Tar. "What'd he *say*?"

The BMW was rolling faster now.

"Jeb Quinlin, you're a bastard!" Madeline screamed, catching a final glimpse of him through the back glass.

"Be careful, butthole. I love you! Please be—"

Coal Tar was in the den, casting disinterestedly from ESPN to ESPN2, munching nacho-flavored tortilla chips and chasing them with a two-liter bottle of Dr Pepper. Madeline knew sleep wasn't going to come easily, and she was too preoccupied to keep her mind on the latest Michael Connelly novel or the small black-and-white portable in Coal Tar's spare bedroom.

If she put off the wedding to spring, they could get married outdoors at the Dallas Arboretum, one of her favorite spots. On the other hand, Thanksgiving wasn't far off and, God knew, she had plenty to be thankful for. The symbolism felt right. Not to mention grabbing Jeb before he got elusively paranoid again. But would Christine Beckley, her old dorm buddy and best friend from SMU, be out of town for the holidays? Madeline chuckled out loud at the mental image of Coal Tar holding the rings at the altar, standing next to Christine Beckley, a five-foot, hundred-pound Nordic blonde from old-line Highland Park money.

The ten o'clock news was about to go off on the black-and-white, and Madeline automatically thought of Quinlin. The sign-off of the local newscast was his favorite, a campy time he called the "Moron Minute," and it had become a ritual for them to watch it together. The final film clips were totally irrelevant, cutesy, and meaningless, but they provided anchors Chip and Heather their segue into happy talk and gave them the contrived opportunity to chuckle or shake their heads in amazement. Quinlin's personal favorites, delivered with the anchor's phony, dramatic inflection, were the stories about a woman who spent two years in the top of a redwood to keep a lumber company from sawing it down, the trained-killer Doberman watchdog who nursed an orphaned kitten, and the quacking "hero" duck who alerted a man to a prowler in his backyard.

Madeline looked up from her book to catch the lead-in: "Waymon Pritchett, an admittedly *novice* hunter, bagged a *bigger* catch in his first deer season than most die-hard stalkers claim in a *lifetime.*" The screen flashed to a short, fat guy with rimless glasses, clad head-to-toe in Rambo green-and-black camouflage and proudly cradling a rifle across his arm like a Colombian guerrilla. "Pritchett, a Dallas insurance claims adjuster hunting near Granbury, bagged a *sixteen-point* buck that field-dressed at an amazing *one hundred sixty-two* pounds. And while that certainly qualifies the rookie hunter for a *trophy* shot, Pritchett will go into hunting *record* books for killing a solid *white* buck." The film shifted to the grinning hunter straddling a white buck and holding its head up by its rack. "Authorities for the Texas Fish and Wildlife Commission say they've *never* seen a solid white white-tail deer in Hood County."

The book fell from Madeline's lap.

"White Deer!" she whispered. "Damn."

She was swept with sadness. She tried to visualize Jeb, by himself in the pickup, somewhere on the highway in the dark. Alone.

35

Even after forty-four years, Quinlin never ceased to amaze himself. He looked at his watch and saw he was thirty-five minutes early. He had accepted long ago that he was type A, but it still depressed him to know that his compulsiveness irrevocably bound him to the hands of a clock. Over four decades, the thirty- and forty-five-minute blocks of idle time amounted to—what, maybe a month or three months of lost time?

The main terminal at Love Field was thinning out from prime-time arrivals and departures, but at 6:30 P.M., the lanky detective still had to dodge business travelers dragging suitcases and briefcases on wheels behind them. Quinlin hated the wheeled carriers. One ditz, apparently a lawyer, rolled two file boxes across Quinlin's right boot, a relatively new Lucchese smooth ostrich, leaving a furrow like a corn row. Quinlin cursed, but the lawyer was clueless.

Quinlin checked the monitor; the flight was on time to arrive at Gate 14. He headed for the coffee shop, pausing along the way to browse the headlines in the *New York Times*. He got coffee to go, checked his watch—only *thirty* minutes to go—and ambled toward Gate 14, taking a seat where he could watch passengers deplane.

Love Field was primarily a commuter airport now, used almost exclusively by Southwest Airlines for its intrastate routes and for flights to adjacent states. There were still concourses that hadn't been used in years, but before the D-FW Airport was built, Love Field had been north Texas's hub for the world.

The memory came from nowhere, while Quinlin was sipping coffee, and he looked around him to confirm his bearings. Small world; more than twenty-five years earlier, he had left Gate 14 on the first leg of a journey that would land him in Vietnam.

His orders to Vietnam had just about killed Geneva Quinlin. They were all each other had, and, bless her heart, she had been sick for days, convinced that her only son wouldn't be coming back. It was a common sight in the terminal, he recalled—crying mothers, wives, sisters, and girlfriends hugging sailors and soldiers, holding on to them until the last second, when they had to pass security to board the planes. Thank God he'd arrived on the Trailways bus with Clay and Will. That had been bad enough.

Quinlin remembered standing at the glass, staring down at the Boeing 707 that would take him to Treasure Island, the Navy's jumping-off point for Southeast Asia. He'd seen baggage handlers pull two aluminum caskets from the belly of the plane and heave them unceremoniously onto a small trailer. As the tractor took off, Quinlin had walked hurriedly along the glass walls of the concourse, following the caskets to an olive drab army panel truck parked on an apron. Two GIs in fatigues emerged from the truck, unloaded the bodies into the rear of the van, and drove off. There wasn't any playing of taps, and there weren't any solemn color guards like he'd seen on the six o'clock news, just a couple of baggage handlers and a couple of grunts who'd probably drawn short straws. It was, he had suspected, just another day in Vietnam, and halfway around the world, Dallas was getting back part of what it had sent.

Quinlin shook his head. A quarter of a century ago seemed like Monday. He was humming a song. It was something from Buffalo Springfield, but he couldn't remember the title:

There's somethin' happenin' here,
What it is ain't exactly clear.
There's a man with a gun over there
Tellin' me I got to beware.

He'd had to hurry to Gate 14 back then to catch his flight to San Francisco. As he hustled back down the terminal, he'd seen an

Air Canada flight boarding for Montreal. He was in dress blues and carrying his gear, but he walked up to the gate attendant and asked her if there were any seats left. Half the plane was open. He remembered standing there several seconds, looking at the attendant blankly. He was eighteen years old and had two minutes to make the most important decision of his life.

He'd pulled the seabag over his shoulder and run down the concourse. He hadn't gone to Nam for his country. He'd always known that. He went to Nam so he could see his mother again.

Paranoia strikes deep,
Into your life it will creep.

Will Stephens and Clay Moore had made the same trip, maybe even had the same doubts. It wasn't something they'd probably ever talk about, certainly not tonight. But was that why he trusted them so implicitly? Because they'd traveled the same paths, for whatever reasons, and battled the same demons?

Quinlin didn't hear the flight announced on the PA system, and when he looked up, she was standing in front of him, holding her bag.

"So where were you? You were looking straight through me. You're not all that great for a girl's ego, you know that?"

"Zita, you look wonderful."

"Thank you for letting me come," she said. "I think you know what this means to me."

She kissed him on the cheek. He took her bag and put his hand on her elbow, pointing her toward the parking lot.

"What do the shrinks call it?" he asked. "Closure? Well, let's see if we can't get you some."

Quinlin spotted Clint Harper's gray Bronco first, parked near the railing. Clay Moore's banged-up Chevy pickup was two cars down, backed in. Parked next to it was Paul McCarren's personal car, a red Miata convertible. He checked his watch: 8:30 P.M. Everyone was on time, if Will Stephens had landed on schedule and Clay had remembered to pick him up. There were just two other cars and four pickups in the parking lot of the Blue Armadillo, bearing out his prediction that they'd have the place almost to themselves. Big Sue had already herded everyone into the tiny back room.

"We'll get down to the basics after a while," Quinlin said, reaching into a brown paper bag. He produced a bottle of Dewar's Scotch, which he set in front of Zita, and a quart of Jack Daniel's, which he passed to Clay and Will.

"My apologies, Paul," he said. "Cowboy's Cut-Rate Liquor was fresh out of designer water. Clint, you and I will just breathe the fumes."

He gave them time to pour drinks, then raised his glass of tea.

"It occurred to me driving out here that the people around this table are the people I trust most in this world," Quinlin said. "That'll become increasingly obvious as you hear more about why you're here. And as you hear the bizarre details, any of you can cut and run at any point, no hard feelin's. Because I'm gonna tell you up front. This is one of the squirreliest deals I've ever been involved in.

"Beyond the trust I have in you, each one brings something special to this grandiose plan. At the risk of sounding corny, the best-case scenario gets justice done in a case in which there wouldn't be any justice. Worst-case scenario, well, that's another story. If this deal blows up in our faces, we'll either get hurt or be seeing each other at Leavenworth.

"Cheers."

The six dined on Truck's Armadillo Special—chicken-fried steak the size of catcher's mitts and a plateload of fries. Clay and Will were the only takers on Big Sue's coconut pie. After dinner, everyone followed Quinlin and Zita to Lobo Mesa, where everybody except Quinlin parked behind the barn.

Quinlin put on a pot of coffee, stuck the two extra leafs in the dining room table, and gathered everyone around. He found his checklist and went person by person around the table.

Harper produced two four-foot maps that he'd gotten at the Map and Plat section at the Sul Ross County Courthouse. Spliced together with tape, they detailed the layout of the forty thousand acres that comprised Pan Permian Headquarters Ranch.

"Did anyone give you any trouble?" Quinlin asked.

"Nope," the reporter said. "I just left the impression I was working for the Colters."

Moore had a sheaf of smaller maps from the U.S. Department of Agriculture's Agriculture Stabilization and Conservation Service. The government made topographical maps of all its erosion-prevention projects, and Clendon Colter, ever quick to tag the federal government for huge chunks of money, had availed himself of the ASCS's free services to environmentally conscious landowners. The smaller maps showed the layout and elevation of existing structures, runways, and every gravel road inside the ranch, along with the location of hills and arroyos.

"Remember Goose Moreland?" Moore asked. Quinlin had gone to school with Goose's younger brother. "Well, Goose runs the ASCS office. He didn't even ask me why I wanted them."

McCarren had already piled his contribution in a corner of Quinlin's den—six handheld walkie-talkies and Kevlar bullet-resistant vests checked out from DPD's Tactical Operations Division, and six sets of dull black cotton-rayon-blend pants and pullover shirts, six pairs of jungle boots, and six black pullover ski masks, all bought from an army-navy surplus store in Fort Worth.

"Everything's just the way we talked," McCarren said, "with one small exception."

The detective was looking at Zita. "The vest, shirt, and pants are going to be a little big," he said, grinning. "Apparently, most guys your height weigh about a hundred pounds more."

Quinlin could tell by his grin that Stephens was proud of himself. The pilot had shown up wearing a brown flight suit with Texas Air National Guard emblems and his name—Lt. Col. Will Stephens—embroidered over the right side of his chest.

"As a former E-5, I'm duly impressed, *Colonel* Stephens," Quinlin said. "Should we salute?"

"I may be the only person here on official duty," he said. "Kinda."

Stephens, like many helicopter pilots, had reverted to Reserve or National Guard status after Vietnam. It not only gave them a

chance to keep flying but it also contributed toward military retirement and gave them a monthly paycheck.

"There's a requirement that we've got to get thirty hours of training a quarter," Stephens said. "So I logged out a Huey for cross-
country training. You didn't really think I was gonna show up here
with the Jet Ranger? The bank still owns three-quarters of that son
of a bitch, and I figure the lien holder would be a little put out
knowing somebody might try to put a round through it."

He'd also checked out infrared night-vision goggles.

"So if ol' Clay here cuts cheese out there," Stephens said, "well,
that's going to cause some heat, and I'll see it."

"You'll smell it first, guarantee you," Moore said.

After the kidding died down, Quinlin produced a manila envelope, which he emptied onto the table.

"These," he said, "are photographs of the Colters' houses, the
hangar, and the main barn. They're some snapshots Rebecca Colter
took over the years, and she's written some specifics on the back.
She's a pretty cool lady, for those of you who haven't yet had the
pleasure. But at least these shots will give us a rough idea of the
way things look out there.

"And these," Quinlin said, passing photographs to Zita, "are the
stars of our show. The shot of McCray is obviously a book-in shot.
The shots of Clendon, Buck, and Wade are driver's license shots I
got from DPS. Same for Mervin 'Hoot' Gibson, our illustrious
Texas Ranger, and Red McNeal, Sul Ross County's finest. At this
point we don't have a clue how many people the Colters will have
at the scene or who they'll be. But if they're out recruiting people
like they did Clay, you can expect they'll have some extra bodies.

"We also don't have anything to look at on San Martín and his
guys, but from what McCray tells Clay, that set of bad guys will all
be Hispanic.

"Zita's been around these guys before," Quinlin said, "and she's
going to brief us later on McCray, specifically, and on the San Martín group in general."

"Man, this guy's a real cretin," Stephens said, looking at one of
the mug shots.

"Who's that, McCray?" Quinlin asked.

The pilot turned the photograph over. "No, apparently this is the fuckin' sheriff. He gives rednecks a bad image. Bet the sheep ain't safe around this ol' boy."

"Or anybody else," Quinlin said. "Okay, so we'll spend the next coupla hours getting the specifics down, we'll get a good night's sleep, and late tomorrow, based on the timeframe McCray has given Clay, we'll move everything to the airport in Comanche Gap.

"Anybody getting cold feet yet?"

"Oh, hell yes," Clay Moore said. "That's the kick, right?"

36

The grinding of metal on metal startled the young U.S. Customs agent, and he looked toward the Piedras Negras bridge and saw headlights. Half a thermos of coffee and walking around the booth in the fresh air wasn't working. Apparently, he still had dozed off, one of the several disadvantages associated with working the overnight in Eagle Pass. He could see through the glass at the terminal, and Sampson had his feet on the table, reading. At least he was awake.

The headlights were getting larger, and he could hear the groan of a straining engine and the metallic sound of a clutch about to go out. NAFTA may have been a boon for international relations and economies, but it also opened the gates to thousands of Mexican junkers that were unsafe at any speed. He was a probationary agent, but he'd already seen a fleet of Mexican trucks that he didn't want his wife and child meeting on any highway. But NAFTA guaranteed that Mexican truckers had carte blanche to hurtle down American roads at seventy miles an hour on bald tires, depending on slick brake drums to stop them.

The pair of trucks was fifty yards away when the agent got his first whiff. He cursed as he pushed the intercom button to the terminal. "Our lucky night, Sampson. We got two more loads of sun-dried beef, like last night." There was a corresponding curse from the other end.

The old Mexican in the first truck got out, handed the young customs agent a manifest, and began straining against the heavy tarp covering the trailer. The bill of lading was made out to Trans-Rio Grande Rendering Company in Quemado, just up the Rio Grande from Eagle Pass. Forty-thousand pounds, the bill said, of assorted beef, hog, and goat by-products. The rancid stench was unlike anything the agent had ever endured, and he got the full effect as he climbed up the side of the trailer. He was nauseous and he could feel the bile backing up in his throat as he shone the flashlight into the pile of animal parts. Quickly, he ran the light back toward the rear of the trailer, the beam taking in nothing but hooves, heads, internal organs, and intestines.

"That's enough," the agent managed in Spanish. The old driver was probably seventy, and he was relieved not to have to pull back the rest of the tarp.

Sampson was on the ground with his drug-sniffing dog, Nifty, who was pulling at his leash and whimpering to get back to the terminal.

"He wouldn't go near that shit last night," Sampson said, "and it ain't gonna be no different tonight. Let 'em roll."

The two customs agents stood in the middle of the international bridge as the first driver reattached his tarp and his counterpoint pulled in behind him.

"There can't be any money in cleaning up dead animals," the young agent said, taking a whiff of his shirt sleeve.

"Probably not a lot," the older one said, "which is why meskins do it. But where you think you get soap and leather?"

They inspected the bill of lading and waved the second truck through.

"Makes you wonder, doesn't it?" the young agent said. "That'd be a hell of a way to get dope through. How'd we ever know?"

"The goddamned dog won't even go near that shit," the veteran said. "They want it that bad, I say let 'em have it."

An hour later, the decrepit old trucks turned east off U.S. 83 onto a ranch road and into a field. Six men converged on each trailer, ripping off the tarp and shoveling three feet of animal parts off the top and rear, exposing two huge metal containers that resembled Dumpsters. A Caterpillar with a front-end attachment nosed in, lifted the containers, and moved them into the field where two Mexicans in hip waders used a portable high-pressure compressor to hose them down with water and disinfectant.

The dozer picked up one, then the other, moving them into refrigerated trailers already connected to idling Freightliner tractors, which bore the logo of Trans-Rio Grande Beef Packers, Inc. The metal vaults slid in beneath forequarters and hindquarters of beef already hanging from the ceiling. Once the metal boxes were shoved in the vans, a pickup backed up to the tailgates and three men hung more beef from ceiling hooks at the rear and stacked in cartons of chilled beef, concealing the ends of the metal vaults.

In precisely forty-three minutes, the two Freightliners pulled onto U.S. 83, hauling silver trailers with signs that read BEEF—IT'S WHAT'S FOR DINNER. They headed north, trailed by a black Land Rover with blacked-out windows.

Quinlin's hand reached for the phone, and he noticed the digital reading on the clock—6:25 A.M. Not that he'd been sleeping all that soundly anyway. Involuntarily, his mind manufactured questions, and he'd have to grope to make sure he had answers. It'd gone on all night.

The phone rang again before he could find the receiver.

"Jeb, sorry for the hour. It's Roger Wilmon. There's been some developments that you need to be aware of ASAP. The clock's running."

"No shit, Roger. That's why I was up all night. What do you mean, 'some developments'?"

"Well, I, uh, did something I've never done in nineteen years," the FBI agent said. "I went out of the chain of command. I made a phone call to Washington. We're in the game."

"How's this going—"

"Look, it's still all screwed up," Wilmon said. "We've got to lay a plan; that's the main thing. I got an FBI SWAT team on hold, and a Title Three wire-tap authorization, based on the tape recording and journal you gave us. But there's some, uh, frayed feelings and political fallout we've got to work around . . ."

"You gonna be heading this deal?" Quinlin asked.

"Oh, Lord no," Wilmon said. "This is way over my head. The boss is going to be on the ground, and Stokes, too. Washington didn't give him a choice."

Quinlin groaned. The whole operation was turning into a group grope.

"So how long will it take you to get to Dallas—an hour?"

"More like two," Quinlin said. "But it's gonna take a lot longer to unfuck this."

37

R ebecca Colter worried about how her only child would take the news that, in effect, she was selling out his father, opening him up to a lifetime in prison or, potentially, even getting him killed. But whatever biological allegiance the teenager had for his father apparently had long been eroded by Buck Colter's brutality, disinterest, and drunkenness.

Chad's flight was actually ten minutes early from San Antonio, and she was waiting on him at the Southwest terminal at Love Field when he deplaned at 4:55 P.M. She'd given him the plan then, studying his face for a reaction. She related everything Jeb had told her, even about the federal government probably seizing every asset they had—land, houses, bank accounts, cars, planes, everything. That's the way drug laws were. She also told him about Charley Blake leaving his ranch to them. In less than twenty-four hours, their lives would change dramatically. And there'd be the long-term stigma of living with what his father had done. It wasn't going to be easy.

Chad Colter was mentally tough for a sixteen-year-old. He listened quietly as they drove from the airport and turned south on I-35. When she had finished, his reaction brought tears to her eyes.

"I'm proud of you, Mom," he'd said, patting her shoulder as she drove. "I've known that Dad and Grandpa and Uncle Wade weren't doing everything right. I didn't know what, but I could tell something wasn't right. And Dad didn't treat us the way he should have, that's for sure. I thought a lot of times about, well, just leaving.

"Yeah, I know we have a lot of things, but they're not worth it, not the way things were going."

She could hear the enthusiasm when he talked about moving to Charley Blake's ranch. "Guess you and me'll be running our own place," he said. "We'll get by just fine, Mom. And we won't have anything to be ashamed of. We're doing the right thing."

Rebecca checked her watch. It was 6:25 P.M., well within the thirty-minute time frame Jeb had given her. She pulled the Suburban off U.S. 281 behind the abandoned general store. Night had settled in in earnest, and the moon was still too low to shed much light, but she saw movement behind the store. She felt her hands shaking, and she reassured Chad before she opened the door.

Two figures in black uniforms, their faces painted in nonglare black, appeared beside Rebecca.

"Good timing," one said cordially, "we were about to freeze. I'm Paul McCarren, with the Dallas Police Department, and this is Zita Morales, who's an assistant district attorney from Laredo."

The realization hit Rebecca Colter that she wasn't in control.

"We're Jeb's friends," McCarren said, reassuring her.

"Yeah, I know. I'm just not used to any of this, and I guess I'm scared to death."

"Your part's going to be over real soon," Zita said. "You're doing great."

Chad's bag was tucked behind the driver's seat, and the third set of seats in the Suburban was already collapsed. McCarren and Zita crawled in the back, and Rebecca pulled the accordion cargo cover over them, latched it, and closed the rear doors.

"You guys all right back there? Anything I can do?" asked Chad, wanting to play a role.

"We're fine," Zita yelled. "And you're already doing your part. You're our ticket in."

They barely had time to settle in, when they felt the Suburban slow, felt the left-hand turn, and heard the crunch of gravel.

"How are you, Mrs. Colter?" asked the gate guard.

"Great, Robert. How about you?"

"Have a nice night, ma'am." From the back, they could feel the acceleration.

"Any problem?" McCarren yelled.

"Don't think so," Rebecca said. "He seemed fine."

The Suburban drove exactly two miles down the gravel road and swerved to the side. Quickly, Rebecca threw open the door and ran to the back, letting McCarren and Zita out. The pair in black crept immediately into the shin oak beside the road. Rebecca spun gravel as she left.

"Two and Three," McCarren whispered into the walkie-talkie. "We're in big-time."

"And we're gonna freeze our asses off again," Zita said after McCarren put the phone back on his belt.

They walked a quarter of a mile from the road, dodging brush and cactus, then turned parallel to the road and continued walking. It was slow going, not being able to use flashlights.

"Shit!" McCarren said.

"Yeah, I know. They didn't mark the goddamned cactus on Jeb's maps."

Within minutes, they saw lights ahead. They made a wide circle, ending up twenty-five yards behind a huge two-story house.

"No mistaking this," Zita said. "It's Clendon's."

McCarren checked his watch: 7:12 P.M. "Show time," he said. He crept off, leaving Zita in the bushes. He made it to the cabana, then to a small servants' quarters, and stopped. He ripped the Velcro seal on his bag and retrieved a tiny transmitter, grabbed a quick breath, and, crouching, ran to the northeast corner of the big house. He scraped two lengths of phone wire with pliers and attached the transmitter. Seeing no one, he crept back to the bushes.

"Two and Three," Zita whispered into the walkie-talkie. "We're hooked up."

They stayed in the brush, moving eastward past the mansion to the hangar. They found a stand of shin oak and settled in.

"Don't you love cop work?" McCarren grinned. "Protect and serve. Hurry up and wait."

"I hate this shit. It's turning me into a whiny bitch."

• • •

McCray was surprisingly succinct in his rundown, talking in bursts as he drove from the square in Comanche Gap. Clay Moore was concentrating, trying to remember every detail.

Deal was supposed to go down about 2:00 A.M. Now they were figuring four hours earlier, around 10:00 P.M. Two refrigerated tractor-trailers, maybe a trail car or two, probably ten meskins, including the honcho. Deal would go down in the main barn. Two large doors on either end. The head meskin would take the cash, then his guys 'd drive out with their tractors. Colters' guys would back up to the trailers with their own rigs, then be gone. Done deal.

"How many guys we got?" Moore asked.

"Me, you, the two truck drivers—they're totin', too—two or three other cowboys, Buck and Wade. That's it."

"The ol' man don't want to see what he's gettin' for his money?"

"That's what Buck's for," McCray said. "He don't have to touch the stuff no more. Too big for that.

"Now you, you're the backup, know what I mean? I'm gonna want you outside the barn, checkin' shit out. You see a bunch of meskins runnin' out the place real quick, grease 'em and ask questions later."

"I can handle that."

"You mind I ask you a personal question?" McCray said. "See, I got a place all picked out for you, but I ain't sure. I mean, that leg of yours—can you climb up in a tree, cause I—"

"If my leg's all you got to worry about, you ain't got no problems," Moore said. "That leg'll take me where I need to go."

"Well, I was just askin', you know what I mean, 'cause it's a good place, but I want you to be comfortable with everything and all."

They drove past the two guards at the main gate, the compound where the Colters' houses were, and the hanger, ending up at the main barn. Moore had never seen a barn that big, easily more than two stories high and large enough to accommodate two tractor-trailer rigs parked side by side, with plenty of space left over.

"That there tree's the one I was thinkin' about," McCray said. "Dark's it is, nobody gonna see you up there. Shit; ain't no need to look up there. Think that'll work?"

It was a towering blackjack oak and it sat south of the door. On the other side of the door was the thirty-foot butane tank Moore had seen in the snapshots.

"Don't know why it wouldn't," Moore said. "Got a good field of view. Even if somebody comes out the other end, they're gonna be headed for the road, and I'll have 'em covered. What you need to do is show me ever' friendly we got here and where they're gonna be. I don't want to hurt the wrong people."

They walked around the barn, McCray introducing him to Colters' people and pointing out where they'd be. Buck and Wade wouldn't show up with the money until the trucks were in the barn. If everything was cool, McCray would appear in the door and give him a sign; if he didn't show, no one was allowed to leave.

"Just part their hair with that Russki piece I gave you, know what I mean?"

Moore was getting buried in detail. He needed to sort it out and get it to Quinlin.

"I'm just gonna roam around, get the lay of the land, and go take a leak," Moore said. "Back in a few."

He headed back for the blackjack oak, and when he saw McCray talking to another guy, he crept into the brush behind the barn and activated the walkie-talkie under his vest. He looked at his watch: 8:23 P.M.

Part their hair? Right, Moore said to himself. Gimme a half-assed reason, Snake Boy, and I'll put one between your runnin' lights.

"This is Four," Moore said in a coarse whisper, never taking his eyes off McCray. "Listen quick. It's going down in about an hour and a half in the barn. About ten meskin bad guys, and eight or nine Colters', including Buck and Wade. Daddy ain't coming. Your best shot is gonna be on the northeast corner of the barn. Just one guy. Repeat: northeast corner of the barn. One dude. I'm long gone, buddy."

Quinlin leaned against the armored van, shaking his head. At the spur of the moment, the FBI had managed to mobilize enough agents and firepower to retake Ho Chi Minh City. There were four agents posted at the east gate off the dirt road, four in the ditch across from the main gate, and twenty-two milling around the mobile command post, a converted Winnebago painted dull black, with three-foot yellow letters that said FBI. The detective assumed all of the agents were armed like those around him—.45-caliber sidearms, M16's, and tear-gas canisters and masks. He even spotted a few grenade launchers.

Special Agent in Charge Michael Whitt, U.S. Attorney Ronald Stokes, and some deputy assistant attorney general from Washington, whose name he hadn't caught, were inside the command post, talking on a secure line to someone in Washington.

The only problem was, the command post and battle-ready FBI agents were stashed in the brush atop a hilltop a full mile away from the valley where the drug deal was going down.

"All dressed up and nowhere to go," said a bemused Quinlin.

"What?" Roger Wilmon asked, slapping at his sides against the cold. The top of the hill was bald and the wind from the west was gusting at forty miles an hour, creating a chill index of twelve.

"I said I don't see how this is going to work."

"Looks like a circle jerk, doesn't it? No more time than we had, our SWAT people say it's the best we could do," Wilmon said. "This is as close as we could get."

Not that they hadn't tried. Quinlin had intercepted two agents just as they tried to cut into the fence, which he had already warned them was wired with motion-detector devices. He was beginning to understand the Branch Davidian fiasco.

"It'll have to be a containment operation," Wilmon said. "The squads will deploy once the trucks get in. With any luck, the Mexicans will get their money and leave the barn. We're still depending on your guy inside to let us know."

Guy. Singular. That's all the FBI knew—that Clay Moore was down in the valley with the bad guys. They'd already heard the tape with his voice and McCray's. Quinlin hated misleading Roger Wilmon. He was a decent guy and a friend. But Wilmon wasn't calling the shots. That fell to Larry, Mo, and Curly inside the cozy command center.

"We grab the Mexicans as soon as the last one clears the gate," Wilmon said. "Then the second squad surrounds the barn, arrests the Colter group, seizes the drugs, and secures the crime scene. Not the way we'd want to do it, but at least it cuts the number of bad guys by half and puts a few miles between them."

"Everybody's seen the picture of my guy, Moore, right? He can't get caught in the middle of a firefight."

"Yeah, and everybody knows to look for a guy with a limp. With only one CI to look out for, it won't be a problem."

CI, federalspeak for cooperating individual.

When Wilmon had called twelve hours earlier, Quinlin was variously frustrated and relieved. He and his team had a workable plan, albeit one that stretched everyone's talents and imagination. But driving to Dallas to meet with the feds, he realized he was off the hook. If the FBI was there and the operation went up in flames like Waco, it was their deal, not his.

By the time he'd gotten to FBI headquarters, he'd been ready to turn everything over and walk away with his fingers crossed. But that was before he met Ronald Stokes, the chief federal prosecutor for the Northern District of Texas.

Early in the meeting, Stokes lamented that federal authorities were having to jury-rig a sensitive operation at the eleventh hour. "It didn't have to happen," he said pointedly, "if DPD had gone through regular channels."

"Regular channels were clogged up with sewage," Quinlin had said. "You were doing the traveling road show with the key suspect, giving testimonials on his behalf. If you fuckin' people enforced ethical standards, you'd be brought up on charges yourself. I'm supposed to trust you? Bullshit!"

Roger Wilmon had interceded, but Quinlin could tell by the assistant AG's face that he had struck a sensitive chord. The Washington bureaucrat had hauled Stokes off, leaving Quinlin alone with the FBI. Quinlin made a decision then. He told the feds enough to get their sanction, but not enough that they could screw it up. He had a few objectives of his own, and they weren't necessarily all that compatible with the federal government's.

What the FBI didn't know wouldn't hurt them, and Quinlin hoped it wouldn't hurt anybody else.

The crack of the command post door startled Quinlin and Wilmon. The Department of Justice attorney motioned them inside, and Quinlin could feel the warmth that bathed the doorway.

"Mr. Stokes and I think it would best accomplish the goals of the mission if you didn't go down to the barn," he said. His inflection was on Stokes, and the message was that the U.S. attorney of the Northern District of Texas was still in control.

"That's not what we agreed on in the briefing," Quinlin said.

"We have to consider safety," he said. "In that regard, we've reconsidered."

"Reconsider this," Quinlin said. "The only eyes and ears you have down there belong to my guy."

He held up a walkie-talkie—not the one the FBI had issued him a half an hour earlier. "I'll have his ass over the fence before you can say Ruby Ridge."

The Justice attorney huddled briefly with Stokes, who was shaking his head and talking in muffled grunts.

"We'll stay with the original agreement," the Washington lawyer said.

"So I'm still going down when the trucks are spotted?"

"Not a problem."

Quinlin paced at the edge of the hill, wondering how long it would take him to get down to the barn in the darkness. The half-moon was well into the sky now, shedding a little light. Once his eyes adjusted, it wouldn't be bad. He checked his watch for the umpteenth time: 9:14 P.M. One minute later, he heard static through his right earpiece. He had to concentrate. Right ear was his guys; left ear was the FBI frequency.

"Five and Six," Will Stephens said. "The bird's poised."

It was exactly 9:15 P.M.

The terrain was too rough to risk a night landing without lights, and the Charlie-model Huey was louder than a freight train in a tunnel, so Stephens and Clint Harper had put the helicopter down just before dusk. They came in fast and low, barely clearing the scrub brush beneath the range of hills, and landed in a field of winter oats a mile south of Pan Permian's fence line. They hung out for nearly four hours, monitoring the radio, until it was time to check in.

Quinlin breathed deeply. Everyone was where they were supposed to be. He checked his watch. *Still 9:15.* Waiting was worse than a commode-hugging hangover. If he'd turned over the whole damned mess to the FBI, he'd be at home in front of the fireplace with Madeline, and his friends wouldn't be lying in bushes or hiding in trees. He hadn't felt so out of control since Vietnam.

Rebecca saw him out of the corner of her eye. She'd been watching him all night. He slipped her car keys off the kitchen counter, where she always kept them, and tucked them in his jeans. He opened the hall coat closet and retrieved his insulated vest and ball cap with the Pan Permian logo, putting them on as he headed for the garage door.

"Rebecca," Buck Colter said, "I'm gonna take care of some business for two or three hours. What I want you to do is stay in the house, and that goes for Chad, too. Some folks are coming in, and I don't want you around them. That's all I'm gonna say. I don't want you outside or leavin' or anythin' else."

She heard the garage door open and then the Ranger Rover start up.

She groped in her jeans pocket until she felt the spare ignition key.

"It's happening, isn't it?" Chad said, appearing in the den.

"I think so, son," she said. He already had on his heavy boots. "Get your big coat and put it by the back door with mine. Then come over here and sit with me on the couch. I could use some company. How 'bout you?"

"Two and Three," Zita said. "Buck's on the road."

Quinlin monitored the transmission from the hill, then checked his watch: 9:39 P.M.

At 9:44 P.M., he heard Clay's voice through the ear jack: "Four. I got a red Range Rover with two men at the barn."

Buck had stopped at Wade's to pick him up. They must know the trucks are close, Quinlin thought.

Quinlin's stomach rolled and he felt the adrenaline. He'd already picked his descent down the steep hill, but he checked a final time for a quicker path. The terrain looked the same as it had the thirty other times he'd checked. At least the moon was higher now; the path was clearer than before.

He heard a mike click in his left ear, the FBI frequency. Quickly, he checked his watch: 9:47 P.M.

"Scout to Command. We've got two blue tractors with reefers going through the gate, trailed by a black Lincoln Continental and a black Range Rover."

"Roger."

Three minutes later, rock sliding beneath his jungle boots as he descended the hill, he heard McCarren's voice on his own frequency: "Two and Three. Two trailer trucks, a Lincoln, and some kind of SUV coming your way."

Quinlin cursed under his breath. He twisted his left ankle on cliche, and the crunching rock sounded like an avalanche.

Calm down. Stay cool. They probably didn't hear it at the barn. There are all kinds of noises in the country, he told himself, cattle, deer, fuckin' everything. One foot in front of the other. No sweat. What was it he told rookie patrolmen? If it was easy, anybody could do it.

Zita elbowed McCarren, who let out a startled grunt. They were on their stomachs, and she held the small console in front of her on the ground. The tiny red light was pulsating, and she pushed on her ear jack to make sure it was in tight.

The voice-activated recorder whirred, and she cocked her head, listening intently, like a startled cat with a paw in the air:

"Daddy, they'll be here in five minutes. What's it gonna be?"

"Keep the money."

Zita made a clenched fist in the air. "*Yes,*" she whispered. Clendon Colter didn't have to be in the barn with the dope. Answering Buck's question had just established him as the kingpin in a RICO indictment. She strained in the dark to make sure the recorder was working.

"You sure? It's gonna cause—"

"I said, keep the money."

The phone went dead. McCarren could tell something was wrong.

"What is it?"

"I . . . I'm not sure," Zita said, pulling the walkie-talkie from her vest. "Two and Three. Daddy's in the soup. But Jeb, we may have a problem."

Quinlin was two-thirds down the hill, close enough that he could see the silhouette of a man holding a shotgun at the northeast corner of the barn. He crouched behind a cedar bush.

"*May* have a problem?" he whispered, watching the guard below him. "We do or we don't, goddamn it."

"Daddy said, 'Keep the money.' "

"What's that mean?" Spitting distance from a man who'd blow your stones off wasn't a good place to be having this conversation.

"It could mean, you know, keep the money and call off the deal," Zita said frantically. "Or it could mean rip-off. Take their dope but keep our money. I couldn't tell."

"Four, you copy that?"

Moore didn't answer. Quinlin's eyes were locked on the guard at the barn. Moore was at the other end, diagonally across, and out of sight.

"Clay, you there?"

Quinlin cursed and hit the transmit button: "Just stay put. We'll have to sort it out down here."

Clendon Colter's state of mind was academic. Whether he planned to call off the deal or rip off the meskins, Quinlin still had to be on the ground. He crept on, trying to watch his step and the guard.

The guy with the shotgun was standing on the other side of a small gully about four feet wide, his back to Quinlin. The detective knew he couldn't slosh through the water without being heard. He reached in his back pocket for the blackjack. He'd have to hurdle the gully and hit Shotgun in midair to make it work.

He took a deep breath, the frigid air stabbing his chest. He fought off a cough and leapt as far as he could with the blackjack above his head. Quinlin overcompensated, his knee hitting the cowboy in the shoulder and knocking him forward with a gutteral moan. He brought the blackjack down on the crown of his head before they hit ground.

Quinlin lay on top of him, breathing hard and listening as he pulled the SW 99 from its holster. All he heard was the wind. He pulled duct tape from the Velcro pouch, taped Shotgun's mouth, then bound his hands and ankles.

Clay Moore's voice came through the ear jack.

"This is Clay, uh, Four. Fuck it. Jeb, there's about to be a blood-bath down here. McCray's lost his shit, says no meskins are leaving the barn alive. The Colters are gonna rip 'em off. Told me he'd make it up to me, but to kill everything that moves that's meskin."

Quinlin could hear the sound of diesels gearing down in the background.

"How far are you from that butane tank in the pictures?" Quinlin asked.

"Maybe forty yards."

"That's too close. Let everybody get in the barn; then get out of the tree," Quinlin said. "Get some distance across the road. When I click the mike three times, you shoot the regulator on top of the tank, where the gauges are. We're gonna need to put down some H and I."

Harassment and interdiction, they'd called it in Nam. Create a diversion. The butane tank was a big one, a thousand-gallon steel reservoir of flammable gas. A god-awful fireball ought to be a sufficient diversion.

"Roger that," Clay Moore said. "I hear you."

The vet's voice was confident again. All he needed was a plan.

"Five, you there?"

"Five's here." Will Stephens was calm and cool.

"Crank, wait three minutes for the trucks to get in the barn, then get airborne," Quinlin said. "When y'all see the fire, you hold on the south side—I'm sayin' the *other* side of the barn from the fuckin' FBI. You read me?"

"We're cranking."

"Three."

"Yo," McCarren said.

"Follow the road to the barn," Quinlin said. "Get across the road, and back up Clay when he comes down from the tree."

McCarren was carrying an M16 assault rifle.

"Ten four."

"Two."

Zita's voice came in immediately.

"You stay with the original plan," Quinlin said. "You'll just have to do it by yourself. You handle that?"

"No problem here," she said.

Quinlin heard car doors slamming and unintelligible voices on the other side of the barn. He dragged the bound and gagged cowboy to the edge of the gully and kicked him off the bank with his boot, watching him go rigid as he hit the water. It was only three or four inches deep, but the fucker fell in face-first. Quinlin cursed, bent on one knee, grabbed him by the collar, and rolled him over to keep him from drowning.

He heard rollers running on metal rails and knew they were bringing in the trucks from the far end, where Moore was posted in the tree.

The FBI frequency was constant with traffic; the agent in charge was moving his squads into place to seal off Pan Permian. Quinlin knew half the agents had started down the hill behind him, and the others were headed along the ridge toward the main gate. They'd be useless at the main gate; no Mexicans would make it that far, not with the Colters' change of plan.

Quinlin grabbed his FBI radio and put it to his mouth, staring through the window of the barn as the first semi pulled in. Colter's men were on the ground and in the rafters, armed with what appeared to be MAC-10 machine guns. The Mexicans looked edgy, and they carried automatic pistols pointed at the ground. McCray, wild-eyed and grinning, was standing in the door of the barn, a MAC-10 cradled in the crook of his arm. Buck and Wade Colter were ten feet away, watching the trucks move in. Four large aluminum briefcases were stacked behind them. As the second tractor pulled in, Wade moved to the other side of the barn, closer to the huge door at that end.

Changing the FBI's plans would create chaos. Not enough time to tell them about the rip-off. They'd bring all the firepower on the barn, putting Clay Moore, maybe even himself, too, in more jeopardy. McCarren would be in the bushes, and they didn't even know about him. Quinlin stuck the radio back on his utility belt. He couldn't risk it.

Juan Carlos San Martín, trademark black suit, boots, and hat, came through the door, encircled by five Mexicans carrying automatic pistols. If San Martín was worried, Quinlin couldn't see it. The graying drug smuggler was grinning as he shook Buck's hand, looking like a distinguished guest showing up at a dinner party with old friends.

"One. I'm on the ground across the road," Moore said.

"Is McCarren there?"

A pause. "No, not yet."

"Watch for him, and Clay, watch your ass."

Quinlin looked through the window as Buck crouched on one knee and opened all four aluminum briefcases, laying them on their sides. He stood and backed off, allowing San Martín to inspect the contents. The Mexican picked up several bundles of bills, smiled, and returned them to the cases, which he closed. As he stood, Buck made eye contact with McCray, and both moved casually toward the idling diesels, distancing themselves from the smuggler.

It was a signal; the rip-off was imminent. Quinlin pressed the transmitter button three times.

Quinlin glanced at his watch out of habit. There was a muffled pop and an almost-spontaneous earsplitting explosion. Quinlin flinched instinctively as a red-and-orange fireball slammed through the far wall like a tornado, spewing flying timber, nails, and shingles from its epicenter.

The FBI frequency went off in his ear. "What the hell?" someone yelled. Another: "Get down and *stay* down." A team leader: "Jacobs, Ricther, *go!*" They would be the snipers, probably headed to the barn to reconnoiter the area, figure out the explosion. He heard hurried footsteps on the hill and gravel and rock sliding.

Quinlin ran across the double doors to the other side, stopping at the corner. There hadn't been a single gunshot, unless he'd missed it in the pandemonium. The bad guys had other things to worry about.

The whine of an accelerating diesel screamed from within the barn. As he started back toward the door, Quinlin saw the two FBI snipers at the other corner, crouched with M16's on their shoulders. One recognized him and waved in acknowledgment. He'd stay put.

The blue hood of a Freightliner pulled from the doors, and in the glow of the flames, Quinlin saw Wade Colter behind the wheel.

"Halt, FBI! Stop or we'll shoot!"

Wade Colter ducked his head and hit the accelerator of the big rig, jolting it forward. He was still in Quinlin's line of sight, and the detective saw Colter's body slump at the sound of two bursts from an M16. The rig slowed and veered left, out of control, coming to rest against a blackjack oak.

Quinlin saw a figure lurch from the side door of the barn. Buck Colter was easy to spot in the holocaust, his insulated vest covered with soot and the right leg of his jeans bloody and ripped at the knee. He limped frantically on the bad leg, slowed even more under the weight of the three metal briefcases in his hands and under his arm.

In the fiery melee, one brother had gone for the dope, the other the money. Daddy would be proud.

"I'm behind you," McCarren said, catching his breath. The area was illuminated with fire. "Gawd *damn.*"

Clay Moore didn't turn around, his eyes locked on the scene in front of him. The tree where he'd hidden only minutes earlier had been seared in the blast, the top-two thirds of its limbs blown away, leaving only a soot-charred trunk; the half of the barn behind it was engulfed in flames.

"What the shit?" McCarren said, tapping Moore's shoulder and pointing.

"That's McCray," Moore said, recognizing the snakeskin boots and belt.

The man's torso was in flames, and the smoldering remnant of a two-by-four stud protruded at a forty-five-degree angle from his shoulder. He ran blindly, reversing himself, turning abruptly, flailing his arms, stumbling, and staggering on, a steady high-pitched scream coming all the while from within the flames.

Moore put the Russian sniper rifle to his shoulder and peered through the scope fifty yards away. McCray's shirt and jacket were burned off; it was skin that was burning. There were no recognizable eyes or lips on the head, just skin molten like hot lava, exposing extraordinarily white teeth.

Moore slid his index finger into the trigger guard of the Dragunov SVD. It would only take three pounds of pressure on the trigger and the man's agony would be over. He slid the crosshairs over the heart, took a shallow breath and held it.

McCarren watched the burning man, waiting for the blast that would put him out of his misery.

Abruptly, Moore moved the rifle from his shoulder, letting the barrel slide toward the ground.

"What are you doing?" McCarren asked.

"Nothing," Moore said, his eyes fixed on McCray. "I ain't doing nothing."

Zita Morales slipped through the unlocked back door of Clendon Colter's mansion. The place appeared deserted as she crept room by room through the first floor, holding the .45 automatic upright in front of her. She could hear her heart pounding, as if it were hooked to a stethoscope and an amplifier.

Just like Rebecca had told them. The servants were off and Clendon would be puttering around by himself. *But where?* She glanced at the winding stairway, hoping she wouldn't have to go to the second floor. The staircase was open, leaving no place to hide. The mansion was huge, with hallways snaking off in every direction. Methodically, slowly, she followed each of them.

She had worked her way to the front without finding him. She stood in the foyer, panting, wishing McCarren hadn't been pulled out of the original plan. He'd know what to do. She scanned the winding staircase. It was all that was left, and she dreaded the prospect.

A raspy cough broke the silence, and she tensed. Then another. From outside? She moved her back along the wall of the formal sitting room until she could sneak a peak out the window. The automatic pistol felt like it weighed twenty pounds. Clendon Colter was at the eastern corner of the front porch, his back to her. He was watching the fire in the distance, holding a cell phone to his ear. The front door wasn't closed all the way, and she moved it slowly to see if it would creak. She nudged it gently, only wide enough to ease through sideways.

"Fuck," he said, tossing the cell phone and reaching into his pants pocket. She was ten feet behind him when he pulled the car keys from his pocket.

"Freeze and don't turn around," Zita Morales said, wincing. She had meant to sound menacing, not singsong, like some goddamned Pollyanna.

Clendon Colter turned, his face puzzled.

"I said freeze, goddamn it," she said, leveling the .45 at his midsection.

He stuck his arms out beside him, parallel with the porch. A slow, confident grin appeared on his face and he stared at her utility belt.

"You need to call Mr. San Martín on your little radio," Colter said. "Tell him he ain't got a chance in hell of gettin' off this ranch alive. A woman? Juan, Juan. Didn't know he was so politically correct. Nice try, but . . ."

He thought she was one of San Martín's group. Of course. She was Hispanic. Had to be a drug smuggler.

"You can tell him yourself if he's not already dead," Zita said, reaching for the handcuffs on the back of her belt. "Lie facedown right now so I don't have to shoot you. 'Cause I'm not supposed to have so much fun."

He stood defiantly, staring the petite woman in the eyes. Finally, he stooped to both knees and leaned forward on the porch, breaking his fall with his palms. She made a wide half circle around him, holding the automatic in her right hand and sliding the cuffs on his wrists with her left.

Clendon Colter rolled onto his back and managed to sit up as she moved away from him. "Aren't you supposed to read me my rights?" he asked, a smirk on his face.

"I'm not a cop," she said. The furrows reappeared on his brow. "So who the fuck are you?"

She holstered the .45 and grabbed him beneath both arms, dragging the big man backward to the steps. She leaned him against the ornamental iron railing and used a second pair of handcuffs to lock him to the iron post.

"Just your garden-variety vigilante," Zita said.

She bent in front of him, unbuttoning his shirt pocket. She produced a microcassette from her vest and stuffed it in his pocket.

"What's that?"

"Just a little memento of your conversation with Number One Son," she said. "Think it'll make you real popular with the FBI, which, if everything goes well, will be the next face you're gonna see, Gotrocks."

"One. Did you see your guy hit the bush?"

Quinlin had been held up when Buck Colter headed into the tree line across the road. One of the FBI snipers went to the truck to secure Wade, but the other had yelled at him, wanting to know if he was all right. Quinlin didn't want the snipers seeing him go into the brush.

"Yeah," he yelled, giving a thumbs-up.

The FBI frequency was hot. The squad from the hill was surrounding the barn, readying to secure any of the survivors. The other was headed east on the road from the main gate, making sure no one from the barn was escaping.

The sniper yelled from the truck, drawing the other's attention long enough for Quinlin to get across the road.

"This one's a fatal," the agent yelled. "Gimme a hand."

Fifty yards into the brush, Quinlin knelt on one knee and grabbed the walkie-talkie.

"Four. I saw him. It's Buck."

"You want some help?" Moore asked.

"No," Quinlin said. "You and Paul head for the site. Pick up the plan. But watch it. There's a squad of FBI coming your way from the main gate. Don't want anybody shot."

"Two. You read that about the squad on the road?"

"Yeah," Zita whispered, checking Rebecca and Chad behind her. They were hunkered in a clump of shin oak twenty-five yards off the road, and she was listening to hurried footsteps on the road. "See you at the site."

Quinlin stared into the brush, letting his eyes adjust as he pulled the black ski mask over his head and put on leather gloves. The land sloped downward, and as he crept deeper into the trees, the light from the burning barn grew dimmer and dimmer, until he was totally dependent on the moon. He moved quickly and as quietly as he could, pausing periodically to listen and to choose his route. Buck had less than a five-minute lead, he was hurting, and he was carrying the briefcases. Catching up with him shouldn't be a problem—unless he turned off or doubled back. Quinlin counted on him heading deeper into the brush, as far from the chaos at the barn as he could get. There was only trouble for him at the barn; he had to know that. Quinlin moved on.

Two hundred yards down a cattle trail, Quinlin heard twigs cracking. He knelt on one knee and listened. The sound came again, from his left, not far off. He reached for the SW 99, running the tip of his little finger under the grip to make sure the clip was still locked in. He stared ahead, in the direction of the sound.

He saw a muzzle blast and heard the *zing* at the same time. Before the sound died, a white-hot pain hit him like a laser below his ribs, just above his pelvis. The impact knocked him backward, landing him on his back. He rolled onto his stomach, holding his side with his left hand, feeling the hot moisture seeping over his fingers. He lay there staring at the position where he'd seen the muzzle blast. In the quiet, he couldn't see anything but trees.

He held his left hand close to his face, but it was too dark to assess the blood. The burning sensation was constant, but manageable. Too low for a lung, and he couldn't think of any other organs on his side. It was probably a flesh wound, in and out. Unless he bled out, he'd probably be okay. He hadn't seen Buck, but Buck had obviously seen him, well enough to put a slug through his torso. He had to stay focused. He couldn't afford a second screwup.

For a good ten minutes, Quinlin lay still, listening. He challenged himself to make sure he wasn't drifting off from blood loss—multiplication tables, visualizing Madeline's face, trying to remember his last bank balance. He heard rustling up front and to his left. If Buck had seen him fall, he might have assumed that he'd killed him. And he might come back to make sure. The cop couldn't see shit, and he tightened his grip on the Smith & Wesson, straining to listen. Footsteps on leaves and twigs. The noise was growing fainter; Buck was moving on.

Quinlin pulled himself to his knees. He saw the heavy branch of a cedar tree springing back in place fifteen yards in front of him. He fixed on the tree and crept toward it, the 40-caliber automatic poised in front of him. Every time he put weight on his left leg, he felt a burning cigarette in his side. A ligament, an artery, God forbid? He craned his head around the tree and watched Buck drop one of the briefcases. Quinlin moved quickly in a wide circle to his right, hugging the stand of cedar trees until he was ten feet ahead of his prey, as close as he was going to get without showing himself.

Buck picked up the briefcase; juggled it with the others, and moved on down the narrow path, heading on a diagonal to Quinlin's position. The cop put the automatic back in its holster and retrieved the lead-loaded blackjack from his back pocket. Buck was within eight feet of him, as close as the trail was going to carry him.

Quinlin grabbed a deep breath and sprang from the trees, his foot snapping a dry two-inch branch as he redistributed his weight. A startled Buck Colter heard the limb crack and swung the aluminum briefcase as hard as he could in that direction, catching Quinlin beneath his chin. The detective went down hard, feeling the pain of his teeth cutting into his tongue and tasting warm blood. He fought to keep his eyes open and on Buck.

Flinging the briefcase had knocked Colter off balance, and he was down on one knee, just beyond Quinlin's grasp. The detective raised himself to a crouch and lunged at Buck, grabbing him in a headlock and slamming the blackjack hard on top of his head. It was a glancing blow, and he lost his footing on the rocks. Buck pushed himself free, clawing at the ground for his gun. He came up on his knees with a flat piece of caliche the size of a pancake and brought it around like a discus. Quinlin felt the crunch of bone beneath his right eye, his head snapping sideways. There was ringing in his ears and everything went pitch-black. Wait, he thought. How could he be unconscious? He still felt the pain in his face and side. He put his hands to his face and felt the ski mask. The blow had twisted it, moving the eye slits.

He realigned the mask just as Buck Colter located his gun. He was bent over, his right hand two inches from the automatic pistol, when Quinlin yelled.

"Touch it and you're dead!"

It hurt to talk. The fucker had broken his cheekbone. He was propped on his left elbow, probably getting dirt in the gunshot wound on his side, the SW 99 trained on Buck's back.

Buck was frozen in time, still crouched over the automatic pistol.

"I'm telling you, Buck, you move, it's the last second of your fuckin' life. They'll haul you outta here with a tag on your toe."

Seconds turned to minutes. Finally, Colter shifted his weight backward, falling onto his butt, keeping his wounded right leg outstretched in front of him and groaning in pain.

"Back up against that scrub oak," Quinlin said. "Do it *now*."

Quinlin cuffed one hand and pulled it behind Buck, then grabbed the other. The tree was bigger than it looked, and Buck's arms barely made it around the trunk. He howled in pain as Quinlin ratcheted down the final cuff.

Quinlin collected the three large aluminum briefcases and dropped them in front of Buck, unlatching one. He pulled off his backpack, retrieved a Maglite, and ran the light over the open briefcase. He picked up one of the bundles of hundred-dollar bills and flipped through the stack. What were they—a hundred bills to the bundle? He didn't have time to count.

"Who the fuck are you?" Colter asked.

Quinlin ignored him. He produced a black drawstring bag from his backpack and loaded two-thirds of the money. He relatched the case and stacked it with the other two beside Buck Colter.

"The fuck you doin'?" Colter asked. "Help me, and you can take it all."

"I could take it all anyway, dickwad."

"Well, you can't just leave me here. I'm bad hurt, and I can't last in this cold."

"You won't have long to wait," Quinlin said. "The FBI will find you by morning. Or maybe the coyotes, if they smell the blood. I was you, I'd hope for the coyotes."

"You see 'em yet?" Stephens was flying the Huey and watching the fire to the north. The FBI could have called in air support after the explosion. He didn't have time to mess with the night goggles. Harper was in the right seat, the infrared goggles strapped around his flight helmet.

"Yeah, just to the right of the clearing," the reporter said. "Two, three, four, yeah, all five of 'em."

Stephens set the helicopter into the clearing, just as he had a hundred times in Nam. McCarren was the first one in, reaching his hand out for Rebecca, then Chad, Zita, and, finally, Clay Moore. Moore was only half in when Stephens pulled in the torque, lifting the helicopter at a forty-five-degree angle. They'd been on the ground less than twenty seconds.

"You all right, One?"

"Yeah. Our boy's not a player anymore."

"Where are you?" Stephens asked.

"Don't know for sure," Quinlin said. "I figure I'm about half a mile into the brush, south of the barn."

"Keep heading south and find me a clearing. I can't hover long that close to the barn, not without rousting the FBI. We'll give you ten minutes, then head your way. But we can't hang around. Read me?"

"I'm moving."

Quinlin was headed away from the barn and the FBI, and he risked turning on the Maglite. He could make better time if he could see. The terrain was rough and sloping, grown over in cedar and scrub oak. He looked at his watch. Ten minutes. He ran the light out in front of him. Nothing but trees and rocks. A clearing was going to be a problem.

He heard rustling in the brush to his left, and he stopped abruptly, grabbing the automatic from its holster and crouching on one knee. Could someone else have fled the barn? Who? Quickly he jerked the light toward the direction of the noise, following the beam with the pistol in his right hand. Two armadillos, illuminated by the glare, stumbled blindly off into the brush.

Quinlin moved from a brisk walk to a jog, training the light on the ground ten yards in front of him. He stopped periodically, scanning the sides of the cattle trail for a clearing in the trees. He sloshed through a shallow creekbed, then ran up a slope on the other side. At its top, the land flattened in front of him. He scanned the immediate horizon with the Maglite. There was maybe three acres of grassland in front of him.

"Five. I've got your clearing. Don't know how to tell you to get here, but it's plenty big to set down in."

"Gimme two minutes," Stephens said, "and put your light straight up in the air. When we get close, you flick it on and off. We'll find you."

Quinlin realized he was exhausted. As he sat, the movement triggered the pain in his left side. He groaned loudly; his face hurt, too. He shined the flashlight on his side. The blood was dried and smeared over the hole, which was the size of the tip of his little finger. He touched his cheekbone lightly, and the bottom, rounded portion moved under his fingers. It was broken.

He heard the unmistakable rhythmic *pop, pop* of the Huey growing closer, and he headed into the clearing with the Maglite raised skyward. In less than two minutes, McCarren and Moore were pulling him through the wide door, to the sound of applause. Rebecca, Chad, and McCarren sat in webbed jump seats behind the cockpit, and Moore and Zita sat opposite them. All of them were grinning and holding their thumbs up.

"What's this?" Stephens said, keeping his left hand on the stick.

"A map that you need to follow," Quinlin said. "It'll only take fifteen minutes. It's the last hurrah, I promise."

The pilot stuck the map under the light on the console, looking at Quinlin quizzically, and steered sharply to the right, accelerating and handing the map to Clint Harper.

In the passenger-cargo compartment, Quinlin took off his backpack and removed the black drawstring bag, dumping an avalanche of bundled hundreds knee-deep onto the floor. He was too busy to see the shocked reactions or to notice their chatter had abruptly turned to silence. The detective counted out the money, shoving two-thirds of it back into the bag. He dug in the backpack for a cell phone and raised his left sleeve to expose a clear plastic band with white paper around his wrist. Studying a number off the band, he dialed the cell phone.

"Jeb, what the fuck is this?" McCarren asked finally.

Quinlin held up his hand for silence.

"Susan Bettman? Susan, this is Jeb Quinlin with the Dallas Police Department. You remem—"

He was yelling into the phone and had his index finger in his other ear to shield the rotor noise.

"Great. The Colters have just been arrested by the feds. I knew you'd want to know. I'll call with the details later. But listen to me now. I don't want you and the kids to be alarmed. In a few minutes, a helicopter's gonna hover in your front yard. That's gonna be me. I've got something for you. It's a black bag. Make sure you go get it just as soon as we lift off. You hearin' me?

"Good. And Susan, you ever say anything about this, and I'm gonna be eating beanie weenies every Thursday in a mighty small room. You understand? *You can't say anything to anybody.*"

They flew twelve minutes south-southwest. As the helicopter started its descent, Stephens hit the nose light, illuminating the yard in front of Susan Bettman's house. From the right seat, Harper saw white dirt flying and, beyond that, a small woman in the shadows, shielding her eyes with her hand. Twenty-five feet off the ground, a black bag with half a million crisp unmarked bills went out the door.

It was nine minutes to the airport in Comanche Gap, and it took every moment of it for Quinlin to accomplish the last goal of the mission.

"Why?" he asked, crouched in front of Rebecca Colter. "Because the federal government's gonna take everything you've got, that's why."

"It's dirty money," she said. "I can't."

"If you can't do it for yourself," Quinlin said in desperation, "you have to do it for Chad here. How you gonna pay for insurance for this boy? Or send him to college? Or feed him, for that matter? Morality's great; I'm damned glad you've got it. That's what's straightened out this mess. But you got to think about Chad.

"Rebecca, the boy hasn't got a daddy anymore."

She was crying, and Quinlin put $250,000 in her lap.

Quinlin could feel Stephens slowing the helicopter on a gradual descent into the airport, and he saw the lights from Comanche Gap in the distance. He looked up, to see Clay Moore standing over him, extending his right hand.

"Thank you, buddy," Moore said.

"Thank *me*? Hell, you—"

"Thank you for giving me a chance to win," he said, his voice breaking. He nodded toward Zita Morales, who was strapped in her web seat, and corrected himself. "Thank you for giving *us* a chance to win."

In three minutes, everyone in the helicopter would go their separate ways in the darkness, dispersed like so much caliche dust in the wind.

38

I t was noon, and the third-floor district courtroom of the Sul
Ross County Courthouse had standing room only. Clint Harper
slid in at the back amid a cluster of onlookers leaning against the
wall of the antiquated high-ceiled courtroom. All four Dallas-Fort
Worth network affiliates were there. He spotted his old competitor,
Brett McCaleb with the *Fort Worth Light,* a couple of Houston
newspaper reporters, and even Jeremy Weiss the *Washington Post*'s
Austin-based political correspondent.

The glare of television lights spotlighted two tables loaded with
evidence the U.S. Department of Justice had confiscated a night
earlier in northern Sul Ross County—four aluminum briefcases,
one partially melted, unlatched in order to show rows of bundled
hundred-dollar bills; a chest-high stack of clear plastic bags of cocaine; and nine MAC-10 machine guns. An easel, bearing end-of-
the-world type that said "The El Gato–Pan Permian Cartel," held
a huge map with hopscotch arrows from Colombia to Mexico to
Comanche Gap, and three more that ended in Atlanta, New York,
and Detroit.

A SWAT team of DOJ flaks, Harper figured, had been up all
night. World premiere time for the DOJ-FBI made-for-TV production, starring Deputy Assistant Attorney General Lawrence Berg-
man, U.S. Attorney Ronald Stokes, FBI Agent in Charge Michael
Whitt, and the FBI SWAT team commander, all wearing blue wind-
breakers with official federal seals.

The Washington bureaucrat played the lead, reading lines that billed the bust at Pan Permian Headquarters Ranch as "the single most important inroad ever by the federal government into international drug smuggling and public corruption." Some of the scenes: the arrests of sixteen Americans and Mexican nationals, including Juan Carlos San Martín, "one of the most powerful drug lords in the history of smuggling"; Clendon and Buck Colter, "father and son multimillionaire Texas entrepreneurs"; a Texas Ranger; and the sheriff of Sul Ross County, Texas.

Unfortunately, a massive explosion, "apparently triggered by an errant bullet from a drug smuggler's gun," had resulted in the deaths of two Mexican nationals and one American. Wade Colter, Clendon Colter's youngest son, had also been killed in an attempt to evade arrest.

The AG waited for the drama to sink in before he moved everyone to the next scene: "While all the suspects in the cartel will face federal racketeering charges, San Martín and the Colters also will be charged with capital murder in the homicides of a Dallas journalist, a commercial pilot, and a bank courier in Aransas County, Texas."

The FBI used its tactical expertise and "confidential informants," the DOJ lawyer noted from his script, to intercept nearly three tons of cocaine "before it reached mid-America" and to confiscate more than $20 million in illicit drug money.

Ronald Stokes cleared his throat in the microphone in preparation for Act II.

"The U.S. Attorney's Office in Dallas has diligently pursued this intensive, complex investigation involving Clendon Colter and his family for more than ten months. . . ."

Clint Harper stopped to light a Marlboro Lights on the courthouse lawn. Six old gentlemen sat around a cement table and benches, plopping dominoes on a green felt cloth. He recognized one, a rickety old curiosity seeker in a plaid shirt, who had been upstairs at the press conference. He was holding court with the spit-and-whittlers.

"Those fed'ral agents say it was just the FBI," the man was saying. "But my brother-in-law's sister, Gussie, works at the hospital. She says a young guy came in last night, shot with a gun. Tried to say it was a huntin' accident, but he was wearin' those solid black uniforms and his face was beat to hell. Nobody'd hunt in black clothes. It's a fact his insurance card said he was a Dallas cop. Tell you what. Sounds to me like somebody's shadin' the truth."

An old man caught Harper listening.

"You a guv'ment agent?"

"No, sir, I'm a newspaper reporter."

"You reckon those ol' boys are telling the truth upstairs?"

"You believe your government, don't you?" Harper grinned.

"No, sir. Matter of fact, I truly don't—not after Nixon. I 'spect there's some things about ol' Clendon Colter and that deal that we'll never know for sure. What you think, Mr. Reporter?"

Harper flicked the cigarette on the sidewalk and ground it out with his boot.

"Gettin' justice may be like makin' sausage," he said. "You don't want to know what goes in it; you just want it to leave a good taste in your mouth."